After We Fall

Books by Deborah Clack

SHELTER AND SKY

Even After This

After We Fall

SHELTER AND SKY • 2

After We Fall

DEBORAH CLACK

Haven
a division of Baker Publishing Group
Grand Rapids, Michigan

Published by Haven
a division of Baker Publishing Group
Grand Rapids, Michigan
HavenFiction.com

Printed in the United States of America

ISBN 978-0-8007-4695-7 (paper)
ISBN 978-1-4934-5565-2 (ebook)

This book is a work of fiction. Names, characters, places, and incidents are the product of the author's imagination or are used fictitiously. Any resemblance to actual events, locales, or persons, living or dead, is coincidental.

Cover illustration by Nate Eidenberger
Cover design and type by Laura Klynstra

Baker Publishing Group publications use paper produced from sustainable forestry practices and postconsumer waste whenever possible.

26 27 28 29 30 31 32 7 6 5 4 3 2 1

To my dad,
the first person I ever knew who
wrote a book. I love you.
So very much.

P.S. Thank you for letting me
steal the pickup line you used
on Mom for this story.

Dear Reader,

I'm delighted to share Penelope and Luke's story with you. As with all stories, theirs holds a multitude of beauty and pain, love and loss. If you would like to read the content warnings for this story, which may contain spoilers, you can view them at www.DeborahClack.com/contentwarnings.

With love,
Deborah

1

HOW HARD WOULD IT BE to locate a bulletproof stained glass window?

Standing at the foothills of the Rocky Mountains on the far edge of the Holcombe property, I scan the outside of the quaint chapel. I could find one, but not before the Thanksgiving Day wedding that starts in—I flip the sleek band of my gold-link watch—sixty-eight minutes.

Besides, such a precaution would be overkill.

The on-call security consultant arriving soon will cover my bases for the last-minute situation I discovered. Another item completed on the list attached to my black acrylic clipboard.

Efficiency is my love language.

The wind catches the corner of the message that arrived sometime during the night. At least I think it's a message. I found it this morning amid a shattered floral arrangement at the front of the chapel. The gust grabs the fluttering edge from my hand, whisks the glossy paper through the air, and plasters it around a fence post that delineates the property lines. Before it can take flight again, I snatch the paper, smooth the edges into submission, and secure it under the clipboard's clamp.

Once I manage this detail, everything will be in place for my boss's nuptials. Bosses'. Both of them. My professional multitasking duties straddle the property line on which I currently stand. West of the fence rolls out the vast acreage of Harlan Holcombe's childhood home, where he now runs a consulting company. East of the fence sits Twelve Bluebells Ranch, his fiancée's boardinghouse for young women aging out of the foster care system.

A master's degree in business administration prepared me for work with Harlan's company. A master's degree in misery from a group home during my teenage years prepared me for work with Meredith's halfway house.

West of the fence holds my expertise. East of the fence holds my heart.

And it's almost time to ask the soon-to-be newlyweds for my dream job.

I stride toward the white wooden chapel, crunching the brittle grass with each step of my four-inch heels. As if a personal wedding gift to the Holcombes, the sun breaks through the smoky clouds, streaking well-wishes across the grounds for the noonday ceremony.

Upon entering the one-room building, I proceed down the aisle and study the floral decor. Bound by brown ribbon, modest wildflowers adorn the ends of each of the eight pews. Light fragrance dusts the room with a romantic autumn perfume. Bold colors complement the fall palette of the golden aspens and Rocky Mountains outside the church windows.

An out-of-place daisy catches my attention.

I hike up my knee-length trench coat, and flares of boysenberry chiffon fabric peek from underneath, hinting at the hidden cocktail dress. Before I can crouch down to fix the flower, someone at the chapel entrance clears his throat.

Leaning against the doorjamb, arms crossed, eyes glittering, he chews on a toothpick. "Luke Granger."

Two words. It only takes two words to appreciate this man's electricity. Something's vaguely familiar about him, but I need to focus on the task at hand. Cargo pants accentuate his tall, muscled body but aren't enough to throw me off my game. Even if the black fleece he wears causes those green eyes to pop. But I don't recognize his name.

"I'm from the LG Security Team," he says. "I know Logan usually handles your account's on-property needs, but he has the day off to celebrate Thanksgiving with his family."

"Of course." With a calming exhale, I approach the back of the room and extend my hand to him the way my education taught me. Palm neither up nor down. Straight across and equal. "Penelope Reid, Harlan Holcombe's assistant. Thank you for coming on such short notice, Mr. Granger. I'm sorry you're here on a holiday but grateful your company offers on-call services."

"Not a problem. Call me Luke." He matches my firm grip. "The after-hours operator briefed me with the basics. She mentioned we don't have long before the ceremony begins. Show me what we're dealing with in here."

"Today's wedding is a small family affair. Several of us worked yesterday to set up the chapel. We finished by 7:30." I place my palm firmly on the door. "I'm positive I shut the door before we left the premises. But when I arrived this morning, it was cracked open."

Luke crouches down, inspecting the latch. "Entry doesn't look forced."

"No need," I say. "The family keeps the chapel unlocked."

He stands, runs a hand up the dark-stained wood, then closes and reopens the sturdy door. "The wind wouldn't be able to budge this thing open."

"I don't think so either. Everything appeared to be in place with the exception of a shattered floral arrangement on the stage.

While cleaning the debris, I found small pieces of ripped paper. I gathered them and taped them back together." Earlier, I'd painstakingly pulled each scrap from the pile of flowers, glass, and water. I hadn't needed to tape the pieces of the puzzle together before I recognized it as a shiny brochure for Twelve Bluebells Ranch.

I slip the mangled leaflet from the top of the clipboard and pass it into Luke's hands.

He shifts the toothpick to the opposite side of his mouth while studying the paper.

"I'd like for this to be handled without burdening anyone else." I lift my chin and say firmly, "Harlan and Meredith deserve a day to celebrate without this added stress."

With a curt nod, he takes booted steps across the hardwood planks and inspects the front of the chapel.

Outside the open doorway, a flash of color catches my eye, and I see the three tenants of Twelve Bluebells Ranch skittering across the field. Meredith purchased each of the women burnt-orange taffeta dresses for today's occasion. Three beloved giggling pumpkins scurry toward the barn for the upcoming group pictures.

One yells in my direction, her hand flailing in the air with excitement. "Hey, Penny Lady."

My heart warms, and I hold up my clipboard in a responsive wave.

Once today's celebration is complete, I'll be in charge of the boardinghouse tenants for nine days while the Holcombes are on their honeymoon. Ample time to prove I'm more than capable of being the new program director at Twelve Bluebells Ranch.

This morning's mess in the chapel reeks of prank more than threat. Still, my uncertainty nudged me to call the ranch's security company. We need to shut down the matter at hand so I can proceed with the schedule for today and the goals for the coming week.

"This is interesting." Luke's comment recalls my attention,

and I turn toward him, hugging the clipboard to my chest. "If it was just a broken vase, it could be an accident. But this brochure you found ripped up is for the ranch next door? Is that right?"

"Yes. The groom lives on this property, and the bride owns the neighboring halfway house." I keep my tone neutral. "Do you think we have an issue?"

"What issue?" asks a voice from behind me.

At the sound of my boss's question, I close my eyes.

Harlan Holcombe. The groom.

After pasting a fake smile on my face, I turn. "We were discussing a matter with the grounds." I cringe inwardly at my terrible attempt to lie.

Harlan raises his hands in surrender and offers me an easy smile. "I recognize that look, Penelope. But I come in peace. Scout's honor." He shifts his attention to Luke, and his face lights up in surprised recognition. "Hey, man. Good to see you." Reaching past me, he grabs Luke and pulls him into a hug, each man pounding the other on the back. "Shouldn't you be globe-trotting? I didn't think I'd catch you until the New Year's Eve shindig."

Every muscle in my body tenses. Today's ceremony is limited to immediate family, the pastor, the girls, and me. The official wedding celebration with friends and extended relatives will be at the Broadmoor in five weeks. Luke Granger is on the guest list?

Trying to gain ground on the scene in front of me, I rack my brain for Luke's connection to the Holcombes. Dread claws at me as the reason for his familiarity stays just out of my mind's reach.

Luke pulls the toothpick out of his mouth. "Penelope called the company about your last-minute wedding problem here. I came to check it out."

My entire torso jerks in shock at his audacity.

Harlan's body stiffens. His gaze moves to me. "Do I have a last-minute wedding problem?"

I exhale and make my tone confident and light. "Not you. I'm taking care of it." Pressing a hand to his shoulder, I attempt to usher him out of the chapel. "Family photos are in a few minutes. Please don't be late."

But he doesn't budge. Rather, he draws his tuxedo jacket back and splays his hands on his jeans-clad hips. "I know what Luke does for a living. What's going on, Penelope?"

As I open my mouth to make another attempt at sending Harlan away, Luke leans in and hands my boss the patched brochure.

Anger spots dot my vision. Who does he think he is? I know I called him, but this is not what I expected. We were supposed to shield the bride and groom while we privately handled the situation.

I squeeze Harlan's forearm, trying to redirect his attention. "I'm handling everything."

Frowning, he examines the vandalized leaflet.

Luke's stoic focus doesn't waver from Harlan, and he misses the death glare I aim in his direction.

Harlan snaps his head up. "I don't understand. What is this?"

"Last night someone came into the chapel and destroyed a flower arrangement and vase," I say. "They left this brochure torn to pieces on top of the debris."

"Meredith came over here last night." He cringes. "She loves this place. Wanted a few minutes to herself. What if something had happened to her? Did you call the police?"

"No." I stand tall, trying to fortify myself yet remain calm. "I can if you want me to, but I was trying to avoid squad cars at the wedding."

His focus darts around the chapel. "Where is the broken vase?"

I swallow. "I cleaned it up."

"You cleaned up all the evidence?"

No, I ensured the ceremony would happen on time. I hold up a hand. "I took pictures on my phone, caught the broken vase from all angles. The pieces are in a trash bag in the dumpster if someone wants to take a look, but there really wasn't much to see."

Harlan gapes at me, but Luke takes a step forward and says,

"With the door unlocked and very little touched, I'm not sure the police would've found much anyway. Probably nothing to fingerprint either." He nods to me. "Still, it's a good idea to notify them after the ceremony."

"This is a private family gathering. Only eighteen people are attending, and we didn't send invitations. Who else would know about today?" Harlan shoves the brochure in my direction. "And why would they do something like this?"

My boss's rare display of frustration isn't the only factor causing a nervous lump to fill my throat. But I straighten my shoulders and push past the feeling of foreboding that this might have something to do with one of the girls at the ranch.

"My best guess? An uber fan from one of your superhero movies. Or an obsessed person who caught wind of your viral YouTube video." I shift to address Luke. "A little over a year ago, Harlan saved a teenage girl from drowning. The footage went viral."

Luke nods. "Yes. I believe two and a half million people deemed him Hercules." To his credit, his face remains blank when he mentions the embarrassing moniker.

Harlan's glower shoots from Luke back to me.

"In the beginning, he had a few obsessed teenagers contact him," I say to Luke. "It was all very benign. Other than that, nothing. The bulk of the social media attention subsided after a month. Other than normal fan mail, we've never dealt with anything like this before." I study Harlan and take a breath. My boss has never been anything but honest with me. "I hope it's a teenage prank. But I called the security company to come evaluate the chapel just in case."

In spite of the crisp Colorado Springs autumn morning, the air in the room hangs heavy.

Harlan runs a hand through his hair, a combination of frustration and worry etched in the lines around his eyes. "Luke, what do you think?"

Luke plants his feet wide and crosses his arms. "I'll point out that this incident wasn't aimed at a specific person. It could be meant for anyone on either property associated with the halfway house."

"It has to be for Harlan," I say, the pitch in my voice higher than I prefer. "He's a fairly well-known celebrity. This is just a local wayward adolescent acting on the dare of a classmate. Something for attention. I think you might be blowing this out of proportion."

"You're the one who called me," Luke says.

"Because I wanted discreet monitoring of the chapel. Not because I wanted to escalate the situation an hour before the wedding starts."

"Listen, I don't know what happened in here. But this feels a little personal. Why didn't the perpetrator unleash a can of spray paint? Why only destroy one flower arrangement, leaving everything else in place? It seems controlled. Intentional."

I curl my hand into a fist, fingernails digging into my flesh.

"It's too vague to assess if there's a true threat," Luke says. "I don't know what this person's endgame is. It could be nothing."

Pressing a palm to his forehead, Harlan turns and takes two steps. "What needs to happen next?"

Luke sticks the ridiculous toothpick back into his big mouth. "Your existing security on the ranch is all solid. No sensors or alarms were set off, so that's good. I'll walk the property and look for signs of stakeouts, additional damage, or unwanted visitors. I'll also stick around today and keep watch. It'll all be fine." His eyes glitter when he adds, "And if you're interested, I can send two undercover bodyguards with you on your honeymoon."

Harlan angles back in our direction, shaking his head. "I'm not double-dating on my honeymoon."

Luke laughs, the sound grating on my nerves. Why is he having this reaction? Not one thing about this is funny.

Rubbing the stubble on his cheek, he downgrades his outburst to a chuckle.

Wait a minute.

The stubble. The green eyes. That dumb toothpick attached to a cocky grin. And Harlan's thirty-third birthday party. The one where I met a man named Luke who asked me to dance. Whose intoxicating energy and sincere interest pierced right through my typical negative response to such a request and tempted me to say yes. As I recall, I took a breath to accept, but his phone rang before I could utter a word. He barely apologized as he hurried out of the restaurant, leaving me with the taste of watered-down lemonade and bitter embarrassment.

"All right. No roommates on your honeymoon," Luke says. "But I think while you're traveling, someone needs to keep an eye on the ranch in case this joker shows up again."

"I know you're usually on the road," Harlan says, rubbing the back of his neck. "But can you stay on the property? Beef up our existing security system? Watch the place?"

My entire body jerks back. What? Stay on the property? I know I called for help, but this is not what I meant. My control of the situation seems to be unraveling, and the snag is a man named Luke Granger.

"Not a problem," Luke says, chewing his toothpick like it's cud.

How hard would it be to yank that thing out of his mouth and stab him with it?

"I want you next door at Twelve Bluebells with the girls." Harlan hitches a thumb toward the adjacent property across the wooden fence line. "My fiancée's halfway house serves young women who've aged out of foster care assistance but need help getting their feet on the ground. It doesn't officially open until next spring, and we have yet to hire a program director to run the place. But Meredith can't turn anyone away, so we already have three boarders."

The girls. *Nothing can touch those girls.*

"Sounds like Meredith's doing good things," Luke says.

Harlan nods. "The women work hard. They just need a little support. We're grateful Penelope agreed to look after them while we're on our honeymoon. She can smell when rules aren't being followed."

I peer at Harlan out of the corner of my eye. "We're trying to have a civilization here."

"I know. It's your life's motto. It's also why you're in charge while we're gone." He wraps one arm around my shoulders and squeezes.

In charge while they're gone. Hopefully in charge long-term after they come home.

Harlan returns his focus to his friend. "Thanks for handling this, man. I'll let you work out the rest of the details with Penelope. But, you guys"—his intense stare bounces between Luke and me—"Meredith knows nothing about this. She's been through enough in her lifetime. I'll tell her later, but I want today to be perfect for her."

I square my stance to him, and for the first time in five years of employment with my boss, I make a promise I'm not sure I can keep. "This won't go anywhere near her."

As soon as Harlan leaves the chapel, I spin on my heel to face the man who stole my breath away three years ago at a birthday party. I point at his chest. "I knew there was something familiar about you."

A blinding smile breaks over his face, and he winks.

Whoever said lightning doesn't strike twice was dead wrong. His sway is as powerful now as the first time I met him. Maybe more so.

"So, you do remember me," he says.

"Yes." With my arms outstretched, clipboard still attached to one hand, my voice rises. "How could I forget your opening line? 'Excuse me, ma'am, I don't think you've had the pleasure of meeting me. I'm Luke.'"

"The one and only." He grins. "At your service."

My face flushes with heat. Will he bring up his disappearing act? I don't have time to be embarrassed. I have a job to do.

I lower my voice. "This situation isn't a joke to me, Luke."

All hints of humor leave his face, and he aims his fierce eyes at me. "It's not a joke to me either."

"I can't let anything happen to them." My whisper carries the weight of my world. This job is my home. The only place I've felt like I belonged since I was twelve. "The Holcombes. Meredith. The halfway house girls. Any of them."

Luke moves one heavy cargo boot a step toward me. "I'm a professional, Penelope. I specialize in the security of large-acreage property. You took great care of them when you called the company for reinforcements."

I proceed to a pew. Aware of his scrutiny of me, I study the floral arrangement with the out-of-place daisy hanging on the end of the bench. After setting my clipboard aside, I bend down to rearrange the flowers. Maneuvering the blooms with a gentle touch, I shape the arrangement into perfect symmetry with the bow. My boss trusts this man. I need to trust him too.

I rise and turn to him, dusting my hands off. "All right. What's your plan?"

He scowls while staring at the brown ribbon I adjusted. "Like I told Harlan, I'll walk the property. I've got some temporary cameras I'll strategically place for additional short-term monitoring. I've also got one drone ready to go. Everything is linked to my colleague's computer at the office. He'll be in constant contact with me."

I step to the next pew and repeat the reorganization process with the next floral decoration. "Where will you be?"

"Not far. Watching. No one will get anywhere near the door to the chapel unless they're supposed to be here." He picks up the newly pristine spray and messes with my rearrangement.

"What are you doing? That bouquet was perfect." I grab at the bundle in his possession, but his quick reflexes evade my reach. "I need to introduce you to Hank, the main ranch hand on duty for the holiday. He'll need to know you're on property."

"Thanks, but not necessary. I met Hank through the Holcombes a few years back. I saw him earlier on my way to the chapel and briefed him. He'll have eyes on this building too." He rehangs the flowers and moves to the second bouquet. I dart an arm out to snag the decoration, but he uses his body to deflect my effort.

Shifting my foot one step, I attempt to reach around him. To no avail. His brawny mass is a wall. A giant, regrettably attractive wall.

"Well, good. Then you probably already know he's hard of hearing and often has difficulty understanding others. Half the time, he refuses to wear his hearing aids." I grunt with the repeated effort of stealing the bouquet, this time grazing his solid bicep.

"I told him to send up a flare if he found trouble. He thought I said something about his underwear." Luke chuckles and pushes a cream-colored rose in front of a deep-orange daisy. While this is a definite improvement to the arrangement, his finger catches on the brown grosgrain ribbon and pulls one of the loops free.

He pauses, examining his bouquet handiwork. After an approving nod, he flashes a confident grin my way.

I roll my eyes. "Hold still and let me at least fix the ribbon." Leaving the flowers in his hands, I lean in and, with practiced precision, retie the bow. The fresh floral scent combined with something manly teases my senses. "Hank's an honorable man. But I swear he misinterprets things on purpose to get a good laugh."

"He's hilarious." Luke crunches the ribbon I just tied, relieving it of its perfection and somehow creating depth to the display.

I pick up the clipboard and tap my finger on the shiny, smooth surface. We need to be aligned for the next nine days to run well, but everything seems to be a joke to this man. "I can't handle you here with us every day if you don't take the welfare of those girls to heart."

He turns and locks his gaze to mine. "The only reason I'm staying is because I'm concerned about the welfare of those girls."

"Right." I nod. "I appreciate your help today. But you must know that we follow a purposeful regimen around here. I don't want your presence over the next week and a half to disrupt the girls' lives." *Or mine*, I want to assert, tracing my index finger along the tattered edge of the ranch brochure.

"All I'm going to do is secure and monitor the grounds. The rest of my time here, I'll ask around, see if anyone has any leads on today's incident. I'll get my job done, then I'll be out of your hair. And"—he leans an inch toward me and nods at my clipboard—"I won't disrupt your purposeful regimen."

Before I can respond, his eyes dance, and a heavy dose of confidence zaps around the room. "But you can't fire me if someone happens to smile while I'm here. Even if *you're* the one who's doing the smiling." Bending over, he hangs the flower arrangement on the end of the pew.

The swirling, giddy sensation in my stomach is an unfortunate reaction to this man. Studying the two pews seems like a favorable distraction. But when I take in the stunning result of Luke's floral creations, I shake my head in utter disbelief.

"I must admit," I say through gritted teeth, "the arrangements look better your way."

He crosses his arms over his chest, eyes never leaving the flowers. "The beauty's in the wild."

Something in my soul aches to reach out and grasp at the fragments of his words. Words I don't understand, but ones that somehow hang on wisps of hope.

The beauty's in the wild.

I tighten the belt of my coat. "I need to check on the wedding preparations. I trust I won't see you until this evening. But if you need anything, you have my number."

As I stride through the doorway and onto the path, he calls after me, "Penelope."

I turn to face him.

Luke raises his forearm over his head and leans his weight into the doorjamb. His gaze, full of intensity, bears down on me. "If there's a threat, I'll know. And I'll take care of it."

A flash of something unfamiliar streaks through my chest. What is that? Fear? Comfort? Tuning out the uncomfortable feeling, I offer a slow nod.

"I'll catch you later." He knocks the doorframe twice with his fist before he heads down the edge of the property line.

My stare lingers on his exiting form just a tad longer than I intend.

2

"NO. THAT DID *NOT* just happen," the bride says to me from across the chapel porch. Her head hangs as she stares down at her wedding dress.

My eyes are fixed on little Alex, Harlan's four-year-old daughter, as she enters the chapel. Her orange poofy skirt heaves with each skip-step toward the groom, her beaming daddy. The precious girl's lack of inhibition captivates me.

But at Meredith's alarming words, I jolt back to reality and turn around.

Meredith's panicked eyes shoot to mine. "Gum."

"Gum?" In two strides I cross the wooden planks to the bride and the father of the bride, then assess the situation.

In spite of the significant funds available to her, Meredith found the perfect on-sale, off-the-rack dress at David's Bridal. The long-sleeve gown stretches to the floor and fits her body as if custom-made. Nothing extravagant, but everything beautiful and demure with guipure lace skimming the top of the ivory dress.

And on her collarbone, stuck in between the thick threads, sits a grayed piece of gum.

I didn't realize I needed to institute a no-gum rule on Meredith's wedding day.

"I know. I know." She nods, the garland of tiny wildflowers holding its place while her wavy locks of brown hair dance across her shoulder blades. "I make it to fifteen seconds before I walk down the aisle, and disaster strikes." Using the matching bouquet, she points in the direction of the wad.

The culprit is positioned right above the sweetheart cut of the dress. If I can distract Meredith from moving, I might be able to retrieve the piece without leaving a mark.

"I'm not even a gum chewer. But one of Hank's guys offered me a stick." Meredith spews her words, her arms flailing in nervous energy. "And all I could think was of all days, my wedding day is not the day for bad breath. So I took the gum. Why couldn't he have had a mint?"

Notes from a violin drift through the doors of the chapel and onto the tiny wooden-plank porch. Little time remains before Meredith's niece finishes the prelude and begins the bride's procession.

I grasp her shoulders, my focus locking with her wide eyes. "Meredith, you are a vision. This is your day to marry the man you love."

A blinding smile breaks across her beautiful face, and she releases a heavy exhale.

"A piece of gum"—I glance down, plucking the menace off the gown in one swift movement—"cannot touch today. Neither can anything else."

Both of us shift our focus to the dress. No evidence of a stain.

"You're a miracle worker," she whispers with brightened eyes. "I can't imagine what I'd do without you."

I'm hoping those words will be etched in stone when she returns from her honeymoon and I ask for the program director job. But in this moment, she remarks these words on a personal level, and she can't possibly know what they mean to me. Clearing the lump from my throat, I nod. "It's time for you to get married."

Meredith lifts her gown and taps one of her feet in front of her, revealing her trademark Texas flag cowboy boots. She flashes a smile at me, then says over her shoulder, "Let's go, Dad."

Her father steps forward, loops his daughter's arm around his, and guides them to make an entrance into the chapel.

The pastor nods to Meredith's mother. She takes her cue to stand, and the rest of the family follows her example.

As they walk down the aisle, varying degrees of smiles, several wobbling chins, and a few tears adorn the small congregation's joyous faces.

But it's Harlan's heated gaze of pure adoration that gives me pause.

Tempts me to hope. That maybe. Maybe someday.

Someone would finally choose me.

A picture of a toothpick-wielding security consultant with mesmerizing green eyes pops into my head.

No. No way. He had his chance three years ago when he asked me to dance and then ditched me. Harlan called him a globetrotter. I don't need someone else in my life who will leave me. That list already includes too many names.

Pursing my lips, I shake my head back into the moment. I lead a good life. A fulfilling life, doing something at which I excel. I'm needed by those around me.

And that is enough.

Before heading into the chapel, I turn around and peruse the nearby grounds one last time. I skim the landscape, searching for any kind of movement.

Hank stands nearby, pretending to work on a fence. And though I can't see him, I sense Luke's presence. Why do I find that comforting?

With no answers to my question, I back into the chapel, drawing the doors closed.

Everybody needs to eat, I tell myself as I maneuver a small mountain of mashed potatoes onto a plate. Even annoying security consultants.

Standing at the buffet table set up at the main house on the Holcombe ranch, I release a long breath. The ceremony went off seamlessly, the celebratory meal was enjoyed by all, and little Alex got to shove delicious wedding cake in both Harlan's and Meredith's mouths before they left for their nine-day honeymoon.

I can't imagine Luke had an opportunity to eat today. Maybe a few bites of a protein bar he had stowed away in one of the pockets of those well-fitting cargo pants. If pressed by hunger, someone who looks like him could probably wrestle a wolf to the ground and make his own jerky, all while keeping the land around him safe.

Whatever the case, I'll just take him this plate of food to butter him up before I send him on his way.

"What's up with you?" Tanya Purtle approaches the long granite kitchen counter with an armful of Tupperware.

As a wedding gift for Harlan and Meredith, the tenants at Twelve Bluebells created a makeshift catering company to help with the celebratory dinner. They can't cook to save their lives, but they made effective, albeit humorous, sous chefs while the two families prepared their traditional Thanksgiving recipes for the wedding feast. The sole item purchased for the event was an exquisite pumpkin-flavored wedding cake lavished in a thick layer of buttercream frosting.

The family devoured the cake an hour ago, before the newlyweds left the premises. The only remnants of the delectable dessert are the three figurine toppers. A miniature Harlan, Meredith, and little Alex.

Now the halfway house girls serve as the cleanup crew. If their straightened shoulders and confident air are any indication, it seems they have taken proud ownership of their gift to the Holcombes. A small token of gratefulness to the people who offered them a safe home.

I study the young woman in front of me. Her light brown skin, tawny eyes, and long legs could put her on a runway somewhere. Tanya typically hides her beauty under hats and baggy clothes, but today's simple A-line dress to the knees accentuates her natural beauty.

"Miss Penelope? You doing okay?"

"I'm well, thank you," I say. A giant hunk of green bean casserole clings to the serving spoon, and I shake it onto the plate.

"That's just it. You seem almost too well. Almost relaxed."

Refusing to give her the annoyed response her playful jab was meant to produce, I continue to forage through the leftovers. "Well, why wouldn't I be? The wedding was lovely. The meal was wonderful. And cleanup is now in your capable hands. Of course I'm relaxed."

Other than a headache I've been working on all day, I'm relaxed and relieved. There were no signs of any threat during the ceremony. I smile to myself. A certain security consultant could soon be discharged of his duties. And I will be discharged of the attraction. I shake my head. *Dis*traction. I will be discharged of the *distraction.*

Tanya places the tall stack of containers on the counter. "There's enough food on your plate to feed a pack of wolves."

"Only one wolf," I say under my breath. More of a panther, actually. One towering, dark, svelte panther named Luke.

The top two pieces of Tanya's storage containers teeter, and sticking out a hand, I stop the portending avalanche.

Tanya shoves a serving dish aside and divides her pile into two shorter stacks. "Well, I'm glad to see you're eating. I was worried you caught the arbitrary and got a stomachache."

I don't correct her assumption that the food is for me. There's no need to alert the girls to Luke's presence if he's leaving.

I reach over the counter to nab the last piece of cornbread, thinking through Tanya's word choice. She performed well on the GED, but her lack of vocabulary is hurting her SAT practice scores. Ever since she purchased a word-of-the-day calendar, we've had some confusing, if not interesting, conversations. "I think you mean dysentery," I say.

"Right. Right. That's what I meant." Tanya's responses to her word mix-ups always include a distant stare and a head nod. As if she's trying to calculate a complex math problem, only to realize the answer she needs requires letters, not numbers.

After wishing good night to the girls, Hank, and the Holcombes, I pull my hair into a bun, wrap myself in my trench coat, and slide on my gloves. The trek from the main house on the Holcombe property to neighboring Twelve Bluebells isn't too far, but the chilly gusts coming off the Rocky Mountains usually shoot straight through to my bones. Armed with the plate of leftovers, I head out the door.

The sheer force of the howling wind almost knocks me over. I tighten my grip around the edge of the plate, pinning the flopping foil in place. But as I walk across the fields, the chills running down my arms have less to do with the decrease in temperature and more to do with instinct.

Am I being watched?

I scan my surroundings. Well-lit houses pepper the ranch grounds, but darkness seeps between each building, the overcast moon refusing to help my visibility. The guesthouse wind chimes frantically clink as I pass.

The nearby bushes shake.

I freeze and glance in the direction of the noise. Many small- to medium-sized critters live on this land. That has to be a raccoon. Heart pounding, breath labored, I quicken my strides toward my destination.

Passing the chapel on my left, out of the corner of my eye I catch a shadow on the move.

A hulking, dark figure fast approaches. He yells, but the wind carries his words away. Whatever message he meant for me is indecipherable.

I cry out and throw the plate of food at my attacker.

Closer to Twelve Bluebells than the Holcombe ranch, I take off running toward the boardinghouse. The fence separating the properties will slow me down, but heading in that direction is my best shot at finding safety.

The barren, hardened field of late autumn challenges my high heels, and I struggle for balance with each step. On my next stride, my ankle turns. I hit the ground, nothing but my palm breaking the fall. A cry escapes as pain sears from my wrist to my elbow. Trying to gain leverage, I dig the pointed toe of my right shoe into the grass. But my foot slips and I go down on my knee.

A massive shadow bears down on me.

Solid arms hook around my waist, pull me to stand, then yank my back to his front. A gloved hand covers my mouth, muffling my effort to scream. "Penelope," he growls in my ear. The grip at my middle squeezes, and air is forced from my lungs. He half drags, half carries my kicking body to the seclusion of the shadows on the side of the chapel. "Shh. It's—"

With everything in me, I raise my knee and thrust the spike of my heel back into his shin. It's not a direct hit, and my foot shanks off the fabric of his pants. A hiss sounds from behind me, but the lock across my belly doesn't loosen. My arms flail uselessly.

Jagged breaths can't provide me with enough oxygen, and I start to shake. I'm losing my ability to fight back. Stars dot my vision, and my weakened body sinks lower.

My attacker releases my mouth from his hold.

I know I should scream, but if I can't get more air into my lungs, I'm going to faint.

Strong hands cover mine while thumbs stroke the tops of my knuckles.

One choppy breath in. One shaky breath out.

One short breath in. The stars dissipate. One longer breath

out. My line of sight is clear again. My other senses return, and I feel the hard wall of a chest at my back.

"Penelope." The deep, gentle voice fills my ear. "You're safe. It's Luke."

Luke. Luke Granger. I blink and inhale cool air, unable to fill my quick-moving lungs to capacity.

Pull yourself together, Penelope.

Luke's hold remains solid. And for a few seconds, suspended in someone else's strength, my burdens no longer mine, I relax. As the adrenaline drains from my body, I allow my head to rest on his shoulder.

"That's it." His minty breath tickles my cheek. "You're safe."

"I'm safe." My breath shows in the crisp air. I am safe. My breathing slows, and Luke loosens his hold.

Wait. I'm safe?

The events of the last ninety seconds replay in my mind. "I'm safe?" My yell travels across the field. "What is wrong with you?" I ram my elbow into the side of his gut, his grip loosens completely, and I whirl around on him.

This would have been a solid move, except for my lightheadedness and the ankle I twisted. I falter, and to my utter embarrassment, Luke grabs my elbows to steady me.

Blazing eyes stare back at me.

With all the vast land around us, how can his energy possibly fill the fields?

"Whoa there." He grinds his words.

"What—" I lose my balance again and grasp his forearms. Closing my eyes, I grit my teeth. "What were you doing?"

"I was trying to keep you out of the line of sight of an unidentified vehicle. That is, until you initiated the world's most ill-timed food fight."

My eyes pop open, and I stare at his chest. The one plastered with swashes of turkey, gravy, and mashed potatoes. Wonderful.

The back of my trench coat is likely covered with the other half of the meal.

"What do you mean? Whose line of sight?" The last words are shaky at best, and darn it if his hands don't tighten.

The sound of spinning tires draws my attention across the field. On the opposite side of the wooden fence, a black SUV I hadn't noticed before reverses and peels off, spraying gravel down the driveway of Twelve Bluebells Ranch.

I return my gaze to him. "Who was that?"

"I don't know." He studies my face. "How much pain are you in?" He releases one of my arms and pulls his phone out of his back pocket. His attention only leaves me to make a call. Once he draws the cell to his ear, he raises his eyebrows.

"I'm fine." I hold my glare in place and hope it masks my extensive discomfort.

His nostrils flare. It isn't an attractive feature on most people. Annoying that with Luke, it only enhances his masculinity. After he reports the make, model, and plates of the SUV to the person at the other end of the line, he shoves the phone back in his pocket.

I pull my arm from his grasp and massage my wrist. "Who was that on the phone?"

"A guy who works for me." He chomps on his gum and his eyes dart around, taking in our surroundings.

Choosing to ignore his vague answer, I rub the scar above my eyebrow. "Can we revisit the part before you almost killed me?"

"Do you mean the part before you walked toward a Peeping Tom in an unknown vehicle and I saved your life? Sure. Let's revisit it."

"Was attacking me necessary? You could have just yelled my name."

"I didn't attack you. I extracted you from a possibly dangerous situation. And I did yell your name, but you didn't hear me."

Stupid thundering wind.

How did I miss the SUV? But its presence doesn't mean I was in any danger either.

The gum pops between his teeth, causing my hackles to rise. Is there anything more obnoxious? As if to answer me, my mind recalls the toothpick from earlier today, and I sigh. The sooner we solve this, the sooner I can rid myself of this man.

I step back, placing weight on my good foot. With a swift yank, I smooth out the front of my coat. "Can you please give me the rundown of what just happened?"

After a beat, he offers a curt nod. "From my viewpoint, the wedding went as planned. Hank and I were in constant contact." He shifts his head and points to some kind of earpiece. "After the ceremony, I tracked everyone from the chapel to the main house and kept eyes on the grounds during the meal. Meredith and Harlan left the property, and my guy has since reported they made it to the Broadmoor and checked in without incident. Nothing suspect happened the rest of the day. Until a few minutes ago, when that black Suburban showed up, parked, but left the engine running."

My gaze travels to the empty driveway. "Do you think it's the intruder from last night?"

"Can't say. We'll know more when we run the plates."

"It could be the press." I hug my arm into my chest, massaging the pain in my wrist with gentle motions. "If someone heard a rumor about Harlan's wedding, his agent would have been contacted. We've heard nothing from her. But if someone in town found out, it could be local media. You probably made a big production over nothing."

"Like I said, we'll know more when we run the plates." Luke narrows his gaze on my wrist. He runs his knuckles over my forearm. "You okay?"

My entire body jerks away from the contact. "I'm fine."

He widens his stance and splays his hands on his hips. "I know the last few minutes weren't ideal, but today went well, Penelope."

"It did. Everything went well," I say, thinking of all the details that fell into place rather nicely over the course of the day. "I think the most stressful thing happened right before the wedding. Thankfully, we avoided a gum disaster with Meredith's dress." I glance at his gum-chewing mouth. An eerie sensation crawls over my scalp, and I straighten my spine. "*You* gave Meredith the gum. You have no idea what you caused. She was so nervous, she accidentally spit out that gum, and it stuck to her gown."

He scratches the stubble on his cheek, unsuccessfully trying to hide a sheepish smile.

"What were you thinking? You can't give a bride a stick of gum right before she walks down the aisle." I throw my arms out, vaguely aware of how ridiculous my argument sounds. "How does that play out, Luke? Does she hand someone the wad of chewed gum right before she says her vows? Or later before she kisses the groom?"

He chuckles and opens his mouth to answer, but I hold up my hand. "Wait. Why did you even see her before the wedding? You were supposed to stay out of sight."

"Hank and I accidentally ran into her, and I had to improvise." He shrugs. "I've never met her, but I didn't want her focusing on me. The gum bought me a short distraction, and then we hightailed it away from her. How was I supposed to know she couldn't chew gum and be a bride at the same time?"

"Because she's Meredith." She's lovable from head to toe. Something in the deepest part of me envies her ability to be imperfect and yet completely endearing.

"I set up surveillance in the chapel this morning so I had eyes and ears on the service. It was a nice ceremony." He grins. "My favorite part was when she pledged her eternal love to Hercules."

In spite of the pain radiating down my arm, I smile. "Yes. That is classic Meredith."

Only lovestruck, awe-inspired, winsome Meredith would say

her vows using the name Harlan was known by on the big screen and YouTube.

I press some weight into my ankle to test its strength. Our conversation gave the sting some time to dissipate, and when I distribute more weight to it, only a minor protest from my foot remains.

"Tomorrow I'll get to the bottom of who owns the SUV," Luke says. He nods to my wrist. "In the meantime, you need some ice on that."

A strand of my hair blows in the wind and I pull it into submission, tucking it behind my ear. What I need is for Luke to leave.

Forget the questionable vehicle. I am in real trouble if a man can make me feel better with one simple gesture of attention and care.

Notwithstanding the toothpicks and sticks of gum.

3

NOT TODAY.

Please, I beg my body, *not today.*

Hunched over the kitchen counter at the main house on Twelve Bluebells Ranch, I rub my forehead, willing the headache that woke me in the dark of predawn to go away. *Think, Penelope. What is the minimum you have to accomplish today? Prioritize. Then you can go hide.*

"Good morning, sunshine."

I snap straight at Luke's obnoxious greeting, and the sharp pain at my temple reprimands me for the movement. Biting back my distress, I face him with calculated control. "Good morning." Even my quiet acknowledgment pounds a hammer into my head.

Luke flips on the overhead lights, and he might as well have taken an ice pick to my eyes.

Trying not to grimace, I direct my gaze to the floor as I approach the panel on the wall. "I like the natural light in the morning." A grunt accompanies my complete lie. While averting his stare, I throw my hand out to slap the switch to the off position.

Only I forgot about my fall last night and pain shoots up my arm. I curl my aching wrist into my chest.

With one glance at Luke, I catch his narrowed eyes. The energy radiating from him is more blinding than the canned lights. I'm tempted to ask if he has some kind of off button. At the very least, a dimmer switch.

Two long strides in my direction, and his huge body stands in front of me. "Are you okay?"

My migraine welcomes his soft tone. So does my soul. I have to be careful. My defenses are down a little today, and it would be easy to want someone to wonder if I'm okay. Easy to forget that I'm perfectly capable on my own. Without someone to care for me.

I take in his attire. "Are you wearing the same clothes as yesterday?" His foul aroma answers my question, and I cover the lower half of my face to keep the odor farther out of range. "Oh my gosh. You are."

"It's my new cologne. Nature's Delight." He gently pulls my injured arm toward him and inspects my swollen wrist, cradling it in his tanned, veined, calloused hands. His tender touch tingles up my arm, warming me. After a final sweep of his fingers across my forearm, he releases me. "Just a sprain."

I grasp the spot he touched and wipe off the leftover sensation. "Did you sleep at all last night?"

"No. Surveillance." He crosses his arms in a macho-man stance while his eyes scan my face. "What's wrong with you?"

"It's nothing." I rub the scar over my left eye, and it welcomes the pressure. "Did you find anything significant?"

"No. But I got a feel for the property and its security needs." He pulls a thin beef stick out of his back pocket, removes the wrapper, and tears off a bite.

The strong stench of teriyaki invades the kitchen, and my stomach roils. I sidestep away from him. Why do my senses have enhanced powers during a massive headache? A supersonic sense of smell would serve me better at roll call. I could sniff out any possible drinking, drugging, or questionable activities.

The girls. *Focus, Penelope.*

Placing more distance between Luke and myself, I move backward until my hips rest against the counter behind me. "The tenants will be down in a minute to check in for the day. I'll make introductions."

"I take it they're all staying here in the main house?"

"For now, yes. The boardinghouse is under renovation and won't be ready for several months, but when it opens, it will have space for fourteen resident rooms."

Meredith has been working with a renowned architecture firm to create efficient square footage in the unique space. Fourteen rooms and four bathrooms upstairs. Downstairs holds an open floor plan with a mammoth kitchen, dining room, and great room to encourage a family atmosphere. Several closed rooms off to the side of the house will have multipurpose function for tutoring, professional development, yoga classes, art classes, and whatever else Meredith can come up with to give these women skills and support.

Across the kitchen here at the main house, double doors open to a beautiful deck. In spite of the closed blinds, light streaks through. The sun must have come out from behind a cloud because the brightness in the room multiplies, and my optic nerves want to shrivel into the far recesses of their sockets. Unable to continue speaking, I close my eyes and swallow.

"Migraine?" Luke asks.

I grunt my affirmation.

"Go to bed, Penelope," he orders. "I'll figure everything out."

"Today is the girls' day off. I think all three of them will leave the property." Did the house just shift? I grip the edge of the counter. "Curfew's at ten."

With each step Luke takes closer to me, the monstrous fragrance of his jerky gets stronger, but thank goodness he at least sets it on the counter. Gently, he draws one of my hands off the granite. He drags his thumb over my palm, then rubs the spot between my thumb and pointer finger.

"What are you doing?" And why is my voice breathy?

"My grandma got migraines. She said this helped."

I want to protest his proximity. But the massage causes the headache to decrease by two percent, my first semblance of relief in hours. Keeping my eyes shut, I inhale a shaky breath. "I apologize for not getting you a proper breakfast this morning."

"What are you talking about? You threw a wonderful plate of food at me last night." His quiet, rumbling voice reverberates in my ears, almost as if he reined in his intensity so he could soothe my pain. His next statement is definitive but somehow softer, as if he's reprimanding me with the kindest thing he can say. "Don't need you to take care of me, Penelope. I have a job to do."

With my eyes closed, I nod. Right. Stay focused. "We should talk about your plan for the day." The jackhammer in my head slows a bit. His hands are magic, and God help me, I want to lean into his chest and let him take away this misery. I'm grateful his teriyaki death breath prevents me from acting on the ridiculous thought.

"Got a guy who's delivering the updated security system to the ranch. We'll install it today."

"But nothing happened yesterday. It's over. Crisis averted."

"Harlan wanted me to stick around while he's on his honeymoon. So that's what I'm going to do." Using his thumb, he increases the pressure on my hand. "After I finish the install, I'll gather intel on anyone with access to the ranch."

"Why's that?"

"Only a handful of people knew about the wedding. Intentionally or accidentally, someone had to leak the information. That could lead us to our vandal."

What sounds like a herd of elephants descends the stairs. Only they speak in high-pitched English with intermittent giggles.

The girls.

I stifle a groan and open my eyes. "I need to introduce you to the girls."

Luke nods, releases my hand, and turns to rest his hips against the counter next to me. He crosses his legs and arms, but his alert eyes give a hint to the harnessed power hidden underneath his relaxed stance.

I don't think this man misses much.

Then again, there's no way he can miss Finley's entrance. She bounces her beautiful eighteen-year-old self into the kitchen, and it's hard to believe she isn't using a pogo stick. "Good morning, Miss Penelope."

Her sheer enthusiasm could cause me to have a stroke. I flinch and hold out a hand as if it could stave off the decibels traveling toward me at light speed.

"Oh." She skids to a stop, gorgeous brown hair waving forward, chocolate eyes widening. "Do you have a headache? Is it as bad as the last one? It looks as bad as the last one."

Bianca, looking over her shoulder to talk to Tanya, slams into the back of Finley. "Whoa."

"Shh. Miss Penelope has one of her headaches." Finley, my sweet caretaker, shoots her arm out during this declaration.

"Who's this?" Bianca doesn't try to disguise her disgust. Her glare rakes over Luke from head to toe and back again. She holds her body taut.

The other two girls freeze.

Introducing Bianca to new men always constitutes a challenge. With her past, no one can blame her.

"Bianca, this is Luke Granger." I use a calming voice. "He's going to be on the property working on the security system. Mr. Granger, this is Bianca Miller."

The air in the room goes static. No one moves. To Luke's credit, he waits with the rest of us.

"Bianca." My call to her is a whisper as I coax her into action with my words. "Luke can back a trailer."

Whatever I might think of Luke and this situation, Harlan chooses his friends wisely. He would not have left us with someone he didn't trust implicitly.

At the sound of our safety phrase, Bianca shifts her stare from me to Luke and inhales. In a moment more courageous than Luke will understand, she takes two steps toward him and offers a hand.

He returns her greeting with slow movements.

A wisp of relief floats through the room, calming the charged energy to a dull roar.

Finley bounces in front of Bianca and holds out her hand. "I'm Finley Harris, Mr. Granger. So nice to meet you."

Luke keeps his eyes on hers as he shakes her hand.

She claps her hands in exuberance. "So much fun to have someone new at the ranch!" Her feet almost flitter off the floor.

"Don't get all unkempt." Tanya slides in between Luke and Finley, shielding her friend from any more attention. "Hi, I'm Tanya Purtle." She pumps Luke's hand.

"Luke Granger." His lips twitch.

"Tanya, I wonder if you meant to say 'verklempt'?" I ask. "I think that was the word of the day last Tuesday."

"Right. Right." Her blank-faced gaze moves to the kitchen window, and she adjusts her sweatshirt hem over her black yoga pants. "That's what I meant."

Finley turns her long-lashed doe eyes to Luke. "Tanya is studying for the SAT, but Miss Penelope said this was a good opportunity for all of us to work on our vocabulary. I just don't know when I'm going to use the word 'verklempt.' Has anyone ever used the word 'verklempt' in their life?"

Tanya crosses her arms and huffs. "I just did."

The group collectively chuckles, and I grit my teeth as the sound causes another round of pain to pelt my brain. Unfortunately, Luke chooses this moment to grab his beef stick and take another bite.

Finley shifts to create a circle with the five of us. "Shh. Penny Lady has another migraine, you guys."

"You look like you're going to puke. Is it the beef jerky?" Tanya scrunches her face. "But, Miss Penelope, just because Meredith's gone on her honeymoon doesn't mean we're okay with you puking."

I close my eyes as stifled giggles circle the room. If I didn't feel like I was on my deathbed, I'd admonish them. While Meredith's vomit phobia is a common topic of conversation in the house, the reality of it is not entirely fun.

Feeling a presence in front of me, I open my eyes and Luke fills my vision. On my next inhale, the scent of his jerky fills my nostrils. My exhale includes an unfortunate gag. As I tip toward him, I reach out, grab the offensive-smelling snack from his hand, and hurl it in the direction of the sink. My self-preservation move causes me to lose my balance, and I am forced to clutch his biceps. His well-formed, hard-as-a-rock biceps.

"Right." Luke transfers me to his side, keeping a hand on my elbow. "Nice to meet you all," he says to the girls. "But I need to get our girl here to bed. I understand you have the day off today. I'll be here for check-in at ten o'clock."

Our girl? What did he mean by that?

Bianca scowls at Luke. Tanya gives him a thumbs-up. But it's my sensitive Finley who sees more than the other two. Her bright eyes fixate on Luke's grip, and she glances at me with a grin.

I give her nothing in return. It's best for no one in the room to know how much I enjoy Luke's warm touch on my skin. Myself included.

He guides me down the hallway that leads to my bedroom suite. At the back of the house, the mother-in-law quarters are equipped with a full bath and an outside door to the garage. I can almost pretend I have my own efficiency apartment. No one is allowed to come back to my room. Not without reason. And because I know no one will enter my domain, I have allowed myself to make it my own. Decorate. Enjoy the safety of a cocoon no one else will enter.

"Please stop here," I say. I'm not proud of my pitiful tone, but it gets the job done. He doesn't move closer to my private quarters. "I apologize for needing your help today. I know this is not what you were hired to do."

"It'll kill two birds with one stone. I need to get to know the girls and question them anyway."

The sharp jerk of my head is involuntary, and I pay for it. A piercing stab starts at the base of my neck and travels around my cheek, over my temple, and up through the crown of my head. "What kind of information could they possibly know that would be helpful?"

"I'll go in soft with the questions, Penelope. But word of the wedding got out somehow. Tracking down that answer will help our cause."

"They're good girls who are—" My world spins, and I place a hand on the wall to steady me. "Doing the best they can. We're teaching them new life strategies."

He steps closer, his body towering over me. "Are you okay?"

I exhale, ignoring that he once again asked how I am and that I once again liked it, and direct my attention to the task at hand. "Do not give them a reason to make poor choices."

"Do you have appropriate medication to take for this?" Concern laces his question.

Disregarding it, I focus on taking care of my girls. "Do not confuse them."

His soft chuckle floats through the hallway. "What does that mean?" He lowers his voice. "Do you find me confusing, Penelope?"

I take two steps backward toward my room, my hand grazing the wall. Once I reach the door, I clutch the knob and release a heavy breath. "Do not smile at them."

"My smile's confusing?" Another chuckle.

I'm not trying to be funny. Is he flirting with me? Why does it feel like I might *want* him to flirt with me?

I swallow.

I'm a woman who doesn't make mistakes. I only make choices.

And I make a deliberate choice when I glance back at Luke.

"My smile's confusing?" he repeats. His eyes glitter, and the sparkle hurts my head.

But this time it isn't the migraine.

As his grin fades, his eyes spear their intensity at me. "I'll take care of the girls while I'm here, Penelope. And I'll take care of you too."

4

"CLAP, CLAP, TA-BLE, ta-ble, clap, up, down. Clap, sweep, top, ta-ble, bot-tom hand, down." The chant moves through the wall and into my bedroom.

Tucked into the warmth of my bedspread, I pry my eyes open and peek at the bedside clock. 10:13 p.m. Only four minutes have passed since the last time I checked. I'm not surprised I can't fall back to sleep. Without turning on a lamp, I sit up, testing my headache. The only thing pounding is the game going on in what sounds like the dining room. I sigh in relief. Migraine gone.

Time to get back to work and figure out what's going on outside my four walls.

As I slide my feet into the nearby house slippers, I throw my hair into a ponytail. My gray Pepperdine sweatshirt and navy sweatpants will have to do.

Once I enter the dining room, it all becomes clear. With the padded fabric walls as their background, in high-back chairs with light wood scrolling etched at the top, the girls sit at the end of the matching donated dining room table. All this dining room needs is a painting with abstract brushes of pastel colors and it could be launched back to the 1980s.

Luke, whose army-green cargo pants and black Henley shirt imply that maybe he showered since the last time I saw him, tromps along the area rug, circling the girls and chanting the directives to a game that involves nothing more than plastic cups.

He looks good. Somehow relaxed and still commanding the room.

He spots my entrance and makes his way to my side. His eyes peruse my face. "How's the head?"

I turn my eyes to the girls. "Fine. You smell like you found your way to your accommodations in the master suite."

He shifts his attention to the table. "You like the way I smell?"

"I like that you showered. And I hope you can get some sleep tonight."

"Penny Lady," Tanya says. "Hope you're feeling better."

"What are they doing?" I ask Luke out of the side of my mouth.

"Sobriety test."

Sobriety test? How can he assess anything with a game?

"Is playing cups standard operating procedure with the LG Security Team?" I snap and shoot him a glare.

Almost in slow motion, he turns his head to me, eyes glittering, a smile tugging at the edge of his lips. "Did you just make a joke?"

"What? No. I—" Did I? Did I just make a joke? I don't make jokes. I stare at him, perplexed. Must be a residual side effect of my migraine medication.

"Playing cups isn't SOP, but it sure is more fun than a boring ol' Breathalyzer test." He throws the judgmental comment at me like a grenade and returns his attention to the middle of the room.

I scan the moving cups on the table, then dart my eyes his way. "We have to ensure they're making appropriate choices. It's a requirement for staying at Twelve Bluebells."

He nods. "Well, as you can see, it looks like everyone made good choices today."

To my dismay, this method of assessment seems logical. I turn to stand in front of him, shielding our conversation from the room. Luke cranes his head down to look at me, and the heat coming off his body engulfs me. The girls chant and giggle off and on, engrossed in their own world. Still, I keep my voice low. "What kind of progress did you make today in regard to the vandalism?"

"Got word that the plates from last night's unidentified car are registered to Katherine O'Rourke." His quiet voice rumbles between us. "That name ring a bell?"

"She's a reporter for the local news. I wonder if she received a tip about the wedding." The muscles in my shoulders tighten. I don't know whether to be angry or relieved at the thought that someone from the media was on the property last night. Maybe it wasn't her. I've met her family. Maybe it was her teenage son. But none of those answers matter. "Bottom line is that the car wasn't a threat, right?"

He cocks an eyebrow. "It was a threat to my jacket."

My face flushes with warmth as I remember the plate of food I launched at him. I straighten my posture, running my hands around the hem of my sweatshirt. "I'm sorry about that. I will happily pay for your jacket to be cleaned if we can stick with the topic at hand, please?"

"From a tactical standpoint, today was productive. The cameras and sensors for the new security system are live. I also placed some new motion-sensor lights around the property. But with this being the day after Thanksgiving, the Holcombe ranch was deserted. No one to talk to about who might have leaked wedding details."

With each back-and-forth of the conversation, I'm drawn just a hint closer to him. Everything in my life revolves around solving problems. For myself. For others. Alone. Even in my solid working relationship with Harlan, the tasks are always *for* him, not *with* him. My whole goal is to do everything I can to help in such a way that it makes his life easier. That's the job, and I've loved every minute.

But I've never been a partner with someone, working through an issue. There's something foreign, uncomfortable, but altogether attractive about the process. About Luke.

"With Harlan and Meredith on their honeymoon, the rest of the Holcombes went to Disney World as a post-wedding celebration," I say. "Other than Hank, all ranching staff are off for the weekend. And the construction crew working on the boardinghouse is also off until Monday. I'm sorry there's no one for you to interview."

"Until now." He steps around me, breaking our small connection, to address the table. "What did everyone do with their time off?"

I bite back a smile. He's a little bit genius. Get the girls distracted. Get them talking.

Moving in sync with the others, Tanya focuses on the cup in front of her. "Well, it was between seeing my drunk, angry mother or taking Bianca shopping." She sweeps the red Solo cup a little farther than usual. "I chose Black Friday shopping."

Luke leans back, cocking a leg to press one booted foot flat against the wall. He crosses his arms while his assessing eyes follow each woman's movement. "Find anything good?"

Tanya traps her tongue between her teeth in concentration. She's the most coordinated of the three at this game. "We found a lot of awesome stuff, but Bianca wouldn't buy anything."

"It's not you, it's me." The unexpected comment comes from Bianca. Her handling of the cups is more stilted than Tanya's, but she has a surprising grasp on the rhythm and her head bobs with the beat of the cups.

Interesting. Bianca has three ways to communicate. When she perceives a threat, she doesn't speak at all. If she's unsure but wants to participate in a conversation, she speaks in relationship-breakup clichés. *It's not you, it's me.* We've seen this choice of communication style the most since her arrival at the halfway house. But if she feels safe, her brilliant, wise inner self draws you to her. I've only been privileged to witness it once, and I hope I'm afforded the opportunity to see that beauty again someday.

It's noteworthy she's chosen to speak in Luke's company tonight. It says a lot about him. I hope he honors her effort in return.

Luke pulls a mint out of his pocket and pops it in his mouth, then shifts his focus. "What about you, Finley?"

Finley is uncharacteristically quiet this evening, but she doesn't lack coordination in the game. I don't think she's imbibed any substances, but something isn't quite right.

Tanya lets out a judgmental-sounding "Hmph."

Finley bangs her cup down and bursts out, "We were in a group, Tanya."

"Whatever." Tanya doesn't miss a beat. "You know your ex is bad news."

Technically, Finley isn't supposed to see her old boyfriend alone, but it doesn't bode well for her to have seen Marcus at all.

Bianca claps and sweeps through the game while she says, "You can't help who you fall in love with." Her tone mocks the clichéd dating sentiment.

Luke narrows his eyes.

I temper my original annoyance at this setup. His little game might prove productive after all.

Finley falters her table taps, and her cup almost falls. "I'm not in love with Marcus anymore. I just miss him as a friend." She shoves the cup over, and as soon as the pattern starts again, she rejoins the game.

Tanya, fixated on the game, raises her eyebrows. "As a friend? A friend who sleeps around on you?"

Bianca adds her cliché. "There's too much of him to be tied to one person."

"He only cheated *once*," Finley says, her tone exasperated.

Tanya's pained red face grimaces. She slaps both palms on the table, the sound bouncing off the walls of the room as she brings the game to a complete halt. "Oh, okay. How about the time he hit you—he still your friend after that?"

Luke's torso jerks with the announcement.

Pushing herself up from her chair, Finley throws her cup across the room. It bounces off the wall and falls to the ground. "He didn't mean it!"

When Tanya stands, she squares her shoulders to face her friend. "Is he still mad at you?"

"He says he's not mad at me." Finley shifts back a few inches and picks at her fingernails. "But he's still upset I chose to come live on the ranch."

"He's an idiot if he hasn't figured out *he's* the reason you came to live on the ranch."

"He's not the reason." Finley flakes polish off her thumb. "I am. Miss Meredith says I have a bad picker. She and Miss Penelope say I can learn how to make good choices."

"How would Miss Penelope know?" Tanya places her hands on the table and leans into them. "She's like a robot. Good choices are probably programmed into her."

The words are like arrows, hurtling toward me but shanking off my armor. It's all right. Sometimes people need target practice before they hit their intended bull's-eye.

I just wish she hadn't said it in front of Luke. For some reason, I don't want him to think I'm a robot.

Luke crunches his mint and grinds the remnants. He glances at me, but I give him a small shake of my head. As long as they don't start pulling hair, it's best to let them continue the showdown.

Looking displeased, he returns his focus to the girls.

"Good choices or not"—Finley puts her hands on her hips—"I bet Penelope's never gotten flowers like mine today."

Flowers. A demoralizing thought presses on my chest. I've never received flowers from anyone other than my boss.

Wait. Finley received flowers today? The hairs on the back of my neck rise.

"Gah." Tanya rolls her eyes with dramatic flair. "You don't even know those were from him. There wasn't a name attached to the delivery."

Pushing off the wall, Luke stands, hands ready at his sides, his fingers twitching. "There was a delivery today?"

"Yes." Finley's face transitions to a dreamy daze, but concern etches her brow. "Though the card didn't make sense."

"What'd it say?" Luke spits out his words, his intensity choking the room.

My heart races. What has him so stressed?

"Something like, he was glad I enjoyed the wedding . . . and just wait until the time was right . . . because he has something planned for us. I texted him when I got home but didn't hear back." She scrunches her nose. "I'm more of a jewelry person than this kind of thing."

Luke clears his throat. "What kind of thing?"

"Well, there were a dozen red roses in a plain vase. And a stuffed animal that cuddles a clock." Finley shrugs. "Flowers die, so why would you spend money on them? The bear is cute, but the ticking on the clock is so loud. Totally annoying."

Luke steps forward, urgency surging in his raised voice. "Where's the arrangement, Finley?"

At the harsh words, Bianca shoves to standing, her chair crashing to the floor behind her. Her chest heaves with frantic breaths.

He swallows, appearing to rein in his urgency. He holds out a placating hand to her. "I'm sorry, Bianca. Hang in there with me, okay?"

With jittery movements, she nods.

Finley's widened eyes dart between each person. "It's in my room. First one off the hallway. What's going on?"

Luke turns to me. "Penelope, take the girls outside, and walk all the way to the property gate at the road. Do not come back. I'll come to you after I check this out."

"Let's go, ladies." In spite of my desire to ask Luke questions, in spite of my initial hesitation to work with him, and in spite of my refusal to accept another dance with him, I trust him to take care of us. Professionally.

I usher everyone in my direction. "On your way out, grab your coats off the rack." Glancing at their feet, I'm glad none of them changed clothes when they got home. Everyone still has their shoes on. But only two of the women are moving.

Bianca stands stock-still, staring at the table, almost comatose.

"Bianca?" I call.

In the background, feet shuffle, jackets are yanked on, voices spike with anxiety. However, in this moment, in this room, the air is eerily still.

"Bianca, can you hear me?"

Nothing. How do I solve this? How do I convince her to evacuate the house?

"Miss Penelope and Bianca, I've got your coats." Finley's voice travels through the house to us, but it doesn't penetrate Bianca's world.

"Bianca, look at me, please." My solid voice doesn't betray me like my shaking hands do. I place myself in her line of sight, and thank goodness, she stares back at me. "Bianca, it's Penelope. Can you hear me?"

It's slight, but she nods.

"We have to go." I take her cold hand in mine.

Her body tightens and her face becomes hard. "I am not going anywhere that *man* tells me."

I don't blame her. Men have never led her to safe places. But I need her to leave.

"Bianca, Mr. Granger's here to help us. And I will explain everything to you once we are out of the house." I give her hand a gentle tug. "But you must come outside with me first."

She releases a noise that can only be interpreted as a growl. "I'm not doing anything for that man."

"Don't do it for him." I stare into her flat blue eyes. "Do it for me. Do it for Tanya and Finley. Do it for yourself. But whatever you do"—I move an inch closer and lower my firm voice—"do *not* do it for him."

After a beat, her features soften. "Okay." She swallows. "I'll leave because you're asking me to."

I squeeze my eyes shut. "Thank you, Bianca." Gripping her hand, I pull her through the living room, to the front door, and out to the dark gravel driveway.

Tanya and Finley wait near the entrance to the ranch, huddled under the spotlight of one of Luke's newly installed motion-detector lights.

"What's going on, Miss Penelope?" Finley's breath fogs in the chilled air.

Did cold weather arrive while I was in bed all day? I catalog our surroundings. No snow, but the temperature is lower than last night. And a cool, westerly wind curls itself around the group.

Could someone be watching?

Tanya thrusts a coat at an unresponsive Bianca.

I grab the black fleece jacket, shake it out, and wrap it around her shoulders, trying to bide my time to figure out how much to tell them. I'm not exactly sure what Luke is up to in the house, but I know enough to follow his lead. "Okay, girls. We need to discuss Mr. Granger's occupation here at Twelve Bluebells."

"No kidding." Tanya's under-the-breath remark is unwelcome, and I flash her a glare to let her know.

"The night before the wedding, there was some minor vandalism in the chapel," I say. "I apologize for not telling you all sooner. I wanted to handle this without it disrupting your lives. However, not communicating this with you was a mistake."

I cannot believe I didn't anticipate this kind of scenario. I may have put them in jeopardy.

Bianca opens her mouth but says nothing.

After explaining the incident and our concerns, I look them each in the eyes. "Luke installed state-of-the-art surveillance systems on both the Holcombe ranch and Twelve Bluebells Ranch and is now keeping an eye out for us." Squeezing Bianca's arm, I gentle my words. "He's here for your safety."

Finley tilts her head to the side. "And why is Mr. Granger interested in my bear?"

"For whatever reason, I think he interpreted it as a possible threat," I say.

"But how . . ." Finley's eyes grow big. "A clock. He thinks it's a bomb?"

I stare back at the house, my brain finally calculating the scenario. My stomach drops. Surely he's not checking out a possible explosive by himself. There's a difference between someone who is a loose cannon and someone who doesn't value their life. Which one is he?

"Marcus wouldn't have sent a bomb," Finley says.

"Finley!" Tanya stomps, her hands fisted. "For the love of God, there wasn't a name on the card. The bear might not have been meant for you."

"But it might still be from Marcus. He still loves me." A breeze carries Finley's hushed words away. I wish the wind would take her expectations with it.

Tanya groans. "You have got to be kidding me." She leans in to hand me my trench coat.

After whisking it around my body, I dive my arms in, yank the lapels closed, and tug the tie taut at my waist.

"What do you think he's doing in there?" Tanya says to the house.

"Assessing the situation."

Before I can figure out what we can do to help, Luke's massive, shadowed figure fills the doorway. "Okay, ladies. Come on back."

As we make our way toward the lit-up house, I glance back to check on Bianca. She trudges behind the rest of us, her stoic face pointed to the ground, hands in her pockets.

When I cross the threshold, Luke grabs my wrist. I stop, causing the other three to pile up behind me.

"I think we all need to sit down and have a talk." Without sparks of humor in his eyes, he is almost unrecognizable. The protective beast I've known was in Luke stands in front of me.

"May we please wait until morning?" I slide my eyes to indicate the girls.

"Not sure that's a good idea."

Finley peeks around me. "Is my bear okay?"

A muscle in his face twitches. "The bear is fine. Except the delivery wasn't for you."

Her shoulders slump as if his words poked a hole in her spirit. "Then who was it for?"

Luke's searing gaze shoots to me. "Penelope."

5

"ALL RIGHT. It's just the two of us. You got something you want to tell me?" Hands splayed on his narrow hips, expansive chest puffed, Luke's commanding presence fills the kitchen.

"Shh." I shush him with my hand. "Settling the girls took long enough. I don't need your voice to alarm them. Again." Though I am glad he relented and postponed asking the girls more questions until tomorrow.

I pull the rubber band out of my ponytail. "Finley looks at me like I ran over her dog. I almost wish those flowers were from Marcus." Running my fingers through my hair, I regather it into a ponytail, swirl it around, and tuck it securely into the elastic.

He scowls at the bun I created. I don't know what that's about, so I smooth the strays flat against my head and tuck some wisps around my ears. "What is going on?"

"Who's Jason Livingstone?" His clipped words are full of irritation.

I cock my head to the side, trying to put all the pieces of the night together. "What?"

He steps toward me. "Who is Jason Livingstone?"

"I grew up with him." That statement's not a lie. "We're close." Neither is that one.

His gaze narrows. "He sent the bear. To you."

Relieved, I exhale and roll my eyes. Jason's been known to send gifts over the years. But I don't want to get into my past. "Of course he did." To avoid Luke's scrutiny, I walk to the opposite side of the kitchen.

"Is this someone you're involved with?"

My heart stops. He thinks I'm involved with someone? Why do I care if he thinks I'm involved with someone?

I open a cabinet, studying the shelves, calming my nerves. "Jason's a friend, Luke. Why does this matter?" Describing Jason as a friend is easier than describing who he really is to me. Too many questions.

Luke thrusts the florist card under my nose, causing me to lean back to bring the words into focus.

I'm glad you enjoyed the wedding. Just wait until the time is right because I've got something planned for us.

No name is attached to the message.

Confused, I glance at him. "This is what you're upset about?"

He seems angry. Is he—is he jealous? That can't be right.

"Wait a minute." I glance at the card. "How do you even know it's from him? There's no name on the card." I return my focus to the cabinet. No one emptied the dishwasher today, and the mug I need is at the back of the shelf. Grimacing, I stand on tiptoes to reach.

"I made some calls." He leans over me and grabs two cups. In doing so, he brushes his chest against my back.

My body stiffens, and he plants the two mugs on the granite. Recovering from his touch requires a few extra seconds and a deep breath. I slide a canister of tea closer to me, open it, and retrieve two bags of chamomile. "You made some calls?" I prompt him.

He crosses his arms and leans a hip against the counter, standing perpendicular to me. "Even though we didn't file anything formal with the police, the sheriff was briefed on the situation. When I updated him tonight, he offered to have a word with the florist. She passed along the delivery details."

I twist my neck and glare. "You asked him to wake the florist on a Friday night for an unidentified bear delivery?"

"For a suspicious package delivery." His lips quirk. "And waking the florist wasn't hard. He's married to her."

Of course. I slap the tea bags against my palm. "Jason's harmless."

"Are you dating him?"

I grab the handles of the two mugs and walk them to the stove. What's more upsetting—that he's asking the question, or that I want him to know the correct answer?

I can't deal with this right now, so I go on the offensive. "Are *you* dating anyone?"

"No one sent me a delivery today."

"Come on, Luke. Is there a woman somewhere, waiting for you to come back for a dance?" I hold his stare and raise my eyebrows in question.

He pauses. His expression softens. "I'm sorry," he says quietly. "Were you waiting for me to come back, Penelope?"

I've misplayed this conversation, and his question feels like a kick in the gut.

I set one mug down and hold the other under the hot-water spout. What the dining room lacks in needed decor updates, the kitchen makes up for with its modern amenities. The hot-water spout is one of my favorite indulgences, but it doesn't offer me much comfort now. As steam rises from the cup, I try to figure out how to maneuver out of this disastrous conversation. "I'm not dating anyone. Delivery or otherwise. Why is this so important?"

"At the very least, he's interested in you."

"That's not true." An uneasy feeling creeps down my spine. "Our friendship is . . . complicated."

He steps toward me, making it harder for me to breathe. "No man gives a woman a gift unless he has feelings for her."

I shake my head. Not only does he not understand the history and dynamics behind my friendship with Jason, now he's spouting more ridiculous things. "That's not true either."

He smiles, something knowing and a little bit cocky in his tone when he says, "It's completely true."

Reality hits me between the eyes. How would I know? I've never dated anyone. Dating is kind of hard to do when you're moving from one group home to another. Or later, when you're the adopted daughter of a public figure. And now, with the unforgiving spotlight aimed at the assistant to a megawatt superstar. Other than when Luke asked me to dance, I can't think of a time in my twenty-nine years that afforded me any kind of opportunity. Much less the butterflies that had invaded my stomach when Luke smiled at me.

I have to move us past this topic. "I'm going to ask again. Why is this important?"

"Between your admirer, Tanya's hateful alcoholic mother, Finley's ex-boyfriend, and goodness knows who haunts Bianca's thoughts, I don't know what we're dealing with or who to focus on. Not to mention anyone else who lives or works on the ranch." He knocks on the counter twice.

I turn to him, shooting daggers with my eyes. "I don't have an admirer. He's just a friend. And no one you named has connections to Harlan. The incident happened on his property. Why would any of them be the vandal?" I fill the second mug until the tea bag floats to the top.

"Our search isn't about interest in Harlan. Back up a step. How did the person who vandalized the chapel find out about the wedding in the first place? The information leak could point to the person of interest." He steps forward and takes the cup from me, brushing his fingers against mine. "I'll start by talking to the girls tomorrow morning. But looking into everyone with access to both properties will take time. And to be honest, this could lead to a dead end."

Looking away, I rub the knot in my shoulder. He's doing his job, but I hope he doesn't dig too deep into my personal life.

I pick up my drink, drawing it closer to take in its warmth. "You're talking about a needle in a haystack. For all we know, Mrs. Holcombe accidentally mentioned the ceremony to her hairdresser."

Luke lifts his mug to his lips and pauses. "Agreed. If there are obvious suspects, I'll check into them. But I'm not expecting answers this week."

"Then what *are* you expecting to accomplish this week?"

"To check off all the boxes. To keep you guys safe." He takes a sip of tea. "Then move on to the next job."

When I tighten my hold on my mug, I burn my hand. But the pang that shoots through my chest sears far worse.

Right. Check off all the boxes.

This is a job for him with defined parameters.

Then he will move on. Of course.

Absolutely. Hadn't I wanted that just yesterday?

To my detriment, I allowed myself to appreciate working with someone. Sharing the burden of a migraine today. Partnering tonight for the safety of the girls. But this is just a job for him. A job for me.

I shake my head once, ridding myself of the regret passing through me. I always work alone, and I always do a fine job by myself. Excellent, even. "Well, Bianca will be pleased that your time here is short. Yelling at her earlier really set her back."

He winces. "About that. A little heads-up would have been nice."

"I apologize." I place the hot drink on the counter. "But it wasn't like I could hand you their files."

"In my experience, observation reveals much more pertinent intel than a piece of paper."

I clasp my hands in front of me, holding my body taut and my eyes directly on his.

"But considering how little I get out of you, I might welcome a look at *your* file," he says, his solid stare holding mine with an intensity that warms me from the inside out.

No. No way.

He's leaving like the rest of them. He does not get the luxury of knowing me and leaving me. "You don't need a file on me, Mr. Granger."

He rests his cup on the granite and stands straight, expression alert. "Mr. Granger?" he asks in a low, unhappy voice.

"The girls have an activity tomorrow morning and will be available for interviews at ten o'clock." I pour the remainder of my tea down the drain and rinse out the mug while I give directives. "I'll attend your meeting with them. We can convene in the living room." Leaving the cup in the sink, I turn sideways to slip by him.

He touches my arm. "Penelope."

Without looking at him, I strain to maintain a level tone. "Thank you for your help today. And this evening."

"Penelope." His growl is almost a plea.

My stare remains forward. Always forward.

Looking behind me is too painful. And I sense that looking to the side at Luke will only compound the anguish.

So I focus ahead. Because there's always something to do next. Someone to help. Something to fix.

I can't fix anything behind me. I can't depend on the man beside me. I can only move forward. And when I do, he releases my arm.

6

MY CELL PHONE RINGS, offending the peaceful atmosphere of the at-home yoga class. The noise bounces off the walls of the empty room, lands on the scuffed-up hardwood floors, and dies in the four foam mats.

Natalie, the long-haired, fluid-moving, fabulous-bodied instructor, shoots me a glare. It's a peaceful glare, causing no wrinkles in her porcelain, blemish-free skin, but a glare all the same.

The noise can't surprise her. This scenario happens most Saturday mornings when she visits the ranch to teach her class.

I make no apology, exit the room, glance at the screen, and take the call.

"Jason," I say, pushing the door to the makeshift studio closed. "I meant to call yesterday. I apologize."

"No problem." His friendly voice fills my ear. "I figured you needed your rest after all the wedding stress. Did you end up with a migraine?"

Jason always understands me. He would. He's known me longer than most. Been through more with me than most.

"Yes." I sigh, rubbing the scar at my left eyebrow. "But I'm fine now."

"You always end up being fine. I still hate that you have those migraines."

The silence between us fills with flashbacks to the accident that caused my headaches. "Accident" is a gracious word for it. "Attack" seems more accurate. An attack that Jason still believes he should have saved me from.

I pull the phone down to glance at the screen. The clock continues to tick off the seconds of the call. "Jason?"

He clears his throat. "Yeah."

"I got the flowers. They're lovely." If anything Luke said last night about Jason having feelings for me has an ounce of truth to it, I need to steer Jason clear. "But you didn't have to send them."

"I know. But with the wedding, I knew it was a big day for you."

Big day.

Big week. Once I show the Holcombes how well I can manage the ranch without them, I will pitch them my vision as a candidate for program director. But I'm not sharing my plans to ask for my dream job with Jason. He has his own dream plans for me that involve moving to Denver to be near him. A move I'm not even considering.

"Did everything with the ceremony go like you planned?" he asks.

"Almost everything." I bite my lip, recalling the vandalism. It's odd not to share everything with Jason, but I don't want him to worry. I'm not even sure there's anything to worry about, but if Jason gets a hint of the slightest concern, he'll hover.

"What's going on, Penelope? Did something happen?"

One of the family portraits hangs unevenly, and I reach to straighten it. "Nothing I couldn't handle."

For the most part. Minus one regrettably handsome security consultant.

"Are they still waiting five weeks to have a reception? I think that's odd."

"It's not a true reception. Just a party. Meredith has a tough history. They didn't want an overwhelming wedding day. In spite of it being a delayed celebration, I think it will be a fun event. Plus, they'll be able to enjoy it more."

"Have you decided if you're going to invite dear old Mom and Dad?"

I press my palm flat against the wall, and my head drops. "You know I hate it when you call them that."

"You'd rather I call them our dear old adoptive parents?"

"Call them the senator and his wife, please." No matter how noble their adoption of a few strays looked to the public, those vipers don't deserve the word "parent" attached to their name.

"Okay." He clears his throat. "Are you inviting the senator and his wife to the reception?"

Squeezing my eyes shut, I lower my voice. "Yes. I will be inviting the California state senator and his wife to the reception."

"I knew you would." He doesn't disguise his disappointed tone.

My head shoots up, and I glare at the painting of a family having a picnic. "You know as well as I do that they're coming to town on business. I wasn't going to get around having to see them. Including them is a calculated decision, Jason. There will be less grief if I offer an invitation than if I don't."

"And how does your boss feel about his high-maintenance guests?"

"He told me to do whatever made my life easier." I turn away from the happiness portrayed in pictures on the wall. "Which is why you're invited too. I need reinforcements."

"I'll protect you from them."

His confident words cause a twinge of guilt. He always did try to protect me.

"Thanks, Jason," I whisper.

"Have you given more thought to moving to Denver after the reception?"

More guilt. Each time he mentions his hope that I'll join him in the Mile High City, I cringe. Jason and I aren't related by blood. Only a terrible foster care system story. But for me, he's the closest existing faction resembling family.

Other than Harlan and little Alex. And now Meredith. And possibly these exquisite tenants at the ranch who, against my will, make great efforts to plant themselves firmly in my heart.

But joining Jason in Denver has never felt right to me.

The studio door opens and the girls pour out of the room, their moans filling the hallway.

"I've got to go," I say to Jason as I huddle closer to the wall. "Your invitation to the party will arrive in the mail soon. Make your reservations at the Broadmoor now because they book quickly for New Year's Eve. I'll talk to you later."

Pulling my phone down, I press End before he can respond. As much as I love Jason, he requires boundaries. And I'm done discussing a move that isn't going to happen.

"Everyone grab something to drink, then proceed to the living room for a family meeting." I hold my arms out and usher the ladies down the hallway.

Family meeting. Not a term that comes naturally to me.

I resisted it at first. My adoptive family used the label for meetings filled with tension and ridiculously high expectations. But Meredith asks that we use the term to establish the desired culture of the house. Her gatherings are full of love, acceptance, and community. It helps the girls as they discover their place in this world. Or possibly it helps me as I discover my place in their world.

Whatever the case, I am grateful for the new definition of the concept.

After grabbing waters from the kitchen, the three girls enter the living room. Bianca and Tanya shuffle across the Berber carpet and plop themselves on the oversized blue denim couch.

The wide black letters on Bianca's baggy white T-shirt announce "Namaste in Bed Today."

Finley, whose bouncing energy has been reduced to a slight spring, slumps into the remaining space on the middle couch cushion. "Penny Lady, why do we have to do yoga?"

"We're learning to take care of ourselves." Tanya mumbles the words I've said to the girls on repeated occasions.

"I can learn to take care of myself without playing the adult version of London Bridge." Finley twists the cap off a water bottle. "Seriously. Downward dog?"

As Finley speaks, Luke enters the room with a swagger, wearing black cargo pants and a well-fitting black fleece with the LG Security logo on the left side of his chest. There doesn't seem to be a lot of variety in Luke's wardrobe, but I'm not complaining.

"I'm sorry I missed London Bridge," he says.

A serene Natalie appears in the door, her doe-eyed focus on Luke. "Well, if you're here next Saturday, you can join us."

I bet he's *really* sorry he missed London Bridge now. Natalie is a knockout.

Watching Natalie give the most minute attention to Luke makes my skin crawl. I clear my throat. "Thank you, Natalie," I say, not masking my dismissive tone. "We will see you in a week." I step toward the side table and straighten the coffee-table books, aligning each spine with precision.

"Thank you, ma'am"—Luke grins at Natalie, displaying a mangled coffee stir stick protruding halfway out of his mouth—"but I don't do yoga."

In spite of his newest annoying chew toy, the roguish appearance of his dark stubble and the potency emanating from his broad frame offer a vivid picture.

He belongs on a wrestling mat, not a yoga mat.

That isn't correct. He belongs in the wilderness, wrestling a bear on the cool, loamy mat of the forest.

Natalie's stunted smile puts a ding in her zen, but she still manages to exit the room, long limbs graceful, as if she's floating on a cloud of tranquility.

I perch on the edge of one of the dark leather–covered Louis XV armchairs. It flanks the bricked fireplace with a matching partner on the other side. An empty-nest couple in the Springs donated this room of furniture to the ranch when they decided to update their existing home decor. Meredith accepts every donation with open arms. Therefore, each room in the house seems to be decorated or furnished as an homage to a different decade. This room bows down to the 1990s.

Luke studies me, his eyes traveling over the impeccable brown wool slacks that I paired with a thin ivory cashmere sweater. "Why are you all decked out?"

"I'm working."

His eyes glitter. "Did you wear that outfit to practice yoga?"

"No." I flick a piece of lint off my pants. "I was supervising yoga."

"That's not a thing." The plastic stick moves with each syllable, highlighting his jaw muscles.

"What's not a thing?"

"No one supervises yoga."

"Are you going to start this meeting or am I?"

"Do you ever relax?"

I scowl. "I relaxed yesterday. Today, I need to get back to work."

"Yesterday, you fought a migraine." He leans in, the obnoxious stick within my reach. "That's not relaxing. Today is the Saturday after Thanksgiving, and your boss isn't even in town. What could you possibly have on your to-do list?"

"Do you want to see the list?"

"No." He pulls the stir stick out of his mouth and points it at me. "But I want you to be available to me at lunchtime today."

My mouth gapes. "I have to—"

"Nonnegotiable." He transfers his attention to the girls before I can respond. "Ladies, if I could have just a few minutes of your time, please."

Something swirls in my stomach. Do I have a lunch date with Luke? No. A working lunch. Do I want a lunch date with Luke? No. But what if the swirls mean I do? Maybe a little companionship would be nice. Just for lunch. Just this once.

Luke sits in the matching armchair across from me. He straightens his legs, crossing them at his ankles, and folds his hands across his abs. His body is relaxed, but his piercing eyes are alert. Cargo pants are to Luke what high heels are to me. A daily necessity. Dressed in black attire from head to toe, he resembles a resting panther.

"I need your help," he declares to the room.

Finley sits up straight, Tanya cocks her head, and Bianca grants him a curious perusal. With four words, he disarmed them, offered them responsibility, and gave them significance.

In complete awe, I dart my glance from the intrigued girls back to Luke. He continues to prove he's good with them. Trustworthy with them.

"The floral delivery last night was legit. No worries there." He scratches the stubble at his chin. "But I've got to figure out how information about the wedding leaked outside the gates of the ranch to the person who committed the vandalism. Anyone overhear anything that might help me?"

Bianca and Tanya turn their gazes to the middle of the couch.

Finley gapes. "What? You guys think I told someone?" Her pitch rises as she shifts her focus to me. "Miss Penelope, I made a promise not to tell anyone. I know the wedding was supposed to be kept under wraps. I keep my promises."

I nod to her, then redirect my focus to Luke. He's running this show. I won't wade in until there's a problem.

"I need each of you to think through your interactions with people. Any offhand conversations you might have participated in or heard," he says.

Finley points her thumbs to Tanya and Bianca. "They're still looking at me."

Luke returns the stir stick to his lips. He turns his intense green eyes to me. "Penelope? Can you think of anyone you told about the wedding who wasn't on a need-to-know basis?"

He's starting with me, which causes the tension in the room to defuse. Luke should be hired to negotiate peace in the Middle East.

"I mentioned the wedding to three people," I say.

Finley gasps.

Bianca raises an eyebrow.

"Did you have a good reason?" Tanya asks.

I level my voice. "I discussed the wedding with a trustworthy acquaintance. And for business purposes, I consulted a senator and his wife about the dates of the reception. Each of them knew there was an impending ceremony, but they didn't know the time or location."

"How come *your* friend is worthy of telling?" Tanya throws her head around with sass. "But no one *we* know is worthy?"

"This is my job, Tanya. There are pressures on me I need to release. Finding safe people to confide in helps me cope with the stress. I've trusted this particular person in the past with sensitive information, so I knew it would be safe."

The girls ponder my answer while I exhale, grateful no one is pressing anything I mentioned further. Acquaintances and senators in my life are not topics I discuss. With anyone. But glancing at Luke, I catch him observing me. Why do I get the feeling that he wants to know more about my acquaintance and the senator?

Crossing my legs, I fold my hands in my lap.

"Thank you, Penelope." Luke puts his boots on the ground, leans in, and rests his elbows on his knees, his hands dangling between them. "Anyone else think of anything significant?"

Bianca's and Tanya's heads turn to home in on Finley a second time.

"Again? Why me?" Her shriek carries through the room.

"I'm asking each of you," Luke says.

In a giant gesture, she sweeps her pointer finger in a semicircle at every one of us. "You're all staring at me."

Tanya rolls her eyes.

Finley slumps back into the couch, her expression filled with hurt. "You guys think I told someone?"

I inch toward the edge of my chair. "No one thinks you told."

"I think she told," Tanya says.

I dash a glare at Tanya.

"I have no reason to think you did, Finley." Luke's laser focus doesn't waver. "But I need you to think through your interactions. Did you mention a wedding to anyone? Maybe it wasn't about the wedding, but instead a comment about Meredith's family coming into town? Or changes around the ranch?" He leans back. "There's no blame here. I'm looking for innocent conversations."

"You're always talking to that cute guy on the construction crew," Tanya says.

This new announcement slices through the fragile peace in the room, and my posture stiffens.

Finley turns a deep shade of red and bounces off the couch to her feet, fists clenched. "I would never cheat on Marcus!"

Tanya matches Finley's stance but adds a finger point. "You can't cheat on someone you're *not dating anymore*."

"She's just not in a good place for a relationship right now," Bianca says, but her muttered breakup cliché goes unnoticed by the other two girls.

"Ladies, take a seat," Luke says with a commanding tone.

With huffs all around, the women return to their places on the couch.

"Finley, I'm not questioning your honor, yeah?" Luke waits for her to nod. "Think through anyone you've talked to. It could have been recently. It could have been two months ago."

She stares at the coffee table.

"That goes for the rest of you too." He glances at the other two girls.

An uneasy silence falls over the room, everyone seemingly in thought.

Tanya, chewing her thumbnail, aims her vacant gaze at the rug. "This is a nefarious situation."

SAT prep work strikes again. Proud of her for trying even now, I lean toward her and whisper, "This might be an evil situation, Tanya, but I'm wondering if you meant to use the word 'precarious'?"

"Right, right." She nods to the floor. "That's what I meant."

"Bianca?" Luke's voice gentles. "Have you talked to anyone from your family?"

A flash of pain crosses her face.

"You don't need to ask her that," Tanya snaps. "Or me."

Luke waits a beat, then nods. "I'm glad to hear you're both making healthy choices," he says while he pulls out business cards and hands them to everyone. "This has my number on it. Program it into your phone. If anyone unsafe contacts you, use it. Immediately. If anyone receives a package, a letter, a special delivery—anything—hang on to it and let me check it out before you open it. In the meantime, if you remember something helpful, send me a text or give me a call."

Bianca shoves a hand in her pocket and pulls out a long, silver-wrapped stick of gum. Without looking at Luke, she holds it out to him.

He takes the peace offering from Bianca, unwraps it, and trades it out with the stir stick.

Tears sting my nose while a warmth fills my chest. How did he do that? It took me weeks to gain her trust.

To step away from their moment, I zero in on Finley, raising my eyebrows in question.

"I haven't told anyone, Miss Penelope." She sinks into the couch cushions. "I promise. Not Marcus. Or anyone else."

"I trust your word, Finley. Thank you."

This is a dead end. I look at Luke.

"I appreciate your time, ladies." He drops the stir stick and gum wrapper on the side table.

Finley finishes putting commands into her cell, and her head shoots up. "What about Miss Olivia?"

Luke chomps his gum. "Who?"

"Mr. Holcombe's ex-wife," she says a little too enthusiastically, bouncing on the couch cushions.

"I'll need her contact information," Luke says to me.

"It wasn't her," I say.

"What makes you think it wasn't?" He stands and stretches his arms above his head. "I met her once and it wasn't pleasant. I could see how she might have it in for Harlan."

"Because that's not her brand of chaos." I gather Luke's trash, grateful he gave up the stir stick but now concerned about the annoying smacking noise he makes with the gum. I glance up at him in time to catch his lips twitching and a sparkle in his eyes. "What's so funny?"

"You are," he says before he exits the room.

Am I? Am I funny? I've never been called funny in my life. Well, not since my mother. But I thought the memory was too hazy to be true—that I might have wished it instead of remembered it.

What does it mean that Luke thinks I'm funny?

Shaking my head, I smooth the already perfect crease on my pants leg. Nothing. It can't mean anything, because he'll leave when the job is done.

So why do I hope I'll make him laugh again at lunch?

7

"I HAVE SOME ground rules for this lunch," Luke says.

Standing in front of the menu posted at Trivelli's Hoagies, I peer at him out of the side of my eye. "You have rules? The kind you live by? Not just the kind you break?"

"Of course I have rules. We are, after all, trying to have a civilization here." He throws my motto in my face and winks.

Ugh. That wink. That wink that will leave town soon.

The simple decor of the restaurant, located in the old Alexander Film Studio Building, mirrors the down-home feel. The walls are decorated with various pieces of antique projectors and black-and-white photos. History chinked with age, but perfectly placed all the same.

Luke knocks on the wooden counter. "The rules are, you're not allowed to order a salad, a vegetarian meal, or anything labeled as lite."

I gape in horror. "What? Why are those the rules?"

He leans in and aims his mouth for my ear. "Because everyone's got to live a little, kitten."

Kitten? A cross between offense and thrill trickles down my back.

I straighten my spine and take a high-heeled step toward the cash register. "Fine. I excel at following rules."

"What can I get you today, ma'am?" The teenager behind the counter smiles a mouthful of metal at me.

I clasp my hands and rest them on the wooden block, leveling my voice. "I'd like the Rock Star, please."

He nods, his long brown hair brushing the shoulders of his faded restaurant T-shirt as he writes down my order. "A half or a whole?"

Glancing at the menu, I note that at $11.25, half of this monstrous steak, ham, salami, cheese, and sauce hoagie costs almost twice as much as the other sandwiches.

"I'd like a whole, please," I say without changing my facial expression. That should be plenty to make winning this challenge extremely satisfying.

Luke barks his laughter. "A whole? Where are you going to put all that food?"

I slide my gaze to his and glare.

He holds his hands up in surrender, then turns his attention to the shocked kid behind the counter. "I can't be outdone by a pint-sized city girl. By all means, I'll have the same."

"Uh-huh," the kid says without writing anything down, his perplexed eyes darting between the two of us. "Anything to drink?"

I nod. "Water, please."

"Water? With your three-thousand-calorie hoagie?" Luke pulls his wallet out of the back pocket of his pants, shaking his head and chuckling.

"Three thousand is my lunch calorie-intake limit."

This time his laughter comes from deep within his chest, and as I stride toward the drink station, I can't help myself when a smile curls my lips.

Once seated, I smooth out the vinyl blue and white checked tablecloth. A spot refuses to stay in place and wrinkles back.

"These walls have stories," Luke says, glancing around the restaurant. He sets his drink on the table and next to it plunks the plastic sign denoting our order number. He pulls out the chair opposite mine and sits. His body moves with extreme control and power, but somehow he makes it look casual. He leans back, crosses his arms over his chest, and stretches a leg into the aisle. "So. What's your story, Penelope?"

I fold my hands in my lap, out of Luke's sight. "What do you need to know?"

He grabs three packets of sugar from the rectangular plastic box of sweeteners. "Where are you from?"

"How does that pertain to the vandalism?"

"You never know what details might help." Holding the packets at one end, he bats them against his other hand.

I'm never comfortable discussing myself. My past. What exactly does he want to know, and, better question, how little information can I reveal and still satisfy him?

Buying me a little time before I have to approach the topic at hand, the cashier from earlier delivers our food. He places the monstrous meals and silverware in front of us, his eyes bouncing between Luke and me.

My sandwich sits in its full state, staring me down, while the accompanying potato chips flank it like they are its loyal subjects. The proud, sturdy roll holds an enormity of meat, and the oozing cheesy sauce divulges the tight fit inside. A tomato had slipped out of the side, and after I tuck it back in, I say, "This looks wonderful."

When the teen doesn't move from his spot, I raise my eyebrows at him.

He tucks the tray under his arm. "I was kind of hoping you'd let me watch you tackle that beast of a hoagie."

"Maybe I should sell tickets," Luke murmurs, smiling down at his food. He claps his hands loudly and rubs them together.

I unroll the silverware from the napkin. "I think we have everything we need. Thank you."

The boy's shoulders slump, and he trudges to the front of the restaurant.

While I smooth the napkin across my lap, Luke reaches over and slides my fork and knife away from me.

I snap my head up. "What are you doing?"

"No silverware allowed." He gathers both of our sets and drops them on the tray of a passing busboy.

"What? You didn't state that rule at the beginning."

"Would you have ordered differently if you'd known?"

"No."

"Do you want me to get you a bib? The sauce tastes good, but it probably won't wear as well on your fancy sweater."

I glance down at my ivory cashmere top. Not an ideal choice for this meal. I gingerly pull my sleeves up a few inches, then lean in just a touch to inspect my plate. I pick up my hoagie, causing sauce and varying chunks of meat to slip out the back. Then I stretch my jaws to capacity and sink my teeth into my lunch.

With each chew, the flavors of heaven fill my senses. I close my eyes and moan. Somewhere, my vegetarian mother is rolling over in her grave. I offer her a mental apology, and the precise moment there is more space for food in my mouth, I take another bite.

I return the sandwich to the paper plate, pick up my water, and guide the straw between my lips. But with one glance at Luke, I freeze.

His lips twitch. "Should I let you and that sandwich have a nice, cozy lunch together? I can just do some background research on you to fill in the gaps I don't know."

"You're the one who issued the challenge to eat the thing. I'm just delivering on that challenge." I place my cup on the table. Using my napkin, I dab at the corners of my mouth. I'll give him just enough information to satisfy his curiosity, things he could find out on his own—that way I won't infringe on my own privacy. I'll scatter a few pieces of my history. He'll never know the picture they paint is incomplete. "I'm afraid you won't get far researching my past. My records are sealed."

Luke's eyes flash, but the rest of him stays stock-still. "Are you safe?"

"It's nothing that dramatic, Luke. My mom died when I was twelve. I was placed in the California foster care system and lived in several temporary settings until a family adopted me."

He waits a beat, his eyes narrowing. "That doesn't sound like it's without drama."

"I was well provided for. My circumstances allowed me to attend college. I had jobs here and there and landed in Colorado Springs." I shrug. "It's pretty simple." Leaning over my plate, I take another bite of my sandwich.

His actions mirror mine. "You are anything but simple," he says between chomps.

Maybe. But he won't be around long enough to know for sure.

For a few minutes, we eat in silence, the playfulness of the meal lost in the unasked questions.

After several mammoth bites, Luke sits back and gulps down some of his drink. "You didn't say anything about your father."

With just those seven words, my appetite deserts me. This sharing thing isn't working out for me as well as I hoped. For the sake of getting through this conversation, I need to isolate my feelings and focus on the facts. I set my sandwich down and push my plate away. "I don't think he's worth mentioning. He left my mother and me just after I was born."

Luke grinds his teeth, causing the muscles in his cheeks to jerk. "I'm sorry." Those two words seem to carry more weight than just his sympathy.

"My mother, Caroline Reid, was from a small town in Oklahoma. Her family lived almost at the poverty level. Poorer than dirt, she used to say. She met my father and fell madly in love." I rattle off the basics of my family history as if reading a checklist. "She became pregnant, and his poet's soul inspired him to take us to California. He uprooted us, dragged us across the country, then abandoned us when I was six months old. I haven't heard from him since."

Luke swipes his lips with his napkin. "Does he have a history with the law?"

"Not that I know of."

"Probably a stretch, but is there any chance he's come back to town and is trying to get your attention?"

"I can't imagine he would even know where to find me." Sitting back in my chair, I purse my lips, allowing time for the acidic wave in my stomach to pass. I don't think of my father often. It serves no purpose.

Luke balls his napkin and throws it to the side. "Okay. What about your foster homes? Anyone worth looking into?"

"I think in the vast foster care system there's always someone who might be unstable. It can be a disconcerting environment."

"Does that mean you have a person in mind?"

"Luke, the vandalism has nothing to do with me." I grasp the edge of the table and lean toward him. "It's about Harlan. No one from my youth knows or cares where I am." I rub the scar on my brow, swallow the lump in my throat, then quietly say, "No one's looking for me."

He cocks his head. "Except Jason Livingstone?"

This again.

"It's not what you think."

"What is it I think?"

I know he's baiting me. But I can't help myself. "He doesn't have feelings for me."

"Then how is it?" he asks in a tone that I know means he doesn't agree with me.

"Jason and I were in a group home together, then we were adopted by the same family."

He narrows his eyes, seeming to consider this information. "When was the adoption?"

"I was sixteen when the Nelsons welcomed us to their home." The simple statement swirls in my stomach. The Nelsons are a different minefield to tiptoe through.

With no forewarning, Luke pushes out of his chair, grabs both of our cups, and heads to the fountain for refills.

"Will you please get me a Sprite instead?" I call to him when he's three steps away.

"That sandwich causing an upset stomach?"

"You guessed it," I say, offering a manufactured sheepish smile.

It's the sandwich. The Dysfunctional Adoptive Family on Rye with a side of Abnormal Love is the root of my acute digestive distress.

In the few minutes it takes Luke to pay for and grab me a Sprite, my brain swirls along with my stomach. I've never had to discuss my life story like this before. My college application essays hold some of the pieces of my history. Harlan and Meredith hold a different set of the pieces. Jason thinks he holds all the pieces, but he only has the ones I've carefully chosen to share.

Luke won't get every piece either. No one gets that from me. Just because I trust him professionally doesn't mean I trust him with my personal story. Besides, he's leaving and will take it with him. Everyone leaves eventually, taking something from me along the way.

Except Jason. I think he holds on to his pieces of me too tightly, without meaning to.

Upon Luke's return, he slaps my drink down, the fizzing liquid sloshing up the sides of the plastic cup. "Do you trust Jason?" he asks as he sits.

"With my life." My words are slow and deliberate, reining in my anxiety about each question that probes further into my past.

"What about your adoptive family?"

"What about them?"

"Could they have anything to do with this?"

I place my hands in my lap once again and squeeze them together. "You're really stretching now, Luke. Phillip and Cynthia Nelson would never do anything to scratch their perfect public persona."

"Okay, maybe not them, but do they have any biological children?"

"No." My glare shoots to him, putting a final stamp on this portion of the conversation. "Now, is there anything else you want to ask me that pertains to the ranch or halfway house?"

Luke grabs his sandwich and inhales the remaining portion.

I sample a few of the potato chips, but I taste nothing. Mentioning my adoptive family usually robs me of my appetite.

In between the salt and pepper shakers on our table stands a vertical wooden holder stocked with thin, brown paper towels. Luke rips one off and wipes the bottom half of his face. "What does 'back a trailer' mean? You used that term yesterday when talking to the girls about who I am."

I exhale a sigh of relief. Good. The girls. A topic of neutral territory.

"At the halfway house, we discuss that there are two kinds of people in the world. One group can metaphorically back a trailer. Backing a trailer takes skill, moving valued belongings from one place to another without fuss. They are solid, dependable, and trustworthy. The second group of people fakes it. They tell you they can back a trailer, but in reality, they scratch the vehicles, sometimes damage the contents inside. At the very least, they're dishonest, not worth our time. At the worst . . ."

He runs his tongue over his teeth. "Yesterday you told Bianca I could back a trailer."

I nod. "It's our safety phrase. Bianca has a hard time trusting people. If one of us tells her the person in question can back a trailer, she knows she doesn't need to vet them. Or fear them.

She can trust our analysis of the person in question. Trust that they are safe."

"So if I'm a safe person"—he rests his forearms on the table and leans toward me—"why are you avoiding my questions?"

"I'm not. I provide the necessary information as warranted, Mr. Granger."

His head jerks. "Mr. Granger, again?" He draws his words out while leaning back.

Grasping the top of the paper towel holder, I pull off another piece, allowing it to rip one tiny perforated section at a time. I avoid eye contact while briskly wiping my fingertips. One at a time.

When I gather the courage to glance at him, his stare travels to something over my shoulder, and his face hardens.

I freeze, not understanding what's happening.

From behind me, a sinister voice laced with curses says, "Who do you think you are?"

Luke shoves to his feet so fast, his chair falls backward and lands with a resounding crash. "Can I help you?"

Twisting in my seat, I catch a view of a seething man, his chest rising and falling, a feral expression darkening his eyes.

Marcus.

With stringy hair, gravity-defying baggy jeans, a ratty T-shirt, and clenched fists, Finley's ex-boyfriend is intimidating. A dragon tattoo runs up Marcus's neck, its mouth open, releasing red, orange, and yellow licks of blaze around his right ear. By the scorch in Marcus's eyes, I'm positive he would unleash that dragon on me if he could.

He points to Luke but doesn't move his fiery glare from me. "I'm not talking to you, man."

"Careful," Luke warns.

The hairs on my body stand on end, and pricks of awareness skitter from my scalp to the ends of my limbs. He's less than two yards away from me. I'm trapped between the chairs of neighboring tables.

Luke maneuvers in front of me with a wide stance, body wound tight, hands ready at his sides.

I push my chair out and stand, half my body concealed from Marcus by my personal panther. Luke brushes his knuckles against my thigh. A warning? A touch of support?

I clear my throat. "May I help you, Marcus?"

The only encounter I've had with him was when I helped Finley move out of her apartment. As I recall, his eyes were just as fierce. However, today they have a glassy effect that doesn't bode well for our conversation.

"Yeah." Marcus scoffs, body swaying forward. "You can stop filling my girlfriend's head with lies and tell her to get herself back home."

"I'm not sure to what you're referring," I say.

"It's always 'Miss Penelope this' and 'Miss Penelope that.' You two seem pretty tight. And now she won't even take my calls anymore. And I know it's *your* fault." Spit flies from his mouth with the sneered words.

Fear courses through me, and I clutch the back of Luke's shirt. I promise myself that if he needs to move, I'll release my hold. But it's becoming evident that Marcus is under the influence of a substance.

"You need to back off, man," Luke says in a lethal tone.

Marcus's explosive cursing sears the placid restaurant chattering, leaving silence in its charred wake. An evil grin crosses his face, causing the dragon at his neck to move, its breathing fire somehow coming to life. "You think you're some kind of fancy hero here to save everyone? You'd better get ready. 'Cause I'm comin' for my woman."

I offer a placating hand. "Think about this, Marcus. Finley is doing well at the ranch. She's using this time to improve her life. Don't you want her to be somewhere she can flourish?"

"Flourish?" He throws his head back and unleashes a mocking

laugh. "You guys and your fancy words you keep shoving down my woman's throat. You don't know the first thing about Finley."

I release my grip on Luke's shirt and shift to step in front of him. "She just needs a little space, Marcus. A little help to get her feet on the ground. She needs a safe place. She needs—"

"Shut up!" Marcus's hand slices through the air. "I'm done givin' her space. She doesn't have a clue what she needs." With each declaration, his volume increases. "*I'm* what she needs." He beats his palm on his chest.

Luke grabs the back of my sweater, drawing me into his chest, while I say, "She doesn't need you. She's stronger than you think."

"Careful, woman." Marcus's glazed eyes roam my body from head to toe in a disturbing manner. He lowers his voice. "I'm stronger than you think."

"Enough," Luke says.

Marcus finally shifts his focus to Luke. He bares his teeth, revealing a gold-capped eyetooth. "You're new to the savior brigade, man. Did you come in town for the super secret wedding?"

Ice travels down my veins. The wedding.

"I don't remember seeing you at the ceremony." Luke leans toward Marcus, his voice lowering to a growl. "Or were you hiding like a coward?"

A middle-aged lady with a restaurant-themed T-shirt approaches on the opposite side of Luke, seeming to keep a safe distance from the situation. "Excuse me." Her timid voice matches her wringing hands. "You're disturbing the other customers. I'm . . . I'm afraid I'm going to have to ask you to leave. Or I'll need to call the police."

Marcus doesn't even do the woman the courtesy of looking at her. Instead, his attention remains on me. "I'm done with you." He spits on the floor, then turns his attention to Luke while he points to me. "Just make sure she stays outta my way."

"You lay a hand on anyone at the ranch," Luke says, his expression dark, "I'll come after you myself."

Luke and I cruise down the highway toward the ranch, mountains filling the frame of the windshield. Their dark clouds swallow the afternoon sun, keeping the light hostage.

From the passenger seat of Luke's black Ford F150 Raptor, I try to wrap my mind around the firestorm that just occurred at the restaurant. My inability to perform well during unplanned scenarios is unfortunate. However, with Finley's well-being at stake, my inability to perform well feels grave. In truth, I don't think either Luke or I handled the situation well, and I'm worried about the consequences. Did he have to threaten Marcus? In a public venue, no less?

I turn to Luke. "What is wrong with you?"

"Probably a lot." Luke shifts a toothpick from one side of his mouth to the other.

Ugh. Another toothpick.

"You just threatened someone in public. With numerous witnesses."

Luke does a double take. He runs his hands from the top of the wheel and around the sides to the bottom. "It wasn't a threat."

"What do you mean it wasn't a threat? You told him you'd come after him yourself."

"It wasn't a threat." He chews twice. "It was the truth."

After Marcus had stomped out of the restaurant, Luke and I checked on the staff and remaining customers, smoothing over the situation. If I had known he was going to grab a toothpick on the way out, I would have requested the manager confiscate them.

After a swift unzip of my purse, I reach into the side pocket and pull out a peppermint. When I hold out the offering, Luke glances at me, grins, and takes it.

He hits the button to roll down his window, snags the toothpick out of his mouth, and chucks it outside. After rolling his window back up, he unwraps the mint and pops it into his mouth.

Acres of dried grass roll by, and an uneasy concern settles over me. "I set him off," I whisper. "Marcus said, 'I'm stronger than you think.' I set him off. It puts Finley at risk. *I* put her at risk." The weight on my chest presses me back against the seat.

"She put herself at risk the second she started dating him." He reaches to squeeze my arm. "This isn't on you, Penelope."

His grip is warm, but I pull my arm away and brush a strand of hair off my cheek. He can't understand this situation the way I do. I was left in charge of the girls while the Holcombes are away. The sole responsibility for Finley's well-being lies on me. "Do you think Marcus is the one? The vandal?"

"I think the odds are high that he did it. He's nursing a healthy hatred of Twelve Bluebells, and he could have been making a statement that night with the broken vase and the scattered brochure pieces." Luke looks into the rearview mirror, adjusts it, then returns his focus to the highway. "But that information isn't what concerns me now."

"Why wouldn't it concern you now?"

"While you were working this morning, I interviewed everyone I could who knew about the wedding firsthand. No one owns up to leaking the information, whether it be accidental or otherwise. With all the physical evidence cleaned up and no true leak of the wedding to an outside source, we're not going to know who vandalized the chapel. It doesn't really matter, though. If Finley really didn't tell Marcus about the wedding, the fact that he knew means the information was never secure in the first place."

"All right. So if that's the case, what concerns you now?"

Luke shifts the mint from one side of his mouth to the other, the candy rattling against his teeth. I would give good, hard-earned money for him to stop his constant movement.

"He's fixated on Finley," Luke says. "I'm concerned with how he plans to get her back. But he's also got *you* on his radar. And I don't care for that either."

A flash of warmth hits me. He might annoy me, but it feels

good to have him around to help handle this situation. Safe. Secure. Something I might want on a regular basis.

But my shoulder muscles clamp down tighter with each passing mile toward the ranch. Pain creeps up the back of my neck. A migraine clawing around my temple threatens to take over the rest of my day. I rub the scar above my eyebrow, begging the headache to stay away. "What do we do now?"

"When the girls check in tonight, we need to update them. Make sure Finley understands how volatile the situation could get with Marcus. I can let my contact with the local authorities know to keep an eye out." Leaving his hands on the wheel, Luke shrugs. "Other than that, we just keep moving forward. Live life. And keep our eyes open."

My stomach sours, and I think of the mammoth hoagie I abandoned at the restaurant. There's a reason I couldn't keep all the ingredients tucked inside the sandwich.

I ordered more than I could handle.

8

SEVERAL HOURS LATER, my bleary eyes refocus on the digital document in front of me. The names of Meredith and Harlan's wedding reception guests are a jumbled mess. Which table assignment would best obscure my dysfunctional adoptive family?

The thump of a bass guitar resonates through the walls to my bedroom. My fingers pause on the keyboard. What in the world?

I glance at my watch. This musical outburst is right in time for curfew. The girls aren't late, but if the disco funk sing-along is any indication, they're up to something. With each beat of the harmonized brass instruments invading my room, I'm more certain I won't accomplish anything else tonight.

Still in my professional wear from earlier today, I slip on my heels and head to the living room. When I reach the entrance, the scene before me breaks my stride.

The couch, coffee table, and chairs are pushed to the walls to allow for a stagelike area near the hearth. Filling the room with music is a small, portable speaker on a shoved-aside table.

Bianca sits on an ottoman, her fluid movements suggesting

she's playing an invisible set of drums. Her head sways back and forth. A blank expression covers her face except for the sliver of tongue she bites between her front teeth. The rhythm pounds through the imagined drumsticks in her fingers. As bizarre as it sounds, she appears to be very good at this.

After making a mental note to research used drum sets for Bianca, I shift my focus to the rest of the "band."

Finley's body gyrates, her hands lifting a fake trumpet, cheeks expanding as she blows along with the music. When she spots me, she plays the next measure in my direction, wild eyes widening with the whole-note hold.

A smile tugs at my cheek.

Tanya, a half step in front of her bandmates, leads this motley crew. While playing the air guitar, she directs the others in their singing and non-choreographed dancing.

Leaning against the wall, legs crossed, arms folded on his vast chest, Luke appears to be their manager. He glances at me and lifts his chin in greeting.

My stomach leaps, but I ignore it and move next to him, copying his stance. "What's happening here?"

"You're being treated to a performance of 'Thank You' by Sly and the Family Stone."

A warm sensation spreads through my chest.

Family.

Yes.

I slide my gaze to him. "And are we the groupies?"

"Yeah." He speaks out of the side of his mouth. "We're also conducting a sobriety check. In the event that they made unwise choices on their day off, they're too distracted with the performance to censor themselves from a stumble or a slur."

"That's unconventional," I say. "Unconventional, but genius."

"High compliment coming from you, Miss Reid." He glances at me, his lips curved in a slight smile. "I'll be sure to remind you of your stellar assessment of me when it comes in handy."

"You don't get to throw my words back at me when it's convenient for you."

"Oh, I absolutely do," he says, his tone laced with amusement.

What is this? Flirting?

We need to focus on the task at hand. I press the pleats on my slacks flat. "And what is your assessment of the ladies' sobriety?"

"Our girls are just fine tonight."

Our girls.

A piece of solidarity fleets through my core. It's unfamiliar. Almost uncomfortable. But it calls to me just the same. Is this what it would be like to partner with someone? Someone to shoulder just a little of life's weight.

I offer Luke a smile and, for one fraction of a second, allow myself to study the warmth in his eyes. The beauty. The sincerity. And if I'm not mistaken, a hint of vulnerability.

Then a boyish grin crosses his face, and he nods, redirecting my attention to the band.

The performance is charming, spirited, playful, and full of quasi-melodious voices belting out in earnest, right up until I hear the actual lyrics of the chorus. Then the whimsical nature of the moment is replaced by something deeper. Something profound and meaningful.

Tanya points to me, her finger bouncing with each word of gratefulness in the song.

There can be no mistake. She's singing the sentiment to me.

I pull my stare from her and glance at the other two ladies.

They are all singing. Pointing. To me.

Every fiber of my being wants to allow the magnitude of the moment to wrap me in its cocoon. But Meredith should be here. She deserves their gratitude. Twelve Bluebells Ranch exists because of her vision. She's the one who created a safe haven for these women. How is it possible that they're singing to me?

Luke nudges me with his elbow. He leans in and fills my ear

with his deep voice. "They picked this song for you. Kept talking about what you've done for them since they arrived at the ranch."

A lump forms in my throat, and I swallow. What I've done?

I've done my job.

I might have offered a listening ear or a piece of guidance a few times. But they're the ones who do the real work.

So, yes.

Yes, I decide, standing in the living room watching a band of silly, lovable girls lip-synch to me. "I'll be their groupie," I whisper. "For the rest of my life."

Luke brushes his knuckles against mine, a sweet movement, almost as if he's asking permission to take hold of my hand. Unable to peel my eyes off the beauty in front of me, I take his hand and squeeze, but instead of releasing him, I hang on tight. He doesn't seem to mind, his grip firm. His presence solid.

After a few more measures, Tanya grabs my wrists, breaking my connection with Luke, and yanks me to the "stage" at the front of the room. She links our fingers together, throws our arms in the air, rears back her head, and yells, "Sing it, Penny Lady."

The soundtrack repeats the chorus, and Bianca's and Finley's giggle-filled, slightly off-key crooning gets louder as they close in around us.

"Come on." Tanya shakes our hands above our heads. "Don't disappoint us. Let it out. We know it's in there."

In spite of my efforts, the lyrics break free. They're only a whisper, but the words escape my lips to entwine with the girls' voices.

A pronounced, collective "woo-hoo" sounds, and Luke's laughter barks over the chaos.

A grin splits my face, hurting my cheeks. The neglected muscles protest as they stretch to capacity.

The song comes to an end, and a group hug ensues. Sweaty arms, heavy breaths, and no small amount of love fill my senses.

With grins, giggles, and high fives, the pack disbands.

As the next disco song grooves through the room, Tanya says,

"Somebody turn that stuff down. I had fun, but I put my foot down at Barry Manilow."

Finley shifts to the side table where the Bluetooth speaker sits adjacent to her phone. Using her cell, she turns the volume down.

After observing the cups game last night and the lip-synching tonight, I'm beginning to appreciate the value of enjoyable sobriety tests. Luke's loose-cannon ways could teach me a thing or two. Meredith often instigates discussions with the girls about safe options for having fun. Maybe terrible singing accompanied by air guitar is the path to making good choices.

I peek over at Luke.

A proud grin breaks across his face as if he heard what I was thinking.

Brushing the hair off my forehead, I look away. Goodness. When was the last time I felt bashful?

I place my hands on my hips and survey the room. There's always something to do. There must be something to do here. Bending over, I grab the edge of the coffee table and drag it to its original spot in the room.

Luke nabs Bianca's attention, offers a chin lift to indicate the couch, and they slide it behind the table.

"Finley, are you okay?" Tanya asks.

A displaced cushion on one of the Louis XV chairs had caught my eye, but at Tanya's concerned tone, I redirect my focus.

Finley's shoulders hunch over as she stares at her phone. She snaps her head up and locks her blazing gaze with mine. "What did you do?" She whispers the accusation.

My spine stiffens.

"What. Did. You. Do?" Her eyes flash.

Every molecule of oxygen has been sucked out of the room, and no one moves.

"Finley. What's going on?" I take a step toward her.

With a stiff arm, she shoves her phone a few inches from my face.

I can't make out anything on the shaking screen.

"You told Marcus I didn't *need him*?"

"Careful." Luke utters his warning as his imposing body shifts closer.

A puff of air escapes my mouth, but I'm caught frozen in her allegation.

"You saw Marcus today and told him I didn't need him?"

I clasp my hands in front of me and square my shoulders. "Yes. I did."

Her face contorts. "Why? Why would you do that?"

"Because you're a strong woman. You can stand on your own two feet."

Tears fall as she pounds a text into her phone. "I'm out of here." With her hair shielding her face, she squeezes past me.

Tamping down the rising panic in my chest, I stride toward the hallway after her. Footfalls of the others follow me. "Finley, it's not that you don't need Marcus. It's that you don't need anyone to tell you you're okay."

After entering her room, she yanks a large, tattered blue duffel from under her bed. She pulls at the zipper, so caught up in emotion it takes her three tries to open the canvas case.

One of the girls behind me gasps.

As I stand in the doorway, the impact of what I'm witnessing threatens to paralyze me. Is she going to pack? She can't leave. "You are flourishing here, which is what I told Marcus. Finley, listen to me. You're growing and learning, and soon you'll be a force to be reckoned with."

She turns to the dresser, jerks open a drawer, and scoops out the contents. "You don't know me. You don't know anything. I signed up to be here so I could sort some things and *go back* to Marcus." She dumps the armful of her belongings in the duffel, then turns to open the next drawer.

Bianca slides past me into the room. "Girl, you do not want a piece of that man anymore."

While moving a load of clothes to the luggage, Finley drops a pink T-shirt. She snags it off the floor and jabs it at her friend. "What do you know, Bianca?"

Bianca snarls in disgust and leans against the wall, arms crossed.

Finley makes fast work of clearing out her sparse closet, hurling shoes and wadding up her few hanging items.

The fearsome reality of what she's about to do hangs heavy. "Finley, has it ever occurred to you that if you let go of Marcus, you might discover something better on the other side?"

She mashes the top of her luggage down, items spilling out. Furiously, she shoves the contents back, zipping behind each effort to close her life inside the bag.

I lean forward, straining to gentle my pleading voice. "What if what's next is beautiful?"

"I don't know anything about you, Penelope." She slings the strap of the duffel over her shoulder and glares at me. "I don't know who didn't choose you. But you don't need to project your life on me. Find your own beautiful. Marcus wants me."

I press a fist into my belly. It takes five full seconds to regain my breath after her devastating blow.

She moves past me, her bag shoving me aside.

"Finley—"

"Why are you here, Penelope?" She angles her body back toward me, spewing her acerbic words. "In the middle of nowhere ranchland, hanging out with us? You have no friends. No family. At least I have Marcus. Which is more than I can say for you."

The sting from her first blow numbed me from the full uppercut of the second one.

She huffs and storms to the front of the house.

The girls part for me to squeeze through and follow. Luke stands against the hallway wall, arms crossed, his eyes boring into mine as I pass. He keeps his distance, but he also keeps a careful watch on the chaos. Again, I hear everyone's footsteps traipsing after me.

Finley pulls the front door open and stomps across the white wooden porch planks.

"He cheated on you." Tanya's shaking voice emerges from behind me. "He abused you. Do you get that? He *hit* you."

As Finley's foot hits the first step off the porch, I grab her hand. "Please don't leave. We've been working through your aptitude tests. You are incredibly talented. You have support here. Tanya, Bianca, me, Meredith, and Harlan. We're all here for you." I reach my unsteady hand to rub the scar at my eyebrow. "I'm worried you're making a mistake."

"Good news, Penny Lady." Her seething words drip with defiance. "I'm one less thing you need to worry about."

The motion lights on the driveway illuminate as she half drags, half carries her duffel to the end of the gravel road. Her overpowering shadow follows in her wake, dwindling smaller and smaller as she reaches the street, where a car awaits her.

My breathing becomes labored as she swings open the back door and hurls her bag inside. She climbs in, pushing it further, plops herself on the seat, and slams the door.

Never looking back.

I release a quiet gasp as the car peels away, tires announcing the abrupt getaway.

"She was safe," I say to no one as I amble down the stairs. "She was safe here."

Murmurs sound from the porch behind me, but I don't look back. I can't look back. My eyes are glued to the road. I shake my head in small movements, a desperate attempt to make sense of the drama.

"Penelope?" Luke's deep voice sounds from behind me. "I sent the girls inside. You should come too. It's getting cold out here."

Clutching my chest, I pace. Five steps to the right. Five return steps to my original spot. "How could she . . . how could she leave?" Five steps to the right. Five steps to return. "I . . . would never have left here if I had been given the opportunity to have the Holcombes. Friends." Five steps again. Five back. "Almost a . . . family. A chance to . . . to feel safe. To maybe even feel loved." Unable to claw out of my confusion, I cease moving and catch Luke's concerned gaze. "I would have stayed and never left."

With one stride, he's in my space. He places a hand on my arm and with a gentle voice asks, "When was the last time you felt safe?"

I cock my head and stare in Luke's direction. It's not a difficult question. The answer is immediate. "Twelve. Before my mom's aneurysm. Before she died."

"Twelve." His thick, gruff voice should mean something to me in this moment, but it won't penetrate my anguish. He runs his hand down my forearm and grasps my hand. "You said earlier you were in foster care. Where was the rest of your family?"

Shifting my stance, I face the driveway. Maybe Finley will come back.

That's it. She'll get down the road, realize what she's done, and she'll come back.

"I had an aunt," I answer, "but she didn't want me. There wasn't any money in it for her."

He squeezes my hand. "You said you were adopted."

"Not immediately. My first foster family had me for six months. I got sick—expensive. They started paperwork to put me back in the system before I got out of the hospital." I rub my chilly arms and strain on my tiptoes to search farther down the empty road.

"Where did you go next?"

"Group home." I sigh. "I waited. I waited so long. Who wants to adopt an emotional teenager? It's too much of a risk. So I learned not to become a risk. Do exactly as I was told. Be needless. Wantless. Find something useful I can offer. Show my worth."

A car turns the bend and comes into view. I hold my breath, but it doesn't slow. I cannot fathom this has happened. "All Finley had to do was stay," I whisper.

"But you have an adoptive family now."

"Yes. I was sixteen. A California state senator and his wife. What better way to appear generous than by adopting two unwanted teenagers? But I showed them. I showed them my value. Excelled at everything they needed me to be." I make a fist and press it to my chest. "I was a perfect addition to the picture-perfect family of Senator Nelson and his wife. We were. We were the perfect addition. Jason and me."

Luke stands perpendicular to me, scrutinizing my face.

I can't hold his stare, so I squint and keep watching for headlights. "All she had to do was stay. She thinks Marcus is her family. If she stayed, she would have a true, safe family."

"That means you were in the group home for about four years. What wasn't safe there?" Luke's gentle tone infiltrates my thoughts, coaxing me to answer.

I rub the scar above my eyebrow, the reminder of my unstable roommate and her baseball bat. "It's okay. Jason made me safe."

He places his solid, warm hand at the small of my back.

"Finley was safe," I whisper, the soft easterly breeze carrying my words. "She only had to choose to stay."

I've lost Finley. Her life will derail, possibly in ways that are permanent.

And when Meredith returns to discover Finley gone . . .

I've taken away part of Meredith's family. Something unforgivable, considering her history.

I should not have talked to Marcus today. It cost me Finley.

Cold seeps through me. It cost me everything. Now I won't be able to apply for program director.

My chin trembles, and I bite my lower lip to contain the pain.

I'll offer my resignation. Search for a new home.

Because family is always a fantasy. Something in songs. In dreams.

Unobtainable.

9

TODAY HAS BEEN a special brand of misery. After a night of tossing and turning, I hoped my Sunday routine would soothe my weary bones.

The repetition of yoga attempted to stretch my worry into submission. The steaming shower tried to pound out my anxious thoughts. Even a certain cargo pants–wearing man couldn't distract me from my concern for Finley.

Nothing helped.

But per my usual, I put one foot in front of the other. Moved forward. Completed the next step. Hoping that the progression might lead me to Finley. To an apology. A do-over.

Her return.

Will she remember we're attending the Christmas tree lighting tonight?

Tanya works in the Alzheimer's unit of a retirement community. Every year, they put on a Christmas program the Sunday after Thanksgiving to light their tree. A local band plays carols while different tenants of the community lead their favorite songs. Tanya's not working tonight, but she invited us to come.

I want to be here to support her, allow her to show off her job. I get the feeling Tanya hasn't had many opportunities to share with anyone the pride she has in her work.

The four of us sit in folding chairs in the second row, waiting for the program to begin. Garland wrapped in tiny white lights lines the stage, each five-foot strand separated by a poinsettia. The staff all wear black scrubs with various Christmas sweaters.

All I can do is think of Finley and wonder if she'll show.

Tanya leans over me to speak to Luke, the strings from her hoodie dangling in my lap. We might be stretching the come-as-you-are dress code, with both Tanya and Bianca wearing jeans and sweatshirts. I'm the only one of us not adorned in denim. Instead, I'm wearing my typical business attire. Somehow, though, Luke's wine-colored Henley and black cowboy boots make more of an impression than my Christmas-inspired green silk shirt.

I may be worried, but I'm not dead. He looks good.

"Mr. Granger? Do you have family nearby?" Tanya asks.

He presses his shoulder against mine, moving closer with his answer. "Not anymore."

I grind my teeth, tightening down my annoyance. To my dismay, I find myself intrigued by his answer. More to my dismay, I find myself enjoying the warmth of Luke's arm against mine. And his smell. Something masculine and confident. How someone can smell confident is beyond me, but it oozes from his pores. And it isn't altogether unpleasant.

Tanya slants toward him again. "Did you grow up in the Springs?"

"Yeah."

"What part?"

"Garden Lake Village."

She scrunches her face. "The trailer park?"

"Yeah."

"Was it as awful as everyone says it is?"

I gasp at the intrusive question. "Tanya."

"I didn't mean it in a bad way," she says.

Luke aims his eyes to the stage. "Growin' up, it was tough sometimes, I guess. Not sure where to belong."

Not sure where to belong. My soul feels like it wants to reach out and touch him.

"I'm half Black. I don't fit anywhere either." Tanya's whisper tells me her soul might want to reach out to him too. She stretches her arm across my lap and offers her hand.

He slowly turns his head to her, glances down, and takes hold of her hand. "It seems like you found a good place to belong now, Tanya."

"You have too, Mr. Granger," she says in a whisper. "You have too."

They release each other and face the stage while I close my eyes and deep breathe against the tears stinging my nose.

Twelve Bluebells seems to give everyone who darkens its doors a place to belong, no matter where they come from.

Finley once believed she belonged here.

Twisting around, I scan the room for the fifth time, searching for her long brown hair. The dull ache in my stomach upgrades to a pronounced throb.

"Finley's not here, Penny Lady." For the first time since we sat down, Bianca joins the conversation. She shifts forward and curves her weight into Tanya, my left side now holding them both at bay. "She won't be showin' her face here. We figured out last night she blocked all of our numbers."

"I'm hoping she came to her senses. She might arrive late." I crane my neck to bring the back corner of the room into view. "She's always running late."

"She's meritorious for running late," Tanya says, picking at one of her fingernails.

Meritorious? What word was she looking for?

"While it's true that Finley deserves an award for her tardiness," I say, settling back into my seat, "I think you meant 'notorious.'"

Luke leans into me and murmurs, "Maybe she meant 'laborious.'"

My lips twitch.

The director of the facility walks to the edge of the stage, his smile plastered on a little better than his black toupee. "Welcome to the annual Christmas tree lighting. We're so glad you're here. We're also glad that Colorado Springs' Mountain Nirvana Band is here, led by our very own Pearl Hellman's grandson, to accompany our celebration for the third year in a row. Will everyone please stand? Pearl's going to lead us in a modern rendition of 'Joy to the World.'"

An electric guitarist, adorned in sleeves of tattoos and a Santa hat, opens the first few measures of the familiar carol. I whisper to Luke, "I think this song is going to be *glorious.*"

Amusement crosses his face, and he breaks out in laughter as we all rise. "That's the spirit, kitten."

Whatever bizarre happiness I gleaned from making Luke laugh whooshes out of me. That's the second time he has used the odd nickname. "Don't call me kitten."

He stares at the ground and rocks back on his heels, shoulders shaking.

"And stop laughing." I hiss my rebuke.

Luke carries an unapologetic air of freedom in his life that should be infuriating—except I find it alluring. After years of living a stringent life full of nearly suffocating rules, I want to breathe in the oxygen of the man next to me. I want to know the story behind those piercing eyes and how he found his freedom.

As if he knows I'm thinking about him, he glances down at me and flashes a dangerous grin.

I clear my throat and skitter my focus to my shoes. Shaking off thoughts of laughter, beauty, and green eyes, I bring my attention to Bianca.

Her lack of singing is not a surprise, but I follow the path to where she's staring.

The drummer. The drummer in the band is a woman. With her eyes closed, she pounds out the rhythm, locked in her own world. She's the mirror image of Bianca playing her air drums last night.

Perfect. More confirmation I need to research drum sets and lessons.

I pull a piece of scrap paper and a pencil from my purse and start a new to-do list.

While the audience transitions to the chorus, Luke leans over to me, pressing his shoulder against mine. Again.

And I like it. Again.

"Are you working?" he asks, his tone one of disbelief.

"No." I jot down details about the drum set. Five drums, three cymbals, Yamaha brand. "Just making a note."

"Does your brain ever stop?"

Turning to him, I lower my voice. "This week will be full of tying up loose ends, and I don't want to forget anything."

"Tying up loose ends?"

"When Meredith and Harlan return, I will explain how I lost Finley"—regret climbs my throat, and I swallow the uncomfortable lump—"and hand them my resignation."

A look of surprise crosses his face. "Penelope—"

"It's of the utmost importance to me to leave my job and Twelve Bluebells well organized. I want my exit to be seamless so I don't give anyone an extra burden."

"They might not react the way you think—"

"Meredith will want to know about Bianca's interest in percussion." I don't pause in my explanation, and Luke releases a frustrated groan. "If my memory serves me, Meredith has a connection who might know how to get Bianca an inexpensive drum set and possibly place her with an instructor. Who knows? Down the road she could plug Bianca in somewhere as a music intern." I'm liking this plan more and more. It's a shame I won't be around to see it to fruition.

He peeks at my list. "You forgot the high hat."

"The what?"

"The high hat cymbals."

I search the stage. "The two cymbals that look like a hamburger?"

"Yeah," he says, a hint of humor in his voice.

A plump woman in the row in front of us glares over her shoulder. "Hush."

I offer a polite smile, and she refocuses forward. "I cannot believe you got us in trouble," I say to Luke out of the corner of my mouth.

He winks at me. "It might do you good to get in a little trouble sometimes."

Laughter. Beauty. A little trouble sometimes. Why is it that the man who is supposed to protect me this week scares me to death?

Luke and I pause our discussion and stand in silence while the song winds down.

The director takes the stage to welcome everyone. He asks us to turn to someone next to us and greet them this evening.

Luke runs his hands over his face, sighs, and turns to me. "All right. I need the lay of the land this week. I know what you're working on and where you'll be. What about Tanya's and Bianca's schedules?"

"Tomorrow they'll go back to their respective jobs and chores around the house." I fold my to-do list, running the edge between my finger and thumbnail to reinforce the crease. "Other than job searching and packing my belongings, our week will be relatively normal. I don't expect any surprises."

"Don't you think it's a little premature to be packing? I wouldn't be so sure Harlan and Meredith will accept your resignation."

I angle my body toward him, shielding Tanya and Bianca from our conversation. "Keep your voice down. I don't want the girls to know anything is wrong. If I were the Holcombes, I would fire me. It's simple. I didn't do my job. And I accept the consequences."

"That doesn't even make sense. You can't control Finley. That's not on you."

He opens his mouth to continue, but I blurt, "Luke, I was going to ask for a promotion."

He says nothing, and I sigh. "I wanted to be the program director at Twelve Bluebells. This was it. This was my big trial run to show the Holcombes I could handle the job, and I failed. They won't hire me for that position, and then what am I supposed to do? Stay in a job that no longer fulfills me?"

"I didn't know you had so much riding on this week."

I curl a stray hair around my ear. No one knew I had so much riding on this week.

"I still think you need to talk to Harlan and Meredith. They sing your praises. Their response might surprise you." He studies my face. "Are you going to go after Finley? Try to talk to her?"

Of course I am. This is not up for debate.

Catching the eye of an elderly man sitting behind us, I plaster a fake smile on my face. "Good evening. So glad you're here."

The man returns my greeting.

Before I can find another way to avoid the conversation with Luke, he wraps his hand around mine. "Penelope. Are you going to try to track down Finley this week?"

His hand is warm. Strong. And a flash of wanting to hold tight shoots straight through me.

Instead, with an uppity air about me, I lie straight through my teeth. "No. I'm not going to try to find Finley."

Luke's eyes narrow and he releases his hold. "Marcus is not your biggest fan. If you go looking for Finley, I need to be with you."

"Well, this might not be the time to discuss this, but I think your services are no longer needed. You're relieved of your duties and can leave the ranch. We'll be fine." I ignore his glare.

"The wedding went well, and there have been no other signs of vandalism or other such threats. It's been peaceful at Twelve Bluebells, and it seems we're in the clear from any impending danger."

Crackling anger emanates from him. "This is my job."

"I know, Luke. You're checking off the boxes," I say, throwing his words from two days ago back in his face. "All I'm saying is, you've completed the list. You can go now."

"I'm not leaving the ranch. And I'm not leaving you."

His words reach into my heart and squeeze, the sensation somehow both comforting and painful. *I'm not leaving you.*

But you'll leave at the end of the week, I want to say to him.

I shake my head, chastising myself. What do I care what he does at the end of the week? He was always leaving at the end of the week. Heading to a new location. A new job.

Even if he did stay, I've ruined everything.

I'll most likely be leaving too.

Tears well in my eyes. I sit and drag my purse out from under the chair. "Stay if you must. You'll probably be bored. With everyone gone to their jobs, the halfway house is pretty quiet during the days. But most nights we eat dinner together. You're welcome to join us."

"Penelope—"

"The concert is starting." After placing the scrap paper in the inside pocket of my purse, I zip it closed. I nod to the stage where the director stands, hands clasped in front of him, clearly waiting for the crowd to settle down.

Luke folds into the seat next to me. "Penelope, I could—"

"Hush." If we continue this discussion, the tears will break free. And I've made too many mistakes lately for me to add emotional breakdown to my list.

He might be declaring that he won't leave me this week. But he will eventually leave.

Finley's not here today, but she'll have to show at her place of work. I'll let things settle down a bit, then I'll pay her a visit. Without Luke.

I will solve this problem on my own. Without Luke.

And then I'll find a new routine and settle into the predictability it offers. Without Luke.

10

A WOMAN IN A QUIET HOUSE is someone to be feared.

I should stitch that on a pillow.

But it would cut into my productivity today. And I am a *machine*.

With the girls back at work and Luke gallivanting off to do whatever it is he does, I'm in my makeshift office at the halfway house, completing projects to make the transition as smooth as possible for Meredith when I leave my job.

Harlan's consulting business is straightforward—a new assistant won't find it difficult to work through my meticulous files.

The New Year's wedding celebration planning is complete. The invitations are on their way to the guests. And I emailed my thorough yet concise notes about deliveries and decor to the Broadmoor liaison.

But sorting out the halfway house particulars is meticulous work. Construction crews are reconfiguring the boardinghouse, fundraisers are in the works, and several staff positions are unfilled. The good news is the grand opening isn't for a while.

Plus, I need to solidify new employment.

I tap my lips with the end of my pen, studying the computer screen in front of me. Maybe LinkedIn will lead me to where I belong.

Acid has been swimming in my stomach since this morning. Leaving my position, my home, and the lovely people who come with them is more challenging than I want to admit. Instead of providing me with peace, accomplishing this particular task list fans the burning in my gut.

The sound of a FaceTime alert startles me out of my thoughts. A message on my laptop notifies me of an incoming call from my adoptive brother, and I click to answer. My screen fills with his familiar face. "Hello, Jason."

He smiles. His dark blond hair seems to have thinned more since the last time I saw him. But he has the same kind blue eyes. Some woman should fall in love with those eyes someday. I wish that for him. And for her.

"Hey there. How are you?" His confident voice booms through my computer speakers.

Running my fingers over the mouse pad, I split my screen in half. Now I can view the Safari app with my searches while Jason continues to talk. My gaze locks on a job possibility. "Do you think I could handle the high temperatures in Phoenix?"

"What?"

"The scenery is undoubtedly nice, but I'm wondering if I need a milder climate."

"What are you talking about, Penelope?"

I shift forward and click on the description. "I'm job shopping. There's an opening for an administrative assistant to someone on staff with the Arizona Cardinals."

He leans in, filling the screen with his face. "You don't know anything about football. I could never get you to care about it."

Caring about the sport would have been easier if he had played. But he doesn't have an athletic bone in his body.

Hmm. Maybe I shouldn't work in a profession where I view

the main activity as barbaric. Or maybe I'll warm up to it once I figure out why throwing a pigskin around a field matters to America. It's not my fault I grew up with a single mother who was anti-violence and took me to community theater on her days off.

"I can do research." I squint at the qualifications of the job. "How hard can it be to learn a game?"

His face full of exasperation, he knocks on his screen. "Hello? You earned an MBA from Pepperdine. You should not be someone's assistant."

I shoot my gaze to his. "Are you upset? I thought you hated my current job."

"I do hate your current job. That assistant job is beneath your capabilities. But I also don't care for the halfway house thing. Why would you want to relive the four toughest years of your life? I certainly don't want to go back there every day for work."

This stings.

I know we each process our foster care experiences differently, but somehow I thought he would understand.

"I've found it cathartic to help people who walked a path similar to ours." I taste the bittersweet truth with each word.

His left eye twitches. It's Jason's tell that he's uncomfortable. "All I'm saying is that I couldn't do it. Are you looking for jobs around home?"

Home. He still chooses to refer to California as home.

"No. Why would you even ask that?"

I know why. Jason's only in Denver on a yearlong work project. At the end of his year, he'll have the option to stay and run the program he started or return to the home base of the company in California. If I applied for a job in Denver, he would be happy. But if I went "home," he could easily do the same. The underlying pressure for both of us to move to the same city is like the third wheel in our relationship. Unwanted but always present.

"Phillip's arms aren't that long, Penelope. He can't control everyone you interview with."

His arms might not be, but his shadow is another matter altogether. The issue of our adoptive parents isn't the only reason I won't go to California. I just can't handle the codependent stress of living in the same city with Jason. I know he loves me. He means well, but he has a smothering effect.

In an effort not to hurt his feelings, I remain silent.

He sighs. "Why don't you tell me what happened at the ranch?"

A sound at the door catches my attention, and I turn my head.

With a shoulder resting against the doorframe, one foot crossed at the ankle of the other, Luke rummages through a snack bag of Lay's potato chips.

How can someone appear that attractive while eating junk food?

"Penelope?" Jason calls my focus back to him. "What happened to your job?"

"Right." I sit straighter, ignoring the loud crunching from across the room. "I'm unable to fulfill my duties."

"I doubt that."

Luke is currently standing out of Jason's sight, but I wouldn't put it past him to enter the camera's view of my call. I lick my lips. "Listen, Jason, I need to let you go."

"Penelope?"

"Yes?"

"Come home." His voice cracks, but he recovers. "Time has passed. He's not that mad anymore."

I breathe slowly and deliberately before I respond. "His feelings about me are none of my business. I'm living my life. Not his."

"And what about me?" Vulnerability with a touch of pain streaks over his face. "You're all I have. Will you come home for me?"

I slide my eyes to the side. "Jason."

"Just think about it, okay?" He smiles, his eye twitching along with it.

"I'll think about it." After my gross overstatement, I click to end the call.

"You have an MBA from Pepperdine?" Luke asks from behind me.

As I turn my swivel chair around, he throws a chip in his mouth. His chomping is so loud, he's going to cause the cattle outside to stampede. And I don't have time to deal with a stampede today.

"And a BA. Were you eavesdropping on my conversation?"

"Absolutely." He crumples the chip bag into a ball and shoots it into my wastebasket. When he looks back to me, he takes a slightly wider than normal stance, crosses his arms, and says in a judgmental tone, "So. Jason wants you to move home? With him?"

I blanch. "What? No. Why would you—he's in Denver—we were talking about California—"

Luke looks so satisfied with himself, I want to throw something at him.

I squeeze my eyes shut, then open them and beam lasers at him. "Why would you even think that?"

He raises his eyebrows and looks at me as if I should know the answer.

"What is wrong with you? You can't possibly think that he wants me to move in with him."

"Whatever he wants, Penelope, is more than you are willing to admit."

What ridiculous version of Luke is this? I get his protectiveness. But this? Not okay.

I cross my arms, digging into my position as much as he's digging into his. "Let's move on."

He studies my face for a beat, visibly relaxes, then smiles. "Okay. What is someone with an MBA from Pepperdine doing in Colorado Springs working a job so far below her abilities she could do it in her sleep?"

"I could say the same about you."

"I don't have two degrees from one of the most prestigious private colleges in America."

Cocking my head, I add a thick layer of sarcasm when I say, "No. You just have an Olympic bronze medal in the fifty-meter rifle."

Job shopping isn't the only research I've done today.

He rubs the back of his neck, eyes locked with mine.

"One hundred and twenty shots, forty of which are prone, forty kneeling, and forty standing, all in just two hours and forty-five minutes." I soften my voice. "It's impressive, Luke."

"It was a long time ago."

"Do you keep up your skills?"

"When duty calls, I can still hit a can from across a field." He lifts his chin toward the computer. "What did Jason mean that Phillip's arms aren't that long?"

"The senator has an interesting definition of supportive father."

"Explain."

I sigh. "If I do, will you leave me alone?"

"Not on your life."

Squaring my shoulders, I push out of my chair, step to a card table, and sift through a pile of printed labels. "Phillip felt like I owed him gratitude for adopting me. He provided me with an excellent and expensive education and, upon graduation, ample opportunities. When I chose not to work for his reelection campaign, he took it personally. And when I declined a position with a prominent donor, he made it impossible for me to obtain employment."

"How could he pull that off?"

"I made the mistake of sharing with my beloved adoptive parents where I was interviewing." I pick up a page of labels and pull off the first sticker.

"And?" Luke prompts.

Focused on my task, I keep my voice level. "I didn't grasp what was happening at first. Three different companies strung me along for a few months, then abruptly dropped their interest.

When I confronted Phillip, his response was to inform me that he still had an opening on his staff."

"That's good publicity for a senator when the grateful adopted daughter returns home to serve in the family business," Luke says.

"I refused his opportunity one final time."

"And you came to work for Harlan?"

"No." I pick up a manila file folder and press the label on the tab with practiced perfection, smoothing it down for finality. "That's when I became homeless."

Ignoring Luke's grunt, I push forward as if I'm reporting the daily news. "Phillip kicked me out of his house. Changed the locks. Cut me off financially." I pause, studying the second label, then pull it free of the sheet. "Well, he drained my bank account, *then* he cut me off. And overnight, I lost everything."

"Why didn't you go public with this story?"

"My connections with the media weren't as significant as a senator's—they made that clear." But that wasn't the only reason. I'd been conflicted. The Nelsons had done so much for me.

Out of the corner of my eye, I catch Luke taking one step toward me.

"So what did you do?" His low, tight voice almost demands an answer.

"Jason told me to come live with him, but Phillip threatened to cut him off as well." I smile weakly down at my work. "But the title to the car I drove was in my name. So I got to keep it and live out of it for six months."

Intense energy emanates from Luke and zaps around the room, but I don't dare look at him.

In the midst of confessing one of the most shameful periods of my life, I'm unable to keep my hands from shaking. To steady them, I attach the label to the next file. Shoot. This one is a little crooked. I swallow. "I spent time at the public library using their computers to research employment opportunities and re-create my résumé. I worked temp jobs. Showered at the community center."

Hiding my unsteady hand behind the folder, I ball it into a tight fist. I exhale, uncurling my fingers.

"I met Harlan when I was temping for an accounting firm he used during his Hollywood days. I had talked him through a few details of his accounts over the phone, then met him twice when he had occasion to come in. We briefly talked shop. I think he liked talking about things other than his career. Anyway, one day he came in for a meeting and happened to see me getting chewed out by one of the partners in front of everyone in the break room. Later, he found me in the parking lot. My car wouldn't start and I was"—I shake my head, almost able to smell the oil leak wafting off the hot California pavement—"struggling. I couldn't help myself, and I blubbered my story to him. He offered me a plane ticket to Colorado Springs, free board, and a job as his assistant. I've been here five years."

"If you've known Harlan that long, then you know he won't fire you over Finley leaving the ranch."

I purse my lips. He might not ask me to leave, but I worry he'll never see me as capable of being anything other than his assistant. I ruined my shot at a promotion, one that I yearned for. I don't think I can stay in my current capacity, even if he doesn't ask me to leave.

Luke touches my arm. "I can't imagine someone who is supposed to be a father figure doing something like that to their kid."

Risking a glance at his concerned face, I offer a smile that I know doesn't reach my eyes. "Well, you won't have to imagine. If you're coming to Harlan and Meredith's New Year's party, you can meet him yourself."

His voice sounds lethal when he says, "Come again?"

"Phillip and Cynthia Nelson will be sitting at table twelve with Jason. You can meet the whole family."

"I'm going to need you to explain that one to me." His voice drips with disdain. "Why would Harlan and Meredith invite them?"

I shrug, as if addressing and stamping that particular invitation didn't cost me something. "Not long after I arrived in Colorado, Cynthia came to visit. Lots of dramatics and apologies for her husband's behavior. She begged me to come home. Over the years, she's done her best to patch things up with the family. They've traveled here numerous times over the years, and they've gotten to know Harlan, and now Meredith, pretty well."

"Doesn't mean Harlan and Meredith would invite them to their wedding celebration." He raises his eyebrows.

My shoulders drop in defeat, and I confess, "Meredith makes me overshare."

His lips twitch. "I can see how she might do that. How does that apply here?"

"Phillip and Cynthia were threatening to come into town for Christmas—a plan, I might add, that coincided with business for the senator. Meredith caught my emotional reaction to that news, which was . . . unpleasant. As a solution, she offered to invite them to the reception. It's a way for me to have a public appearance with them as if it's a personal holiday gathering and, by the way, happens to be a work event for me."

He nods.

"So there won't be much time to spend with them, seeing as how Phillip has to go home for a New Year's Day event. He gets his publicity stunt with the adopted daughter he's supposedly trying to bridge the gap with, and I get very limited interaction with him where he won't risk confrontation. Win, win." I sigh, thinking of how complicated that night will be, but how it's also the best way to solve their unwanted family attention. "And then it will be over for a while."

"Over for a while?"

"The senator has time to see me about once a year."

"What did Harlan think?"

"He's protective, so it was a harder sell, but when he realized it would make my life easier, he agreed."

His eyes narrow. "Is that plan good with you?"

"I don't trust them as far as I can throw them. Cynthia was a PR guru back in her day. There's no telling what her motives are on any given day. But she's the lesser of the two evils." I sigh. "Every now and then I think she has a conscience. But I keep the peace because Jason needs them more than I do."

It's a precarious peace, one that holds on to the loyalty and love Jason has for me, and one that forgives the same loyalty and love he has for the Nelsons.

Luke gnashes his teeth, the muscles in his jaw bulging.

That can't be good for his enamel, and for the first time since I met him, I want to hand him a stupid toothpick.

"You didn't come track me down to learn about my past," I say. "Did you need something?"

He smooths his tongue across his top teeth, something working behind his eyes. "Can't someone talk to you without needing something?"

"Not usually," I snap. "No."

After studying me for a beat, he nods. "That's probably right."

"Well?"

A slow grin crosses his face. "I have something to show you."

Glancing at the clock, I internally cringe at the time. I have the feeling that my to-do list is going to take a hit with whatever he has to show me.

But that grin. That grin is full of everything fun, free, and just a little bit mischievous. I exhale. Fine. For the grin, I will go see what he wants to show me.

After slipping my feet back into my heels, I only have to follow Luke a few feet down the hall to the living room.

At the sight in front of me, I open my mouth to say something, but nothing happens. Just like two nights ago, the furniture is moved to the walls. Only this time, a complete set of drums sits in the middle of the room on full display.

Luke turns to me, a gleam in his eyes. "What do you think?"

"What did you . . . Where did you . . ." Squeezing my eyes closed, I shake my head. After I gain control, I fire my gaze at him. "What is this?"

"It's a drum kit."

"I can see that, Luke." I thrust a hand in the direction of the five drums and two cymbals. "Why did you do this?"

With subtle movements, his face softens, giving a hint of unexpected sweetness and vulnerability. "Now you can check one thing off your to-do list. It's for Bianca."

A lovely sensation wraps around me like a blanket. He thought about the conversation we had last night and in turn did something kind for one of the girls. But the blanket turns scratchy like it's made of wool, the uncomfortableness almost choking me.

His eyes narrow, and he cocks his head. "When's the last time someone did something for you, Penelope?"

The fibers of the blanket wrap around my throat, impeding my breaths. Short of Harlan's heroic act of getting me off the streets and into Colorado as an employed woman with provided housing, I don't remember the last time someone did something for me. That's not how my life operates. *I* do things for others. *I* prove my value. This? This unrequested, unexpected generous move on his part to help me? This feels like suffocating.

As if he can sense the torture, Luke shifts his focus to the instrument. "I found this kit at a pawn shop. Total steal."

This announcement jerks me out of my choke hold. "You can't do that. You can't spend that kind of cash."

"Why not?"

"It's too much," I practically yell. "It's too much money." The only valuable thing my adoptive father ever taught me was that no one gives anything without expecting some kind of benefit in return. I can't possibly allow him to help me, or anyone around me, without some kind of payment.

He crosses his arms. "You been looking into my bank accounts?"

"No. I just . . . Okay." I nod to myself, finding the solution. There's always a solution. "Okay. Maybe I can get you a tax write-off. I don't know how to do that with a gift of goods to a nonprofit. But it can't be much different than a monetary gift. I'll do some research and contact you when I can create a valid donation statement."

"Penelope." He takes one powerful stride toward me. "If you give me that paper, I'll just rip it up." He hitches his thumb toward the drums. "I didn't do this to create more work for you."

In spite of his proximity, I refuse to shrink back. "It's too much, Luke. It's too generous."

"No, it's not. It's not that big of a deal." With a mischievous glint in his eyes, he pulls drumsticks out of his back pocket, steps to the set, and straddles the stool. He looks insanely attractive and just a little bit dangerous. "It's an opportunity for me to show you my mad skills."

I blink. "You play the drums?"

"Yeah. And since I'm running out of things to do around here, I thought I'd give Bianca a few lessons."

Does he mean he'll give her lessons this week? Or does he mean that after the job at Twelve Bluebells is done, he'll continue to come and give her lessons? Will it be a long-term commitment from the man who claims his time at the ranch is short-term?

Whatever the answer is, it's more unexpected generosity.

Luke's head moves back and forth to an internal rhythm for a few beats, then he unleashes.

I don't know a lot about the instrument in front of me. But he is a cross between a cool jazz drummer and Animal from the Muppets band. His controlled, deliberate motions pound out the sounds, but there's a move-with-the-spirit element to his playing. And the spirit is some sort of wild beast.

I have no idea what to do with the man in front of me. He's attractive. He's generous. In spite of his globe-trotting reputation, he's done nothing but be completely all-in here at the ranch.

Helping the girls when he can. Buying this drum set. Offering lessons. Tethering himself to them, whether he realizes it or not.

Is he also tethering himself to me?

Tightening every muscle in my body, I resist the desire to move with the beat because I can't afford to enjoy the scene in front of me.

With the addition of the drums, the house will no longer be quiet.

Rather than lamenting the future pounding percussion, I feel my stomach tighten, and I close my eyes, trying to barricade the flood of regret. I am leaving. I have to leave. I failed Finley. I failed the Holcombes. One thing I've learned—there's no room for mistakes.

But what if I could find Finley and fix my mistake? Then I could stay at the ranch. And maybe Luke would return to the ranch and give Bianca more annoyingly loud drum lessons. Maybe Luke would return to the ranch to see me.

If I can find Finley.

11

INHALE.

Fumes from the parking lot fill my nostrils, and I adjust my purse strap over my shoulder.

I can do this.

Exhale.

My breath crystallizes in the cool air, and I tighten the trench coat belt around my waist.

Yes. I can do this.

It's Friday morning, twenty-five minutes after ten. Finley's shift at Safeway started almost three hours ago. She should be going on break soon.

A break that could afford me time to convince her to come back to the ranch.

A break that could give me the opportunity to keep her safe.

A break that could solidify the chance to stay in the only place I've felt like I belonged since age twelve.

A break that could help bring about my dream job.

A break that's loaded with potential, but whose weight bears down on me with such massive pressure, it feels like the dam is going to burst. I strain to hold back the rushing rivers of apprehension, anxiety, and angst. Despite my fortified efforts, doubt forces its way through the cracks to break down my defenses.

It's just a guess, but I'm betting Finley will head straight to her usual break spot, her beloved bench. Leaning a shoulder against the outside brick wall of the Safeway grocery store, I stare at the automatic sliding doors.

Around the corner of the building sits a patch of grass with a few trees. Some of the employees created a beautiful space. They pooled together a little money, weeded the area, set out some potted plants, and installed a bench that now sits proudly in its own poured cement block. From a distance, the Rocky Mountains offer a friendly wave, beckoning anyone who looks their way to escape to their majesty. Even if just in their thoughts.

Finley is the self-appointed mayor of the break time escape. She chides those who dare smoke a cigarette in the mere vicinity of the blessed bench. With her own money, she purchased holiday decor to stick in the planters. She even asked me to help her create an Excel spreadsheet assigning employees chores to keep up the area. It's a precious piece of ownership for her in a world that's left her little to boast about.

And it's an area she's headed toward this very second.

The doors slide open, and Finley, staring at her phone, drags through the exit. The grocery store apron peeks out under the fringes of thread from her long, weathered peacoat. Her hair is slightly stringy, skin pale, shoulders hunched over. She appears older than her fledgling eighteen years. Where is the precious girl who bounces her way through life like Tigger on a pogo stick?

A sinking feeling hits me in the pit of my stomach. Am I too late? I waited six days before I made my approach, thinking the time would give Finley space to miss the camaraderie of the ranch. The safety of the ranch. The hope. I didn't think Marcus would wear her down during the honeymoon phase of her return.

With a quick scan of her face, I can see there's no sign of

physical bruising. But the dark bags under her eyes tell of emotional bruising.

I tamp down my nervousness, push off the brick wall, and straighten my shoulders.

Just a few feet from me now, she still doesn't see me. She taps something into her phone, pauses, and frowns at the screen.

"Finley," I call.

She glances up and comes to an abrupt halt. Recognition and relief, with a tinge of resistance, cross her porcelain face. "What are you doing here?"

"I came to check on you."

When she takes a step toward me, she plants a foot in a puddle of water and makes a splash. She shifts her focus to her feet. "What in the world?" Just behind me, a tiny river of water flows from a tall freezer storing large bags of ice for purchase. Intermixed with the water, patches of ice lurk on the concrete in the shade of the bulky metal container. "I told them three days ago to fix this stupid machine. If it floods over to the break patch and ruins anything, I'll kill someone."

"How are you, Finley?" I ask.

Vulnerability flashes in her eyes and she crosses her arms, hugging them to her chest. "I'm fine."

"How are things with Marcus?"

"That's none of your business."

"No, you're right. It's not anymore." I swallow. "But I care about you. And I miss you."

"Why?"

My heart hammers, as if it knows I'm about to bare its soul.

"Because I know what it's like not to be wanted. As a child, I spent time in the foster care system. I know what it's like to have nowhere to belong." My words waver, but I clench every muscle in my body, trying to remain statue-still. "And I need to tell you that you're wanted. You're valued. Just as you are."

Moisture glistens in her eyes and a single tear streaks down her cheek, watering the tiny seed of hope I brought to this meeting.

"Please come back to the ranch. There's a place for you. You'll be safe. There are . . . possibilities for your future."

And just like that, Finley's face screws up with hardened defiance.

Wait. What did I do? What did I say? Panic hammers my heart. I have to fix this.

"Possibilities? Whose possibilities, Penelope? Yours? Meredith's?" The tears that threatened to spill only a few seconds earlier are replaced with an obstinate stare. "You hide behind your judgment and act like you have all the answers. How come you get to be all holier-than-thou? What has that gotten you? You're completely alone."

Each word pummels my heart, but my body remains still.

"That's what you want for me?" she asks. "Your pitiful, lonely life? No thank you."

My mind scrambles, searching for anything that might keep her in my presence, that might redeem this and allow her to come back to me. My rising panic blurts something I know nothing about and cannot promise. "What if I can also help Marcus?"

She wrenches back, almost in horror. "Oh, so now you're going to save Marcus too? What is it with you? Just because someone doesn't do life the way you think they should doesn't mean they're wrong."

I cringe. What have I done? "That's not what I mean. I just—"

"Then what do you mean, Penelope?"

"The ranch has connections. People who can help him. Mentor him." My hands tremble as I state possibilities on the fly that I hope are true. "Maybe find better work for him."

She gnaws on the edge of her thumbnail, and I hope that means her wheels are spinning. Over the last few months, Finley has voiced concerns about Marcus's possibly shady vocations. Maybe

I can lure her back to the ranch with the prospect of getting Marcus a better job. A legal job. A safe job. For him and for Finley.

"But he hates you," she says.

I nod. "Yes. Yes, that's probably true. I think we just got off on the wrong foot. I can change that. Apologize to him. Make it right."

"I don't know if he'll even talk to anyone associated with the ranch."

I release a relieved breath. Good. Okay. At least we're entertaining the idea. We're headed the right direction. "I think we could have a conversation with him in whatever way might make him feel most comfortable."

"Finley, babe, who are you talking to?" A low voice sounds from the parking lot.

Finley's eyes widen, but she recovers quickly to mask her surprise. In its place is an eerily blank face on a girl who typically exudes expression from her pores.

Marcus comes into view. By the looks of his hair, he hasn't showered since the last time I saw him. To accompany his baggy jeans, he wears a ratty long-sleeve waffle shirt covered by a dark red flannel shirt with its sleeves cut off. He slips between two parked cars to saunter onto the curb and hook his arm around Finley's shoulders. With one look my way, he recognizes me and throws a grotesquely insulting name in the space between us.

Alarm bells clang in my head, and I rub the scar at my left eyebrow. If Marcus doesn't kill me, then Luke will gladly sign up for the job. I should not have approached Finley alone.

Marcus clutches Finley's shoulder, turning her into him, his fierce face inches from hers. "I thought I told you not to talk to her."

My eyes dart between them. "Marcus, I think we got off on the wrong foot."

He turns toward me and puffs out his chest. His nostrils flare.

The weight of his glower bears down, suffocating me. My chest rises and falls with its effort to find oxygen's relief.

"Marcus." I clear the fear from my throat. "I was—I was wondering, would you b-b-be interested in a job at the ranch?" Harlan's going to kill me. But I can't help it. I'm just spouting anything that might sound remotely intriguing to Marcus. Or at the very least anything that could distract his aggression. "I know the foreman and could arrange a meeting—"

"Unbelievable." The word drips with burning incredulity. "You wanna save me too? That's fresh." He prowls one step toward me.

The putrid smells of cigarettes and my own terror assault my senses. "No." My eyes widen, and I put out a placating hand. "No, I don't want to save you. I just want to help. Job security is often hard to come by and—"

"Job security?" He flashes a smile that, at the root of all it offers, can only be described as evil. "Oh yeah. I've got job security. Everybody wants what I have."

This conversation is sliding from bad to terrible quicker than I know how to handle.

His dark aura transitions from evil to sinister, he loses the smile, and his face turns to stone. "Listen to me, *Penny Lady.* Because I'm only going to say this once. I don't need you. Finley doesn't need you. You come anywhere near us again, I have no problem making myself more clear with you."

My last hope slips off the edge. My last hope for Finley. My last hope for me.

"Please." I lace my whisper with an earnest plea. "Please, Marcus. What if you could have a healthy relationship with Finley? Work together to provide a good life for the two of you? We have resources to help you find a better way."

"A better way?" he roars. The boy-man in front of me literally roars so loud that my body shakes. "Who do you think you are, telling my woman there's a better way than me?"

I've made a mistake of epic proportions in coming here.

I shift my weight, readying myself to bolt sideways between two parked cars, across the parkway to the next row, and to the safety of my car.

Marcus leans toward me and shoves my shoulders.

Finley screams.

The angle of his push propels me toward the ice machine. I try to get my foot under me, but my high heel hits ice and slides. Fast.

Before my arms can catch anything to gain ground, I free-fall for the fastest second of my life. Then my eyebrow slams against the metal corner. The scorching pain doesn't last long because gravity yanks me to the sidewalk. My shoulder and elbow make a valiant effort to cushion the blow. But they can't stop my head from banging against the wet cement.

Striations of blood seep through the cracks.

And then everything goes dark.

12

“OHMYWORD. Ohmyword. Ohmyword.”

The mantra echoes through a tunnel.

I don’t want to go anywhere near the sound. It’s accompanied by a fierce pain that pounds closer and closer with each word. I turn my head to distance myself from the agonizing noise. But instead of quieting the problem, it causes a piercing misery to sear through my temple.

I cry out.

“Miss Penelope? Are you awake? Ohmyword. Oh no. It’s so much blood, Miss Penelope. I don’t know what to do.”

Blood.

What?

“Miss Penelope? Can you hear me? It’s Finley.”

Finley.

She needs help.

On an inhale, I take in fumes of gas, hints of iron, and the crisp air of the mountains. For some reason, I’m unable to open my eyes. I grind out a whisper. “Nine.” Oh, help me. That hurt. Gritting my teeth, I continue, “One. One.”

"I can't—" Her voice, full of distress, rocks toward me with each word. "Marcus. The cops. Oh no. You're bleeding. It's so much blood, Miss Penelope." She shifts, and I hope that means she's pulling out her cell phone. "Yes. Okay. 911."

Marcus? What is she talking about? Is he here? Where is here? The simple act of trying to remember causes a vise to grip my skull. I lift my left arm to touch my head, and my shoulder screams so loud, the ambulance should come without Finley's call to emergency services.

What happened?

I have to figure this out. Have to help Finley.

With extreme care, using just the fingertips of my right hand, I graze the cold, hard cement to test for movement and sensation. I'm relieved I can accomplish this without the protest of pain. All right. That's a positive sign. Now let's figure out why I'm bleeding. Without great confidence, my shaky hand crosses my torso and aims for my face.

"No, Miss Penelope. Don't touch it. You're— Hello? Are you there? She fell. She needs help. What? It's Miss Penelope. She fell."

Yes. Good. She's talking to 911. What did she mean don't touch it? Don't touch what? What's wrong with me? I can't keep track of her words. I can't open my eyes.

Wait. Why can't I open my eyes? I swallow. *Don't panic, Penelope. Don't panic.*

Finley's voice rises and moves away from me.

Where is she going? In her absence, bitter wind brushes against me, sending a chill to my bones. Okay, maybe it's time to panic.

"Yes, ma'am," Finley says nearby. "I got my coat off. I'm putting it on the spot."

The spot?

Before I can ask, rough fabric is shoved against my left temple and agony shoots through my brain. Oh. That spot.

"There's more blood coming from somewhere else," she exclaims to the operator.

More blood. My chest heaves with a fearful sob that threatens to rip me in two. I can't do anything to help. I can't even see. Why can't I see? With everything in me, I attempt to draw my lids open, but it's as if they're glued shut.

"I think this other blood is coming from the back of her head. But there's not as much there." She pauses. "No, ma'am. It's not pooling at the back of her head." Another pause. "Miss Penelope? I'm supposed to tell you we can't move you. They're on the way."

"I-I can't—" I swallow and draw in a ragged breath. "Open. Eyes."

"Oh my word! She can't open her eyes! When will the ambulance get here?" Another pause. This one longer. "Oh. Let me see."

I feel her body heat. She's hovering over me.

"Okay. Wait. I think your eyes are okay. Oh no. It's the blood, Penny Lady. You have a cut above your eyebrow. The blood is caked over your eyes." She shifts her weight. "Did you hear that, ma'am? I think Miss Penelope's eyes are okay. Can I wipe the blood off?"

In a few minutes, I won't need her to wipe the blood off. My streaming tears of fear and agony will wash the blood away for her.

"She said I'm not supposed to touch anything else, Miss Penelope." The hand holding her coat to my head presses in, and I moan. She curses. "Sorry. Sorry! I-I am just so sorry, Miss Penelope." Her voice cracks.

I want desperately to help her. To say so many things to her. To comfort her. Is she hurt too? Why can't I remember what happened?

The sweet sound of sirens fills the heavy air.

Okay. It's going to be okay. Someone will take care of Finley.

And me. I whimper on that thought.

"Oh my gosh. Do you need help?" A voice I don't recognize calls from elsewhere. A bystander?

Before Finley can answer her, the ambulance blares its announcement into the parking lot. If I could shoot out the siren wails with a shotgun, I would. In an effort to roll away, I curl my good arm into my chest as if I can create a barrier between myself and the hideously loud noise.

"Don't move, Miss Penelope. They're coming." Finley's voice bounces next to me. Is she perched on her haunches? Is that her shin rubbing against my thigh? If I wasn't so grateful to feel a part of her bubbling personality rubbing up against me, I'd chastise her for moving.

Then, in an instant, life becomes a commotion of swirling responders.

After assessing my general condition, a gentle-voiced male EMT uses swift movements to wipe away the blood that binds my eyelids closed.

When I finally pry my eyes open, I'm punished with streaking light that pierces my optic nerves. I groan and struggle to use my good arm to shield my face, but the EMT is crouched over me in a way that restrains any movement.

"Hang in there with me," he says as he shines lights into my pupils, compounding my agony. "Can you tell me your name?"

I can only whisper pained answers to a few of his multitude of questions. I know my name. I know Finley. I know the day of the week. I know the president's name. I think I'm at Finley's place of work, but I have no idea why I'm on the ground in an emergency situation.

The questions. The questions devour my meager shreds of energy reserves.

My eyelids droop. Maybe if I can rest for a few minutes, the answers will come to me.

"Miss Reid? I need you to stay awake for me. Okay?"

No. No. See, he doesn't understand. Exhaustion envelops me in a dreamy blanket and promises me that if I simply let go, it will sweep away the pain.

The voice turns stern. "Miss Reid."

I struggle to focus on the image in my line of sight. The man's baby blues are kind and alert. Graying hair and distinguished whiskers frame his face.

That's enough. That's all I can do. My eyelids float down.

"Miss Reid. Open your eyes, please."

Several sets of assessing hands move over my wounded body. Various patches of medical supplies are applied to the cut at my eyebrow and to the wound at the back of my head. A foam brace is strapped around my neck. A flat board slides under my body. There's a sharp prick on the top of my hand. Is that an IV?

Each movement jolts me from my efforts to rest. I just need to close my eyes for a second or two. What can't they understand about that?

With the board secured in place, I almost succumb to the weary calling of sleep when Finley's panicked voice fills my ears.

"I don't— His name is Marcus Skelly. He ran away. I don't know where he is." She pauses. "Yes. That's him. He's wanted for what?" Another pause. "My Marcus would never do that."

My eyes pop open and dart around in search of Finley.

"Hold still, please, Miss Reid. We're securing you to the board."

I open my mouth to call to Finley, but nothing comes out. Words require too much effort.

Her tone rises, and placating voices answer her. Back and forth, back and forth.

"We just need to bring you in for some questions," one voice says.

Bring her in where? Are those police officers? Wait. To the station? She didn't do anything wrong. I mean, I don't remember what happened. But I know Finley. She didn't do anything wrong. She wouldn't have done anything wrong.

"Wait." I groan. "F-F-Finley."

"Your friend?" asks one of the paramedics. "The police are taking care of her."

"Please." I move my head, and biting pain tells me I can't slide it against the tight strap over my forehead.

The kind face from before enters my line of sight. "Miss Reid, we need to get you in the ambulance. They'll take care of your friend."

"Wait."

No one responds to my plea. Tears sting my nose.

No. I can't leave her here. She didn't do anything wrong. I'm positive that's true.

On someone's count, they lift the board with my strapped-on body and place it on a stretcher.

The world tilts.

And I can no longer help Finley.

13

FINLEY. I HAVE to find Finley. She needs me.

No one in the emergency room seems to comprehend my urgency to get to Finley, including the unsympathetic nurse in front of me whose frigid personality matches the ice-cold hand she just placed on my wrist. "Who can I call on your behalf?" she asks.

"I-I think the police were on the scene. Are there any officers here that I can speak with? Maybe they would be able to update me on my friend."

Her lips form a thin line. "I'll check to see if there's an officer on the floor in a minute. But right now we need to focus on finding an emergency contact for you. Who can I call on your behalf?"

She wants to know who she can call on my behalf?

That's not an easy question on a good day. But today?

Today, the answer to that question is impossible. I don't dare contact my adoptive family. Unfortunately, this includes Jason. I can't know if he'll call Phillip and Cynthia. The senator's expectations, presumptions, and personal entourage are hard enough to deal with on a normal day. And with Meredith and Harlan on the last day of their honeymoon, and Harlan's family away from the ranch on vacation, I'm left with limited acquaintances.

Or Luke.

Another wave of nausea rolls over me. Only this time, I can't attribute it to the head injury. This time it's the built-like-a-brick-wall man who ordered me not to approach Finley without him.

Apparently I went against his instructions and met her at her place of work. I still can't remember what happened. Evidence in this ER leads me to believe it went wrong. Very wrong.

"Ma'am?" The nurse tries again. "We'll be taking you down to CT soon. It might be good to notify someone now so they can be here when you return to the room."

Luke? At the hospital with me? I close my eyes. How humiliating.

But maybe I can talk to him without this being a big deal. I need to make sure someone checks on Bianca and Tanya at the ranch. I will call him and focus on the girls.

"Can you please hand me my phone? It's in the inside front pocket of my purse. I think the paramedic told me it made it to the hospital."

She crouches low and rummages underneath the bed. There must be storage down there. "Found it," she says as she stands.

Words have started coming easier. And the pain isn't radiating through me anymore, instead stalling at a dull roar. I can't receive pain meds because the extent of my head trauma is unknown. But thank goodness my neck and back are stable, and I'm no longer lying on that uncomfortable board.

My head, on the other hand, seems to be causing everyone a considerable amount of stress.

My lack of short-term memory alone seemed to get me on the CT schedule quicker than the blood from my previously gushing wound.

The nurse hands me the phone, and I glance down. Because I already know there are square apps filling the screen, I can almost make out the edges of the shapes. But everything else is just a frayed mishmash of colors. I blink, but refocusing does me no good.

My blurred vision also sped up my CT orders.

"It's no problem for me to make the call for you, Miss Reid. Would you like me to relay the information to someone?" the nurse asks.

"No, thank you. I'd like to do the talking. But I can't make out what's on my screen. Would you please dial the number for Luke Granger? He's in my contacts list."

After she dials, she hands me the phone. Only my shaky hands can't hold it steady, and I almost drop it.

"I'll just put it on speaker," she says as she pulls it back, punches a command, and sets it on the tray in front of me.

Another nurse pokes her platinum-blond head in the room. "Can I borrow you for a moment?" she asks her colleague.

Both nurses leave as my cell rings through to Luke, and I inhale, gathering any scraps of composure that I didn't leave on the grocery store sidewalk.

I can do this. This doesn't have to be an ordeal.

"Granger."

The moment Luke's strong, confident voice fills the room, tears hit the backs of my eyes. Because the reality is this *is* an ordeal.

I'm in trouble.

And I don't know what to do.

"Penelope?" he calls to me, demanding an answer.

"Luke." My voice trembles, and I close my eyes. *Pull it together, Penelope. Please.*

"What's wrong?"

"Um." I clear my throat, grasping for control. "Could you, um, please handle curfew check-in with the girls tonight?"

His voice softens. "What's wrong, Penelope?"

I'm not fooling him. And the truth is, I'm not fooling myself either. With each word I speak, pieces of fear, anxiety, and pain release into the space between us.

"Um, I'm not going to be home at the appropriate time. Will you please take care of the girls tonight?" My wobbly words match the tears streaming down my face.

"Baby, where are you?"

Baby.

The word makes me ache. For him.

I want to crawl into the lap of that gentle word and let the strong arms of his care-filled tone wrap themselves around me and soothe my frayed nerves.

What I really want is him. With me.

"Luke," I release on a sob.

Squeezing my eyes shut, I draw from the depth of my gut to whisper three words I've never said to anyone in my life. "I need you."

"Where are you, Penelope?" Urgency amps his tone.

"I'm—I'm at the hospital."

"Which one?"

"Don't be mad at me. I know—"

"Penelope, baby. I promise I won't be mad at you. But I need you to tell me where you are."

The nurse returns and says within earshot of the phone, "Miss Reid, it's time to take you down to CT."

"CT?" Luke's grinding voice hits the room. "Penelope?"

My tears bring with them throbs of pain. It's as if I can feel each individual vein of blood coursing through my head.

"Miss Reid? Are you okay?" The nurse steps toward me, glancing at the machine behind me monitoring my vitals.

"Will you please handle my phone call?" I ask her.

She retrieves my phone, and two orderlies enter the room, pull up the side rails, and unhinge the brakes on my hospital bed. They gather the rolling IV and vitals monitor, and as they wheel me out, the sounds of the nurse's conversation with Luke fade behind me.

14

MY BRAIN IS BLEEDING.

Dr. Anthony Gallo's words ricochet off the walls in my ER room and land in the pit of my stomach.

My brain. Is bleeding.

I squint at the grandfatherly doctor, the movement uncomfortably stretching the skin at the cut near my eyebrow. But it blocks out the neon white of the ER doctor's coat, so I count it as a positive. How can something so benign laser into my retinas with such severity? With the curtains drawn in my room and the fluorescent lighting turned off, only the green screens and tiny flashes of the monitoring equipment illuminate the small space. Except for his screaming lab coat.

That is, until the door opens and a brawny flash of lightning appears.

Luke.

One look at me in all my hospital glory, and his body locks tight. In the shadows of the room, his face is dark and stormy. When he takes one heavy step toward me, with a little better focus I see that I'm wrong. His face isn't dark and stormy. It's downright thunderous.

Why does he look so enraged? I haven't even told him yet why he should be angry.

He scans my body, pausing on my left arm strapped to my chest, with another pause on the bandages surrounding my head. His attention shoots to the doctor, and he grinds out his question, his voice sounding rough. "How is she?"

Dr. Gallo, standing just a foot away at my bed rails, looks to me. While the years have textured his hair in silvery streaks, his thick black eyebrows have refused to age, throwing a stark contrast against his olive-toned face. A facial feature that even my blurred vision can't miss. He raises those bushy eyebrows to me in question, I assume in regard to Luke's presence in the room.

Am I honestly going to let Luke stay to hear the doctor's report?

If I thought I could make sense of all the information being relayed, I would kick Luke out of the room. However, for the time being, concentrating is challenging at best. Plus, I need to talk to him about the girls. And finding Finley. I don't want to give him the impression that I'm a complete invalid, but I don't think I can handle all the details by myself.

I nod to the doctor's question and, using my right arm, pull myself to a more upright position. The second I shift my weight, the room rocks as if I'm on a ship in the middle of a storm.

"Another wave of dizziness?" the doctor asks.

Eyes closed, I grunt an affirmation. Tears of frustration sting my nose, and I inhale to temper them. "Please continue," I say.

"I'm looking through your intake. The nurse told me she helped you with your history. I wanted to clarify." He peruses a few screens on his tablet. "You've experienced migraines since you were fourteen?"

"Yes."

"They started with a concussion?"

"Yes."

"What were the circumstances surrounding that injury?"

I swallow. This is exactly what I didn't want to get into in front of Luke. In front of anyone. "I was hit by a baseball bat."

Luke takes another step forward, his taut body zapping stress through the room.

"Where on your head was the impact?"

"Above my left eyebrow." From years of habit, I want to make that first move to rub at the familiar scar. But it's now split wide open with a new wound.

"What were the circumstances that caused the injury?" he asks.

Shame and embarrassment slither into my nerve endings. I ignore the sensation and, without emotion, deliver the story. "I was living in a group foster home at the time. On a fairly regular basis, my roommate felt like I should let her copy my homework. One day, she tired of my refusals and laid into me with a baseball bat."

Luke grunts.

The doctor nods. "What kind of medical treatment did you receive?"

"I got stitches and was sent home."

"A CT scan or MRI?"

"No."

"Anyone talk to you about a post-concussion protocol?"

"No."

"Did you have follow-up appointments with any medical professionals?"

"No."

The doctor pauses, removes his bifocals, and studies me. "What about the stitches?"

"I took them out myself." The rote words don't feel like they're coming from my body. It's not a story that I have any practice telling. Jason is the only one who knows.

Jason. He's going to panic when he finds out I'm in the hospital.

I glance around the room, then back at the doctor, hoping that sharing time is over.

He peruses additional information on his tablet. "Okay. The good news is that there are no breaks in your arm. Your shoulder popped out of its socket, so once we reset the joint, it will be fine." He taps several things on the screen while he murmurs, "But your head requires a little more attention."

I clutch the beige waffle-weave blanket at my waist, gouging my thumbnails into the cloth fibers.

"My understanding is that you lost consciousness at the scene. That's always concerning. But it's the details of your two points of impact that I'm talking about now. When you fell, you hit your head in two places. The contusion on your eyebrow was the first point of contact. Apparently"—he squints at his notes—"you collided with the edge of an ice machine on the way down?"

With no true memory to confirm the accuracy of his statement, I offer a half shrug with my uninjured arm.

"It's going to need sutures. But looking at the CT scan, that area in and of itself appears to look good." He tucks the tablet under his arm. "The spot on the back of your head was the second point of contact—with the cement. That's the one that's got our attention. The contusion needs a few stitches as well. However, underneath the wound is the real concern. The CT shows a subdural hematoma. A bruise."

A bruise? Earlier he said brain bleed. But bruises are no big deal. "Does that mean I can leave?"

"A bruise is a brain bleed. And we never take blood near the brain lightly, Miss Reid," he says with gentle authority. "There's no evidence of a skull fracture. But there's blood pooling around an area of the dura, also known as the outer casing of the brain."

Oh.

"I also don't like the symptoms you're experiencing. The nausea, dizziness, loss of memory. Plus, you've got a history with concussions. One that didn't include a proper post-injury protocol. I'm going to admit you to the hospital so we can keep an eye on you."

Panic sweeps through me. We have to find Finley. The girls are at the ranch on their own. Harlan and Meredith are coming home tomorrow. It's too much. I can't be here now. "For how long?"

"We'll be watching for signs of neurological distress. We'll do a repeat CT to monitor the hematoma. It could be a couple of days, maybe a little longer. I want to be cautious since this isn't your first head injury. We'll take care of you and get you out of here as soon as possible." He pushes through a few more screens on his iPad.

A couple of days. A couple of days might as well be a year. I don't have a couple of days. My bosses come home tomorrow. I have to get back to the ranch and pull things together to resemble some sort of order.

"It says here you're reporting some pain," the doctor says. "Because of the severe concussion, I can only give you acetaminophen. But the local anesthetic for the stitches should help some." He pulls the tablet into his chest, securing it with his crossed arms. "I'm afraid the nurses will have to wake you to check on your vitals every so often. It's part of the protocol. Hang in there with them, they're just doing their job. Any questions?"

"No. Thank you," I say quietly.

His giant eyebrows furrow in concern, but he smiles just the same, then leaves the room as if he didn't just turn my world upside down on my head.

How did this happen?

Spotty patches of memory of the event flash through my head. That is to say, they flash when the blinding pain isn't strobing like a 1970s dance floor.

Luke stands solid, hands splayed at his hips, his authority holding the room captive.

In light of my condition, I'm going to need his help at the ranch. But can he forget everything he just heard about my childhood and help me come up with a plan?

I take a fortifying breath. Let's just face this head-on and get it out of the way.

Using my good hand, I fold the worn hospital blanket over and press on the crease of the fabric. "I wish you hadn't been in the room to hear all of that."

"If you had asked me to leave, I wouldn't have." He nods to me. "How bad's your vision?"

"I know your pants are army green, possibly camo, but I don't know if they're your signature cargo pants."

"My signature cargo pants?" he asks, his question laced with amusement.

Good. Yes. I can banter a bit. Let him believe I'm okay. Let him know I'm capable of moving on and handling this. "Yes. Please tell me that all is right with the world, and that you are wearing cargo pants."

"I'm wearing cargo pants."

"Well, that's a relief. For a minute there, I thought today was going to throw me a curveball."

A pained look crosses his face, and he whispers, "Penelope."

I swallow. "When I tell you what I think happened, you're going to be mad at me, but I need you—"

"I'm not going to be mad at you."

We'll see. "I-I can't recall everything that happened. Yet. The doctor said my memory will return. I have these flashes . . ."

Terrible flashes. Flashes of an upset Finley. Of an irate Marcus. Of a free fall. It's like watching one of those old movie reels with film that's missing huge chunks of frames. The picture is erratic, jerking with choppy edits that eliminate whole pieces of the story.

I finally draw my eyes to meet his.

Compassion etches the lines of his face. He takes a step toward me, but I hold up a hand.

"I need you to find Finley," I say. "And Marcus."

His eyes flash.

"And Bianca and Tanya." My voice cracks. "Please, Luke. I need you to help my girls," I whisper.

"So far, you haven't said anything that's made me mad."

"You will be." I stare at my hands, trying to work through my words. "I'm pretty sure I went to see Finley this morning. She works at Safeway. I-I think. I think Marcus was there and he pushed me."

He sighs, his demeanor softening just a bit. "I already know. When I hung up with you, I called my contact at the police department."

I try to hold my head high, but the injury weighs it down, and I struggle to maintain eye contact with Luke. "Do you want to tell me 'I told you so'?"

"No. I want to throttle Marcus."

Oh.

"I want to throttle Marcus." He moves one step closer. "And I want to erase a time when you had to pull stitches out yourself. I want to fix your head. I want a year to pass, us sharing a pizza, watching a game, and laughing. Then. Then, while holding your hand, I want to tell you 'I told you so.'"

He wants to hold my hand? The thought of that gives me a warm feeling inside.

Wait. He wants to talk to me a year from now? In a social setting? *He wants to hold my hand?* What does that mean? Harlan said Luke never stays in one place for very long. What was the word he used to describe him? A globe-trotter. If Luke doesn't stick around in one place for very long, how can we enjoy a slice of pizza together in a year?

I can't think about that now. At the moment, there's too much at stake, and, of all things, I'm laid up in a hospital bed.

I lift a shaky hand to curl a strand of hair behind my ear. "We need to discuss Finley. I think the police were going to question her. But the stupid ambulance took me away before I could help her."

"Penelope—"

"No, Luke. Listen. I don't know what happened to Marcus. Maybe the authorities have him in custody by now. But I think he needs help. I was trying to tell Finley that I thought we might be able to work with him too, like we do the girls. Oh." I touch my fingertips to my lips. "The girls. What time is it?" I search for a clock on the wall. Not that I could read the numbers if I found one.

"Penelope, stop for a second—"

"You've got to drive back to the ranch and do curfew. Don't tell them about the incident. They'll only worry. What day is it?" I gnaw on my bottom lip. "It's Friday, right? On Fridays, Bianca gets off work and grabs pizza for everyone on the way home, but I don't need her to pick up any food for me. And Tanya works late—"

"Penelope." Luke stomps two steps toward me and plants his fists on the mattress on either side of my hips. His face is so close to mine, I could reach out and brush his jaw. "I get that you want to take care of everyone else. And we'll discuss those things in just a minute. For now, though, I need you to stop talking. You have serious injuries."

His words blow in like a strong wind, gusting up the dirt of today's events. I swallow, afraid of the swelling emotion inside my chest.

A fierce mixture of pain and concern fills his eyes. "Besides the obvious, are you okay?" he whispers.

No.

No. Not now.

A knot forms at my sternum.

I don't want to fall apart now.

My eyes sting with fresh tears.

I'll fall apart later. Not now. Not in front of Luke.

My chest heaves with each breath as torrential waves force themselves to the surface.

No. Not in front of anyone.

But not in front of Luke.

A merciless whimper breaks free. “I’m sorry,” I say, my body shaking. A surge of tears spills down my hot cheeks. In horror at my emotional outburst, I raise my uninjured arm and place my hand over my face. “I’m sorry.”

“Baby.” Gingerly, Luke wraps one arm around my waist and the other across my shoulders, scooting his body closer to engulf me in his protective hold.

I clutch a chunk of his shirt and pull him toward me, burrowing the unharmed side of my head into the safe wall of his chest. Loud, fractious sobs fill the room. The release causes excruciating pain to throb in my head, but if I don’t surrender the fear coursing through my veins, it will swallow me whole.

“I was so scared. I’m so scared, Luke. I didn’t know. I couldn’t see. Then I couldn’t remember. I can’t remember.” My nonsensical words spill out through hiccups and shudders. “And I don’t—I don’t know. Finley. Where is she? Is someone helping her? And—Luke. It hurts.” I squeeze my eyes, trying to block the pain pulsing through my skull. “It hurts so much. I hurt.” Hiccup. “I hurt.”

Luke pulls me forward and drops his head over my shoulder, curling his body around me as if he can somehow absorb my agony.

Wrapped in the safety of Luke’s cocoon, I empty my soul into his arms. The dam that held back the reckless waters of this morning breaks, and a ferocious flood of tears spills over the walls. For Finley, yes, but also for me. For the twelve-year-old who lost her mother. For the fostered teenager who had no one to remove her stitches. And for the woman in a lonely hospital room who has no emergency contact. Rivulets of grief for my past flow into the current of today’s calamity, and I am powerless to do anything but cry.

Luke’s hold on me tightens, but he pulls back just enough to put his mouth to my ear. “I’ve got you, Penelope. I’ve got you. Yeah?”

I nod, my cheek rubbing against the dense cotton of his shirt.

The final anguished drops of my story fall onto his chest, and my breathing slows. The pounding headache has worsened with my outburst, but maybe my slowed pulse will steady the blood scurrying through my veins.

“I’ve got feelers out for both Finley and Marcus. I will find them.”

His voice is so sure, so confident, there’s no other reply than to nod again.

“I also talked to Tanya. She called someone named Daphne Fielding. Said she’s worked with the girls before?”

Daphne. I completely forgot. She’s volunteered a few times teaching art lessons at the ranch.

“Daphne is going to do curfew check-in with the girls and will stay at the house tonight. Hank is the ranch hand on call just in case we need him. Also, one of my men is there. He’ll keep out of sight but will monitor the property. And I’ve got another guy at the office watching the security cameras.”

I take in a broken breath. “You took care of everything.”

He runs a thumb over the apple of my cheek. “I took care of everything.”

I pull back to look him in the eyes. “If you won’t be at the ranch tonight, where will you be?”

Luke slides his warm hand to the back of my neck and squeezes gently. “Hunting.”

“Hunting?”

“I’ve been keeping tabs on Marcus. I know a few places to look for him.”

My eyes widen and I open my mouth to protest, but Luke continues. “I’m not the law, Penelope. I won’t make an approach. But I can help the police by sharing information I find.”

15

HUNTING.

I'll give Luke something to hunt.

How about he hunts down the person who decided to wake concussion patients in timely increments to check neurological responses? After that, let's hunt down the person who declared concussion patients can't utilize electronics while they're intentionally deprived of sleep. Finally, let's hunt down the person who decided that concussion patients can only take Tylenol while they're fully awake and in pain during said torture.

My shoulder, temple, and the back of my head all throb to the beat of my heart. My anger and frustration only cause the tempo to increase. I close my eyes and inhale through my nose, trying to lower my blood pressure.

Shortly after Luke left, my life became a bustle of activity.

A grandmotherly nurse made the rounds to stitch up the two cuts on my head. Her wrinkled but steady hands administered the local anesthetic. When the throbbing subsided to a more manageable range, I became her biggest fan.

I was not, however, a fan of the cocky young nurse who came

armed with a cache of skeleton jokes, which he took great joy in telling me while he popped my shoulder back into place.

Once my admissions paperwork went through, orderlies rolled me to my room. A stereotypical drab room in the corner of the redbrick building. The double windows probably offered a striking view of the Rockies, but I was grateful for the double-enforced curtains that blocked out the streaking sunlight.

Streaking sunlight that, thankfully, surrendered to the more forgiving whisper of the moon's glow. I've eaten next to nothing. The meltdown I experienced earlier today has morphed into a ball of frustration so profound, I can hardly manage anything. The constant pain from the injury cracked open a path for crankiness to seep into my bones and infiltrate every fiber in me. My lack of control over the situation is grating on my last nerve. Worry shreds my last pieces of sanity.

In full migraine mode, I lie on my uninjured side, turned away from the door. My body curls into itself as I grasp the chafing sheet, hoping its cheap cotton can absorb some of the misery.

A line of light travels slowly across the darkened wall, indicating the door behind me is opening.

"Is it time to check vitals again?" I ask. That would mean the last half hour flew by, a minor gift in the scope of today.

Silence.

Quiet footsteps patter around my bed. A sob. "Miss Penelope?"

My eyes pop open. "Finley?"

"Oh my gosh, Miss Penelope. Are you okay?" She crouches down, her tear-streaked face filling my vision. "I'm so sorry. I'm so, so sorry."

I swallow. "It's all right, Finley. I'm okay."

"You don't look okay, Miss Penelope." She takes in my face, the bandages, the IV pole, and the screen with my vitals. "I'm so sorry. This is all my fault."

I open my palm, and she places her hand in mine. "I'm okay, Finley."

"No. You're not. You're in the hospital. That was so much blood, Penny Lady. I was so scared." She pauses, gnawing on her bottom lip. "Marcus didn't mean to do it. You know that, right?"

I can piece together that he was there, he was upset, and he pushed me. However shoddy my memories are, his intention seems clear to me.

"You know that, right, Penelope? He—I mean, yes, he pushed you. But he didn't mean for this to happen."

"Did you talk to him? After the incident at the store?"

She shakes her head.

Searching her face, I try to decipher if her response is trustworthy. The events of today cloud my brain, and I have no idea what kind of storm I'm dealing with.

"The cops are after him." Her voice cracks. "But I'll make this right. I'll find him, bring him in. Make him tell the police that this was all an accident. Then it will all be okay. I'll fix it, and everything can go back to normal." Her eyes move wildly as she discusses each part of her plan.

"Look at me." I wait for her to comply. "This is not your responsibility to fix. You did nothing wrong."

"It's my fault," she whispers. "All of it. But don't worry, Miss Penelope. I'm going to fix it."

I lift my head but drop it the second pain shoots through my eyebrow. Dang it. I'm bound to this bed, and she's probably about to do something stupid. Something that could backfire in astronomical proportions. "Finley—"

"I'm going to fix it. I'm going to get Marcus to turn himself in. Then the cops will understand it was an accident. It will be okay."

Panic hits me, and I tighten my grip on her. "Finley, don't go anywhere near him. Go straight to Twelve Bluebells."

A heart-wrenching combination of regret and longing fills her face. "I can't go back there."

I push forward. "Do you remember Miss Fielding?"

"The art lady?"

"Yes. The art lady."

She sniffles, wiping her nose on her sleeve. "I really like her."

"Yes. She really likes you too."

"She does?"

"Yes," I say, hoping the truth tethers her back to the ranch. "She says you show a unique perspective in your artwork."

Finley looks down at our hands.

"She's staying with Tanya and Bianca tonight. Go there. Stay at the ranch. Stay safe. I'm safe here. You'll be safe there."

She exhales, possibly relaxing into my words, giving me hope.

Maybe in some bizarre way, this painful day was necessary to bring Finley home. A beacon for her inside the storm of abuse. If that's the case, it was worth it. Every last second.

"It's going to be okay, Finley. I promise."

Alligator tears fall down her pale cheeks, and she plants her face on our bound hands. "I was so scared, Penny Lady. All that blood. And you weren't answering me." She sobs. "I don't know what I would do—I couldn't live with myself—if something ever happened to you."

"I'm okay. Just some bumps and bruises. It looks worse than it is. Promise." I rub the top of her hand with my thumb. "Luke's going to track down Marcus and take care of everything. It's going to be okay."

She jerks back. "What? Luke?" Her eyes grow big and round. "No. He can't do that. Marcus hates him."

"Finley—"

"He *hates* Luke." Yanking her hand from my hold, she stands, shaking her head. "No. No. I have to go. I have to find him first. If Luke finds him, he'll just run again. Then the cops will think he's guilty."

"You can't go after him. It's dangerous. Don't you get that?" My voice rises, and pain radiates from the base of my skull. I bite my lip and lower my tone. "Head to the ranch."

"I have to go. I think his boss helps him out sometimes. I have to find him."

"Finley, Marcus's job is questionable at best. I don't think asking his probably drug-dealing boss is wise."

"Marcus—he hasn't been himself this week."

"How hasn't he been himself this week?" Maybe I can keep her talking. Keep her in this room. But the stress of this conversation is spiking my adrenaline and pumping painfully through my injuries.

"I don't know what's going on. I think—I think he has a gun."

"What do you mean you think he has a gun? He either has a gun or he doesn't."

"I saw one. I saw a handgun in his dresser. I asked him about it, but he said it was a friend's. But that can't be right. Why would he keep a friend's gun? And if it's not a friend's gun, why would Marcus have a gun?"

"Yes, Finley. Why would he have a gun?" I close my eyes, silently begging the throbbing to quiet so I can have this conversation. All I know to do is push the nurse button. They can't make her stay either, but maybe they can call Luke. "Please. Please don't go to him."

"I'll fix it, Penny Lady." She touches my leg as she walks backward.

The last I hear from Finley is the sound she makes shutting my hospital room door.

That's odd. Usually the nurse takes my pulse and blood pressure with the machine next to my bed. Why is she holding my hand for this round of vitals?

Now she's stroking her thumb across my palm. That's nice. Probably not in her job description. But it's lovely all the same.

What *is* in her job description is administering medication. A delightful medication that currently dulls the sharp corners of my injuries. Concussion protocol won't allow for normal pain meds or muscle relaxers. But when the nurse entered the room and found me burrowing the injured side of my forehead into the unyielding mattress just after Finley's dramatic exit, she took pity on me. Or, more accurately, she contacted my doctor who took pity on me and ordered a tiny dose of Dilaudid.

I am now thinking about proposing to my doctor—but this nurse is so *nice.*

I shift my weight, pulling her arm into my chest and curling my body into the fetal position.

Her hand seems hairier than a woman's should be.

With a monstrous effort, I pry my eyes open. In a hazy halo is the most beautiful man I've ever seen.

"Luke," I breathe.

His face, pulled close to mine because I'm holding his arm hostage, is a fascinating combination of concern, amusement, and question. "Heard you've had a rough night."

"You're so pretty."

A smile tugs at his lips. Lips I can't take my eyes off of. "You okay?" the lips ask.

"I'm okay." I sigh, petting his warm hand. "I'm receiving some excellent drugs."

"I can tell."

"Do you need some too? Hospital policy won't let me share, but you never know. I've gotten a lot accomplished in my life by simply asking."

"I bet that's right," he mutters.

"Sometimes I think I might want to kiss you," I whisper.

His eyes flash.

"But then you do something annoying."

He chuckles. "Then maybe I should stop doing annoying things."

I lean toward him, our faces only inches away, and offer a sly grin. "Did you know that I'm very good at my job?"

His cheek twitches. "I'm afraid tonight's going to be a story I'll tell you in years to come and you won't believe me. But I really hope you'll be able to remember this later."

I don't know what that nonsense is about, so I continue. "Not surprisingly, I'm also excellent at *your* job."

"What are you talking about, kitten?"

"I'm a better hunter than you."

He lifts his chin. "And how's that?"

"I found Finley."

Luke's hand spasms. He sits up, his arm sliding out of my hold, his piercing eyes alert. Pretty, piercing eyes. "What do you mean, you found her?"

"Well, she came to see me. But it still counts. I found her." I beam, quite pleased with myself.

"When?"

A brilliant thought comes to me, and I point my finger in the air. "I should charge you a finder's fee."

"Penelope, baby. Focus. When did she come visit?"

Gosh, he's demanding. And his urgency is kind of a buzzkill. But his calling me "baby" feels lovely. Okay. When did Finley come to visit . . . "Right before I got my medication."

Craning his neck, he glances at the whiteboard on the other side of the room. The nurses update it every time they check on me. "You got this dose thirty minutes ago," he murmurs. "Did she say where she was going?"

I close my eyes, trying to concentrate. Feathers of a memory tickle my consciousness. "Marcus. Something about finding Marcus." Finley's fear-filled face materializes in my mind. "She said she was sorry. She blames herself for my injuries."

Since the administered medication, I've been enjoying a peaceful state of rest. But the sound of Luke's grinding teeth frays the edges of my nerves.

"She said she wanted to make everything okay. She's going to look for him."

"Did she say where?"

I claw through my muddy memory. "Something about going to his boss."

He leans over me, his hand holding my face, thumb skimming my cheek. "I got this, baby. You just rest."

"Wait." I exhale, trying to concentrate. "Luke, I don't know this for sure, but Marcus might be working for a drug dealer."

"I got this."

"And Finley said Marcus's friend has a gun." This detail seems important. I squint, trying to make the memory focus. "No, maybe Marcus has a gun?" Yes, that seems important. "Wait. Do you have a gun?"

"Penelope—"

"Do you keep it in your underwear drawer?"

Luke quirks his lips just a bit. But an intensity emanates from him, seeping through the bedsheets and into my core. "You just focus on letting that beautiful, tenacious, brilliant brain of yours"—he kisses the top of my head—"heal. I'll be back later."

I graze a finger over the spot where he kissed me and sink into the leftover affection.

And as Luke prowls out of the room, the tentacles of Dilaudid draw me back into its sleepy cradle.

16

IF I WERE PERUSING paintings in the Denver Museum of Art, I might think the strokes of blue, purple, and rusted red against the pale white background in front of me were beautiful. As it is, this particular masterpiece is the brushwork of the injury spattered across my face.

With one arm bound in a sling, I brace the opposite hand on the basin of the stainless steel sink and stare full-on into the hospital bathroom mirror. I opted to leave the glaring fluorescent bulbs off. But a ray of light beams through the small crack in the door, shooting a diagonal line down the reflection and splitting my face in half.

On the plus side, my vision is starting to clear. However, the tears pooling in my eyes now blur my view.

I draw a slow inhale through my nose, taking in the lemon-like fumes of hospital cleaning supplies, then exhale out my mouth.

I can do this.

With shaky movements, I reach for my purse to extract the makeup bag. This simple task takes an exorbitant amount of energy. Between my useless arm and the IV hep lock taped to the other hand, this is a perilous activity. Nonetheless, I need to apply the beginnings of my battle paint. If Meredith and Harlan come visit today, I don't like the idea of being caught in the vulnerability of a hospital setting.

In the darkness of the room, I ignore my jittery hand and trace a path over my mouth with deep-red lipstick. My signature color. The only one I carry. A magazine article once promised me this particular shade spoke of confidence. I hope that's true today. Once it's applied, I attempt to rub my lips together, but my tight, swollen face protests. With my blurred vision, I don't dare try to apply mascara. And applying cover-up might infect the cuts on my face. The lipstick will have to do.

After three tries, I successfully place the cap on the tube. When I glance in the mirror, I notice the halo of my untamed hair. Lovely.

Without the use of my bound arm, I won't be able to tie my hair back into my usual taut ponytail. But maybe I can lean my weight into the sink for balance and somehow manage something more presentable.

With two sets of stitches to avoid, stroking through the tangles is more difficult than I anticipated.

On the third run through, my brush gets caught in a nest of snags. The harder I try to release it, the worse it becomes. My chest rises and falls with my frustration, and sweat breaks across my forehead.

This is ridiculous. I am ridiculous.

Two soft knocks sound through the cracked door. "Penelope? It's Meredith."

I close my eyes, but that causes me to sway. After opening them, I clutch the basin and steady both my body and my voice. "Hello, Meredith."

"Hi. Uh, hi." Her voice wavers with nervousness. "Do you, um . . . Is everything all right?"

"I'm fine. How was your honeymoon?" I ask my boss's wife.

The woman I want to be my future boss. The person who needs to think I have it all together.

She chuckles, but it sounds more incredulous than sincere. "Um, my honeymoon was great. Should I come in?"

"No, I'm okay." My words falter. I pause and cringe. "Really. I'm fine."

"Penelope." She sighs. "Okay, don't hate me. I'm coming in."

I shuffle my feet to turn her direction, plant my hip against the sink, and muster a smile. The rogue hairbrush hangs from my head with a gentle swing, mocking me while I prepare to placate Meredith with a short conversation. "So you enjoyed Hawaii?"

At the first sight of me, her eyes widen. She shakes her head, then plasters on a fake, perky smile. "Fabulous. Yes. Kauai was amazing. Absolutely." She swoops her arm down across her body, showcasing the red Hawaiian tunic covered in white hibiscus flowers. Leave it to Meredith to take a tourist cliché and wear it well. With the shirt belted at the waist of her skinny jeans and a pair of cream Converse tennis shoes, the casual ensemble exudes her personable self. As does her next move when she approaches me and makes quick business of detangling the brush from my head. "I'm just going to help this out a little bit."

Before I can protest, she holds my hair at the root and attacks a lock full of tangles. Her movements are swift but somehow gentle. Once she rakes through the most challenging pieces, she brushes the length.

Long strokes smoothing away the rough spots.

The list of things I lost at the age of twelve when my mother died is quite extensive. But I never considered that I would miss someone brushing my hair. The affection is a memory forgotten somewhere in what became my daily survival of the foster care system.

Tears brim, and I don't know what's worse—the fact that I can't tend to myself or the realization that it's nice when someone else does.

"Stop that," Meredith says.

"Stop what?"

"Stop shaming yourself because I'm helping you. This isn't anything you wouldn't do for anyone else. I will get it done, we won't talk about it, and we'll move on."

Meredith knows me well. So well that she doesn't acknowledge the tear I swipe from my cheek.

The problem is it's not just my pride. With each stroke of my hair, my chance to be the program director at Twelve Bluebells Ranch brushes away.

"It wasn't that long ago," she murmurs, "in a different hospital, that you sat on the tile of a bathroom floor with me, handing me tissues while I cried. You're always taking care of everyone else. It feels good to finally get to do something for you." She studies my face. "Though, maybe we should consider having our big moments someplace other than a room with a toilet."

A half-hearted smile tugs at my lips.

After finishing with my hair, she wets a paper towel. "Your lipstick color always packs a powerful punch," she says as she wipes outside of my lip lines. "I just need to wrangle some of it in."

With one last perusal, as if she can't hold back her heart any longer, her eyes fill with tears and her face crumples. "I can't believe this happened to you," she whispers.

"Meredith." My tone doesn't come out as stern as I want it to. "I'm fine."

"You're not fine, sweetie, but you will be. We're all here for you."

"Everything okay in there?" Harlan's question comes through the door, and my body tenses.

Meredith wipes a tear from the corner of her eye and gives me a confident, curt nod. "Yes," she calls. She raises her eyebrows at me in question.

I straighten my spine and inhale. "I'm ready."

Only I'm not remotely ready.

Meredith assists me to the bed, and by the time I settle into the firm mattress, the room and my stomach are swirling. I reach for the plastic bedpan.

Wringing her hands, knuckles white, Meredith forces a strained and terrified smile. "Do you feel nauseated? I mean, it would be okay if you did. I'm perfectly fine helping you. If you need it. Do you need it? I mean, right now? Do you need help?"

The story of Kim Sterling throwing up on Meredith's head in the second grade is more than simple folklore at the ranch. This grown woman becomes a panicky eight-year-old at the mere mention of nausea.

"I'm fine, Meredith." For her sake, I grit my teeth and hope I'm not lying.

She straightens. "B-because I could do it, you know. I could totally be there for you."

Harlan puts an arm around her waist, pulls her close, and tucks her into the crook of his shoulder. "You don't have to act brave, sweetheart. Between the nurses and me, she has plenty of people to help her."

"Oh, thank goodness." She wraps her arms around him and sinks her weight into his side.

For the first time since I returned to my bed, I can take a breath and focus on Harlan. He sports the man version of the same red Hawaiian shirt, paired with worn jeans and boots. The two of them look like a cheesy advertisement for a luau for beautiful people. And yet somehow they pull it off.

"I'm here to help her too," a familiar deep voice calls from the door.

I close my eyes. Perfect. Luke's here in time to discuss my pending nausea.

"Evidence suggests your help didn't go so well," Harlan chides his friend and nods toward me.

Luke sidles to the bed and lifts his chin in my direction. "You ever try to help Penelope do anything?"

"No," Harlan says. "I value my life more than that."

"There's a steep learning curve. But I'm onto her now, so this won't happen again."

Harlan faces Luke. "Just out of curiosity, where'd you go wrong? Did you underestimate her?"

Luke scoffs. "I value *my* life more than that. No one underestimates Penelope and lives to tell about it."

"Gentlemen, I'm still here," I say, folding a piece of hair behind my ear.

Luke takes two steps closer to my bed and leans over me, almost hiding me in the protective shadow of his presence. His bright eyes soften, and he says in a gentle, husky voice, "How are you feeling? Did you get any rest?"

"Finley?" I ask.

He ignores my question and studies my face. "You didn't get any rest."

"Finley?" My voice is stronger this time.

"The bruises are coming out today. But your hair looks nice when it's down."

I purse my lips and nod in the direction of Harlan and Meredith. In a whisper, I ask, "Do they know what happened?"

Meredith clears her throat. "Um . . . we're also still here."

"They know. It's okay," Luke says as he squeezes my hand and turns to address the room. "About an hour ago, police detained Marcus and took him down to the station."

"How'd they find him?" Harlan interjects.

Luke crosses his arms over his chest and lifts an eyebrow, but he says nothing in response.

Harlan shakes his head. "You always were good at tracking people."

He shrugs. "People are predictable. Finley reports all of her activities and locations on Instagram. With the help of her previous posts, I checked out a few places where she hung out with Marcus's posse. The third location was pay dirt—his boss's house."

My stomach lurches. "Was Finley there?"

"Yeah. It wasn't a pleasant scene, but she's okay. She followed the patrol car to the station."

"Charges filed?" Harlan asks.

"They're working on it."

"I have to talk to her before she leaves the station," I say. "She has to go back to the ranch."

There's a knock at the door, and my doctor walks into the room.

"When can I be discharged?" I ask.

He peers at me over his bifocals, his dark, bushy eyebrows lifting, and smiles. "Well, good morning to you too."

"Hi. Sorry. Good morning, Dr. Gallo." I steel myself against the nausea, shove the bedpan away, and hit the button to sit straighter in bed. "When will I be released?"

He initiates introductions to everyone in the room, scans a few screens on his iPad, and glances back at me. "Would you like some privacy for this discussion, or may I speak freely in front of your guests?"

"You can speak freely," Luke says.

The glare I shoot him bounces right off his smug face and into the great beyond. I fold the top of my sheet into a straight line across my lap. While I smooth the edges, I say, "Go ahead."

"How's your pain level today?"

"Better. Much better." I'm stretching the truth. But the quicker he can evaluate me, the sooner I can get to Finley.

"I'm glad to hear the Dilaudid made a dent in your discomfort last night, but I must confess . . ." He leans in to whisper, "I'm happily married and cannot accept your proposal."

Oh my word. Apparently proposing to my doctor wasn't merely a weird dream.

"She *proposed* to you?" Luke asks, clutching a hand to his chest with feigned hurt. "She only told me I was pretty."

Not a weird dream. A nightmare. Because I remember staring into those long-lashed green eyes and telling Luke he was pretty. And that sometimes I thought I wanted to kiss him. Unfortunately, I meant every word of that particular drug-induced confession.

The doctor points to a poster on the wall. "Give me a number. How would you rate your pain right now?"

I study the chart of numbers corresponding with varying degrees of smiley faces for the lower numbers and frowny faces for the higher numbers. Who designed this system?

For me, there are only two categories of pain. Pain that you can function with and pain that you can't. Most of life lands under the first. Push through. Complete the task at hand. Move forward.

The faces on the poster mock me. "I don't know," I mumble.

The doctor leans in, holds one of my eyelids open, and inspects my eye with his penlight. "How's your blurred vision?"

"Better."

"But not gone."

"No, sir."

He inspects the second eye and returns the penlight to his white coat pocket. "Do you have any new recollections of what happened yesterday?"

"I have flashes, but not the entire picture."

After running me through a few more post-concussion tests and asking several questions, he nods. "You're showing signs of recovery. I'm going to check on you later and probably order a new CT to evaluate the hematoma. If you continue to improve, I might let you out of here tomorrow or the next day."

Tomorrow or the next day. So much could happen to Finley in that amount of time.

"But I have to tell you"—Dr. Gallo levels his gaze at me—"life is going to be a little different for you in the foreseeable future."

The tone of the conversation shifts to something significant but unidentifiable. Luke splays his hands on his hips. Harlan and Meredith exchange an indecipherable glance. The hairs on my arms stand on end.

"We take recovering from a concussion and brain bleed pretty seriously around here. Especially for a repeat customer." He sets his iPad down next to the sink, leans against the counter, and crosses his ankles. "Your activities will be limited for a while."

An eerie chill crawls down my limbs. "What does that mean? And for how long?"

"That depends on you." He nods in my direction, his solemn face communicating more than his calm words.

"But I'm feeling better this morning." My statement is untrue on only a few levels.

The doctor starts to speak, pauses, and studies me. "The quickest way to achieve total healing with a head injury is to be completely honest about the symptoms. If you lie to yourself about what you're dealing with, you will most certainly cause discomfort and prolong your recovery."

I feel more exposed emotionally than I do physically in this hospital gown.

"We'll be measuring and monitoring your tolerance to stimuli through weekly follow-up appointments. Things like nausea, blurred vision, lack of balance, headaches. You'll start off in a dark room, no electronics. Once you can tolerate more, we'll add back activities. Depending on your progress and how you feel, we might supplement with medication therapies or neurofeedback. For some concussion patients, rehabilitation takes weeks. Others take several months to make a full recovery."

Weeks. Months.

Months?

"The most important thing I need you to hear today is this: Head injuries are tricky. If you acquire a third concussion, there's a possibility you'll have irreversible symptoms. And if you reinjure yourself before you've healed, there could be grave consequences."

Remembering my audience, I flick my gaze around the room. Each face wears a varying degree of concern accented by a touch of pity. I stare over the shoulder of the doctor and whisper to no one, "But I can't miss work."

"Work's not the focus now, Penelope," Harlan says. "You are."

I clutch the top of the hospital blanket, dragging it to my waist and gripping it close to my body. I am? I am the focus?

I can't think of anything worse.

"Let's do one step at a time here. First, we need to make sure the hematoma is under control. Then we'll talk about releasing you." Dr. Gallo picks up his iPad, offers a short farewell to everyone in the room, and exits.

My emotional exposure multiplies in the silent room, morphing into its own entity that I want to shove under my hospital blanket.

Meredith steps toward my bed. "Penelope, we'll figure out all the details."

"But—"

She puts her hand on mine, her thumb brushing over my skin. "You just have to rest."

"It's about time for you to take some time off," Harlan adds. He turns to Luke to explain. "She's always on the job. We had to add a mandatory vacation clause to her contract."

Sometimes Harlan's more of a big brother than a boss. Case in point—the vacation clause.

But the doctor wasn't talking about vacation. This would be me sitting in a dark room with nothing to do but wait. Pure torture.

I don't want time off. I have to fix this. I have to find Finley. Second to that, I need to show the Holcombes I'm a solid candidate for the new job at the ranch.

None of which I can accomplish from the darkness of a room.

"I have to fix this. I made a mistake, Meredith," I whisper. Heat hits my face and fierce tears sting the backs of my eyes. "This is all my fault. I upset Finley. I handled the situation completely wrong. She left—"

"I know." She gently squeezes my hand.

"No. You don't. I said some things to Marcus and he reported it all to Finley, but he misconstrued everything. She became very angry and left the ranch. I tried to reach out to her, but this"—I break the connection at our hands and sweep my arm down my body, indicating the hospital bed—"is the result. I mismanaged every aspect of the situation."

Meredith crosses her arms over her chest and hitches out a hip. She clears her throat. "Did you kick Finley out of the house?"

Shocked by her question, I sit up straighter. "What? No."

"Did you yell at her?"

"No. Do you think I would actually—"

"Did you insult her?"

"No."

"Hit her?"

"You can't be serious."

"Sell drugs to her?"

"What is wrong with you?"

"I'm trying to figure out what's wrong with *you*," Meredith snaps back.

Luke chuckles, and Harlan purses his lips, his face growing red with what appears to be a held-back laugh.

The spike in emotions got my blood to flow, causing pain to pulse at my injuries. I inhale a deep breath and swallow down portions of the angst, anxiety, and frustration.

Meredith rests her weight on the edge of my bed and takes my hand in hers. "We knew going in, Penelope, that we have no control over what these women decide to do with their lives. They're over eighteen years old. Adults. If we ran a facility for minors, things might be different. But we chose to help this age group for a reason. We are an uncommon resource for at-risk adults who need a safe place to mature, obtain life skills, and discover community." She tucks a long strand of her dark brown hair behind her ear. "But we do this, eyes wide open, knowing that these precious women get to choose whether they want to stay or go. And we do this knowing that they could break our hearts in the process."

Yes. That's it. That's the ache in my chest. My heart is breaking for Finley. Only there's more.

I draw a shaky hand to my left eyebrow, skimming over the bandage. An old wound giving ground to a new wound. The blood of seasoned grief erupting through the ripped skin of a fresh cut. My heart breaks for an orphaned twelve-year-old Penelope who is begging an eighteen-year-old Finley to embrace the belonging found inside the fence lines of Twelve Bluebells Ranch.

"I interviewed several people who own facilities like the one we're creating," Meredith says. "Every single one of them warned me this could happen. That we could invest in these beautiful souls, only for some of them to return to their unhealthy choices. This isn't your fault, Penelope. This is reality. This is life."

I purse my lips and turn to gaze at the window. The one with the long, gray shades closed to the outside world.

"All right." Harlan claps his hands and rubs them together. "This is great timing. I just wrapped up a big consulting job, so I don't have any business on the table for you right now. Getting someone from a temp agency to stand in your place while you're indisposed shouldn't be a problem."

I rub at a spot over my heart. Someone from a temp agency is going to replace me?

Meredith picks up where her husband left off. "And I know you're so on top of things, Penelope, that any work you've done with the ranch is spelled out in a well-organized manner. Probably color coded."

"Did you talk to Claire any more about taking the program director position?" Harlan asks Meredith.

I blink. "Claire?"

"Claire Stark. Remember? My best friend back in Texas? She's a riot. Also an incredible high school teacher." Meredith ticks off Claire's traits, but I remember her friend.

I just didn't know she was being considered for the job.

"I wonder if we can get her in place sooner rather than later. It would take more off Penelope's plate." Harlan tosses this suggestion to the room carelessly, as if he didn't just spear a javelin through my heart.

I want to stand on my hospital bed and yell at the top of my lungs, *Me. I'm the one. I'm supposed to be the new program director for Twelve Bluebells Ranch.* Instead, I stare down at my hands, one with an IV hep lock, the other peeking out from behind the thick fabric of a sling and bearing scratches from a fall.

"Claire's going to get back to me. She's excited about the possibility, but she wants to finish the school year with her current class. We'll see." Meredith mini-claps her hands. "It would be so fun to have her up here."

My résumé's brilliance is irrelevant. My degrees and personal experience can't compete with the title of best friend. Besides, my résumé is now stained with poor job performance. Meredith's well-intentioned pep talk aside, "lost a halfway house tenant" isn't a resounding endorsement for my qualifications.

"Luke," Harlan says, "with the current crisis under control, what's the update on the wedding day vandalism? Did you find anything concrete while we were gone?"

Luke glances at Meredith, then flicks his eyes back to Harlan.

"You can speak freely," Harlan says. "She knows what happened."

Meredith shoots a glare at me. "Harlan filled me in when we landed this morning. Someday we'll discuss how you kept something important from me."

"I won't apologize for giving you a stress-free walk down the aisle."

"I know." She sighs. "It's another reason you're so good at your job."

Luke pulls something out of his pocket, unwraps it, and shoves it in his mouth. My eyesight might not be twenty-twenty yet, but the way he's chewing, it has to be gum. "The good news is nothing else vaguely resembling that incident happened while you were gone."

"And the bad news?" Harlan asks.

Luke shakes his head once. "I don't have any idea who broke that vase and left the torn brochure. If I could've found who leaked the wedding details, I might've caught a break. But I've questioned everyone working on the ranch, as well as the vendors involved with the ceremony. All dead ends."

"Do you think it was just a leftover Hercules fan?" Meredith asks.

Luke shrugs. "I guess it could be. But then I come back to the question of how that person knew about the ceremony in the first place. I've kept tabs on media and social media outlets. No one leaked it or used it for clickbait."

Meredith releases a loud breath. "Well, that's a relief."

"Could Marcus have had anything to do with it?" Harlan asks.

"Finley swears she didn't tell him about the wedding," I interject. "But he mentioned it to Luke and me. So somehow he knew."

Luke chomps on his gum, at least having the courtesy to keep his mouth closed. "The officer who's interrogating him this morning is apprised of the situation. He's putting pressure on Marcus to get an answer on record."

"It doesn't make sense," I say. "Even if Finley did tell him, what was that incident supposed to accomplish for him?"

"Maybe it's not about doing anything for him," Luke says. "Maybe it's a statement he wanted to make."

Harlan grasps Luke's shoulder. "Well, I guess your work here is done. Thanks so much for taking care of the girls while we were gone."

Luke's eyes flash to me, and he holds my stare. "Wasn't that much of a burden."

"I don't remember the last time you stayed in town this long.

You must be itching to get out of here. Where does your job take you next?"

Luke's attention returns to Harlan. "Not sure. I'll have to check with Mary."

Something unpleasant slithers through my stomach. Is he itching to get out of here? Even after his sweetness to me? And who's Mary? I glance at Meredith, but she's watching the conversation in front of us unfold with the same laser interest I am.

"She still operating your office?" Harlan asks. "I thought for sure you'd have run her off by now."

"She might run *me* off someday. She commands a tight ship."

"You need it with all the travel you do."

Luke shoves his hands in his pockets and shifts his weight.

All the travel he does. The travel that he's not denying now.

The thing in my belly squeezes.

"What's the name of the guy you do your goodwill trips with? Your mentor?"

Luke slides his gum to the other side of his mouth. "Robert Kitson."

"Yeah, Robert. You guys are the Wanderlust Brothers. Any trips on the horizon?"

"He's got his eyes on an orphanage in Costa Rica. We're working on the dates."

The unease slithers from my gut to my throat, robbing me of air. Mary. Robert the mentor. Goodwill trips to Costa Rica. Apparently I don't know anything about Luke. And apparently he really is leaving soon.

I glance at Meredith again, but that proves to be a poor decision. She studies me, her head cocked to the side. I shift my focus back to Luke, who is now examining his boots. In an effort not to make eye contact with me?

But he wanted to share a pizza with me. In a year. Watch a game with me. In a year. Doesn't that mean something?

I rub at the pit in my stomach as the reality of the scenario becomes glaringly clear. I'm not experienced with dating. Luke doesn't feel anything for me. His declaration yesterday meant precisely what he said. He might run into me in a year and share a pizza. Watch a game. Hold my hand. Hold my hand? But that would only be by chance. Not because he chose to hang out with me. Not because I belonged in his life.

That's fine. Absolutely.

I swallow and jut my chin out. "I wasn't aware of your schedule, Luke. I'll make alternative arrangements for Bianca's drum lessons."

Luke snaps his head up, his eyes searing into mine with confusion and possibly a bit of pain.

"What's this?" Meredith asks.

"Bianca expressed an interest in the drums. Luke was generous enough to purchase a used set for her and give her some instruction." I clasp my hands together, albeit with a light grip to avoid upsetting the hep lock.

"Penelope . . ." Meredith draws my name out slowly, her gaze darting from Luke to me. "I have a connection who could help us find an instructor. I'll see what I can work out."

Luke annihilates the gum in his mouth. "I guess that's it for me," he murmurs. He shakes Harlan's hand, then leans in to kiss Meredith on the cheek. With one scan of my body from head to toe, he slaps the footboard of my bed, his palm stopping flat on the thick plastic. "Feel better, Penelope." As he moves toward the door, he drags his hand across the edge of the bed with one final brushstroke.

The beauty's in the wild.

Luke said those words to me in the chapel a little over a week ago.

And as I smooth out a rough spot on my blanket, I try desperately to ignore the piece of beauty walking out of my room.

17

THE DAUGHTER of a lion is still a lion.

That's what my mother told me.

I wonder what she would think of me now, curled on my bed at the ranch, closed curtains holding back the late afternoon light, while I sport stitches, a sling, and a feeling of foreboding.

She and I were polar opposites. My mother, the artsy woman in broom skirts who sashayed through life looking for rainbows, gave birth to a steely daughter obsessed with responsibility and details. We fit together to create an intricate picture. She wasn't irresponsible—she just valued beauty more than concrete answers and planning. I wasn't uptight with her—I just valued the tangible more than the imagination. Puzzle pieces that needed each other.

I once asked her how I could come from a creative mother and a performing father. My existence never quite made sense to me.

"The daughter of a lion is still a lion," she said. "That's true of you and me."

Somehow, my free-flowing mother, who belonged in a field of flowers with a daisy tucked behind her ear, raised me to be proud of who I am. Her strength looked different than mine, but she gave it to me all the same. It came in the form of a single parent who lived paycheck to paycheck, used the bus system, and took her daughter to free community theater. It came in the form of a woman who worked overtime to purchase a used clarinet so her daughter could play in the school band.

My mother also understood that her logical, brainiac, organized daughter needed to balance her fierce left brain with a capacity for ambiguity, creativity, and grace.

Yes, her strength looked different from mine. But it was strength all the same.

The daughter of a lion is still a lion.

I sigh, brushing my hair back from the wound at my forehead. I'll need that strength for this recovery.

Scanning the room, I smile, thinking of the other things she gave me.

Filling my bedroom are vivid colors, flowers, and sunshine. Flowy chiffon curtains dust the windows. Tie-dyed hues adorn a throw rug. Pillows with varying concentric shapes perch on top of a bright pink bedspread with retro daisies.

In the midst of my math team craze, science fair wins, and academic honor rolls, my mother's hippie decorating style rubbed off on me. I can't explain how my decorating choices coexist with my power heels and pencil skirts. I only know that after a stressful day, I crave this cocoon of color, comfort, and hope.

Which is why I am now curled in the fetal position, grasping for the safety of my world.

It's also why, when a knock sounds at my door, I jump.

No one's allowed in my room.

When I lived in apartments of my own, the living room, kitchen, and dining room reflected the latest fads from HGTV. But a closed door to my bedroom kept my psychedelic secret.

"Penelope." A deep voice pushes through the door with three more knocks.

Luke? Until this moment, I've been licking my emotional wounds from his visit to the hospital two days ago. But just hearing him say my name causes relief to wrap around my heart and squeeze.

Traitorous heart.

"I'm coming in there if you don't answer me," he says.

Absolutely not. No way is he coming in here. The girls never come back here, and he is not the exception he's assuming he is. Besides, I view his departure as the brisk cutoff of our relationship.

No. Working relationship slash friendship.

Delete the friendship.

There. I nod to myself, whisking my legs to the floor and sitting up a little too quickly. The room spins, causing the bohemian colors to swirl in my vision.

"Just a minute, please." I blink the final dizziness away. After crossing the room, I inch the door open, blocking Luke's view with my body. "Can I help you?"

His alert eyes study me from head to toe through the crack in the door. "How are you feeling?"

"Fine." I answer in a level tone, as if conversing through three inches of space is my normal routine. As if I'm not wound tight, hoping this man leaves without seeing my room. Hoping he leaves without seeing my heart. "Can I help you with something?"

He narrows his eyes.

On an annoyed exhale, I say, "I thought you were leaving town, Luke. Why are you here?"

He shakes a plastic grocery bag in my face. "I come bearing gifts."

"Thank you. That's thoughtful of you." I slip my hand through the crack and grab the handles. As I pull the bag through, it skims the side of the doorframe.

Luke half smiles. "Don't you want to know what it is before you thank me?"

"I'm sure whatever you brought me is fine. I know you're preparing to leave town. I won't keep you. Have a good night." On my last hasty words, I push the door shut.

Taking two steps to the center of the room, I release a strained breath. I peek inside the bag and pull out a box of herbal tea.

Tension Tamer herbal tea by Celestial Seasonings. What in the world?

The door opens, and I spin around. Shoot! Black spots dot my vision, and I begin to fall to the ground, but Luke slides his arm around my waist and steadies my body against his torso.

I close my eyes and grimace through the pounding in my head.

"You okay?"

I inhale through my nose and nod. I open my eyes and blink several times.

Concern etches the corners of Luke's eyes, but once I'm stable, he steps back. "We need to talk before I leave, and I thought . . ." He turns his head, scanning my room. He jerks with a double take, his eyes catching on the fringe of my bedroom lamp. In what can only be described as painful slow motion, he takes in each element of my room.

My hippie-inspired, quasi-groovy, anti-Penelope, color-infested room.

A grin cracks across his face. It's proud, pleased, and annoyingly attractive. "Did you get permission from the 1960s to use this bedspread?" The grin shifts to cocky, amused, and blindingly handsome.

Heat flushes my face, and I cross my healthy arm over my sling, clutching my bicep. "I would like to ask you to leave."

His face loses its hilarity, and his eyes lock onto mine. "I like the pink."

I stand frozen.

He takes one more step. "I like the flowers."

Oxygen. I need oxygen.

"I like seeing this piece of you."

A puff of air escapes, relieving the pressure in my lungs. I finally inhale so I can speak. "Why are you here?"

"I brought you tea."

"Why?"

"To help your headaches."

"Okay. Thank you. You've come to do what you needed to do." I nod to the door, hoping he'll take his exit. But the gift, the thoughtfulness, the man, are all burning a hole in my resolve.

"I wanted to talk to you about Bianca's drum lessons. I was thinking when I came home between trips, I could—"

"It's probably best not to come in and out of the girls' lives. They need consistency. They need to be able to depend on the people around them." Standing in front of him with a straight, steely spine and what feels like fire coming out of my glare, I dare him to defy me. My responsibility is to protect the girls. If the shield I throw up for them protects me as well, so be it.

The muscles in his jaw tick.

"Miss Penelope? Miss Penelope? I'm sorry. I forgot. I totally forgot." Tanya's urgent voice pulls me out of our stare-down. When I shift my focus to the door, she skids around the corner and braces her hands on either side of the frame.

Bianca, face fuming, stands behind her like a sentry, readying for battle.

When I arrived home this afternoon, Tanya and Bianca greeted me with homemade cookies. Well, they purchased a roll of dough from the grocery store and baked them here at the ranch. But with all the concern and love they packed into their tight hugs, the cookies tasted like they were made from scratch.

"What did you forget, Tanya?" I ask.

"With all of the plutonium this week, I forgot."

"I think you might mean pandemonium. But, Tanya, what did you forget?"

She stares at the sling on my shoulder, then snaps her gaze

back to me. "They called. I forgot to tell you. Now they're here. I didn't know. I didn't know they'd come."

As the next question forms on the tip of my tongue, a waft of icky-sweet, expensive cologne hits my nose. I freeze just before the man I know it belongs to comes into my line of sight.

"Hello, Penelope," my adoptive father says as he stalks into the room, pushing the girls out of his path with his mere presence. Phillip Nelson is rarely seen in anything other than a pristine, tailor-made suit. This particular one is navy with almost imperceptible pinstripes in a lighter shade of blue. I used to imagine he slept in these suits.

In spite of the death grip I plant on Tanya's arm, I stand straighter and level my voice. "Hello, Senator Nelson."

My adoptive mother strides into the room behind her husband. Her heavy Chanel perfume competes with her husband's but loses to its dominance. Clearly it was a travel day for her, as she chose what I know to be her standard casual wear: a pair of black wool slacks and a heather-gray cashmere sweater set. She stops in front of me, her heels lifting her just an inch higher than I stand. "Penelope, your face." While filled with concern, her tone is laced with the tiniest hint of judgment.

"She looks beautiful as always," Jason says as he pats her on the shoulder and they walk farther into the room.

I glance at Jason and raise my eyebrows.

"They messaged me from the air," he says. "I drove in from Denver and picked them up from the airport."

Jason. I shouldn't be surprised. He has always served as a mediator. I could look and play the role of the senator's grateful adoptive daughter, but Jason always fit in just a little better with the Nelsons.

Of course, he was never disowned by them. That always helps relieve the tension between family members.

Despite a small paunch and early-onset balding, Jason looks good in his pressed khakis and hunter-green long-sleeve polo.

He turns to me, a heartbreaking combination of hurt and anguish filling his face. "Why didn't you call me?" he whispers.

I blink, having no idea how to explain the events of the last few days. Or why I never called him, the most loyal person in my life. *I'm sorry*, I mouth back to him.

"Well, isn't this a lovely guest room," Cynthia says, turning in a circle as she takes in the details, no doubt internally devouring them with the criticisms that flow through her veins. She points her perfectly manicured finger at the wall. Her *French*-manicured finger, because flashing color would be tacky. "Do you think we could turn on the light to enjoy the atmosphere a little better?"

"Please don't." My barking answer surprises me, but if someone turns on the overhead light, I will lose all ability to handle this situation. And I have to figure out how to handle this situation.

"This room rocks, Penny Lady," Tanya blurts out with a wide grin. "Did you decorate it yourself?"

Since I won't admit that in public, I dart my gaze to Luke.

He's standing in the corner, arms crossed over his vast chest, running his tongue over his front teeth. He must need something to chew. I confess even I'd take a toothpick right about now. Anything to release some of the stress in this room. With the exception of Tanya and Bianca, lined up in front of me is my who's who of personal disasters.

Meredith slides into the room, and when her head is angled so that only I can see her expression, she bugs her eyes out at me.

"Was there a camera crew with him?" I murmur to Meredith, knowing full well the senator wouldn't pass up an opportunity to be seen, especially at a nonprofit.

"Harlan's smooth-talking the local reporter outside now," Meredith says in a low tone.

"He's a good boss."

"And an even better husband. I also strongly advised the senator's personal assistant to stay in the living room with the cup of coffee I shoved in his hands." She turns to face the room and loops her arm through the crook of my good elbow.

The whole gang's here.

I gather a fortified breath and step toward my adoptive family to begin introductions. "Tanya and Bianca, I'd like to introduce you to California State Senator Phillip Nelson and his wife Cynthia Nelson. Phillip and Cynthia, may I present to you Miss Tanya Purtle and Miss Bianca Miller."

Wide-eyed, Tanya looks at me. "The person on the phone yesterday said they were calling on behalf of your parents. Are these your parents?"

Her question is greeted with a chorus of conflicting answers that come at her all at once.

"No," Jason scoffs.

"Yes," the senator says.

"We love Penelope," Cynthia says.

I clear my throat. "The Nelsons adopted me from a group home when I was sixteen." I omit the detail about them disowning me at age twenty-four. "And this is Jason Livingstone. We became good friends at the group home, and he was also adopted by the Nelsons."

"And how do you know our Penelope?" Cynthia asks Tanya.

"This is our abode," Tanya says, puffing out her chest, presumably for her successful vocabulary effort.

Thank goodness she used the word with a degree of accuracy. The senator doesn't understand mistakes.

Cynthia raises a hand and taps the pearls at her throat. "It's a wonderful facility."

Tanya blanches. "Facility?"

"Home," Meredith says, her firm tone leaving no room for debate. "We do have a wonderful home here, don't we?"

Phillip curls his hand to inspect his manicured nails. "We could bring a little extra publicity today to give the place a boost in public awareness."

"Thank you, sir, but today's timing isn't ideal. As always, though, we appreciate others thinking of us." Meredith's sincere words are convincing, even to me. But I know she's protecting me.

Bianca breaks her seething stare at the Nelsons to focus on me and asks with impatience, "Can they back a trailer?"

My Bianca. She knows unsafe when she sees it.

Before I can figure out how to defuse this impossible situation, Luke steps forward and thrusts out a hand to Phillip with an almost angry "Luke Granger."

While he continues with his curt introduction to Cynthia, Bianca holds her laser focus on me, waiting for my answer. Can the people in this room, claiming to be my family, back a trailer?

No, I mouth to her.

Almost imperceptibly, she nods.

Luke stares down Jason. After a beat, he shakes Jason's hand and says, "Why are you all here?" His words boomerang through the room, hitting everyone with their bluntness.

Jason throws an irritated glare my way. "We're here to check on Penelope."

Luke crosses his arms over his chest. "So far, no one's asked Penelope how she is."

"I-I'm sorry." Ever the PR guru, Cynthia moves toward me to take control of the situation. "We tried to reach you yesterday morning to schedule a possible holiday visit, but instead found out you were in the hospital. We got here as soon as we could."

Luke cocks his head. "There weren't any earlier flights available?"

"The senator's schedule is difficult to coordinate, especially this time of year. He moved several things to be able to come today."

"She had a brain bleed," Luke growls.

"Luke," I mutter and cut a glare his direction.

"Yes, Tanya shared as much with me over the phone. We've been very concerned," Cynthia says. "Penelope, we're here to help you in any way that we can. We have connections to a fabulous neurologist at Mount Sinai."

"In California?" Meredith asks.

"Yes. We want her to come home," Cynthia says.

Meredith looks at me, but I shake my head once. It's best not to say anything until everyone in this group has played their cards.

I shift my focus to Cynthia. It's unclear to me whether she manufactured the tears brimming her heavily made-up eyes. Certainly her high-dollar mascara is holding up to the moisture. Or maybe it really is concern for me. My problem is that I'm not always able to discern the difference between her love for an appropriate public display and her love for the teenagers she brought into her home. I think she walks a fine line.

"You'll be out of work for a while. Your medical bills will be taken care of," the senator says. "Come back home to California with us."

Home? The manicured lawn and pristine white furniture make *their* house more of a facility than a home. And an offer of financial help is never mere generosity. What's his take? I picture the calendar year, and the motive hits me. He's up for reelection next year. A reconciled, happy family would do wonders for his public persona. But he's also the man who brought Jason and me under his roof and provided more than just the necessities in life. The fine line blurs again.

"Miss Penelope?" Tanya whispers and grabs my hand. "Are you leaving us?"

Jason steps forward. "She doesn't have to travel a thousand miles to find a specialist. I found a guy in Denver. She can come live with me."

Luke's head whips around, and he spears a look at me as if to say, *See?*

I don't have time to deal with Luke's accusations about Jason's motives. My heart squeezes. There's no fine line with Jason. From the first day we met, he stomped all over any lines that might have existed, attached himself to me, and has remained loyal ever since. That's the problem with Jason's thoughtful offer. It comes with an unhealthy, codependent string tied to him. But is his pitch the best option for my recovery?

While each offer is generous, I now walk my own fine line between grateful family member and independent woman with her own goals. No one knows I want to stay and work at Twelve Bluebells. And that's the card I'm not willing to play yet.

"I want to thank each of you for the benevolent offers," I say. "I'll have to do some research—"

"Penelope already has a care plan in place." These shocking words come from Luke.

Wait. What? I have a care plan? I look at Meredith in question, but her intense focus doesn't leave Luke. Is she in on this?

"I'm sure you can understand why we believe she can get better medical attention in California than in Colorado Springs," Phillip says with the slightest bit of disdain.

Luke's eyes glitter when Phillip lays down the gauntlet. "I disagree."

A smirk tugs on Phillip's smug face when he addresses Luke. "I'm sorry, I missed what it is you do. How do you know Penelope?"

"I was Penelope's first call after the accident."

The buckshot from Luke's verbal shotgun sprays the room, leaving no one unscathed. But by the devastated cringe on Jason's face, it seems he took the worst of the hit.

"Phillip," I say. "Truly, thank you for your offer. But I feel it's best for me to check out my options here in Colorado Springs. Plus, I can't imagine that my recovery will take too long."

Phillip purses his lips, then nods.

Bianca huffs and directs a shot at Luke. "I thought you were taking off."

"I'm not going anywhere," Luke says, glancing at me, then

back at Bianca. "Be ready for your next drum lesson tomorrow after work."

Her face softens just a fraction, but she keeps her voice strong. "Yes, sir."

What does he mean he's not going anywhere?

"Mr. and Mrs. Nelson, it's so generous of you to want to help Penelope," Meredith says in a soothing tone I've heard her use in many a tough situation. "Would you like to join us for dinner this evening? We're getting takeout from Penelope's favorite restaurant and would love to have you as our guests."

"Thank you, that would be nice. But we can't stay long." Phillip gives a sharp tug to straighten his custom dress-shirt sleeve and adjusts the shiny cuff link. "I've got a meeting in Los Angeles tomorrow morning. Our flight leaves in a few hours."

Either they thought I'd easily agree to return to California or they never believed I'd go, putting on this show. Whatever the case, their effort reminds me that my relationship with my adoptive family is best left to be experienced at a distance.

"Then we'll get things moving," Meredith says. "Tanya, will you please call the restaurant, double the order, and tell them we want the meal delivered now?" She opens her arms to direct the guests to the door. "Let's all go sit down in the living room while we wait for the food. That will give Penelope some time to rest before the meal."

Phillip offers me a terse nod before he exits the room.

Cynthia purses her lips, sighs, and takes my hand. "If you stay here and don't make the kind of progress you need, please reconsider our offer."

"I will." I don't even know if it's a lie when I say those words. What care plan is Luke talking about?

Jason takes me in his arms and gives me a gentle hug. "I have so many questions," he says in my ear.

"I know. I'm sorry, Jason. But now's not the time."

"I know. I just . . ." He pulls back, perusing my bruised face. "Penelope. Are you all right?"

I swallow. "I'm going to be."

"You always are. But I'm just a phone call away." He shakes his head and leans in to brush a light kiss on my cheek. Our thick history may not have granted him my first call, but it will force him to forgive me for not making him my first call.

Bianca stalks over and stands squarely in front of me, shaking her head. "No wonder you needed us." On the tails of her short but very effective verbal assault, she exits the room.

As Meredith walks past, I whisper, "You're a miracle worker."

She flashes a smile. "We'll debrief about this interesting meeting, as well as your fabulous choice of personal decor, later."

I close my eyes. Of course. In the middle of the peace negotiations regarding my future, I completely forgot that a few minutes ago I was outed as a closet hippie.

"Penelope?" Luke's deep voice calls.

I open my eyes, tighten my resolve into my fist, and aim every piece of indignation at him. "Why did you tell Bianca you weren't leaving? You can't play with her emotions like that."

His gaze rakes over my face, studying every inch with a healthy dose of concern. "You're pale. That scene just took it out of you."

"I'm serious, Luke. You can't tell her that you're staying. These girls don't need additional abandonment issues."

"I'm not going to add to their abandonment issues. Come on." He lightly runs his hand down my arm and takes my hand. "You need to get some rest."

The adrenaline rush of my unexpected visitors has deserted me, and my muscles are weak, my bones tired. With a sigh, I allow him to lead me to my bed.

"So, Jason thought you should live with him in Denver," he says casually, but we both know he's anything but casual about that topic.

"Don't start with me about Jason. I've had a day."

He pauses in front of my bed and looks at me. "You have had a day. I'm just wondering if you see it yet."

I don't see it. Or maybe I see a little bit. I don't know. I saw a man who I consider a brother act in a weird way that didn't make sense. And I currently see a different man in front of me who is nothing like a brother to me and might be a little bit jealous. That also makes no sense.

I look at him and say in a small voice, "I'm so tired, Luke."

He nods and gently, oh so gently, runs the back of his knuckles across my jaw.

This makes no sense to me either, except that maybe it does and I just don't want to admit it.

He tosses the decorative pillows carelessly to the ground and shoves the bright pink bedspread back. When he discovers the multicolored pastel-striped flannel sheets and accompanying lime-green blanket, he grins at me. "You have so many layers, Penelope."

"It's winter," I try to snap, but it lacks the heart. "Everyone has layers."

"That's not what I mean, and you know it."

Exhaustion sweeps over me, and I don't have much fight left. I sit on the bed, swing my legs in, and curl my body on my right side, avoiding any contact with my stitches.

He draws the covers over my shoulders, then crouches down, resting his forearms on the edge of the mattress, his face only a few inches away. "You don't belong with those people."

Tears hit the backs of my eyes. "No," I whisper.

"You belong here."

"Yes." I blink, watching Luke stare at my lips.

"I'm wondering if I do too," he murmurs, almost as if he's saying it to himself.

In Colorado Springs? At the ranch? With me? Something in my chest aches. I want him to belong here too.

His eyes shoot to mine. "I'll pick you up tomorrow morning at nine thirty."

"For what?"

"You meet with a renowned, board-certified neurofeedback specialist at ten. Depending on how long that appointment takes, we'll grab some lunch and head over to the DO for a one o'clock consultation."

"What's a DO?"

"Doctor of osteopathy. This one specializes in head injuries."

I put my hand on his forearm. "I don't understand. The hospital didn't mention any of this when I checked out."

"I did some research."

"You did some research?"

He grins. "Not just any research. I spent two days conducting *Penelope-worthy* research of the best doctors for you. But because I knew you would want to see it for yourself, I have a binder full of doctor bios, medical articles on TBI recovery, and different care plan options. For extra credit, there's a pros and cons list, topped off with a cherry in the form of a comparison chart."

"You made a binder for me?"

He peruses my face. "Are you about to pass out on me?"

"You made a binder for me."

Something leaps in my heart. A binder, organized with information that I greatly desire but cannot get for myself. This annoying man has never appeared so attractive to me.

"You have your protocol from the hospital, but there are things we can do to help your healing move along quicker. Both doctors you see tomorrow are the best at what they do in regard to traumatic brain injury. But if you don't like them, we'll work down the list."

He had me at "help your healing move along quicker." The man is speaking my love language. Efficiency.

But . . .

"But you're leaving town."

He sighs, resting his chin on his hands. "I'm not leaving town."

I start to sit up, but he places a warm hand on my shoulder that stops my progress. I settle back into my covers as much as I can. "You said. You said the other day in my hospital room that you were leaving town."

"I said I didn't know what my schedule was, and then you practically kicked me out of your room, making plans as if I was disappearing into thin air."

Oh. I did do that.

"You're not disappearing into thin air?" I whisper.

"No."

I swallow, mustering courage to ask my next question. "Why not?"

"Because there's a bossy, beautiful brunette who might need some help—"

"I'm not bossy—"

"—who I want to spend more time with."

My heart swells. I smile and feign a protest. "What if I don't want to spend more time with you?"

He cocks a smile. "You told me the other night you wanted to kiss me."

Heat rushes from my neck up my cheeks. "I was highly medicated. You can't possibly hold me to things I said under the influence of narcotics."

"It's okay." He leans in and brushes his nose against mine. "I want to kiss you too."

As sweet as he's being, my gut clenches. Too many people who have meant something to me have come and gone in my life. But something in me is so drawn to Luke.

Cautiously, I say, "Luke, your address may be in Colorado Springs, but you don't really live here full-time."

He nods. "I know. There are some changes I need to make. I'll look at my travel schedule and ask Mary to shift some things." He smooths his knuckles down my cheek. "We're going to make a go of this."

I close my eyes, absorbing the affection but still feeling torn. "It's hard to trust that you will stay."

He curls a strand of hair around my ear. "Then I'll just have to show you."

"When did you change your mind about leaving?"

"Do you always ask this many questions?"

My eyes pop open. "You know I do."

"Well, save them for the doctors tomorrow."

"I don't want to see any doctors tomorrow. I just need some rest and I'll be fine."

Something flashes in his eyes, and he smirks. "You're going to make a terrible patient, aren't you, Penelope?"

I tighten my grip on my blankets, pull them to my chin, and glare at him.

"That's okay, kitten. It'll make your recovery more fun." His gaze moves from my eyes to my lips. He leans in, and I feel his breath on my lips. Just when I think my heart is about to pound out of my chest, he shifts directions and presses a light kiss to my forehead. When he stands, he pauses, his stare so full of affection it wraps around me, warmth invading and attacking my doubts about him.

In spite of my complete disdain for the nickname, I feel like a kitten. A warm, fuzzy kitten.

And maybe a confused kitten who can hear the word "wanderlust" but sees a man who is doing anything but wandering. A man who is shifting his life around to be here. With me.

As he turns to leave, he skims his fingers down my arm, the lingering sensation reminding me of the kind, thoughtful, and protective streak he clearly has for me.

A streak that snuggles in, finding just the right spot deep in my soul.

Where is my inner lion?

Somewhere curling up in the warm den of a panther.

18

"THIS IS UNNECESSARY," I say to Dr. Isaac Ridding, head physician at the Neurofeedback Center of Colorado.

"What's unnecessary?" he asks. "The low lighting in the room?"

"No." The light reflecting off the snowcapped Colorado mountains almost killed me on the twenty-minute ride over here in Luke's truck. By the time I walked into this low-lit office, I wanted to curl up in a ball in the corner.

"Do you mean that closing the door is unnecessary? Your body language tells me that sound bothers you. But I can reopen the soundproof door and use my normal-range voice if you prefer."

I slide my eyes to the side. "No, thank you." Jumping out of my skin when the office phone rang was not one of my prouder moments. And I can't be sure, but the timbre of this former college football lineman's deep voice probably has the ability to increase to a powerful volume. Even if he played twenty years ago.

As he sits across the sleek, modern black desk, the doctor's demeanor is relaxed. His folded hands rest on the wicking fabric of a golf shirt bearing a Denver Broncos logo across his heart. "Then can you explain to me what you think is unnecessary?"

I swallow, wanting to choose my words carefully. Respectfully. And assertively. Luke was right. The man is world-renowned. I'm impressed with his credentials, but I just don't think my injury warrants this kind of attention. "I have a problem with your treatment plan."

He nods, his tone calm. "Which part, exactly?"

"I understand you had to do some baseline testing today. I appreciate that you'll be supervising my recovery. But I think thirty neurofeedback sessions are excessive."

"You mentioned you've had a previous concussion?"

"Yes."

"One that went untreated?"

"Yes."

"One that caused you to have migraines on a regular basis for the last fifteen years of your life?"

"Yes."

"Does *that* seem excessive to you?"

I blink. Point for the doctor.

He scratches his cheek. "I tell you what. Let's give it two weeks."

"Two weeks? But I'm telling you I don't want this kind of treatment. It seems unnecessary for me."

He looks down at my file on his desk and murmurs, "I told Mr. Granger it was too soon to see you."

"What do you mean, too soon?"

"Your accident was Friday. Four days ago. You haven't had time to really understand how post-traumatic stress can manifest itself with a traumatic brain injury."

"Please don't tell me what it's like to be me."

He nods again, this time slower, his keen eyes softening, beckoning me. "I would love to hear what it's like to be you."

"This is something I will handle on my own." I will handle this on my own, figure out a way to find Finley, and work toward getting my dream job. And I will handle it on my own because that's how I accomplish everything.

He smiles. It's small and doesn't reach his eyes. Not pitying me. But something else. Something not quite sad and not quite hopeful. "Two weeks. We'll revisit this in two weeks."

I open my mouth to respond, but he holds up his hand. "I can't make you do anything, Miss Reid. Mr. Granger has given me the basics of your background, and it's clear to me that you are an extremely talented and intelligent woman. He certainly thinks so."

It takes great restraint not to roll my eyes at the name of the traitor who ignored my protests and brought me here to begin with. The handsome traitor who apparently thinks I'm extremely talented and intelligent.

"I know you're highly capable," Dr. Ridding continues. "What I'm wondering is if we could give you some tools to help you recover more quickly."

My eyes dart to his. This is the only part of his plan that I like. Let's recover and move on with life. Quickly.

"You take two weeks to think it over," he says. "You're restricted from using computer screens for now, but I've got some printed material and articles about the neurofeedback process that you could read." He leans in, planting his elbows on the desk, and talks over his folded hands. "But more importantly, for the next fourteen days, I need you to pay attention. Record causes of headaches, length, medications used. You'll find a headache chart in the clinic information packet we'll give you before you leave."

I look away. That seems simple enough. Practically everything I've done in the last few days has caused some degree of a headache. When I rise from my bed, my pulse pounds through my temples. Leaning over to brush my teeth causes a searing pain to score through my skull. A noise I don't expect sends a sonic boom pulsating through the membranes of my brain. Flashes of light make me wish the world would end.

I glance around the room, taking in his qualifications. Displayed in matching black frames, impressive degrees from Ivy League schools adorn his wall side by side with certificates of multiple board certifications. Squinting, I make out the words citing additional credentials.

I turn to him. "You're a board-certified neurologist who is BCIA board-certified in neurofeedback, and you're also a licensed professional counselor?"

"Yes."

"Why? Most medical professionals are just that. Medical."

"I wanted to make sure I understood the brain from the inside out." He shrugs. "I find that physical healing and emotional healing can be tied together. And not everyone needs the same kinds of treatments."

"I don't need a shrink."

"What do you need?"

"I need the pain to stop."

Gentleness coats his deep voice when he says, "I believe you."

On one side of his L-shaped desk sit five framed pictures laying out what I assume is his family history. A weathered black-and-white photo with a group of young people full of smiles in front of a wooden church. A family of six posed on the front steps of a conservative-sized home. A teenager in football pads posing with someone who, by the looks of the facial features, could very well be his father. Contemporary photos from beach vacations and a trip to Disney—he must have a family of his own now.

But the picture that catches my attention is one of Dr. Ridding not too long ago. He stands on a red carpet next to a smiling Will Smith. Both men are in suits. It's their smiles that intrigue me. Whatever reason Dr. Ridding had to meet Mr. Smith at the opening of a movie doesn't give them great joy. Rather, the smiles read more about something somber.

Behind the two men hangs a poster backdrop for the movie *Concussion*.

I look up to find Dr. Ridding studying me. He cocks his head. "Have you seen the movie? It's about Dr. Bennet Omalu, a pathologist who discovered CTE, chronic traumatic—"

"—encephalopathy," I finish for him. "He did research on brain-damaged football players who suffered repeated—"

"—concussions," he finishes for me.

Concussions.

"Yes, I've seen it." Scenes of old NFL footage flash through my mind—players packing hard hits, their helmets violently crashing. Scenes that I could barely watch, each clash reverberating through me, reminding me of an old wooden baseball bat that once met my face. Now scenes that remind me of a patch of unforgiving cement. "How did you come to be on the red carpet?"

"I was a consultant . . . of sorts . . . for the movie."

I glance at the picture of the boy in the football pads, then the larger man behind him. Much larger. Say, the size of a professional football player. A large professional football player who isn't in any of the other family photos. "Your father . . . ?" I whisper.

"Played for the Denver Broncos. Undiagnosed CTE. Suicide."

"I'm so sorry," I say through a clogged throat. The progressive degenerative disease involves the buildup of an abnormal protein that, depending on the stage, causes anything from loss of memory and impulse control to dementia. And sometimes suicide. "And so you decided to understand the brain from the inside out."

He nods. "If there's any way I can hit back at a brain injury, I will."

It's not that I'm in danger of CTE. I've only had two concussions. But everyone has made it clear to me that if I get a third, I'm at risk of irreversible long-term damage. Not CTE level, but significant all the same. If there are things I can do to help my brain heal, I need to make every effort possible.

This man isn't patronizing me with a contrived treatment plan. This is his life's work. If my TBI recovery turns out to be more extensive than I think it's going to be, then I need to take Dr. Ridding's recommendations seriously.

I square my shoulders to the boy who lost his daddy living in the body of a man who found his life's mission. "I'll be back in two weeks."

"I think I can walk to the car just fine without your help, Luke." To no avail, I try to pull my elbow from his grip. My appointment with Dr. Ridding showed me one important thing. I'm going to have to prove to everyone that I am well. I've got to be able to perform my duties for work.

"You wobbled getting off the elevator. I thought you were going to go down," he says as he guides me through the lobby to the glass double doors at the front of the five-story office building.

"Well, the maintenance team should check the proper speed of that elevator. It's probably not up to code. My stomach dropped on the way down."

"That's the slowest box I've ever traveled in. And you almost lost your stomach because you're recovering from a head injury."

"I should have lost my stomach all over you," I snap.

We've been doing this all morning. I could win an award for my foul mood. And Mr. Bossy Pants would get runner-up. Whatever connection we had yesterday is on shaky ground.

I'm not sure what his deal is, but I have an excellent excuse. I'm wearing loose black sweatpants today. As out of my element as I am in these clothes, it's nothing compared to the way I feel in my footwear. Tennis shoes, of all things. Where are my heels? My pencil skirts and chiffon shirts? How am I supposed to conduct my day and make an intelligent impression on these new doctors while I'm dressed in this . . . this casual wear?

Almost as disconcerting as my attire is the amount of time it took this morning to put it on. Thank goodness Meredith strolled into my room, chitchatting relentlessly while helping me. I'm certain she was aware of how difficult the process was for me. But Meredith makes an art out of helping others feel comfortable in her presence. She acted like she dresses me every day and even let me be cranky about the way she styled my hair.

Luke also let me be cranky about my hair when he told me I looked beautiful when I wore it down. Where is my tight power ponytail when I need it?

He stops us just short of the exit, flips open one of the pouches on his cargo pants, and pulls out a pair of sunglasses. Abnormally dark sunglasses.

I watch in fascination while he opens the frames and, with great care, slips them on my face. His gaze travels from one side of my head to the other, pausing at the temple on my injured side. "Good," he murmurs. "That doesn't mess with the stitches."

"What are these?" I whisper, afraid my voice will crack. Afraid he is demonstrating his thoughtfulness. Afraid I won't be able to refute his thoughtfulness.

"You were miserable on the drive over here. While you were in your appointment with Dr. Ridding, I ran to the store and grabbed these for you. They were the darkest ones I could find."

I rub the edge of the bandage at my eyebrow. He bought me sunglasses?

"I also got you an Alexa, but it's in the car. We'll get it set up when we get you home."

"An Alexa?"

He takes my elbow and guides me a few feet in one direction to allow a woman pushing a toddler in an umbrella stroller to pass. "An Echo Dot. Smart speaker. We'll hook it up to your phone, your music, some AirPods—"

"I don't own any AirPods."

"You do now. But you might not be able to use them yet. I don't know how much sound you can handle. I got them just in case."

I place a hand on my chest. What is that uncomfortable feeling? Pressure builds behind my rib cage, as if my heart is swelling.

"You asked Siri so many times this morning if you had any

new text messages from Finley that I thought she was going to go on strike. So we hired Alexa."

Oh, right. Makes sense.

My adoptive family wasn't the only set of visitors to the ranch yesterday. The police showed up to help me file charges against Marcus. By the time I got ready for bed, Finley had left a crying, gut-wrenching, expletive-filled message about my supposed betrayal. Then she blocked me.

"Alexa'll help you accomplish all the things you were doing this morning, like checking the time or sending texts and emails. Plus, it's someone else you can boss around during the day." Luke winks. "I think you're going to miss that the most while you're on a hiatus from work. Especially without your prized clipboard."

"What?" I gape at Luke while he opens the door for a delivery man pushing a dolly stacked with cases of printer paper. "What happened to my clipboard?"

"I stole it. You'll get it back when you're cleared to return to work."

"You can't do that."

"I did it this morning."

"You know I'll just ask Meredith to get me another one."

"She's the one who showed me where it was."

Traitor. I'll deal with her later.

"That's fine." I tap a foot on the acid-washed concrete. "I'm sure I can train Alexa to make me a list."

"Wouldn't surprise me." He chuckles, his sparkling gaze of affection almost too much to take in. "Wouldn't surprise me at all if you whipped Alexa into shape."

The pressure comes back to my chest. My heart asking—pushing—to increase its capacity. But I find all of this very difficult to accept.

Luke takes hold of my elbow again and reaches for the door, but I pull back. "Why are you doing this?"

He studies my face. "Doing what?"

"This." I throw my hand in the direction of the office elevators. "And these." I thrust my pointer finger toward the new sunglasses. "All of it."

"I'm taking care of you."

"For how long?"

"As long as you need it."

Which means I'm another box to check. He might leave when I no longer need help. "I don't need you to take care of me."

"I get it, Penelope." He nods, his eyes never leaving mine. "We all get it. You don't need anyone to take care of you. Ninety-nine percent of the time, that's true. You're this unbelievable machine with an iron-clad checklist. I'm so sorry to be the one to tell you, but you need help right now. You may have been able to fool that bizarre adoptive family of yours who left town last night, but you don't fool me. You need help."

They did. They left.

The senator, his wife. Even Jason.

In the dark of my room while trying to fall asleep, I tried to reconcile why they came. Why they left. I do think on some level Phillip and Cynthia love me. Unfortunately, they can't separate that from their self-absorption and personal goals. The limelight of politics stirs up the murky waters of family. Yes, if I had agreed to leave with them, they absolutely would have taken care of my needs. But it would have been the kind of help that included strings that would wind around my life and tether me to theirs.

Even Jason's ties are complicated. He has always cared for me. But we both missed out on that typical season of burgeoning independence during adolescence. Distinguishing who we were as individuals wasn't a priority. Instead, we spent those years trying to figure out who we could attach ourselves to.

I think that's why Jason's bond to me is a bit unhealthy. Why it makes me want to open a window to gasp for oxygen.

As I watched them all walk out the door last night, I couldn't ignore the deep sense of loss. Not the loss of the actual people. They needed to leave. And I did *not* want to go with them. But the loss of not having anyone safe enough who loves me enough, knows me well enough, that they wouldn't walk out that door. Someone who understands me so well that, without my having to say it, they see I'm just a bit nervous and I might need just a bit of help.

I shift my gaze to the man in front of me. He raises his eyebrows, not quite in question, but waiting for my response to his annoyingly intuitive proclamation that I need help.

I want so badly for Luke to be that person I can trust. The struggle against the ingrained inclination to believe that he'll leave just like the three people who did last night is exhausting.

I cross my healthy arm over my injured one. "Don't you have somewhere to be? A job in Montana? A well to dig in Guatemala with Robert? I seem to remember a man who left my hospital room with no plans to return—"

He jerks back. "No plans to return?"

"But suddenly you've created this . . . this *care* plan and want to be my chauffeur, all while buying ridiculously thoughtful things for me."

Blood rushes to my head and pounds. This pain came out of nowhere. I close my eyes and let out a small moan.

"Penelope?" Luke slides his arm around my waist and walks with me a few steps. "Hang on. Let's find a place to sit down."

I peer out of the slits in my eyelids and catch sight of the wrought-iron table and chairs. No, no. The light from the nearby floor-to-ceiling windows strikes through the slats of the window treatments and pierces my retinas. "Can't." I swallow. "Light."

"Sorry." He steers me to the opposite wall, his powerful legs slowing to a protective crawl, and settles us onto a green polyester–covered bench.

Breathing in a deep inhale, I open my eyes all the way. The pain lessens with my slowing pulse.

"What happened just now?" he asks.

You, I want to say.

I glance over his shoulder at the list of businesses posted on the wall next to their suite numbers. My need for Dr. Ridding is becoming glaringly clear.

Shifting my focus back to Luke, I swallow and whisper, with vulnerability laced in my voice, "Are you really staying in Colorado Springs, or are you going to leave?"

His eyes flash, and his answer is immediate. Steady. "Staying."

"Why?"

"Because no one took care of you at age fourteen when you got your first concussion, and that has to be righted."

The declaration shoots an arrow into my heart, only instead of injuring the muscle, it spreads something warm, gooey, and soothing. I shake my head, squelching the arrow and setting it afire with my indignance. "But it's not your job to right anything, Luke."

"And because you spend all your time taking care of everyone else, but by my count do very little for yourself."

Another arrow. Another blaze to snuff it out. "You don't know me well enough to make that kind of statement."

"And because you're mine."

This time the arrow hits, but in my confusion I can only blink. "What are you talking about?"

"I saw those people—your adoptive family—trying to claim you yesterday, and I thought I was going to crawl out of my skin." He rubs the back of his neck.

"*Yesterday?* You decided that I was yours *yesterday?*" Sparse time for him to know if he's committed to staying in Colorado.

"No. I didn't decide this yesterday. You became mine the second you called me from the hospital and whispered in my ear that you needed me."

"You can't base a relationship on a traumatic situation."

He stares off to the side. "No," he says, as if to himself. "It was before that."

"How convenient for you to have figured this out now."

He shoots his attention back to me. "You calling me a liar?"

"No. I think you're misled. And I think you'll spend a week in town, become bored, and catch the first flight out of Colorado that you can."

"I don't think you know me as well as you think you do. I look forward to proving you wrong."

"I know the man who asked me to dance three years ago, then disappeared without an explanation. And I know the man who walked out of my hospital room a few days ago. Again, without an explanation."

His face softens. "Baby," he whispers, "you practically kicked me out of your room."

I did. I did everything in words, tone, and actions except call hospital security to kick him out of my room.

He studies me as if I'm answering him without words. "You wanted me to stay," he finally says. "You wanted me to stay, but I left, and now you're angry."

A battle wars internally with my past between the wounds that want to send him away again and the man who created a binder for me with extensive research about my care plan. I hug my purse close to my chest, squeezing out the memory of his thoughtfulness and fortifying my resolve. But all I can muster is, "I think you should take me home and then leave town. It might be best."

He cocks his head, staring at me. Then he nods, takes my uninjured hand in his, and pulls me to standing. But he doesn't let go. Instead, his eyes sear into mine, and his grip tightens. "Be mad at me all you want. Your anger doesn't scare me. You have a lot of it, and it doesn't all have to do with me. But if you need someone to hate, I will be the safe person for you to hate."

People walk around us, the elevator doors ding open, but all I can do is stare at Luke.

"I'm not going anywhere. Throw anything you want to at me." He takes a step forward, closing the space between us and rubbing his thumb over the top of my hand. "Then, Penelope, when you're finished, I intend to be the safe person for you to love."

19

MY LIFE HAS TURNED into a bad game of Mad Libs. All the wrong word choices are in all the wrong blanks.

At the foothills of the Rocky Mountains sits Twelve Bluebells Ranch operated by _______ (person). Everyone pitches in to help ________ (name) recover from _______ (situation).

The cogwheel of my relationship with Meredith used to run on what I was able to do for her. But post–head injury, the wheel turns on what *she* can do for *me*. It's disconcerting, uncomfortable, and makes me want to scream. Or at the very least, throw one of my tennis shoes at her when she does something in service for me. This is to say nothing of how the girls continue to dote on me or how Luke pops in with unnerving displays of thoughtfulness.

In an attempt to get my people, places, and things back in order, I find myself sitting in Dr. Ridding's office, waiting to discuss my brain map. I didn't make it two weeks until our next appointment. I made it six days.

Barely.

Long enough to get my stitches out of both wounds so I can

handle the red electrode cap. Well, fight tears as I handle it. The metal electrodes push against the raw, healing spots.

Who can blame me for being unable to wait any longer to start treatment? I need my nouns and verbs returned to the correct places.

Cocooned twenty-four hours a day in my dark bedroom without "distractions" (read: any meaningful activity), I'm about to careen over the cliff of boredom, straight toward insanity. I'm considering painting a wall just so I can watch it dry. Anything is better than scrutinizing the dust collecting on my work files.

No one is allowed to ask me for help, Meredith said. With anything. It's by far the cruelest thing she has ever done to me.

Yes, I nap. I'm able to admit that maybe my body needs the extra sleep. I certainly can't ignore my lack of stamina. Completing the simplest task requires me to sit down so the world will stop spinning.

But no one gets to ask me questions?

Whatever Dr. Ridding has planned to speed up my healing, I'm officially on board.

Until he walked me through my first QEEG test. Now I'm wondering what kind of unorthodox treatment plan awaits me.

"Remind me again how this works," I say to Dr. Ridding while I pull a thread at the hem of my oversized tunic, one of the few items in my wardrobe that can handle the bulk of my ever-present sling.

"First, I conduct a brain map. It will tell us how well your brain frequencies are working at different speeds. Sometimes we find blocks in the pathways where the injury occurs, sometimes we find that the brain tried to compensate and work around the injury. Based on the results of said brain map, I create a protocol for your neurofeedback sessions that will retrain the injured areas." Dr. Ridding's voice is patient but not condescending. When he finishes, he scratches at the Denver Broncos logo on his chest. He must have one for each day of the month. Their only variance is the color scheme.

"Brain map? Do you mean when I stared at the wall for ten minutes? Then closed my eyes for an additional ten minutes?" I raise my eyebrows. "That brain map?"

"No. I mean when you were hooked up to electrodes and we ran a QEEG—quantitative electroencephalogram—that measured your brain frequencies. First while you focused on a specific point, then while you focused on nothing at all."

I shoot him a glare. The technical name of the test sounds sophisticated, but during the evaluation process, it seemed useless. What can he possibly decipher about my brain function while I stare at a Post-it note? With a handwritten smiley face on it, no less?

"I'm about to display your QEEG on the monitor in front of you. It's going to look like a colored map of your brain," he says. "We'll go over the exact details, but what you're about to see is how well certain regions of your brain are functioning, in contrast with other areas that are struggling as a result of the injury."

The office setup includes one large computer screen facing the doctor and, on the opposite side of the desk, a separate large computer screen facing the patient. When the monitor in front of me illuminates, I jump, my nerves protesting the jarring change in light. My initial jolt dissipates, but a shock of another kind hits me in the chest.

This one is heavy, weighted with pain.

My personal pain unabashedly displayed in front of me.

"The color-coded explanation is located in the top left corner of your screen," Dr. Ridding says. "As you can see, the red areas are the injury, with the strong orange colors spreading outward."

A little over a week ago, the hospital CT scans of my brain bleed were filled with dark, ominous shadows. Various shades of gray and black outlined my injury. When the doctor showed them to me, I felt nothing but task oriented. The scan stated the facts of my injury, and I immediately wanted to discuss recovery. Bottom line I wanted to ask while I looked at the CT scan: How do we erase the black?

But the vivid screen in front of me now tells a different story. Instead of the grays and blacks of the CT that distanced me from the injury, the colors splayed across the QEEG won't let me escape my reality.

Each page of the report holds images of my brain four rows across and five rows down. Twenty versions of my most important organ on display in high Technicolor. The view is from the top of my head. Inside each image are colors spilling across the brain, reporting the location, depth, and severity of injury.

A bright red glob covers the front left portion of my brain, starting at my temple and reaching tentacles toward the center of my forehead. A second red flare fires from the back of my brain on the right side. The deep colors glare back at me, daring me to ignore their presence.

My hands start to tremble, and I clasp them together firmly in my lap.

Dr. Ridding rounds his desk, pulls a chair next to me, and sits. He uses a pen to point at the screen. "Here is the color-coded explanation. As I mentioned earlier, what we're looking at is how well your brain functions at different speeds on different frequencies. Each piece of the map gives us distinct information."

He points to specific locations of the brain, citing what each area controls. Speech, reasoning, emotions, depression, learning, the ability to do math and use fine motor skills, the sense of smell . . . The list goes on and on as he spouts separate categories and possible symptoms that can be associated when those areas aren't functioning at full capacity.

"This top one here"—he points to my left temple—"is the new injury layered on an old injury. Correct?"

"Yes. I was fourteen. A baseball bat," I whisper, unable to take my eyes off the wounds that wail at me from the screen. New wounds opening old wounds.

Dr. Ridding runs through explanations about each piece of my injury. He shifts into something about where my brain bleed was located. I know he's speaking, but the red blotches screaming at me from the monitor overpower his words. I, the facts-oriented, information-driven woman, can hear nothing but the color in front of me.

My throat, clogged with years of emotion, refuses to work. But something wants to release. My chest aches and my breaths come more quickly. I clutch my hands tighter in an unsuccessful attempt to snuff out the beast of emotion that demands to be unleashed.

Dr. Ridding stops speaking but doesn't move.

One tear of grief streams down my cheek, leading the way for others. The names are different for each tear, but they all stem from the same loss and trauma. Grief, pain, fear, disappointment, loneliness, and terror.

The pictures' robust palate forces something into my cognitive understanding that mere information could never have accomplished. The wild colors reach into my soul and pull out each piece of my story, one tear at a time. A fatherless life. A mother's early death. No place to belong. A barely treated concussion. A performance-based pseudo-family. And now, a traumatic brain injury that I can't ignore.

I am hurt.

I am hurting.

And I don't want to feel this way anymore.

I lean forward and place a shaky hand across the images of my injured brain, my palm unable to cover or hide the entirety of the ferocious colors.

"I need help," I whisper.

Luke lounges in a reception room chair, legs crossed at his ankles, arms crossed over his chest, and eyes closed. It's only been a few days since I've seen him, and unfortunately, he still looks good.

"What are you doing here?" I snap.

He sits alert, rubbing a hand over his face. "Waiting for you."

"How did you know where to find me?"

"I called Meredith. She said she dropped you off here for the day. I told her I'd pick you up. I need to talk to you."

After his last declaration about being the safe person for me to hate, then the safe person for me to love, I have no idea what to say to him. Who says things like that? And why does my stomach lurch but my heart soar at the thought of what his words might mean?

In light of the emotional purge I just experienced in Dr. Ridding's office, I don't have the energy to deal with him. "I don't like surprises, Luke."

He stands, his eyes serious. "I know. That's why I'm here."

Something must be wrong. I take two steps toward him. "What happened?"

"Marcus made bail."

"Oh." I glance around the empty room. "With the events of the last few days, I lost track of that issue."

He opens the door to exit the office and waits. "Someone needs to be with you at all times."

"Isn't that overkill?" I ask as I step into the hallway.

"I don't think so." He takes my elbow and leads me to the elevator.

In the wake of one QEEG and two treatments, I'm quite fatigued, which is probably why I don't mind the support he offers my arm. It's also probably the reason why, when we arrive at the elevator, I lean just a hint of my weight into his side.

At my touch, Luke lowers his head, but I stare ahead and say, "Marcus isn't after me, Luke. He's focused on Finley."

"We can't guess what his motives are at this point. Your charges put him in jail for a few days. Now that he's made bail, I've got feelers out for his movements, but we need to be cautious. Someone will be with you if you leave the house."

I release a long, low sigh. Another blank for my Mad Libs. "Great. Will someone be spoon-feeding me soon? I prefer my mashed potatoes to be creamy, with just a touch of salt."

Luke's shoulders shake against me, jarring me. "Sorry." The elevator dings, and he places his hand on the small of my back to guide me forward while he chuckles. "But you're funny."

"I'm not funny. I'm cranky." And tired. So very tired. I lean against the wall of the elevator, but Luke gently draws me to his side, running a hand around my waist. That feels nice. My eyes drift closed, and a small moan escapes. So tired.

"I take it you started your treatment today?"

I nod. "He says I can do two a day as long as my body can tolerate it, but that I might experience some fatigue." I yawn on the last word, and Luke pulls me in a little tighter.

Today. Just today, I'll lean on him. I'll find my bearings with these treatments and won't need him like this for the entire projected thirty appointments.

"Tuckered you out," he murmurs.

Each time we stop and start at a floor, the elevator jerks a little. Luke tightens his hold, fortifying me to handle the bounces of our short journey to the bottom.

After I put on my sunglasses and get in the car, I'm greeted with a delicious aroma while I buckle up. "Did you eat Trivelli's? Are you trying to torture me?"

Luke grins, stretches an arm into the back seat, then places a to-go bag in my lap. "I figured you didn't have a good lunch in between your appointments."

I rummage through the loot. Chips, a brownie, a bottled water, and an all-too-small sub sandwich. "What is this pathetic hoagie? You know I like to eat whole Rock Stars."

Luke throws his head back and laughs. Twice now I've caused his beautiful smile to show, and twice now something warm has filled my chest. He downshifts to a chuckle, then studies my face. "The sunglasses look good on you."

At his soft words, I touch a finger to the edge of the gift. Dark sunglasses, a sandwich, and two smiles. I might be able to combat those things, but the part where he's tracking Marcus and making sure I'm safe hinders my ability to refuse this man's attention. And I'm so tired today, I'm not even sure I want to try. Without the accusing punch I want to put in the statement, I say, "Where were you the last couple of days?"

"I went by the house a few times, but you were sleeping." He scrubs his hands over his face. "But more so, I've been trying to shift things around at work so I can be in town. I farmed out some smaller jobs to a few of my staff. I'm also working with digital images to help me design a system for a client long-distance, meaning no travel. All of that just takes time."

Oh. He's making an effort, shifting things, so he can be here. With me. Just like he said.

"I'll still have the occasion to leave town for jobs, but there are ways to cut back." His eyes bore into mine. "So I'm cutting back. I'm not going anywhere, Penelope."

I shake my head. How do I trust someone I know nothing about? "But I don't know you, Luke. I don't know anything about you."

"Yeah, you do," he says quietly, confidently.

Dark sunglasses. A sandwich. Two smiles. Protection for me.

Yeah. I do.

If he's really not leaving, it's going to thwart my plans to refuse his kindness.

As he pulls out of the parking lot, I turn to stare out my side window.

My game of Mad Libs is getting worse.

Penelope asked for _______ (noun: a kind of help). Luke and Penelope are now _______ (verb ending in "ing").

20

"IT'S INFURIATING," I say to Meredith three days later.

"Infuriating? How can a neurofeedback treatment be infuriating?" she asks. "The way you describe it, it sounds like a good opportunity to park yourself in a chair and relax."

At the desk in my bedroom, half-eaten lunch on the tray in front of me, I sigh. "Because I can't do anything to make each session go better or worse. I can't try harder. I am required to sit and let the computer do all the work."

She covers her mouth with her fingers but can't hide the giggle. Or her laughing eyes.

"I don't understand why this is so funny," I say. "Twice a day, I sit in Dr. Ridding's office, red electrode cap covering my head, and I stare at a screen. Four rounds, ten minutes each, with a minute break in between."

"Sitting still isn't your thing."

"That's not even half of it."

Dr. Ridding took the results of the QEEG, ran them through several database systems, and entered my protocol into the LORETA

Z-score training, the process behind the neurofeedback treatment. After experiencing trauma, the brain creates new pathways to accommodate injuries. It's a fabulous piece of our bodies' design. However, my brain needs to be redirected to the correct paths to heal the injury.

"The bulk of the work feels uneventful. Infuriatingly uneventful. Four rounds where I stare at one point on a screen doing nothing. Nothing. My only job is to keep my mind blank."

"Uh-oh," Meredith says, because she knows I'm constantly thinking.

"When I start the session, there is a picture of a drab field on the monitor. No music. Each time my brain does something positive, chooses the correct frequency path without my help, it's rewarded. I stare at the screen, and my brain somehow triggers the image to move. The field transitions to a lush green. Music plays. The screen fills with trees, then flowers." I hold up jazz hands as if I'm dazzling her. "But the *second* my brain decides to use the wrong neuropathway, the music ends. The fertile field abruptly recedes and dries up."

"You're like one of those—"

"If you call me a dog right now, it's not going to go well for you."

She curls her lips in, keeping her mouth shut, but bugs her eyes out at me.

"Fine. Yes. I'm like one of Pavlov's dogs." She giggles while I continue. "Rewarded for my good behavior. Not rewarded for incorrect behavior."

"But it's not *your* behavior. It's your *brain's*," she says.

"You know me. I'm a rule follower. I will walk in a straight line with the best of them. However, for this type of treatment to work, I can do nothing—absolutely nothing—to *make* my brain play the game correctly. I have no control. There is no 'trying harder' in the world of neurofeedback, unless it's trying to do less."

"Uh-oh."

"Yeah. 'Uh-oh' is right."

I am in a foreign land, and I don't like it one bit.

I've based my entire life on trying harder. Everything I do is the result of my efforts. My research. My energy. My sacrifice.

So where does this leave me?

In the hands of the LORETA Z-score training. In the hands of Dr. Ridding. In the hands of nothing I can control.

"The good news is that we're moving forward at a solid pace. I'm doing the maximum he'll allow, which is two treatments per day. Dr. Ridding warned me that my body might not be able to handle the strain. Everyone reacts differently." I slide my eyes to the side. "But apparently I have a hard head and I'm exceeding expectations."

Meredith laughs and grabs her side just as Luke appears.

He knocks lightly on the open door. "What's going on in here?"

"Dr. Ridding diagnosed Penelope with a hard head." She giggles through her words.

Luke grins at me. "I hope you didn't pay extra for information we already knew."

"What does it say," Meredith interjects, "that Penelope's brain isn't working as efficiently as it could be right now, but she's still smarter than the rest of us?"

Luke's gaze, full of teasing and affection, locks onto mine. "That we should be very afraid."

"Well," she says as she grabs my tray, "I'll just go put these away."

Ignoring Meredith's more-than-obvious move to leave Luke and me alone, I ask him, "Why are you here?"

"I'm giving Bianca a drum lesson." He struts over to me and pulls a shoebox out of a silver bag.

I purse my lips, trying not to smile. What did he bring me?

Kneeling, he removes the items from the box and slides them on each of my bare feet.

Fancy doesn't begin to describe these shoes. But they're house shoes. Slippers adorned with sleek black sequins leading to a band of silver faux fur across the top of my foot.

I shift my focus from the dazzling shoes on my feet to the dazzling man still crouched in front of me and raise my eyebrows.

"I know you miss your heels. I thought these could suffice until you're back on your feet."

I miss my heels. I miss my life. But giddiness is about to burst out of my chest. Who is this manly man bringing gifts that sparkle?

I sigh, the release sounding more dreamy than I intended. "I miss the original misconceptions I had about you."

"And what are those?"

"You're supposed to be restless. And noncommittal. And distant."

"But what am I really?"

"You're thoughtful. Generous. And you won't go away. I'm not quite sure what to do with you."

He grins.

"Any word on Finley?" I ask.

Luke stands. "No. She and Marcus are lying low at his place. She hasn't reported to work. Other than one visit to his attorney's office and the occasional pizza delivery to his pad, nothing. What about you?"

"She's blocked everyone's numbers associated with the ranch. Tanya tried to check on her at the grocery store once."

Luke stiffens at the news, disapproval written in his eyes. "I don't like the thought of anyone looking for her."

"I know. I don't either. When I asked her about it, she claimed she was in search of coniferous vegetables for a recipe." My lips twitch as I recall the miscommunication. "When we finally concluded she was looking for *cruciferous* vegetables and not, in fact, evergreen trees, I asked her to stop looking for Finley at the grocery store, or otherwise."

"Never a dull moment here at the ranch."

"Nope."

"Does it scare you sometimes that we're the adults in charge?"

"I feel completely comfortable in charge. It scares me that you're an adult in charge."

"There's my girl," he murmurs, his lips twitching. "Do you think Tanya will comply?"

"I do. She doesn't like it. But she understands that with Marcus as a loose cannon, we all need to be careful."

Luke runs a hand down my hair and places a piece behind my shoulder. "I'm going to work with Bianca on the drums for a while. I'll be back later to take you to your next neurofeedback appointment. Get some rest, please."

As he exits the room, he knocks his fist on the doorframe twice, and I grin at my new slippers, wiggling my toes.

Seven.

My pain is at a seven.

Hurtling quickly toward an eight as the wheels of Luke's truck tear up the road between the ranch and Dr. Ridding's office.

The doctor asked me to work on quantifying my headache pain with a number. Zero to ten. Anytime I feel a twinge of pain, I'm supposed to note the exact level. Just like the stupid poster at the hospital with the faces that mocked me, the headache numbers now mock me.

"Penelope, I still think we should go to the ER," Luke says.

"Please." I swallow. "Just the doctor." It takes everything in me to form a word. I can't explain to him that an ER will put me through paperwork and unnecessary tests, and might not understand the best route of medication as expertly as someone who specializes in headaches. Someone who specializes in me. Dr. Ridding's office is set up to administer IVs to patients experiencing a headache they can't manage.

Luke taps his hand on the steering wheel, not unlike the

rhythm of the drums that earlier sent me straight into the pain crisis I'm experiencing. "I shouldn't have given Bianca that lesson. I thought the walls were thick enough that the sound wouldn't touch you."

"Luke." My voice wavers. "Your hand. Stop, please."

An expletive bursts from his mouth. "I'm sorry, Penelope. I'm sorry." He runs a hand through his hair. "I'm really sorry."

Luke's guilt fills the air like it's another passenger in the car. I wish I could explain all the reasons this isn't his fault, including the part where I chose not to tell him the noise bothered me. I thought I could push through, that the building headache would dissipate when the lesson was over. But speaking isn't an option right now.

After a painstaking effort by Luke and myself to walk me into Dr. Ridding's office, I lie on an exam table while the doctor evaluates me.

Luke refuses to leave my side, and I don't have the fight in me to send him away. Also, I don't know if I want to have the fight in me to send him away. He sits in the corner, his glower filling the room.

"What's your current pain level?" Dr. Ridding asks. He's dressed in his uniform, but instead of his typical laid-back demeanor, his eyes are filled with concern as he reviews my chart.

I rub the scar at my eyebrow. "Maybe an eight." Closing in on nine. But I don't want to cause alarm.

He looks at me. "That's a lot of pain, Miss Reid. We're going to get you some relief as quickly as we can." He hits a call button and a young, long-haired, bottle-blond nurse enters the room. She would be all legs if not for her scrubs.

Luke's steely gaze remains locked on me.

Dr. Ridding gives Miss Teen America instructions about administering an IV, and she leaves the room. "On a positive note, my exam shows no sign of your injury worsening. I think the sound trigger sent you into the pain crisis."

The nurse returns with a tray of tools, moves me to the dark blue reclining treatment chair, and rolls up the sleeve on my sling-less arm. One more day until my injured arm is, hopefully, freed of the canvas restraint.

"Let's let that medicine hit. Then I want you to talk me through how your pain got to an eight," Dr. Ridding says.

After wrapping a wide rubber tourniquet around my arm, the nurse taps the veins at my elbows. Not pleased with those options, she moves the rubber band down and finds a vein in my wrist to use. She smells like bubble gum.

I'm tempted to ask Dr. Ridding if I could request an adult instead of this adolescent to poke me with a sharp object. I suck in a breath as the needle pierces my skin. The nurse hooks the IV up to my arm and opens the ports, freeing the sweet liquid relief down the tube. Okay, fine. She hit a vein on the first try. She's a Mensa nurse. That doesn't mean she doesn't look like she should be a backup dancer for Britney Spears.

Medicine crawls through my bloodstream, smoothing the sharpest corners of the pain. After I take several deep breaths, the taut muscles in my shoulders start to release the tension they've been holding captive.

"Feel like talking a little, Miss Reid?" the doctor asks.

I exhale, resigning myself to the conversation. "I don't understand the numbers."

His gaze narrows, but it's pensive, not judgmental. "Help me understand what you mean."

"I don't know." I glance around the room, searching for a way to explain. "I've had migraines since the first injury. I live my life. I function until I can't function anymore."

He nods but waits for me to say more.

"Push through. Finish the task at hand. There's no stopping to figure out what kind of pain I'm in. I just go, move forward, until I can't." I look at the wall with the infamous pain-quantifying poster. The zero-pain face smiles jubilantly at me. The ten-pain face is devastated by life. But they don't mean anything to me. "Numbers zero through six don't exist for me. I'm all of a sudden at a seven and it's hard to function. Before today, I could always push through and finish what I was doing, then go deal with the headache."

"But today?"

"The entire escalation was faster than normal. More intense." *Out of control* is what I want to say. This headache charged through the numbers with no intention of stopping.

"Your recent injuries have changed your normal. You won't be able to cope with your headaches, or 'push through,' as you say, the way you used to." He cocks his head, studying me. "Most people would say that when their pain is at a seven, functioning is difficult. If that's how you define a seven, what would a ten mean for you?"

I blink. "Death."

No one speaks, and the silence falls heavy in the room. Even the nurse, clearing the debris from my IV administration, pauses her process.

After a few beats, Dr. Ridding asks, "And what happened today?"

The medication continues to course through my veins, and I sink a little further into the chair. "I was resting in my room, and the sounds of the drums came through the walls."

"Yes, you mentioned as much. But why didn't you say anything to anyone?"

"Because Bianca was having a drum lesson."

He leans forward, his elbows on his knees. "Yes, but you were in pain."

"Okay," I say, not understanding why this conversation has taken an intense turn.

"Okay?"

"Do you know what kind of life she's endured until now?" I ask. "She's been abandoned. Abused. She's a survivor. Until recently, she hardly spoke to anyone. When she does communicate, her words are ridiculous clichés about men and relationships. It's how she copes."

Luke doesn't add anything to the conversation. He appears to be intently listening, but something else is in the set lines of his face.

I sigh. "But I saw her entranced with a female drummer at the Christmas tree lighting, and Luke bought her a drum set, and now she comes alive at the mention of her lessons. She doesn't have anything except those drums. And lately, she's been speaking in more coherent sentences, trusting us with more words." I point to the doctor. "It's beautiful. And I wasn't going to interrupt her lesson simply because I could hear the drums through the walls."

"That's thoughtful of you." The doctor scratches his cheek. "And what about the pain you were in?"

"I was handling it."

"Did you take any medication for it?"

"No. I thought it would go away."

"Did you feel the pain as it became worse? Were you conscious of its escalation?"

"I don't know. I just concluded I would tough it out until it was over." I shrug. "Then I was at a seven."

"And in a pain crisis."

"Like the wedding," Luke murmurs.

I turn my head to him. "What?"

"You crashed with a migraine the day after Harlan and Meredith's wedding. Did you push through that day too, knowing you would handle it later?"

Did I? The day of the wedding flashes through my mind, but it's hard to remember and quantify the events. I glance at the IV pouring into my body, washing away the pain of today with each drop of medication.

Dr. Ridding makes a few notes on a piece of paper. "Today, we'll get this pain under control. No neurofeedback treatment."

I sit up straight. "No treatment?" If we skip today, it just delays my getting back to normal. My life. My job.

"I'm not going to push your brain today with a neurofeedback session. But I can do a neurofield anti-inflammatory treatment if you would like. That will reinforce what the medication is doing."

Slumping back in my chair like I'm a three-year-old, I nod. "Fine."

"In the meantime, I need you to really work on those numbers. You're so accustomed to the pain, you don't recognize what's happening. In some ways, doing life like this has worked for you." He offers a sad smile. "But your recent concussion isn't going to let you live that way anymore."

I swallow and whisper, "I wouldn't know the first thing about how to do my life differently."

Dr. Ridding nods. "I believe you. We're going to work on that." He points to me with his pen. "I don't know how you started the day, but at some point, your pain registered at a four. There's appropriate medication you can take for a pain level of four. At another point your pain registered at a six. There's appropriate medication you can take for a six. I need you to pay attention to how you're doing at different points in the process. Before the headache becomes a pain crisis."

Luke grunts. "And I think everyone around you would agree that if they can do something to reduce headache triggers, they would gladly oblige."

I pick at a stray thread on my sling.

"From here on out," Dr. Ridding continues, "don't just limit the numbers to pain. Quantify anything you can. Emotions, social situations, the kind of sleep you get at night. Someone makes a dinner you love? What's that number? You get your arm out of the sling and try to open a heavy door? What's that number? A friend says something that makes you angry? What's that number? Quantify anything that you can feel. Both the positive and the negative."

"That's an overwhelming amount of information," I say. "I'm supposed to keep track of all this?"

"Not on paper. I just want you to put a category in your head for how things feel. Good and bad. Sounds, lights, even emotions are going to be triggers for headaches for a while. Post-concussion recovery is different for everyone, but these are the things we need to pay attention to."

"What a terrible thing to have to do," I say, my words slurring just the slightest.

Dr. Ridding grins at Luke. "I think our girl's feeling the medication."

The drugs are now doing their job well, beating back any twinges of pain.

My eyes droop.

"Rest, Miss Reid. We'll check on you here in a little bit."

My heavy eyes open. My heavy eyes close. In and out. In and out. Despite the lack of pain, I can't get comfortable. I shift to my right, curling into the chair.

"Careful of the IV, baby," Luke's low voice rumbles.

I open my eyes to see him freeing the IV tube from between my chair and my knee.

"Hi," I whisper.

He leans in and shifts a piece of hair off my forehead. "Hey."

"How are you?"

He studies my face. "Better than you."

"I don't think so. I have the good drugs."

He offers a smile that doesn't reach his eyes. Eyes so burdened, they cut through the pain meds and it almost hurts me to look at them.

"What are you thinking?" I ask him.

"You've never had anyone to drag you out of your pain."

"What?"

"You've been in pain so long because no one got in it with you and helped you get out."

I inhale, trying to take in what he's saying. Something warm and sweet fills my chest, but it has nothing to do with the sedation. How would he know about helping someone climb out of their pain? "Did someone do that for you, Luke?"

"Yeah."

"What happened?"

"Ever spent time in a trailer park?"

"No." One of the girls at my group foster home talked of her trailer, but I've never visited an actual trailer park.

He grinds his teeth before he answers. "My mom lived in a single-wide. Poorer than dirt. Had an affair with someone in the park and conceived me. The guy was married. Mom's choices didn't sit well with the neighborhood."

"Luke," I whisper.

"We were shunned in the park, but Mom was too poor to move. So it was pretty tough living. Kids roughed me up. People spat on us. Our trailer was vandalized and robbed on several occasions."

The World's Most Beautiful Nurse reenters the room, studies the progress of the IV bag, asks if I need anything, and exits after I say no.

Luke's attention never wavers from me. "One day when I was twelve, Robert Kitson shows up. Young guy, good-looking, in his twenties. Full of life." He shakes his head. "He was clean. Man, he was so clean. That has to sound stupid, but, baby, life in that trailer park felt dirty. I took one look at this guy and I thought, 'I want whatever it is he has.'"

I swallow. "What did he have?"

A hint of Luke's spark returns to his eyes. "Heart and a rifle."

I giggle. "Heart and a rifle?"

"Yes, ma'am."

"What does that mean?" My eyes droop, and I strain to stay awake.

"Story for another day."

"Will you be here another day?"

"I will."

"I'm starting to believe you," I whisper.

"Good."

"Why did you tell me that story?"

"Because I had Robert Kitson to pull me out of my pain." He cups my cheek with his palm. "But you didn't have anyone."

"I did okay by myself."

"You did more than okay, Penelope. You excelled. Flourished, even. But you didn't quite get yourself out of that pain, did you?"

A tear slips out of the corner of my eye, and he skims his thumb through its path.

"That's going to change, baby."

21

FIVE.

No, six. Definitely six.

No. Maybe a seven. Yes. I am positive that I am a seven on the annoyed scale.

Two weeks post-accident, I'm free of my sling. An eight on the joy scale this morning. However, Harlan came over to the ranch and decided to swing dance with Meredith in the living room in honor of my sling removal, and I am highly annoyed.

"It's not even the same word, Harlan. Sling is different from swing," I say, watching the world's worst dancer throw Meredith around the carpet.

Once again, the furniture is pushed back against the walls of the room. I'm starting to wonder why this room is furnished at all.

"Trust me, Mr. Holcombe," Tanya says, "I'm studying for the SAT. Swing and sling are *very* different words."

My heart swells, and I declare a five on the affection scale, in addition to the five on the proud scale for Tanya.

This rating system is baffling. I never understood how many emotions I experienced during a day until Dr. Ridding asked me to pay attention. It's one thing to keep track of my physical pain fluctuations. It's a completely different challenge to quantify every emotional fluctuation.

But as Glenn Miller's "In the Mood" plays in the background while Harlan swings Meredith across the room, reality seeps into my skin, sitting awhile, waiting to be acknowledged.

I'm annoyed with Harlan because his entire presentation is overstimulating my senses. The song is like a friend giving me an unintentionally brutal massage. For a few beats, I enjoy the music, but every note of the trumpets jolts my brain tissue.

I'm not relishing my bosses' performance. Neither is my three on the headache scale.

The appropriate social choice to make would be to allow the happy newlyweds to enjoy their dance. They are, after all, celebrating me. How can I put a stop to this moment? Harlan came in super proud, ready to celebrate me getting my sling removed. It was sweet, well-intentioned, ill-timed, and annoying. As if he was my real-life big brother.

On a typical day, I would simply endure the song and move on to the next task. But my normal no longer exists, my body no longer allows me to push through. If I permit the song to continue, odds are high that a migraine will force its way into my day.

Trumpets build in the melody, teasing me to believe the end of the dance is near. Instead, the song shifts into an additional verse. My headache scale bumps up to a four.

I look down at my wringing hands and take a breath. "I apologize," I say to the room, "but could I request that we put this celebration on hold?"

Everyone turns their focus to me and stares.

Luke enters the room, pauses midstep, and focuses on me. "What's happening?"

I swallow. "I, uh, asked them to stop dancing."

The blinding smile that comes from Luke shoots my proud-of-myself scale to an eight. "Great." He acts like I ask for what I need every day of the week. "Do you want the music turned off too?"

The ends of my lips tip up. "Yes, please."

"Awesome," he says, walking to the speaker and hitting the power button.

I sneak a glance at Harlan and Meredith.

Meredith winks at me. She cheers me on every time I make a choice to take care of myself. But Harlan can only be described as befuddled. He takes in every person in the room, stopping to study Luke's movements.

Luke strides toward me, taking my attention off Harlan. He stops just a few inches away. "How's your head?"

"A four, but calming down to a three."

"Need to take something?"

Over the last week, Luke took time to learn what my pain scale means in the world of headaches. He also took notes of the appropriate medications that correlate with the numbers. He helps me talk through my discomfort levels and what I need to do about them.

"No need for medication yet. If the pain goes back to a four, I'll take something to head it off."

"Okay." He pulls a wrapped gift from behind his back and places it in the space between us. "Happy No More Sling Day."

Wonder Woman paper covers the box, taped in a manner worthy of a preschooler.

"Did my four-year-old daughter wrap that for you?" Harlan asks.

Luke flashes a cocky grin at me but addresses Harlan with his words. "Is she the one who taught you your dance moves?"

I try but fail to stifle a burst of laughter. Harlan is notoriously a terrible dancer. It's a miracle not only that Meredith fell in love with him on a dance floor but that she's never been injured while he's twirled her through the music.

Harlan harrumphs in the background, but one peek around

Luke tells me everyone else is having a similar reaction to mine. All grins and giggles.

Shifting my focus back to Luke, I whisper, "What did you bring me?" As I pick at the tape, my giddy scale rises.

"Penelope, rip it off, baby. Give it your best shot."

A smile breaks across my face as I plant my fingers on the edges of the paper and yank as hard as I can. A seven on the satisfying scale. But when I catch a glimpse of Luke's gift, it tips the balance on a different scale.

The high-end noise-canceling headphones in my hands push the falling-in-love-with-Luke scale to a solid six.

He takes the box from me, wrestles the headphones out of the protective Styrofoam, and holds them out for me to see. "Now Bianca can have her lessons, and you can have your low numbers."

Tears prick the backs of my eyes, and I purse my lips.

"Let's give these a test run." He shifts my hair over my shoulder and places the headphones over my ears.

Can you hear me? he mouths.

I hit him on the arm. "Stop it. I know you're not saying anything."

He clutches his stomach and laughs. "Okay, but you're talking really loud." Through the protection of the headphones, his words are buffered. I can still decipher what he's saying if he's close to me, but the sound is muffled.

"Do you want to play for me?" I ask Bianca.

I glance around the room, and everyone is laughing in varying degrees. Heat flushes my face. The volume of my voice must be louder than I intend.

That is, everyone's laughing except Harlan. His stare bounces from Luke back to me. And it doesn't appear his happy scale is even registering.

Confused, I avert my attention from the brewing volcano that is Harlan Holcombe and shift my focus to Bianca. With a pride

I've never seen her carry, she walks to the drum set, sits, and glances at me just before she closes her eyes and unleashes.

Written all over Bianca's face is a glorious, peaceful concentration as she pounds out sounds she was surely born to create. The rhythm seems to come naturally to her, and even though she doesn't have a melody behind her, she creates beautiful music.

As she ends her set with a powerful crescendo, tears fill my eyes, and my joy scale pushes the upper edge of ten.

The claps of everyone in the room are muted through the headphones, but the beaming faces and robust hugs speak louder than the volume.

Bianca looks at me shyly under her lashes, a girlish gesture I've never seen from her.

I pat my heart three times, then send the love to her across the room with my palm. She repeats the action back to me.

After the group celebration dies down, Harlan points to my headphones, making gestures with his hands that I think mean he wants to talk to me.

When I slide the headphones off, a few strands of hair catch on the plastic.

"I want to know what's going on here," Harlan says to me as I try to untangle my hair.

"What?"

Luke chuckles, taking steps toward me. He puts a finger to my cheek, drawing the hair back and curling the strand around my ear.

"*That.*" Harlan points at Luke. "*That* right there. What is *that*?"

Luke turns to face his friend and lifts his chin. "What's wrong, man?"

"Harlan," Meredith warns.

"I got this, sweetheart." Harlan crosses his arms and takes a wide stance as if he's going to face off with Luke. "I think I'd like to know your intentions in regard to Penelope."

And with one simple statement, Harlan plugs a childhood wound that had been leaking, unnoticed, for years.

No one has ever asked anything like that on my behalf. I have no siblings. My father wasn't in my life. My mother never had the chance. Foster homes didn't afford the opportunity. And the Nelsons wouldn't think to ask someone that kind of question because they were too busy sizing up my dates as future political allies or political risks.

Luke puffs his chest out and steps forward. "Not sure that's any of your business, man."

Before he can say anything else, I curl my hands around his bicep. "Luke, it's okay."

"I think you get that I've known you for years," Harlan says, pressing the issue. "And I've never known you to stick around the Springs for more than a few weeks, much less develop a relationship." He points to me. "This isn't just anybody. This is our Penelope."

Not just a plug. Harlan removes pieces of this particular wound one word at a time.

"Don't appreciate you bringing this up right now," Luke says.

With one glance at the people in the room, I realize this is, in fact, the perfect time to bring it up. I don't know the extent of Tanya's and Bianca's dating experiences, but based on their histories, my guess is that no one ever bothered to ask what someone's intentions were on their behalf either.

Both of their womanly faces have a girlish awe to them as the conversation between Harlan and Luke unfolds.

This is another piece of beauty.

Luke's words come back to me. *The beauty's in the wild.* The unknown. The unpredictable. The letting go. The possibilities.

"Let him ask you, Luke," I whisper.

Luke cranes his neck to look down at me.

"Please." I squeeze his arm. "Let him ask."

He grits his teeth but nods to me, then does the same to Harlan.

"What are your intentions in regard to Penelope?" Harlan repeats.

With a calm, deep, sure voice, Luke states, "I intend to date Penelope."

"Will you treat her well?"

Luke slides a hand around my waist and answers, "Yes."

And just like that, the wound disappears and is no more. Not even a scar.

With no father playing an active role in my life, quantifying exactly what I've missed out on is difficult. But in this moment, there is exquisite pain and exquisite joy knowing that though I never biologically experienced this kind of love and care, it's standing in front of me all the same in the form of brotherly love.

"Penelope," Harlan calls.

"Yes?"

"I get that he's charming." He points to Luke without looking at him. "And I get that he's offering you gifts." He points to the headphones.

I swallow.

"But the second he doesn't treat you right, you let him go."

Luke stiffens next to me, but his hold on me tightens.

Tanya and Bianca, wide-eyed, shift their focus, their eyes darting between Luke and me.

Harlan softens his tone, adding respect and a little bit of humor as he says, "Having said that, *because* I've known Luke for years, I know he's a man of his word. Someone I respect. And if I had a little sister, he's also someone I'd approve of her dating."

The smile bursts from my face, causing my cheeks to ache.

Harlan nods at Luke, and it feels like something thick passes between them.

Meredith claps once. "Okay, everyone. The show is over. No more dancing, drums, or interrogations. I'm sure we all have somewhere we need to be." She steps across the room and pulls me from Luke's hold to hug me.

While in her embrace, I whisper, "In the five years I have worked for your husband, I have never loved and respected him more."

"Me too." She squeezes me. When she releases me, she makes a V with two fingers and points to her eyes, then to Luke's and back to hers. "I've got my sights on you, buddy."

A smile breaks across Luke's face. "Yes, ma'am."

After the room clears, Luke turns to me, taking my hands in his. "How's your uncomfortable scale?"

"Not as bad as you think." I rub my thumbs over his knuckles. "That was kind and thoughtful of Harlan."

He studies me. "I'm seeing that."

"No one's ever done anything like that for me, asked someone their intentions on my behalf. It was like having a brother look out for me." I pause, thinking of my time with the Nelsons and beyond. "Jason's never treated me like that."

Luke glowers but says nothing.

"Jason doesn't consider me his sister, does he." A statement, not a question. I'm just looking for the affirmation I know is coming.

"No."

"Which means he has feelings—"

"Yes."

I lean in and gently rest my forehead on Luke's chest. "I'm an idiot."

He wraps his arms around me. "I don't think you'll find anyone who thinks you're an idiot."

Whatever soap that people are making these days smells good on Luke. It's not cologne. It's not fruity. It's musk. Man. Strong. Luke. "No wonder you were jealous."

"I wasn't jealous." He kisses the top of my head. "So. You gonna give me that first date?"

"Yes," I say without hesitation.

"No, baby. I'm asking if—"

I look up. "I know what you're asking. And you're worthy of a first date."

Relief crosses his face, then morphs into affection. He draws me to him and wraps his arms around my shoulders, tucking me into his cocoon, his heat. He presses his lips to my forehead. "You okay with everything? With you and me?"

I snake my arms around his waist and nod. "I'm a little scared."

"Me too," he says against my forehead.

"Liar," I say, almost scoffing. "You're not scared of anything."

He pulls me in tighter, leaning down to speak into my ear. "I'm just trying to be all manly and not show you any sign of fear. Is it working?"

I rest my face on his chest. He feels pretty manly to me, though I don't say those words out loud.

But something thick hangs between us.

"Be scared with me, baby," he says, his whisper full of a vulnerability that draws me closer to him than the strong arms wrapped around me. "We'll do this together."

Too many feelings skyrocket off the allotted scales all at once, with no way to discern or catalog them. Happiness. Safety. Affection. Attraction. Love. They tear through the walls of my heart, forging uncharted paths, leaving hope to fill the canyons.

"Together." I swallow. "We'll do this together."

22

"YOU'RE SUCH A HIPPIE," Luke says through his laughter.

Smiling so hard my cheeks hurt, I make a failed attempt to counter with, "I am not."

"Olivia Newton-John? Come on."

"'Physical.' 'Heart Attack.' 'Twist of Fate.' None of those identify with the '60s and '70s."

"Nuh-uh." He shakes his head. "I'm not talking about those classics. I'm talking about this playlist you created for yourself with every flower-child song Olivia ever sang."

All I can do is giggle. There's been a lot of giggling lately.

Luke is excellent at unconventional dating. He shoves aside the constraints of my head injury and creates tailor-made quality time just for me. It knocks dinner and a movie out of the park any day of the week.

My days resemble the instructions on a shampoo bottle. Wash, rinse, repeat.

Identify possible triggers. Re-course my day in light of said triggers. Assess the pain scale. If needed, stop my day. Use appropriate medication. Eradicate headache. Reset the pain scale. Repeat.

I still can't watch TV or look at screens of any kind. I spend most of my day in my dark bedroom, but I can venture to the kitchen or living room for short stints without sensory overload causing a headache.

Paying attention to triggers—more than that, understanding how my body reacts to each trigger—is imperative. On several occasions, however, I've allowed too much exposure to trigger elements and ended the day curled up in bed, appreciating the benefits of strong migraine medications.

The learning curve is steep.

The result is that Luke brings his dates to me. And he is proving himself to be thoughtful, creative, and none too playful.

Tonight's date is in my room on the Lovesac.

He insisted on purchasing the monstrous piece of furniture, if you can call it that, declaring that no well-respected 1970s throwback room could exist without a beanbag. It's big enough for two adults and is so incredibly comfortable, I can't bring myself to protest. Even if we did have to rearrange my room to fit the rest of my belongings. Good thing I'm becoming more accustomed to casual wear. Maneuvering around on this cozy beast is easier in jeans and sweaters than it would have been in my skirts and heels.

Our activity for the evening is a conversation through music. Luke bought a double headphone adapter so we can listen from the same phone. The rule is, we aren't allowed to say words. We simply turn on a song from our respective music libraries and allow the lyrics to speak for us.

We play with the caveat that if I get the slightest hint of a headache, I must stop the game.

Noise-canceling headphones are glorious. They block outside stimuli, creating a baseline of silence. Then the speakers provide a crisp sound. Somehow, the combination allows me to listen to songs on low volume without irritating my auditory sensitivity.

I don't anticipate having to play the headache card during this game.

Luke started our musical conversation with REO Speedwagon's "Roll with the Changes."

I countered with "Don't Go Breaking My Heart."

He grinned and played "I Got You, Babe."

"Why is this in your music library?" I asked while laughing.

"Shh. No talking during the game."

My response was Colbie Caillat's "Never Gonna Let You Down."

Luke rubbed my palm while the sweet melody of "You're the Reason God Made Oklahoma" floated through the headphones.

And then I responded with Olivia Newton-John's "Let Me Be There," the perfect song, in my opinion, to tell a wanderlust that wherever they go, you want to be there with them. Which led to Luke grabbing my phone out of my hand and harassing me about my ONJ playlist.

"Fine." I cross my arms in a fake huff. "I like her old stuff. Sue me."

Luke chuckles, scrolling through the playlists. His head shoots up. "No wonder you landed in Colorado, land of the granolas. You have an entire playlist dedicated to John Denver."

"John Denver is an acclaimed artist." Whose tenor voice could cause the most staunch city slicker to love nature and, yes, made me feel right at home when I settled at the foothills of the Rocky Mountains.

It seems my mother's bohemian influence seeped into my life choices without my realizing the extent, a fact that settles well in my soul.

Luke stares at the screen. "What else can I find in here?"

"Give that back." I reach for my phone, and he holds it high above his head. "If you can't respect my secret music stash, you lose the privilege of looking through the lists."

"Oh, baby, I respect the lists. I respect *all* of your lists. But I'm starting to realize you have an inner wild child that might want to be freed."

"That's preposterous."

His flirty eyes shift to awe and affection. "The beauty's in the wild," he whispers. "And you, Penelope, are beautiful."

I smile at him, then look down to pick a nonexistent piece of lint off my jeans, the fancy house shoes glittering at me from my feet. "Have you eaten dinner?" I ask.

"You gotta keep tryin' to help everyone else, don't you?"

Another thing I don't care for in this healing process. No one lets me do anything for them.

"Besides, it's date night," he says. "I'm in charge of the culinary details."

"Culinary details?"

"Yeah. My date traded down to hang out with me, so I have to sophisticate things."

"She must be very patient with you."

"She is."

Not wanting our game to end, I say, "Play me a song that represents your childhood."

Luke nods, scrolling through his phone. We both return our headphones to our ears, and he presses the screen, then sits back and closes his eyes.

Through the speakers sail the opening a cappella measures of Kansas's "Carry On Wayward Son." The electric and bass guitars, drums, tambourine, and electric organ notes drift through my ears, and my heart aches for the boy who identified with these lyrics and the man who continues to hold on to the song.

Without looking at me, Luke shifts me forward to put his hand around my waist and guides me to rest my head on his shoulder. The headphones make it a little awkward, but the Lovesac gives in at just the right places to allow me to sink into the warmth of all that is Luke for five sublime minutes.

The final, eerie note screeches into the silence, and I push up on my elbow, turning to Luke in time to see him shift his gum to the side of his mouth. He must have something to say.

My hearing sensitivity is like having an unfortunate superpower.

When Luke chews on anything, the sound grates right through my ear and scrapes its nails down the chalkboard of my auditory canal. When we figured this out, Luke announced he would only chew on things when I have my headphones on. If I focus on the positive things resulting from my injury, this is at the top of the list.

He pulls my headphones off and curls a stray hair behind my ear.

I pull his headphones off and ask, "Why that song?"

"My grandma paid for me to get drum lessons. It's the first song I learned to play on the drums."

"The same grandma with headaches?"

"Yes."

"You must have been close."

"I wreaked complete havoc in her life. The drum lessons were because I apparently had a lot of restless energy."

I cock my eyebrow. "Had?"

He attempts a grin, but by the somber expression in his eyes, he isn't serious about it. "She was my paternal grandmother."

"Oh?" I ask, remembering the scandal his birth brought upon him and his mother.

He draws me down to him, and I rest my head on his shoulder and curl my arm into myself. "She didn't live in the trailer park. But once a week, she would pick me up in her giant, gas-guzzling Buick and take me back to her house. She said she wanted me to know my heritage, but I think she'd heard the rumors. My mom worked all the time, had a string of men in and out of our trailer. She also knew her son was taking no part in being my father, and I think she felt guilty. Maybe a little responsible."

"And so you learned how to play the drums, as well as how to care for someone with headaches."

"Something like that." His voice rumbles from his chest, straight through me.

"What about the shooting? An Olympic bronze medal in the fifty-meter rifle doesn't just appear around your neck."

"Robert."

I smile, remembering Luke's words. "Heart and a rifle."

"Yeah." He runs a hand through my hair. "Heart and a rifle. Robert and a couple of others from his church would come into the park several times a month. They'd play with the kids, bring snacks, offer donated clothes. One time, he and my grandma had a disagreement about who was going to get me that day."

"Yeah?" I prompt after a few beats of silence.

"It was the first time anyone had fought over me."

I place my hand over his heart and rub my thumb back and forth.

"Anyway, I think my grandma realized she had an advocate in Robert. He took me to church, fed me lunch, then we'd go out to her land and shoot his rifle." Luke shrugs. "The shooting just kind of came naturally to me. Then the two of them paid to send me to marksman camps in the summers, and I got some exposure. With a scholarship to college and a trip to the Olympics, it was my ticket out of that trailer park."

"How'd you start LG Security?"

"My senior year in high school, a buddy of mine from the park was accused of trespassing on someone's property. Minor vandalism. Killing a few of the livestock."

"That's terrible."

"Worse. A kid from the park has no credibility. We were considered lowlife, and my friend was about to go down for it. But I set up a cheap secondhand security camera and staked out the situation. I got solid proof the vandal was a guy who lived two counties away. Apparently the ranch owner had told the guy to stay away from his daughter." He shrugs again. "Over the next four years, I'd come back to visit my ma, and different ranch owners would approach me about taking a look at a problem on their property. I started to get a reputation for knowing what I was talking about, and it stuck."

"You saved your friend."

In response, he lifts his chin.

"You run a company that secures people's property, their livelihood."

Another chin lift.

"And you take trips with Robert to help underprivileged kids around the world."

This time, nothing.

"You appear quite heroic to me right now, Luke Granger." I push up on my elbow again and lean closer. I can see the flecks of yellow in his green eyes. "You didn't belong in that trailer park. The same way I didn't belong with the Nelsons," I whisper.

His jaw muscles twitch, and he gives me another chin lift.

I touch his cheek with my hand. "Don't you ever say again that I traded down to date you. Because you're the best man I know."

He stares at my lips, then says in a cocky voice, "When you were under the influence of heavy meds at the hospital, you told me I was pretty. Do you still think so?"

I give a slight roll of my eyes and start to pull back, but Luke places his hand over mine and holds it to his cheek.

"If I found out that was all an act, my self-esteem would take a significant hit," he says.

I let loose laughter that results in a snort. Appalled, I'm unable to stop the giggles.

"I would pay a hundred bucks for you to laugh so hard you snort again," Luke says with a grin. "But you're just using it as a distraction. Answer the question."

"First, for the record, I've never snorted in my life. Second, I will admit it. That night I thought you were pretty."

"That night? Not now?"

"You're still pretty now."

My problem isn't that Luke is pretty.

My problem is that his soul is pretty. And that's a completely different kind of confession.

"And have you gotten over how annoying I am?"

"That might be impossible." I grin. "Why?"

His eyes flash. He leans in, his lips a whisper away from mine. "Because I'm wondering, now that we have a few dates under our belts, if you still want"—he glances at my lips—"to finally kiss me."

Electric currents pass between us, and I brace as my breathing increases.

"I think . . ." I smile and move just a hint closer. I can feel his breath on my lips, and suddenly I'm bashful, nervous, and I look down.

Luke uses his knuckles to press under my chin and shift my eyes to his. "You think what, baby?"

One swallow to wrestle the butterflies in my stomach and I say quietly, "I think it might make you less annoying if you kissed me."

Luke's chuckle rumbles as he pulls my face to his and kisses me.

The first one soft. The second one sweet. The third one a little longer, with a little more promise.

"And?" he whispers against my lips.

I run my hand down his cheek and leave it resting gently against the side of his neck. "You definitely have a less annoying side."

His face gentles, and he lowers his voice. "I should never have left you that night at Harlan's birthday party. Three years. Lost."

"Why did you leave?"

"My grandma had a stroke. Died later that night."

My heart sinks and I whisper, "Luke."

"I shouldn't have let you out of my sight."

"Luke."

"I should've asked Harlan for your number."

I swallow.

"And you'd better believe I'm claiming my dance at Harlan and Meredith's New Year's shindig."

He leans back in, and just as he places another sweet kiss on my lips, my phone rings. I jump and pull back, a sinking feeling in my belly. Luke's searing eyes don't leave mine.

"That's Jason's ringtone. We keep missing each other." I bite my bottom lip. How ridiculous and apropos that Jason has interrupted our first kiss.

After heaving a giant sigh, Luke says, "You should take his call."

"Yeah," I say, but I can't coax my body to move.

Luke's face shifts into a half smile. He curls us both to sitting. "Talk to Jason. I'll go check on the status of dinner. It's supposed to be delivered soon."

After Luke leaves the room, I command Alexa to answer the phone. "Hey, Jason."

"How is the patient?"

"Making progress."

"Yeah? Are you turning the pastures green? Making the flowers grow?" Jason's tone is laced with a touch of mockery. The first time I explained the neurofeedback process to him, it was clear he had his doubts about the treatment. As well as my choice to stay in Colorado Springs.

"I understand your skepticism, Jason, but it seems to be working."

"You are the last person whose brain needs retraining."

"You aren't here," I say, my voice a little heavier than I want it to be. "This injury has been tough."

"I'm not *with* you because you didn't want to come with me."

"I don't want to argue about this again. I'm getting good, solid care here." I sigh. Trying a change of topic, I offer, "Dr. Ridding has an interesting story."

Silence.

"His dad played for the Broncos for years and suffered from chronic traumatic encephalopathy. He died tragically, and Dr. Ridding made it his life's purpose to work with people who experience traumatic brain injuries."

Jason's breathing is the only confirmation he's still on the call.

"He even consulted on the set of the movie *Concussion*. Worked with Will Smith." My tone rises with hope that the explanation will distract Jason from his disapproval of my treatment plan.

"Did you know that health insurance doesn't even cover neurofeedback?" Jason finally says. "A lot of people don't think this is the correct medical path to go down for a head injury."

"Meredith's from Texas and said the state of Texas requires insurance coverage for neurofeedback in the event of a traumatic brain injury. Not every state legislature has caught up."

Silence.

I drop my head into my hands. "I'm sorry I didn't come live with you, Jason. Your offer was generous."

Jason clears his throat, his words thick. "It's always been the two of us, Penelope. You and me against the world."

I sit up and wrap my hands around the smart speaker, talking to it as if he can see me. "I'm still with you, Jason. I'm just not physically next to you."

"Why won't you let me take care of you?"

His pained voice is almost too much for me to take. I close my eyes, and this time I'm the one who is silent.

He's right. It's been the two of us for a long time. We watched each other's backs at the group foster home, then we endured life in the public eye with the politically motivated Nelson family. Even into adulthood, Jason and I stayed close. But something changed. And somehow I missed when his feelings showed up for me.

Or maybe it's not that anything changed. It's that we never fit the way a normal brother and sister would. The edges of our puzzle pieces could be jammed together to work, but they didn't slide smoothly to complete the picture. If I had gone with him to recuperate in Denver, I think I would have lost pieces of myself.

The Penelope who Luke sees, who Luke draws out, who Luke celebrates, is not the Penelope who Jason knows. She's not the

Penelope who got us through our early years. And she's not the Penelope he's going to understand.

I swallow before I whisper words I know will hurt him deeply. "I need you to let me go."

I'm not sure if the sound I hear is his heart cracking or mine, but I continue. "It feels like you're trying so hard to fix something for me, but what you don't seem to understand is that I don't need fixing."

"You had an accident." His defensive tone blurts through the phone.

"I did. But that's not the only thing you want to fix."

"I just want to help you—"

"If you had your way, I'd be working a different job, living close to you. I don't want either of those things. And I'm tired of talking about it. It's not worth any more discussions. I'm on my own path. And I think I belong here."

For years we've skirted around this conflict. I've never been this direct with him, never wanted to hurt him. I still don't want to hurt him.

He clears his throat, but it's gruff. Deep. "I guess that means you're not coming home for Christmas this year."

I study the opposite wall where Luke hung a hunter-green felt-fabric Christmas tree.

Last week, I voiced my disappointment that this year I wouldn't be able to put up a real Christmas tree. The bright lights would likely cause a migraine. The next day while I was at treatment, he snuck into my room and tacked the felt tree to my wall. I thought that was the only piece of the surprise, but on one of our fabulous dates, he brought felt ornaments. We decorated the tree while drinking hot chocolate, soft music playing in the background.

He declared we would exchange gifts under this tree.

"No," I say, my gaze locked on a reindeer ornament. "I won't be going home for Christmas."

"Agh." The sound coming from the speaker is painful.

"But I'll see you at the New Year's Eve party."

"Yeah." After a long pause, he says, "I'll look forward to that."

"Jason," I whisper, aching to fix this, begging him to bridge the gap.

"I'm okay, Penelope. I'll talk to you later."

I sit, shoulders slumped, staring at the carpet, as the numbers rise in my head.

Luke steps in but stops abruptly. "Everything okay?"

I rub the spot over my heart. "I think I'm an eight. No, maybe a nine."

"Your head?" He makes it to me in two long strides and kneels in front of me.

"No. Sorry. Sad scale. Or conflicted scale? Darn it. I can't even find the correct word."

He takes my hand and rubs the top of it.

"What is it with these emotions? I'm like the girls here at the ranch, riding an emotional roller coaster, but I'm much further from puberty than they are." I clench my fists. "I hate these numbers."

"Nonsense. You love structure. These numbers should be right up your alley."

"They should. But instead, they betray me."

Luke chuckles.

"These numbers are erratic and unpredictable. Do you know what I love most about numbers?"

"Their fancy curves?" he teases.

"Their predictability. But these numbers are anything but predictable."

Right now, this number game is leading me straight into a wall of frustration. So much for Dr. Ridding's "healing" path.

I point an accusatory finger at Luke. "And you owe me a clipboard, mister. I was approved to work with paper today as long as I don't push it." Still no electronics, but I'll take paper. Beautiful, cottony, tree-filled paper that will allow me to do something other than stare at the wall during the day.

"I thought we were talking about the numbers."

"We were. It's on the list of things I'm annoyed with. So is not having my clipboard." I hold out my hand. "So hand it over."

"I'm afraid if I give it to you, you're going to start working too hard."

I open my arms wide in exasperation. "There's nothing for me to do."

"Liar. You know Claire is coming into town over her Christmas break to work with Meredith at Twelve Bluebells. And if I had to guess, you're going to try to be quite 'helpful' to her while she's here." When he says "helpful," he uses air quotes.

I shove his hands down. "I *am* helpful."

"I think your kind of helpful is crossing the border into codependency."

"It's not codependency. It's just a very helpful 'someone is clearly not doing their job' mentality." I use my own air quotes.

Luke throws his head back and laughs. "All right, Miss Helpful. I'll see what I can conjure up in terms of the clipboard. In the meantime, I have Chinese food. Do you want to eat in the dining room, kitchen, or here in your room?"

"Did you bring me vegetable rolls?"

"Do I look like a stupid man?"

No, he looks like a phenomenal, smart, charming, thoughtful man. "No. You don't. Okay. It's date night. Let's eat in the dining room."

"I'll get everything set up and come back to get you."

If our previous dates are any indication, I have a few minutes to myself while Luke sets the table, complete with tablecloth and napkin rings. He'll turn all the lights low on the path from my room to the dining room table. Awaiting me will be candles, but he won't light them until he asks me if my head can handle the stimulus.

Phenomenal, smart, charming, thoughtful man.

While I wait, a warm feeling wraps me in a soft, downy blanket.

Only there's a draft, one that I can't pull the covers over to stop the cold air from chilling my skin.

With Claire actually coming into town, my dream to be the program director at Twelve Bluebells Ranch slips further from my grasp.

23

STANDING ALONE in the dark kitchen of Twelve Bluebells, I lean a hip against the counter and stare out the picture window above the sink. Light flakes of snow coat the ground with a gentle dust of Christmas Eve sparkle.

During the day, snow betrays me. Its glaring reflection stabs my eyes with such sensory overload, a migraine is sure to begin.

But at night . . . at night the earth dims its lights, muting the sharp edges of its creation, inviting me to revel in its beauty.

It's a mirror to my life.

Everything that used to be beauty to me is too much for my injured brain to absorb. However, if it's taken in doses, if it's appreciated from a distance, a different view, or a new angle, I can once again enter its realm and soak in the elements of life that I love.

My significance, my worth in this world, has always been equal to my work. Before the accident, I would have chosen to sacrifice myself for my job. But for the foreseeable future, pushing myself simply isn't an option. I have to see a possible job at Twelve Bluebells in a different light. But I can. Program director isn't out of my reach if I approach it from a different angle. I'm not ready to share this with anyone yet, but delegating—purposefully, strategically—could be a powerful part of my role.

I just hope I get the opportunity to do so before Claire takes my dream job. Claire, who arrives tomorrow and stays through the beginning of January. Claire, Meredith's lifelong friend. Claire, who is not recovering from a brain bleed. Claire, who won't need to ask for breaks, won't need a flexible schedule while she's recovering, and won't need to ask anyone else for help while doing her job.

But these aren't the things I want to be thinking about on Christmas Eve. Not with Luke on the way, and a small, pristinely wrapped box waiting to be opened. It sits in red matte paper, a flat wooden Christmas tree affixed to the top with double-sided tape. Dark remnants of bark on the carved tree give Luke's gift a rustic feel, and I cannot wait to see his reaction to what I'm giving him.

The alarm beeps, alerting me to the front door opening. A giddy shiver runs down my spine.

"Penelope," Luke's familiar voice growls from behind me.

Just the sound of his voice puts a smile on my face. But when I turn to him and catch a glimpse of the seething man in front of me, my glee fades. "Is everything all right?"

Save the two of us, the house is empty. A living room lamp provides the sole gentle lighting through the entrance to the kitchen. Only with Luke's glowering frame filling the doorway, the light casts an ominous, hulking shadow across the room.

"No. Everything is not all right. What's this?" He holds a familiar package out to me.

"It was still out there?" I ask, staring at the red-and-white-striped gift bag with green tissue paper bursting from the top.

"*Still* out there? When did you expect it to get picked up?"

If my defenses weren't going up, I could spend more than a second appreciating that Luke ditched his signature cargoes and Henley tonight. They're replaced with a deep-red flannel shirt untucked and worn jeans that are frayed at the bottom with threads draping over his black boots. A complement to my red cashmere sweater and dark skinny jeans. But it seems our clothes are the only thing complementing each other this evening. Something is seriously wrong.

I open my mouth to respond, but he says, "I'm sorry. Let me rephrase. When did you expect the girl who is living with the man who assaulted you to pick it up?" He paces in the room, his anger sucking every last square inch of air into its vortex. "Or even better, when did you expect the man who assaulted you, the man you pressed charges against, the man who is really not pleased you exist right now, to probably *bring* her to the house to pick it up?"

I hold out a placating hand. I might not be able to work right now, but I still know how to negotiate tense situations. "Luke—"

"I can't. I can't." He shakes his head, still panther-pacing from side to side across the kitchen tile. I'm surprised a black tail doesn't appear and swipe everything off the countertops in a fit of rage.

I clamp my mouth shut, waiting out the tirade.

He stops a few feet in front of me and crosses his arms over his chest. "I can't protect you, Penelope, if you don't do what I say. I thought she was blocking everyone's calls. You were supposed to let me know if you made contact. Then you invite her here to pick something up when no one is at the house with you." He runs his hands over his face. "If she had come to the porch, you would have gone out to talk to her without anyone else here."

"She just texted this afternoon," I explain, my voice rising. "It was the first time I've heard from her in weeks. Yes, I told her I had something and would leave it on the porch. Yes, I have kept a watch out for her since the text. But she wouldn't hurt me, Luke."

"No. But I'd put a hundred dollars down on this counter"—he slaps the granite—"betting that you wouldn't have checked to see if she came alone." He holds his hands up in exasperation. "You are a brilliant woman. Capable of almost anything you set your mind to. But something happens to you when you're around those girls. You just can't help yourself. Your brilliance flies out the window and is replaced by poor judgment."

Spots dot my vision, and I have no idea if this is due to anger or my racing blood and impending headache. I grasp the counter to keep my balance. The last time someone accused me of poor judgment was . . . never. And how did we get so far off track? What happened to falling snow and an intimate Christmas celebration?

"You're not even going to deny it, are you?" he asks.

"I haven't looked forward to a Christmas Eve since before my mom died," I whisper with no small amount of acrimony. "I thought this was going to be a lovely Christmas Eve with the man I like."

"Yeah?" Luke throws his hand out wide. "I don't even remember the last time I stayed in town for Christmas. I thought this was going to be a lovely Christmas Eve with the woman *I* like."

"Really? Well, don't let me stop you. Here." I snap my gift off the counter and slap it against his chest.

"Oh, good." One of his hands wraps around the box while the other yanks something out of his coat pocket. "Since we're doing this now, here you go." He tosses me a four-inch-square box wrapped in hunter-green paper with a simple red grosgrain ribbon around the top.

I bumble the catch but try my best to do it with attitude, and I storm out the back door.

My immediate view of the decor on the covered porch reminds me what an epic failure the last ten minutes have been.

Tonight, the Holcombes took the girls to a Christmas Eve event. With all the visual and auditory stimuli that encompass a celebration of that kind, had I attended, I would have been destined for a beast of a migraine. Luke promised we would have our own special Christmas Eve "event" here at the house and exchange gifts.

Earlier today, I set up an area in the corner of the porch where I imagined we could enjoy our time together. After sweeping, I added decorative Christmas pillows and thick, green wool blankets to the weatherproof cushion of the two-seat glider. A space heater sits in the corner, ready to be turned on, and a soft lamp highlights the Christmas tree—our fabulous felt tree that I moved from my room to the brick wall of the porch.

With slow steps, I plod to the festive corner and flip the lamp and heater on. I sink into the glider and cocoon my body in the blanket.

Even with deliberate attempts to slow my breathing, adrenaline continues to pound out the worsening headache. I've overdone it. I'm going to need the heavy meds. Emotion is one of those things my brain only wants in small doses right now. If any emotion, ranging from fury to joy, bubbles over the precipice, my body simply will not cope.

Dr. Ridding assured me this is temporary. Then he drilled me about what number my emotions were when the incidents occurred, and he questioned my awareness. He wanted to know if I caught the escalation in time to make an effort to reroute the pain.

"Well, on a scale of one to ten, we escalated to a twenty-three in about two point five seconds, Dr. Ridding," I murmur into the night, my breath puffing through the frigid air. Even those quiet words pound the inside of my skull. I draw my hand up to rub the scar at my left temple, but the gift box gets in the way.

I bring the package down, inspecting it from all sides. With great care, I lift the tape from the thick, tightly wrapped paper. I unfold and set aside the untarnished paper and, with unsteady hands, lift the top off the box. Dramatic black tissue paper covers the gift. I take a courageous breath before I lift the paper. This gift is sure to deflate my righteous anger, and to be honest, I'm rather enjoying my righteous anger right about now.

A gentle wind from the east lifts the paper just enough for me to see something shimmer. Maybe sparkle. Slightly.

I don't have much dating experience. Am I one of those women who allows a jewelry purchase to sedate an argument? That would be appalling.

The door to the house creaks open, but I don't turn.

"You got me a toothpick holder?" Luke says.

Staring out at the glittering snow, I nod. Not just any toothpick holder. The size of a thick credit card, the silver case is sheathed in rustic mahogany leather and monogrammed with his initials. With my screen time limited, Meredith spent hours on the internet helping me search for the perfect gift.

Four booted steps sound on the planks. He crouches down perpendicular to me, holding on to the arm of the rocking chair. "You hate my toothpicks."

"I do. I really do," I say, having to clear my throat after my declaration. I turn toward him, pull my knees up, and tuck my feet under me, pressing my cheek against the back cushion of the chair. "But I really like you."

He studies my face, shakes his head, then sighs. "You've got a headache."

There's no point in denying it. I might be able to fool others, but Luke can always pinpoint when I'm in pain. He says the evidence is in my eyes. "I'm sorry," I say.

Regret washes over his face, and he slowly closes his eyes. "This is my fault."

"No, it's not. This is the fault of a baseball bat, an ice machine, and a block of cement. More to the point, this is the fault of Brandi Willis and Marcus Skelly." Old wounds and new wounds. Always these two shall meet.

"But I got you worked up," he says in a quiet voice. "I know better."

"Are you saying we're going to be in a relationship where we never fight? I'm new to this kind of thing, but I'm pretty sure we're going to argue."

"Not necessarily."

"What do you mean?"

"I was thinking you could just always agree with me."

I can feel my lips tip into an almost-smile.

"I'm going to get your meds. The big stuff this time?"

Then I do smile. "You are such a good drug supplier. You know exactly what I need."

"I prefer drug runner. I don't supply them. I just bring them to you."

While Luke is away, I uncover the tissue from his gift. An exquisite bracelet stares back at me. Sets of alternating orange and pink gems pattern the entirety of the bracelet. The colors remind me of my mother, but the design is somehow me. Three small orange stones sit with one larger stone beneath it. Next to it, one large pink stone with three small ones beneath. They are all circular in a symmetrical pattern, and I sense they create something, but I can't quite figure it out.

Luke returns with a water bottle, a box of crackers, and two pills. "I didn't know if you had anything in your stomach. Would you like some crackers?"

"An all-inclusive drug runner."

He bows slightly. "At your service."

"I don't need the snack. I had dinner just before you came." I lift the box to him. "Luke, this is stunning."

He sets the crackers down on the side table, then maneuvers a trade of the items. I take my meds, and he sits next to me and pulls the bracelet out of the box.

He takes the water bottle from my hands and places it on the table, then gently attaches the bracelet to my wrist, the lamplight reflecting the jewels in a sporadic dance on the walls of the porch.

"It's exquisite," I whisper, running my fingers over the gems.

He leans in, his fingers doing the same as mine. We touch in the middle, then run our fingers to the opposite edges. Then we touch in the middle again. "Sapphires. They're paws," he says.

This isn't what I was expecting. "Excuse me?"

"They're paws. Three small stones at the top, one larger one at the bottom. It's a paw. See?"

His description brings the design into focus. The colors alternate, the orange paws facing one direction and the pink paws facing the other. With a simple glance, no one would see the paws. They would only see a pristine piece of jewelry. One that would accent an outfit with just enough pop of color to intrigue but not display an overload of gaudiness. But I know what the bracelet really means. Another piece of beauty from Luke. A bracelet laced in my style, the colors of my mother, and the sentiment of Luke.

"You're a kitten," he says.

"Why do you call me that?"

"Because you fight for those around you with the ferocity of a lion." He runs his fingers over the jewels. "But I know under all that power—under all that protectiveness—you hide the sweet, soft side of a kitten."

Luke's generous words and painstaking insight shove their way into my heart.

"Which is why you will always take Finley's calls and put yourself at risk."

I sit up straight and open my mouth, but he holds up his hands. "Hang on. Let me explain something." He pulls my hand to him and begins to rub at the headache pressure points. His eyes are on our hands, but his voice is far away when he says, "This is not what I do."

Having no idea where he's headed with this conversation, I feel my body tense.

He digs his thumb into my palm as he slides it across the middle. "I don't protect people. My job. I'm not trained to protect people. I go into their homes, onto their land. I set up surveillance. I watch. I report." He sighs heavily, the exhale seemingly deep with burden. "But then I leave."

I remain silent, watching the slow movements of his hands.

"I don't know what to do with you," he says, massaging up to the tip of my forefinger. When he starts at the root of my middle finger, he continues, "I don't know what to do with any of this."

My body cannot hold the tension any longer, a sinking feeling weighing in the pit of my stomach. "Are you—are you breaking up with me?"

He jerks back, surprise crossing his face. "What? No." He shifts to cup my face in his hands. "I'm saying I don't know how to protect you. I'm saying that your fierce love for those girls is causing you to make questionable choices, and I don't know what to do. It was bad enough that I missed you like nothing else when I was in Oklahoma this week. And I was only gone for thirty-six hours."

I didn't care for that thirty-six hours either.

"I'm saying that I care for you, and that you're infuriating."

I close my eyes, allowing the flood of relief to wash over me. He isn't breaking up with me. When I reopen them, I say, "Would it help to know that I missed you too? Though you infuriated me long before the days when I started missing you."

I only get a half smile in return. "It does help. But I need you to work with me on this. I need you to promise me that you won't try to meet with Finley again unless someone is with you. Preferably me."

Clutching his wrists at my face, I rub my thumbs along the tops of his hands. "I promise."

"Anything could have happened, Penelope," he whispers.

Flashes of memory skitter through my mind, of a shove, a slow-motion fall, and eyes that couldn't open because they were covered in blood.

"I know," I whisper back.

His eyes glisten. "If anything had happened—"

"Luke."

He exhales. "Yes."

"I'm sorry."

Raw relief washes over his face. He leans in and gently rests his forehead on mine. With an exhale, he says, "Okay."

He settles us back on the glider, tucking me into his side, my head resting on his chest.

In the silence, I stare out at the field. Two cows moo from the black beyond. I wonder if they're having their own argument.

"Luke," I whisper.

"Right here, baby."

"Do you still like me?"

"Not anymore," he says, humor lacing his words. "I think it was just a phase."

I giggle.

He releases another heavy sigh. "That's my problem, isn't it." It's more of a statement than a question, so I don't respond. "I like you. And it isn't just a phase."

I wrap my arm around his waist and squeeze. "Merry Christmas, Luke." Yes. Apparently I am the kind of woman who allows jewelry to sedate an argument. And liking the man who gifted me with said jewelry isn't just a phase for me either.

He runs his hand through my hair and cradles my head, and I wrap my hand around the back of his neck. He draws me in for a kiss, his thumb sweeping lightly across my cheek. The kiss lingers. Gentle. Warm. Sweet. When he pulls back, he rests his feet on the porch railing, and I sink further into his hold.

"Merry Christmas, Penelope."

A few more beats and the pills start to do their job, smothering the pain in a blanket of medicine and taking the burden of the headache from me.

"When does Claire get here?" Luke asks.

There's that draft in my blanket again, sending cold air onto my cozily warmed body.

"Tomorrow."

"How're you doing with that?"

"Do you think if I short-sheet her bed and put plastic wrap around the toilet seat, she'll get annoyed and not want to take the job?" I may have learned a trick or two during my foster care days.

Luke chuckles. "From what I hear of her, she won't scare that easy."

"I know. She's amazing." I rub my cheek into the soft flannel of his shirt. "That position with the Arizona Cardinals is still open."

"They have a pretty good quarterback right now. You trying out for linebacker?"

I giggle, and he pulls me in closer. "You don't sound the slightest bit worried that I'll interview for the assistant position."

"Are you kidding? Your claws are buried deep into the soil of Twelve Bluebells Ranch. You're not going anywhere." He squeezes me at the waist. "You belong here."

I belong at the ranch? Or I belong in his arms? "I'll have to leave if I lose my job."

"Have you told Meredith that you want the program director job yet?"

"No."

"Why not?"

"I want to show her I can earn it."

"I can respect that, Penelope, but a conversation might do you some good. Put it out in the open instead of you carrying that burden in your head. It's clear Meredith and Harlan love you. What have you got to lose?"

I don't care for this topic. "Did you get ahold of Robert to wish him a Merry Christmas?"

"You changing the subject?"

I'm usually more evasive, but on this medication I'm not as sharp. Better to admit defeat and move on. "Yes, I'm changing the topic."

"I'll give you that play if you agree to think about talking to Meredith."

I nod.

"I talked to Robert about an hour ago. It was a short conversation."

"You sound concerned."

"He wasn't feeling good. Again. Postponed our trip. Again." Luke shakes his head. "I don't know what's going on, but he's better at avoiding a topic than you are, and I didn't get any answers out of him."

"You're worried."

"Yeah."

"Maybe you should go see him."

"You trying to get rid of me?"

"No. But I'm worried." I smooth down the chest pocket of his shirt. "I don't want to tie you to Colorado Springs, Luke—be a burden. You like to travel. You need to get out and go somewhere. Even if Robert doesn't go with you."

He pulls back and studies my face. "You've really been thinking about this."

"Just because we're together doesn't mean you have to give up a huge part of who you are. And maybe someday, when I'm doing better, you can, I don't know, show me the world. Show me *your* world."

Luke pulls me in and kisses me on the temple. Leaving his lips there, he says, "Thank you."

I think the kiss was meant to be sweet, but something warm fills the space between us. Something promising more kisses to come.

"You talk to your non-family family?" he asks.

I smile at his nickname for the Nelsons. "Yeah."

"How'd that go?"

"The senator and his wife gave standard-issue well-wishes. But Jason's still mad at me for not traveling to California for the holiday. I told him I'd see them next week at the New Year's party."

"How'd he respond?"

"He sounded hurt. Just like every time we've talked since I didn't call him after the accident." The medicine dulls my headache but also causes my words to slow. "Dr. Ridding said my treatments are going well, and I can go to the party for a little while if I'm feeling up to it. So that's a good thing."

After finishing treatment number twenty-two, I took today off for Christmas Eve. Secretly, I was disappointed to have to take a day off. Maybe it wasn't so secret since Dr. Ridding openly laughed at my reaction after he told me he doesn't work on Christmas Eve.

Luke shifts me to the side, stands, and offers his hand.

I look up at him in question.

"Come on. You've got to get some rest. I think the medicine's done its job. Your words are slowing like a drunk teenager who's concentrating a little too hard to make complete sentences."

I take his hand and push off the glider to stand. "Well, I never had a rebellious phase. Maybe this is it."

He flashes a smile at me and leads the way.

Once in the house, he walks me to the door of my room and turns me to him. His hands slide around my back and press me to him for a tight, warm hug.

I wrap my arms around his shoulders, stand on my tiptoes, and tuck my face into the crook of his neck.

He bends so his mouth is at my ear. "You'll be at that New Year's Eve party, Penelope."

His low, growly words reverberate through me. "I will?"

"Yeah. You owe me a dance."

I smile and snuggle in tighter, the warmth between us heating up.

For the foreseeable future, the light, the sound, the emotion must be muted, taken in doses. But there is one thing I hope I can always experience to full capacity.

Luke Granger.

24

"PENELOPE." Claire Stark's long athletic legs eat up the marble tile of the main ballroom at the Broadmoor Hotel. Legs currently adorned in a pair of shiny black holiday pants matched with an exquisitely feminine tuxedo jacket. She's dressed to kill and has an expression to match. "Thank goodness you're finally here."

I bite the inside of my cheek to hold back a smile.

For five days, I've watched Claire handle the needs of the ranch with a confident hand. It's petty of me, but it's nice to see the stress written on her face and know she has limits. I was starting to believe that she was a superhero.

Or that I was easily replaced.

"How can I help, Claire?"

"Oh no you don't," Luke says at my side. Strikingly close to my side. It seems my choice of dress for the New Year's party pleased him.

The form-fitting black dress with flutter sleeves falls to just above my knees, but the long, wide, silver zipper up the back gives the dress an unexpected spark. A zipper that Luke is currently running his knuckles over as we stand speaking to Claire. My only jewelry is Luke's exquisite bracelet. And if the grunt and the fire in his eyes are any indication, he likes that detail of my ensemble too.

My four-inch black peekaboo heels with thick black bows around the ankles bring me just a few inches below Luke's commanding height.

He darts his eyes to mine, and my face flushes with heat all over again, just like when he arrived at the ranch to pick me up for tonight's festivities. Who can blame me? If the man looks amazing in his standard-issue cargo pants, he looks downright impeccable in the well-fitting gray suit, accompanied by a black shirt with two buttons opened as if he threw the ensemble on without a second thought. Which he probably did, as indicated by the stubble on his face.

I've never been one to fancy facial hair. Typically I look at someone who hasn't shaved and want them to prioritize their life in a manner that allows for increased self-care. But this look on Luke? I immediately want to run my hands over his face.

A face that is now smirking at me.

"Baby?" he says.

I shoot my eyes from his lips to his eyes, then over to Claire.

Right. Claire. She needs my help. "I'll just work with Claire for a few minutes," I say to Luke.

"We're only here for an hour. I'm already worried the lights and sounds are going to trigger a headache. You don't need to be working on top of that."

"Not working. Just helping. Please, Luke. I sit around all day doing nothing. It's torture. Let me just talk to her for a few minutes."

Luke studies my face, then turns to Claire, who stands before us with pleading eyes and hands clasped under her chin. "You have as long as it takes for me to get Penelope a drink. Then she's back off the clock." With those parting words, Luke stalks to the open bar.

Claire follows Luke's exit with her eyes. He saunters between gorgeous round tables, each adorned with tall clear vases filled with dreamy white hydrangeas and roses, their greenery giving the perfect accent of color. The tablecloths and napkins provide the base for the winter-white motif, but the gold edges around the crystal goblets and porcelain china tie in the darker, shimmering gold of the chairs. A celebration fitting for a palace.

I glance at the artwork hanging on the walls, gorgeous paintings showcasing the depth of the Rocky Mountains. They were picked by the quirky and beautiful volunteer art teacher at Twelve Bluebells Ranch, Daphne Fielding, who also works at the hotel's Contemporary Gallery.

When I glance at Claire, she's not looking at the decor the same way I am.

"Claire?"

"Uh-huh," she says, eyes still on Luke's retreat.

"Claire, he's serious. When he returns, our conversation is over. So how can I help you?"

She snaps her head to me. "He's yummy."

I grin but say nothing because I concur. He is yummy.

"I don't mean anything by it. I know he's yours. It's just that I'm surrounded by teenagers all day long. The occasional male teacher I run into is usually married, or married to his coaching job. I just rarely see all of this"—she sighs—"maleness."

"Claire, is there a problem I can help you with?" I ask on a giggle.

"Okay. Ready for the rundown?"

Crossing my arms, I say, "Go."

"The children from table six are disruptive, and guests are starting to notice."

I've worked on these table assignments for months and know them like the back of my hand. "Those are Spencer and Sally

Dean's children. Prissy Prestidge is sitting at table two with her two college-age daughters. Ask them if we could pay them to take the children down to the movie theater on the first level of the hotel. Then check with the Deans to confirm that they are fine with their children watching the Disney version of *Hercules*. If not, use *The Incredibles 2* as an alternative and notify the hotel we would like movie choice number two."

Claire's eyes grow wide. "You're good," she breathes.

I glance across the room to find Luke tipping the bartender, then grabbing our drinks. "What's next, Claire?"

She nods. "Tanya said she's going to tyrannous the hotel for any signs of Finley. Number one, I have no idea what she meant. Number two, do you think Finley will show?"

"Tanya probably meant 'canvass.'" For weeks, I've been reviewing vocabulary with her and am positive she knows this word. Hmm. Something to think about tomorrow.

While I appreciate Tanya's desire to scour the hotel for Finley, I don't even know if Finley remembers that there was going to be a New Year's Eve party. I haven't heard from her since Christmas Eve.

Beating back the sting in my heart, I swallow. "And most likely, Finley won't show this evening. What's next on your list?"

With two drinks in his hand, Luke weaves through the crowd, stopping to chat every few steps. I haven't seen him in a social setting, and I'm fascinated. He flashes a powerful smile to a few guests, but he never stays in any one conversation for very long, all the while clocking me with his eyes as if to remind me he's here if I need him.

"Penelope?"

I tear my eyes away from Luke. "Yes. Sorry. What's next?"

"I was just saying that Senator Nelson's assistant requested a photo op with the guests of honor."

"I'm sure he did." I sigh. We hired a photographer. I can't very well exclude the Nelsons just because I know they have ulterior motives. “That’s fine. He’ll be requesting a digital copy of the photo. You might as well give his assistant the photographer’s contact information this evening. Save us a call back next week.”

Luke saunters past the last few tables between us and offers me the glass in his right hand.

I smile bigger than I intend, a hint of giddiness climbing up my chest.

Claire touches my arm. “Clearly, I still have a lot to learn before I reach Penelope status. That’s what Harlan calls it. Penelope status.”

“You’ll make a great program director at the ranch,” I say, swallowing down the lump in my throat as Luke rubs a spot at the small of my back.

Claire shakes her head, leans toward me, and lowers her voice. “My mom’s sick. I can’t take the job up here.”

I gasp at her difficult news. I want the job, but not because of Claire’s misfortune. “Oh. Claire, I’m so sorry.”

“Please don’t say anything to Meredith. I’ll tell her after the celebration is over, before I leave town.” She sucks in a breath as if to stave off the serious topic. “Anyway. Thank you for your help.”

“You’re welcome.” Luke puts pressure on my waist to turn us, but I stop and turn to Claire. “One more thing. Will you please check with our hotel liaison about the speakers in the room? The music seems to be a little low.”

“Meredith did that.” Claire shrugs, offering a sheepish smile. “She wants the lights and music low for the next hour while you’re here.”

Something warm slides over my skin, down my limbs, to the tips of my soul. That was kind of Meredith. Thoughtful.

“Speaking of. I can’t find Meredith anywhere, and she and Harlan are supposed to kick off the dancing in”—Claire glances at her phone—“fifteen minutes.”

“You can’t find her?”

"No. I think she got overwhelmed. She mumbled something to me about being right back."

"Ah."

"You know where she is?"

"I know this place pretty well. I have a few places to check."

Luke curls himself into me, one arm around my waist, the other casually wrapped around my shoulders and holding his drink. He raises his eyebrows. "I'm done sharing you. You owe me a dance."

"Can you please be patient for a few more minutes?"

"Three years, Penelope. I've been patient for three years."

Holding on to one of his shoulders, I press onto my tiptoes and whisper into his ear, "I'm worth the wait." When I draw back, his eyes flash.

"Are you flirting with me, Penelope Reid?"

"I don't know how to flirt." It's the truth.

"As with everything you do, you seem to be holding your own." He bends just a hair toward me, his words kissing my lips. "Excelling, even."

I smile, the movement taking me a breath closer to his lips. "I was always good in school."

He growls, shoulders shaking. "Again. Well done."

I giggle, settling my weight back onto my heels. "I'll just be a minute."

After taking the escalator to the ground floor, I bypass the check-in desks. If I don't find Meredith on this floor, I'll call up to her room. But if I know Meredith, she's searching for somewhere to purchase chocolate.

She's not perusing pastries at Café Julie's. The signature shop sells everything from beautiful Broadmoor paraphernalia to travel-sized aspirin to paperback vacation reads. Before I leave, I buy something sweet for her just in case I find her in need of a sugar fix.

I head to the lobby restroom. The stalls, plush little rooms stocked with various toiletry needs, are separated by thick walls and closed in with floor-to-ceiling solid wood doors. Upon entering, I catch a glimpse of the back of Meredith's fabulous winter-white pantsuit. A clearance purchase from Nordstrom Rack worthy of a celebration—part New Year's Eve, part wedding. Huddled in the corner of the small room, she focuses on something in her hand.

"Meredith?"

At the sound of her name, she jumps, turns around, and from the looks of it, tries to hide something behind her back. But in the move, she fumbles and hits the counter, causing her to drop the item.

We both crouch down to retrieve the item, but I get to it first. We freeze, staring at it.

Her terrified gaze lifts to mine, eyes glossy. "Penelope, you can't . . . I don't . . ."

My heart races, and I take in a calming breath. Not knowing Meredith and Harlan's family plans, I can't make any assumptions about her emotional reaction. But I sense something is wrong. I take her hands, rise, and pull her to stand. "What do you need, Meredith?"

She places a palm over her heart and skitters a glance around the restroom. "I don't know."

Thankfully, no one else occupies the luxurious room. This venue offers the maximum amount of privacy a patron can find in a public restroom.

Meredith bites her lip, and worry fills her face. "I've been so busy with adjusting to the life of a newlywed and stepmom and the holidays and getting ready for the party. On the way here, I was going over what I packed in my head and I realized I hadn't packed feminine products, but then I realized I couldn't tell you the last time I needed them."

Turning, I peruse the offered amenities, grab a small plastic cup from the nearby mouthwash dispenser, and gently place it in her empty hand.

Her eyes move from the pregnancy test to the cup, then back to the test. "I bought it on my way here. I know it's weird not to do this in my hotel room. But I want to know for sure before I talk to Harlan about it, and I didn't want to risk him walking in. I need to know."

"There's no judgment here, Meredith," I say.

She skims a foot in and out of her shoe but remains in the same spot.

"You also don't have to do this now."

She lowers her head. "It's not what you think."

"I'm not thinking anything. I'm just here with you."

"My doctor advised me not to get pregnant again," she says to the marble tile, her voice cracking. "It would put me at great risk. I need to know. Something in me just needs to know right now."

Fear trickles down my spine. That's not what I was expecting to hear. They've only been married five weeks. News of an early, unexpected pregnancy has the potential to rock any newlywed. I was already cataloging ways I could help them. But this news . . . this is bigger than me.

"Let's take this one step at a time." I open the door to the largest stall at the end.

Meredith follows my lead, taking the box from my hand as she passes. She turns to close the door but stops it halfway. "Thank you, Penelope."

I retreat to a plush, fabric-covered bench with high rolling sides.

"Is this awkward?" Meredith's voice travels through the door. "You knowing what I'm doing in here, and me talking?"

I cross my legs and pat down the fabric at my knee. "I've never been one of those people who goes to the bathroom with their girlfriends, so I don't know."

"Oh."

But her voice sounds lighter, so maybe I should keep her talking. "I could take a stab at it for you."

"Well, it's just that . . ." She grunts. "I'm wearing Spanx."

Another grunt. "So . . . this is not exactly . . . the easiest task to accomplish."

I purse my lips, containing my laughter. Meredith has always had a way with the awkward.

"Okay." The door swooshes open, and Meredith stands, holding the plastic test out in her hand. "That's done." She steps to the sinks. "I broke out in a sweat doing it, but it's done."

I press commands on my phone to start a timer.

After washing and drying her hands, she sits next to me and crosses her legs in the same direction as mine.

Facing forward, we stare at the opposite wall.

"It might not show anything," she says. "Those tests are best in the morning."

"We'll deal with that when it becomes a factor."

She heaves a sigh. "What am I going to do?"

Without looking at her, I pass the M&Ms I had purchased at the hotel store. "You're going to eat chocolate for the next minute and a half, then we'll deal with the next step."

My chest presses in with the weight of each of the next ninety seconds. A small headache nudges its way to my awareness, and I take deep breaths to keep it at bay.

She rips open the package, pours a handful of candy into her palm, and pops it into her mouth. After a few chews, she grabs my hand. "How does this happen?"

Not knowing how to respond, I remain silent.

"I'll tell you how it happens," she says.

"I don't think that's necessar—"

"You marry a *literal* movie star and go on a honeymoon. That's how it happens. I mean, what was I supposed to do? Marry Hercules and just *look* at him the rest of my life? That would be blasphemous!"

"Meredith." I try to swallow down my giggles. "Keep your voice down. If someone comes in, you don't want them to hear you discussing your honeymoon activities."

"All I'm saying is that you can use every kind of protection and—" She stops talking and covers her mouth. "Oh my word. I did marry a superhero in real life. If we were careful and I still got pregnant . . ."

"Meredith." I hold up a hand and laugh.

She sighs. And just as quickly as the classic rambling and humor that is Meredith appeared, the vulnerable, real Meredith takes its place. She's always about life's simultaneous beauty and pain. "Remember when Alex was in the hospital and we ended up on the floor of the restroom in California? And then together again in your hospital bathroom? We have a thing about big, mushy moments in bathrooms."

"It's where I do my best work."

Her chuckle is muffled with the mouthful of chocolate. She crunches and swallows. "Did you just make a joke?"

I laugh, making no noise, but my shoulders shake. "Probably not."

"Hmm."

I pull the water from the convenience store bag, open it, and hand it to her.

She takes a drink. "I think a funny, handsome security consultant is rubbing off on you."

Something in my belly warms. Is he influencing me, or is he simply finding the real me? Coaxing the real me to come out and play. Providing the real me a safe place to let loose.

The alarm on my phone sounds, and both of us stiffen, but neither of us moves.

Still staring at the wall, I swallow. "Would you like some privacy?"

"No." Her whisper is full of fear. She grabs the test off the counter and hunches over it in her lap, her hair creating a curtain around her face. "Oh my gosh."

My stomach clenches as I wait.

She wraps her arms around her waist and folds over herself in tears, the plastic stick peeking out of the hand closest to me.

Pregnant.

I close my eyes, commanding the tears to stay at bay. Placing a hand on her back, I rub long strokes.

"We were . . . careful," she sobs. "Wasn't supposed to . . . how do I . . ." Her words drown in the sobs.

I'm in over my head here. Acutely aware that I don't have all the pieces to this story, I stay silent, finding it difficult to ignore the fear crawling over me with each passing second. My breathing keeps the pending headache away, proof that my treatments are working. But this isn't the time to focus on progress of this kind.

Once her tears subside, I say, "Meredith, can you sit up for me?"

She adheres to my request, and her watery eyes bore into mine. "What am I going to do?"

"The next step is the fun part." I curl a strand of hair around her ear. "You get to tell your husband that you're going to have a baby."

"But what about—"

"Meredith, I cannot imagine everything a pregnancy encompasses for you." This strong woman in front of me is on a first-name basis with loss. Her two small children and husband died tragically before she met Harlan. But with the news of a risky pregnancy, there must be more to her story. "And in addition to the physical stress of the pregnancy, I imagine there are significant issues you are going to have to deal with emotionally."

A tear streaks down her face.

"The way to work through this is one step at a time. Leave all the heavy stuff for tomorrow. But tonight"—I take her hand—"tonight is the fun part."

She gulps. "Grief doesn't get to steal tonight."

I smile. "You're pregnant."

"I'm pregnant," she whispers, a hint of wonder in her eyes.

"Yeah."

"Yeah." Her face threatens to crumble. "It's so scary."

"It can be scary. But tonight it also gets to be—"

"Fun." She smiles. It wobbles, but it's there.

"Fun." I stand, and she rises with me. "I'll arrange for you to be seen by a doctor. Then he will tell us the next step. But tonight—"

"Tonight is the fun part," she says.

Harlan leads Meredith around the floor in what looks like a dance between a giraffe and a rhinoceros. The disc jockey told Hank Williams Jr. to sing "Texas Women," Harlan's charming homage to his wife. Couples dance around them, oblivious to the scene unfolding between the newlyweds.

"I forgot what a terrible dancer Holcombe is," Luke says, standing by me near the edge of the parquet dance floor. "This is almost too painful to watch."

Without shifting my focus, I nod. "He refused to take lessons."

"I hope Meredith took out extra insurance."

"She thinks it's endearing."

"And what do you think?"

"I think . . ."

Meredith pulls Harlan to the far corner of the dance floor. Couples continue to sway as they pass by.

"You think?" Luke moves to block my view of the floor. "Baby, are you okay? Do you have a headache coming on?"

I step around him. Astonishingly, no. I don't have a headache under this stress. But that's not what's important in this moment. Wringing my hands, I keep my eyes glued on the couple.

Harlan cups Meredith's face in his hands, her lips moving.

Luke doesn't block my view of the floor again but angles his body toward mine. "Penelope?"

"Just wait." The trembling words fall out of my mouth as tears sting my eyes.

Meredith stops talking. Harlan rests his forehead against hers, speaking. She nods. Anguished joy. It's the only way to describe them. They whisper, he wipes a tear off her cheek, they kiss, she wipes a tear off his face. And then they embrace, grasping each other for dear life. Truly. For dear life.

Luke stands perpendicular to me and places his warm hand on the small of my back, his intense stare never leaving my face. "What's happening, Penelope?"

A tear streams down my cheek, and I swipe it away. "She's pregnant," I whisper.

"Shouldn't that be a good—"

"It's life-threatening." I almost choke on the words.

Luke slowly turns his head, shifting his gaze to the newlyweds. He puts his hand on my waist and pulls me to him. I rest my head on his shoulder.

"It's going to be okay," he murmurs into my hair.

He can't know that for sure, but it has to be. It just has to be.

Luke's body tenses. He releases me and pulls his phone out of his pocket. He reads something on the screen and frowns. "I'm sorry, Penelope. I've got to go make a call."

"Everything all right?"

"No. Everything's not fine. I came here for the sole purpose of dancing with my girlfriend, and we have yet to touch the dance floor. I'll be back in a few minutes." He stalks toward the exit, lifting the phone to his ear.

I can't help it. I smile. Wide. The muscles in my cheeks are stretched to capacity. I'm Luke Granger's girlfriend. I'm his. I belong to him.

"You're his girlfriend?" a voice asks from behind me.

I turn around to find Jason standing behind me, his face a cross between crushed and betrayed. He's handsome, his blue suit accentuating his crystal-blue eyes. Eyes that I'm level with on account of my heels.

I touch the sapphires of my bracelet, then fold my hands in front of me. "Yes, Jason. Luke and I are seeing each other."

His left eye twitches, and he opens his mouth but nothing comes out.

I glance around the room, trying to think of a different topic. "Have you talked to Phillip and Cynthia yet? They're sitting at table twelve."

He runs his hands through his thinning hair. "Yes. I'm supposed to tell you that Phillip wants a family photo before the night's over."

"I'm leaving in fifteen minutes." That isn't accurate. I'm leaving after I get my dance with Luke. No matter how long that takes.

"Why?" His brows furrow. "Are you feeling okay tonight? You said in our last phone call that you were almost finished with your treatments."

"I am doing well tonight." I rub the scar over my left eyebrow. "We've seen significant improvements. But I still have to be careful. I'll be sensitive to headache triggers for a while."

"I'm glad you're doing better. Are you still job shopping? I have some leads for you in Denver."

I stand up straighter. This conversation might not go well. "I want to stay here, Jason. After my medical leave is over, I don't know if I'll get my old job back. Or if they'll even consider me for the program director at Twelve Bluebells. But I know I have to try."

He shakes his head. "I don't get it. Why would you want to work at a halfway house? We always said we'd get away from the foster care system and conquer the world together."

"I don't remember it that way. We always said we'd survive together and then create the lives we wanted." I hold my resolve inside the tight grip of my fists. "I know this might sound odd, but I feel like I belong here."

"That makes no sense to me at all." He shoves his hands in his pockets and looks down at his shoes. "And how long have you been dating Luke?"

"Not long."

He takes a step toward me and inhales a deep breath. "Have you ever wondered what would have happened if we hadn't been adopted into the same family?"

I blink. "What?"

He looks at me, his eyes full of painful vulnerability.

Oh. Oh no. "Jason—"

"I love you. I should have told you when we last talked. I should have told you years ago. I've loved you since the day I met you. It was always just the two of us against the world. Then the Nelsons came along and swooped up both of us. Adopted both of us. Declared us siblings." He lowers his voice. "But we don't share a drop of blood. Not one, Penelope."

"Jason. Stop." I hold up my hand.

"Don't you ever wonder?" he whispered. "Don't you ever wonder what would have happened if we hadn't been adopted into the same family? Would we have dated? Married? Had kids?"

"Jason," I say with a firm voice, not wanting to draw attention to our already awkward conversation.

"Don't you ever wonder?" His tone begs me to answer.

I stare into the eyes of the sweet teenager I once knew and say the most honest thing I can conjure. The most direct answer to put a stop to this agonizing conversation. "No." I swallow. "I never wondered."

He darts his gaze around the room. "I gotta go."

When he turns on his heel, I grab his arm. "Wait. Jason?"

He shifts toward me, moisture glossing over his eyes. "I knew this day would come," he whispers. It's a low, raspy sound full of pain and something else I can't identify. Self-condemnation? Resignation? "I knew one day you would break my heart."

"It doesn't mean that I don't love you."

"I know," he says. "That's the worst part."

Jason leans in and kisses me on the cheek. It feels more like a farewell than a casual goodbye. He trudges across the room, his gait heavy and defeated.

Luke approaches from my side, his attention locked on the retreating Jason. "He's in love with you, you know."

"I know." I watch Jason kiss our adoptive mother on the cheek, shake the senator's hand, and make a beeline to the exit.

"Which is tough luck for him."

"Yes."

"Because I'm in love with you."

My whole body locks up, and I turn to him, my mouth gaping with shock. "When did you decide that you—that you were—are—when did you decide that?"

"I don't think I decided anything," he says with a cocky grin.

"What do you mean?"

"I don't think it's something you get a choice in. You just feel it."

"But what if I—I mean, I've never . . ."

"It's okay." He steps closer, lowering his voice. "You just keep thinking about those irritating numbers in your head, and you'll figure it out."

Lyrics cascade across the room, crooning sweet declarations of sentiment—a duet about two people living in opposite parts of the world yet surrounded by reminders of the one they love.

He takes my hands and leans closer, his mouth at my ear. "I sure do hope hippies can appreciate country music, because we're about to dance to this song."

My shoulders shake, and I release a giggle.

"Ahh. Now that's a sound I like to hear."

I glance up at him. "What sound?"

"Your happiness."

"Sometimes . . . sometimes I'm happy with you."

He grins. "Sometimes?"

"Well, yes." I nod. "Other times, you infuriate me."

His grin turns into a blinding smile.

I shift my eyes over his shoulder. "I don't think I'm doing a good job communicating what I mean."

"Oh, no." He chuckles. "I think you're doing just fine."

"But I'm not trying to be funny."

"I know, baby. You can't help yourself."

Baby. *Baby.* Not just an endearment but a claim. A soft, sweet claim that I never tire of hearing.

He pulls me closer, one arm wrapping around my waist, the other around my shoulders. Our movements turn into more of an embrace than a dance. Luke lowers his head, and we dance cheek to cheek, my eyes closed as we sway. I only exist in this safe cocoon. With Luke Granger.

When the song winds down, he pulls back and slides his hands to cup my face, one thumb rubbing with a whisper touch over the apple of my cheek. "I know you don't like surprises, Penelope, so I'll give you a heads-up on this one."

I swallow, his beautiful green eyes drawing me under his spell.

"I'm about to kiss you," he says.

I tighten my clutch on his arms.

He grins, his breath a warm caress across my lips. "Breathe, baby."

I nod, that "baby" cutting a direct path to my heart.

Sliding one arm around me, the other sifting through my hair and cradling my head, he presses his lips to mine. The kiss is tender, sweet, slow, and long, but with just a hint of the power and strength that lie beneath the surface of his touch.

Too quickly, much too quickly, he pulls back, then rests his forehead on mine.

Eyes still closed, I smile. "Luke?"

"Right here, Penelope."

"Kiss me again."

Feeling his lips smile against mine, I lean my weight into his, and he tightens his hold.

"Bossy." His teasing word flutters between us. With couples twirling around us, a country singer twanging sweet nothings through the room, Luke's lips capture mine again, this time unleashing the electricity he carries with him and the love he just declared.

25

FOR CHRISTMAS ONE YEAR, my mother bought me a preowned camera from Goodwill. The Olympus point-and-shoot had a nifty cover that, when slid open, triggered the lens to electronically move forward and prepare for the shot. At eight years old, I considered it my prized possession.

But with it came responsibility.

The film wasn't cheap to purchase or get developed, and periodically, the batteries needed replacing. At first we bought film from Dollar General and processed it at Walmart. But after some research, my mom found a mail-in service that saved us about thirty percent. Waiting almost two weeks for the pictures to return was difficult, but we thought we hit the discount jackpot.

Because I knew it was going to cost us precious money, each photograph I took with that camera was a deliberate choice. I only took pictures I knew would turn out well.

My artsy mother, however, encouraged me to experiment, to look at objects through a different lens. You would have thought she had bought me a 35mm Kodak the way she encouraged me to play with light, color, and texture.

Five months into my novice photography stint, I was tasked with the most important photo shoot of my life, though I didn't know it at the time. All my mother wanted for her birthday, she said, was a picture of the two of us at the beach. So as not to waste money on poor photos, I practiced using the self-timer without film. Once I understood the timing down to a science, I loaded up the camera and gave my mother strict instructions on where to pose and how exactly to time her beaming smile. She threw her head back and laughed at me. "Not today, Penelope. There are no rules today. We're going to use all twenty-four pictures on just us."

When I miss my mother the most, I remember that day. The freedom, the laughter, the joy.

But when I need my mother the most, I remember the day the developed film showed up in our mailbox.

I knew the developing process would take at least eight days, but it could also take as many as thirteen. Each day after school, I would run from the bus to our apartment, straight up the five concrete steps to the double doors, and down the hall to the row of tarnished metal mailboxes lined up in order of apartment number. That week, my mom let me keep the mailbox key in my backpack so I wouldn't have to trudge upstairs to get it off the bulletin board where it usually hung. Our box was 3A.

Day nine was our magic day. I hugged the thick envelope to my chest all the way up to our apartment door.

My mother was running late returning from work that day, and when she found me, I was on my bedroom floor in tears.

Somehow I had made a mistake of astronomical proportions, ruining my mother's birthday gift. I had loaded a used roll of film and taken our beach pictures on top of another set of pictures. Fanned out in front of me were the twenty-four photos. Twenty-four double-exposure snapshots. Images of our day at the beach were layered on top of images I had taken the previous week of flowers in a field. Our faces adorned one layer of the photo, distorted with the second picture on top of petal close-ups. Each picture was a mishmash of combined colors and gelled memories from the two different photo shoots.

The wasted money was almost as concerning to me as the wasted birthday gift.

But my mother walked in, put her hands on her hips, and gaped. She dropped to her knees, picking up various photos for closer inspection. "Penelope," she gasped, "these are stunning."

"I ruined them," I told her through hiccuped tears.

She turned to me, placed one hand on my cheek, and held a picture with the other hand. "Don't you see? The messy combination is what makes these so breathtaking."

In the photo, our faces from the beach peeked through the petals of a flower from the previous week. Spread before us on the floor were layers of loveliness throughout each picture. The double-exposure process had pulled something abstract and textured from our lives, turning chaos into beauty.

Standing in the ranch kitchen, stirring a pot of black-eyed peas on the stove, I smile to myself, remembering those pictures. My mother found beauty in everything. Not unlike a man I now know. A man I am now dating. A man I am falling in love with who reminded me of my mother's words one day in a chapel five weeks ago.

The house alarm beeps in two quick successions, alerting me to someone's entrance at the front door.

"Hello?" Meredith calls. "Penelope?"

"In the kitchen," I call over my shoulder while I set the spoonula down on the counter. I check the oven timer—the chicken should be ready in a few minutes. My feeble attempt at making dinner will be rounded out with a salad and a cherry pie from the bakery.

Meredith and Harlan enter the room, and I turn, studying their demeanors. They've just returned from a visit to the ob-gyn. Harlan heads straight to the fridge and opens the door. Meredith offers me a small smile.

Because I walked into a hotel bathroom at exactly the wrong time—or the right time, depending on how I look at it—I'm privy to the most sensitive information in their lives right now. However, I'm aware that Meredith might not have wanted it that way. The exposure to their personal lives is so great, *they* are double exposed. Layers of her previous life behind her current one. Colors melding together the tragedy of her past and the questions swirling around her current pregnancy.

"Thank you for setting up that doctor's appointment, Penelope," Meredith says.

"Of course. I don't want to pry, but please let me know if there's anything I might be able to help with."

Harlan grabs a bottled water out of the fridge, twists the cap off, and hands it to Meredith. "Dr. Gordon said in spite of it being a high-risk pregnancy, everything looks good. She'll probably be on bed rest at some point."

Meredith glances at me and shrugs with a resigned smile.

"He also wants to deliver early," Harlan says. The lines around his eyes are filled with concern, but his stance widens and he places his hands on his hips as if he is commanding confidence into the room. "But overall, the doctor was very optimistic today."

Meredith nods. "He also said I'm already asking a lot of my pants."

"I believe his remark was that you were perfectly healthy," Harlan says.

"He said I've already gained three pounds since my annual visit."

Harlan walks to Meredith, takes her face in his hands, and gentles his voice. "He said there's a strong possibility that you and the baby are going to be fine." He leans his forehead against hers. "And that's all that matters."

"That's all that matters," Meredith whispers back.

Harlan and Meredith's double exposure is also wrapped in

beauty. One that takes my breath away as I watch them embrace, Meredith resting her cheek on her husband's chest.

I look down, flicking a nonexistent particle off my pressed, dark-stained jeans.

Meredith pulls back, kisses Harlan on the cheek, then while still in his arms, turns to me and says, "And one other thing that matters is that I'm asking a lot of my pants."

"Do you want to . . . go shopping?" I ask, cringing.

"Did that physically hurt to say those words?"

"Yes."

Meredith takes a drink of her water. "Good news for you, I'm not a shopper. How about we forgo the girly activities like shopping and gossip, and you just cut to the chase and tell me what's going on between you and Mr. Drum Set."

"Mr. Drum Set?"

"Captain Cargo Pants," she says with a sly smile. "Or I could just call him the man who delivered a hot kiss to you on the dance floor two nights ago."

Heat floods my cheeks, and I have to look away from the gleam in her eyes.

"Where is Luke, anyway?" Harlan asks. "We saw Bianca on the way in, and she said he didn't show for her drum lesson last night."

He didn't tell her he wasn't showing for her drum lesson? That's new information. I wonder if that's why she stalked out of the house this morning.

The oven timer beeps, and I press the off button. I pull a trivet and hot pads out of a nearby drawer. "He had to fly to Arizona. One of his clients had an issue and insisted Luke be the one to go check it out."

"Perfect," Meredith says with a wink. "Distance makes the heart grow fonder."

I try to smile, feeling only the tips of my mouth lift.

Maybe. Maybe distance makes the heart grow fonder. Or

maybe distance just confirms that you don't need someone in your life. He's only texted twice.

But this is a short trip. He'll be home tonight. And this relationship is new. Luke is probably used to his space when he travels. I just have to learn what to expect.

"When does he get home?" Meredith asks.

"Any minute now." I open the oven door and say to the pan of chicken, "He's coming by for dinner." After I place the dish on the trivet, I close the oven door and turn to find the Holcombes staring at me with looks of amusement and awe.

"You're cooking?" Meredith asks.

"What?" I say, crossing my arms over my chest. "I can cook. How hard is it? You follow instructions. I excel at following instructions."

Meredith takes me by the shoulders and pulls me in for a hug. "I like that Luke brings out this side of you," she whispers into my ear. She pulls back. "Other than Luke, will you please keep the pregnancy to yourself? It's so high-risk, and we need a little time to think through the details. We aren't quite sure yet when to tell everyone. Alex is so little, we don't want to get her hopes up—but if I'm bedbound soon, that might not be up to us. Plus, I've had so many lost pregnancies in the past." Her voice breaks, and her eyes fill with moisture. "It's just hard to know who to involve, and at what point."

"It's safe with us, Meredith. But will you let me know if you need anything?"

"I don't want to put stress on you, Penelope. It seems like your headaches have gotten better, but you aren't one to share when you're not doing well."

I glance away. No, I'm not one to share. Still. "I'll make a deal with you. You tell me what you need, and if I'm not up to it, I'll find a discreet way to get someone else to help you out."

Meredith squeezes my shoulders and releases them. "It sounds like a deal."

Harlan puts an arm around Meredith's waist. "You know what we need is to find someone for the program director slot. And soon." He looks at me. "Did Meredith tell you that Claire officially declined the position? Her mother's not well, and she needs to stay in Dallas."

Meredith looks up at him. "I'm not going to be able to travel as much, am I? Darn it. I think this is going to be a tough cancer diagnosis for Claire's mom. I was hoping I could fly out and be with the Starks every so often while they walk through this."

"No, sweetheart, you aren't going to be able to do that." He shifts his focus back to me. "And Meredith's not going to be as hands-on as she wants to be with Twelve Bluebells. So we need to find someone soon."

My heart pumps quickly, and I take a breath to calm my pulse. Maybe I should just tell them now that I would like to be considered for the job. I was planning to wait and figure out the perfect way to pitch the idea. But this moment feels like it was dropped in my lap.

But then Tanya enters the room, her shoulders slouched with burden and exhaustion. Possibly something to do with her pea-green scrubs being decorated with an orange stain over her left shoulder.

The opportunity to discuss my future with the Holcombes slips away with everyone's greetings to Tanya. I sigh, hoping I can find the right approach, the right time to act, and the courage to follow through.

"We're going to let you go." Meredith squeezes my arm as they turn to leave. "Have a fun dinner."

I look at Tanya and nod at the stain. "Tough day at the old folks' home?"

She sighs. "Mrs. Leibowitz threw her Jell-O at me again."

"Did she say why this time?"

"I couldn't find her hair ribbon. I told her I canvassed her room and it was nowhere to be found. But her daughter Martha explained later that Mrs. Leibowitz hasn't worn a ribbon in her hair since she was a little girl. I guess it's more of that dementia."

Full-time employment is required for residents of the ranch. I once asked Tanya why she chose to work in the Alzheimer's unit of a retirement community. She said she'd lived her entire life with her mother forgetting to pay the rent or to feed her children, but the people in that community didn't have a choice in what they forgot. It felt good to her to help someone who didn't mean to forget things. That might have been the moment I fell for Tanya Purtle.

But right now, I'm rethinking something she just said. I cock my head. "What did you say about her room?"

"I canvassed it. I looked *everywhere*. In between the mattresses, behind the dresser, inside her books. Everywhere."

"You looked everywhere. Searched everywhere. *Canvassed* the room."

"Yesssss?" She stretches out the word with a little exasperation, clearly not knowing where I'm taking this conversation.

I stand directly in front of her and cross my arms. "True or false: You know what the word 'canvass' means."

"You know I know what it means. I just used it."

"And how do you know what it means?"

"Because we worked on it all last week."

"Was that a hard word for you to learn?"

"No."

"Did you ever struggle with its meaning?"

"No. We talked about this. All of those cop shows I like have people canvassing the neighborhoods all the time. What's going on with you, Miss Penelope?"

I level my eyes with hers. "Are you purposefully underperforming?"

"What are you talking about?"

"Your vocabulary." I nod, remembering the times she has confused words. Arbitrary for dysentery, unkempt for verklempt, plutonium for pandemonium. "For months, you've been working on your vocabulary by yourself, but you often confuse similar-sounding words and their meanings when you talk to others. But since my accident, I've been working with you one-on-one. You're sharper than a tack. It takes you very little time to memorize meanings and use the words appropriately. I've never seen you mix up words while you're learning them."

She looks away. Swallows.

I take a step toward her and gentle my voice before I lay out my final piece of evidence. "I know you know the word 'canvass,' which is why I was surprised to hear from Claire on New Year's Eve that you mixed it up with 'tyrannous.' But you just proved my point by using it correctly right here in this kitchen without batting an eye."

Gnawing at her bottom lip, she stares at her uniform tennis shoes.

"Tanya, why don't you want anyone to know how smart you are?"

She shoots her head up, her eyes glistening with painful vulnerability. "Because I don't want to have to leave the ranch," she whispers.

Her answer hits me square in the chest, and all the pieces fall into place. "You think that if you succeed here at the house, you'll get kicked out."

A lone tear falls down her cheek.

That one tear solidifies what I've always known about this ranch. Twelve Bluebells reaches in and wraps its arms around the souls of those of us who don't have anywhere to belong.

"Tanya, there's going to come a day when you won't be able to hide your intelligence and your strength anymore. It already seeps out sideways when you have your guard down. The insight you have for Finley. The fierce protectiveness you show to Bianca. Your commitment to serve others through your job in the Alzheimer's unit. And someday, you're going to finally let the world see the whole of you." I lean in. "And that day will be brilliant."

She wipes her nose with the back of her hand.

"In the meantime, you're not going to lose your place here, Tanya. It's your home. And it wouldn't be the same without you."

In a moment so quick I don't anticipate it coming, Tanya throws her arms around me, squeezing so tightly I lose my breath. "Thank you, Penny Lady," she whispers in my ear. And just like that, she's gone. Taking a piece of my heart with her.

I pull my thin black sweater down, smoothing it out at the waist, and turn to the stove. The black-eyed peas simmer, bubbles rising around the inside edge of the stainless-steel pan.

I belong here too.

Meredith might not see me as an automatic option for the program director. Maybe I, too, have hidden who I am. Maybe I've hidden behind my job at Harlan's consulting business. Maybe I haven't revealed to her the wisdom and strength that I could put into the ranch. I've hidden pieces of me as well.

I don't know if Meredith views me as a candidate for the job or not. I'm not perfect for it. The fact is, Finley was my responsibility when she left the ranch. And as I manage headaches, I'm not as on top of my game as I have been. But I can't hide behind my fears. I have to show Meredith who I am. I have to show her what I want.

And I have an idea of how I could do just that.

I can't wait to run it past Luke.

As I smile into the beans, the alarm beeps again to note the front door opening. I glance at the clock on the microwave. It must be Luke. Butterflies sail through my stomach, and I steady my voice. "Luke?"

I turn the knob of the gas stove, but instead of flipping the burner off, I mistakenly increase the flame. My other hand jerks the spoonula, throwing a small dollop of black-eyed peas on the counter. "Shoot."

Heavy footsteps enter the kitchen but stop at the entrance.

"Hang on a second. I spilled." I kill the flame and grab a kitchen towel off the handle of the oven. As I wipe up the beans,

I say, "I'm so glad you're here. I can't wait to tell you what I just figured out."

Once the beans are cleaned up, I put the towel on the counter and turn. "I hope you had a good tr—"

Destroyed.

It's the only word to describe the man in front of me. With what I guess is three days' stubble across Luke's cheeks, he locks his anguished eyes on me, shoulders hunched, hands in pockets. His stillness is almost eerie.

"Luke?" I whisper.

"Robert Kitson died this morning."

I barely hear his gravelly words. But I did hear them. And something deep in my bones aches at the news about his mentor.

Luke doesn't move, so I take three steps to him, run my hands around his waist, pull him into me, and hold on. Tight. His body rigid, he doesn't respond. But after two breaths, Luke wraps his arms around me and tucks his face into the crook of my neck.

And this beautiful man—this beautiful, strong, seemingly invincible man—lets go. His body bucks in my arms with ravaged sobs.

26

"DID YOU THINK more people were going to come today, Penelope?" Meredith asks, standing in the finished basement of Mountainside Baptist Church in southwest Colorado Springs. Her simple black dress matches the varying degrees of dark-clothed mourners who assemble for today's memorial. Soft-toned conversations about the deceased fill in the crevices of grief around the room. "The service was nice. Short, but nice. I guess I just thought after all the years of Robert's service to others, more people would be here. Is this what you were expecting?"

I dart my gaze around the room, taking in the twenty-some-odd people standing around two long folding tables that offer various homemade finger foods, desserts, and two kinds of coffee. The sweet smell of baked goods collides with the musty scent of sorrow. With the short ceremony and sparse reception, this funeral has a salt-of-the-earth feel. The few that knew him well gave testimony that this is what Robert would have wanted. To love and live well, then die unnoticed. Unadorned.

It's hard to reconcile the scene in front of me with the tales of Robert Kitson. The stories speak of a man larger than life, a gregarious personality that charged into poverty-stricken areas around the world armed with vast amounts of courage and love.

But he was a man with very few strings attached to anything on this earth. Or anyone. A hot-air balloon with no place to land before pancreatic cancer ravaged his body.

Is this what I was expecting? No. Is anything in the last forty-eight hours what I was expecting? No.

"It's not exactly how I thought this would all play out," I say.

"Do you know those people huddled in the corner?"

I glance at the group of five, including an older couple with two young women in their twenties. But it's the woman with the stunning, long silver hair pulled back into a braid who is full of intrigue. From the time of her arrival before the service up to this very minute, she has silently wiped tears away, the other four in her group taking turns consoling her. Robert has no family to speak of, so why is this woman so affected by his death?

The rest of the room is filled with those of us connected to Luke, staff members from Robert's home church, and a few men, most of whom flew in for the service, who worked with Robert over the years on various humanitarian trips.

"I don't know who they are," I say. "Luke said that Robert hasn't lived or served in Colorado Springs proper in years. He had an efficiency apartment and a post office box he would visit between trips. But he was very rarely here."

"Did Luke plan the ceremony?"

"I don't know, exactly. He wouldn't—well, that is to say, he didn't want me to . . . help." That's putting it mildly. I haven't seen him since the night he told me about Robert's death. When he got home, an urgent work situation ate up his time. He flat-out declined my help, almost refusing to talk to me altogether. I've had two short phone calls with him, and I sent three separate texts that he answered with one-word responses.

Meredith touches my arm. "Grief can be confusing, Penelope. It does really awful things to people."

I sigh, staring at her. Meredith understands grief more than most. Has had to deal with grief more than most. I offer a small smile. "I appreciate you saying that, Meredith. I just . . . he said he didn't want to talk about anything until he got through today."

"Well, that's not all bad."

"But he added a warning—that things were going to change."

"A warning?"

"Yes," I whisper. I close my eyes, hearing his words from an earlier call. *"Penelope, I'm giving you a heads-up. Things are going to change between us."* The anger in his voice was disconcerting.

"You're scared," Meredith says, squeezing my arm.

"Yes." I open my eyes. "And so confused."

I touch my lips, remembering the New Year's Eve kiss. A dance-floor kiss full of tender passion. A good-night kiss at my door full of heartfelt promise. *"The best is yet to come, kitten. Happy New Year."*

A tall, lanky man, dressed in full cowboy attire complete with handlebar mustache, approaches Meredith and me. With the gray at his temples and a story he relayed in the service about a trip with Robert to Costa Rica thirty years ago, I'm guessing he's in his mid-sixties. He nods to us. "Ladies. I'm not sure how you knew Robert, but my condolences to you both. I'm Vance Holland."

He offers a handshake, and we introduce ourselves.

"I'm so sorry for your loss," I say. "We didn't know him personally. Luke Granger is a friend of ours and we're here to support him."

Understanding crosses his face, then a grimace. "Ah. Luke. This must be hitting him hard. I was only privileged enough to travel with Robert the one time." He holds up his ring finger, showing a scuffed, wide silver band. "I thought I was going to travel the world with Robert until my Marcy came along and swept me off my feet. She wanted to start a family immediately and said it was either her or Robert. Well, the fact is, Marcy's prettier than Robert."

That's our cue to laugh with him, but something in his words thunks in the pit of my stomach.

"We settled in Montana. She gave me five sons. I got to send three of them on trips with Robert over the years. They couldn't be here today, but if they had been, they'd tell you that what Robert did for them on those trips to grow them into men was more powerful than what he did for the local population they were trying to serve."

Vance's words are thick, and he pulls a yellowed, folded handkerchief out of his back pocket and wipes his nose. When he returns it to his pocket, he looks back at us. "Sorry. I guess it will get to me for a while. There's nothing like a man who builds into your sons and helps them become the men they are today. One of them is finishing up college and wants to join Luke and pick up where Robert left off." His voice garbles, and he shakes his head, murmuring "Sorry" as he again reaches into his back pocket.

Join Luke and pick up where Robert left off? What does that mean, exactly? Instead of the pit in my stomach feeling heavy, now it churns.

This marks the fourth person today who has commented about Luke's travels with Robert. One man flat out couldn't believe that Luke was in town for the funeral because, in his words, "Catching Luke in town is like catching a foul ball at a Rockies game. It happens to other people, but never to me."

Just as Vance makes his exit, Harlan stops in front of us with Tanya and Bianca in tow.

"It's time for me to take all my ladies home," Harlan says.

"You mean, it's time for me to go home because I've been out of the house for too long," Meredith says under her breath, out of earshot of the girls. She hasn't shared her pregnancy news with them, and her comment makes me think Harlan is keeping close tabs on Meredith's activities.

Bianca moves in front of Harlan to offer me a hug. The embrace is stilted. A month passed after her arrival at the ranch before she touched anyone. Today's embrace is progress.

"Thank you for coming today, Bianca," I say. "It means a lot to Luke that you're here."

"It's what family does," she says.

Family.

In the wake of Robert's death comes a miracle. Bianca, a woman wounded by every man she's ever let get close, declares Luke family.

Meredith is the final hug of the group. When her arms go around me, she whispers, "Lean in. Hear what he has to say. Tell him how you feel."

I pull back. "He's deep in his grief, Meredith. Do you really think this is the best time to do this?"

She shoots a look at Luke. "I'm not sure what's best. You'll know when the time comes. But here's what I do know. I hid behind my grief for four years before I came to terms with one of the most painful lies I had been telling myself my entire life. A lie that had nothing to do with my loss. Sometimes we need the hard truth to be able to move forward."

"I don't want to scare him away. I don't want to lose him."

"I know. But your actions, even if they're perfectly planned and executed, can't control what he will do."

Even if I'm perfect, I could lose him. "What do I do?"

"You take a risk."

I don't even know what that means.

She smiles as if she knows what I'm thinking. "Sometimes risking is hardest for those who are intelligent, capable, and independent. It requires letting go of the results."

"That doesn't sound like a compliment."

"It's not."

I rub the scar at my eyebrow. My neurofeedback treatments are infuriating because I can't control the outcome. I'm only allowed to look at a screen and let my brain learn the rest.

This? There's so much more at stake. It's not infuriating. It's terrifying. Why can't I try harder to make everything okay with Luke?

"The only thing you can do is lean in," she says. "Be honest with him."

"I am honest with him."

"So you've told him you're in love with him?"

I draw a hand to my chest. "I'm not . . ."

Am I in love with Luke?

Dr. Ridding continues to work with me, identifying pain and feelings. Categorizing my pain into numbers can be challenging simply because the triggers and the kinds of pain vary. But I can chart that kind of concrete information.

Categorizing my emotions into numbers can be exasperating. It's not linear. I never knew there was such a variety, or that my emotions could overlap with each other or switch on a dime. I've never been given the awareness. Never been afforded, or allowed myself, time to stop and feel.

In love with Luke? How would I know that information? I don't have any comparison. What I have is a giddiness that reminds me of a teenager. Factually speaking, giddiness doesn't equate to love. And I can't base my relationship with Luke on feelings I can't understand or define. Can I?

Meredith squeezes my arm before she joins her husband and the girls to say their goodbyes to Luke.

I glance around the room. Only a few of us left. There must be something to do. There's always something to do. A woman from the church staff is already consolidating the leftover food. I walk the room, gather abandoned cups and napkins along the way, and deposit them in the trash.

Out of the corner of my eye, I watch Luke say goodbye to the mystery family. The woman embraces him, and his body locks tight, his arms barely responding to her hug. She hands him what appears to be a business card. He slips it in his wallet and nods to her. She pauses, raising a hand, looking like she wants to say more, but then exits with her family.

The staff woman carries the last of the food out of the room, leaving Luke and me alone.

He turns toward me, takes one step, then stops and shoves his hands in his pockets.

"How are you?" I ask.

He aims his lifeless eyes at me, and I almost don't recognize him. Luke's energy usually hits a room before he even steps through the door. Today a different man stands before me, in the body of Luke Granger.

"Fine," he says, his voice gruff.

I take two steps in his direction but stop abruptly when he takes one heavy booted step back, holding out his hand as if to fend me off.

I fold my hands in front of me. "I don't know what to do for you."

"There's nothing to be done."

"I would like to—I would like to help you. Comfort you somehow."

"I appreciate that. But he's gone. Like I said, there's nothing to be done about it. I've got to refocus my life. It's time to move on."

His words trickle fear down my spine.

Lean in.

I clear my throat. "What does that mean? Refocus your life. Time to move on."

"This was a mistake."

The fear travels down my limbs into the tips of my fingers and toes.

Lean in.

I swallow. "What was a mistake?"

"This." He throws an arm between us. "You. Me. This." He doesn't look the least bit tortured. He looks . . . he looks blank.

My breath catches, the fear now hitting my bloodstream and running through my veins. “This?” I whisper.

“I’m sorry, Penelope,” he says matter-of-factly. “I can’t do this. I can’t do you and me. I think you’re a good woman. I’m sorry about your injury. I wish you the best in your recovery. But I can’t be with you anymore.”

His declaration rips through me, and I’m paralyzed. I simply stare.

“I wasn’t ever supposed to do this,” he says, pacing, his voice picking up urgency. “It was supposed to be Robert and me.” He pounds his chest. “We could pick up and go anywhere, at any time, wherever we’re needed.”

Luke the panther stalks back and forth, his tail swiping anything that gets in its path. I’m in the room, but I’m not even sure Luke is talking to me.

He stops and scrubs his hands over his face. “I don’t know what I was thinking.”

“You don’t know what you were thinking?”

“I don’t know . . . I was in the Springs for a few days, it was Thanksgiving, I felt a little . . . lonely. And you needed help.”

The panther’s tail swipes at me, hitting me square in the chest for asking for help the first time with the wedding.

“Harlan asked me to stay. So I did a friend a favor. Then you called from the hospital and said you needed me. So I thought, ‘Okay, she needs me here. I can be here.’”

This tail swipe knocks me off-balance for asking for help the second time.

“I stayed too long in Colorado Springs, finding those doctors. I thought I could help you.”

Gaining strength with its momentum, this swipe all but levels me for allowing him to help in my recovery.

I shake my head quickly. “I-I could have—” What? What could I have done differently? Not asked for help? Not accepted his help? If I’ve learned anything over the last month, it’s that asking for help is healthy. Necessary. “I don’t understand, Luke. I asked for help. We grew close. Why is that a bad thing? Why—”

“Because I all but ignored Robert!”

“You said he was hard to get ahold of,” I whisper, my unease almost choking me.

“He took me under his wing. Practically made me into the man I am today. And I have done nothing over the last month but be distracted by you. I put off calling him,” he roars. The panther is unleashed. His sharp teeth bared. Every word dripping with pain. “Not only that, but while I was getting carried away with you—”

Getting carried away with me . . .

“—I didn’t even know he was dying. I ignored all the warning signs. In our spotty communication, he talked about not feeling well. Being tired. Mentioned a doctor’s appointment. And I didn’t follow through with him about it.” He slices a hand through the air. “He kept postponing trips. Told me not to visit him. That he was okay. So I stayed away. I stayed away because I wanted to be with you. And now he’s gone.”

I clutch the side of a chair, regaining my balance after the last blow, when Meredith’s words from earlier whisper to me. *“Grief can be confusing, Penelope. It does really awful things to people.”*

“He’s gone, and I’ve got to continue his legacy. We fly and spread our wings.” He outstretches his arms. “Spread our gifts wide and long, he once told me.”

I clear my throat. “And what about the ranch?”

“Not my circus, not my monkey.” His harsh words slice through me. “I was hired to do a job. I did it. Now I have to move on.”

I take a breath, pushing through the punch he just threw. “Bianca came to the service today.”

“I know.”

“She said she came because this is what you do for family.”

He has the decency to flinch at my statement but says nothing more.

Lean in.

"You're a hypocrite," I whisper.

He pauses, eyes blazing. "Excuse me?"

"You're a hypocrite," I say, my voice gaining strength. "You say the beauty's in the wild, but you can't handle the mess of relationships. You think I'm structured? What is your life, Luke? Make no mistake about it, you live by a set of rules. You don't land long enough in one place to let anything get out of your control. But life's messy with other people in it. *That's* the beauty."

Something in my chest pounds against my ribs, demanding to be let out.

"The numbers," I say to myself, rubbing the spot above my heart. "Those stupid numbers."

"What are you talking about?"

Every emotion and matching number fires at me all at once. Only, instead of maxing out on my scale of ten, they are skyrocketing off the chart. Anxiety is at a twelve. Outrage hits an eighteen. Hurt climbs past thirty-seven. Fear pushes the envelope at sixty-two.

But as my chest rises and falls, I can feel courage. It climbs with a steady pace, handling each feeling one at a time. It nudges anxiety off the rungs like it's weightless. It takes a good swat at outrage, a hard shove at the hurt, then it rears back and kicks fear into the next room. What I didn't understand as courage made each move was that it has a partner. And the second that courage overcame the other feelings, it revealed its power source—the one thing that provided it the strength to push through and dispose of every other feeling.

Love.

Love stands at the top of the ladder, arms held high, conquering every feeling, leaving them destroyed in its wake.

I clutch my chest and whisper, "I love you."

He blinks, his fierce eyes locked on me.

"I love you, Luke. I'd tell you that I love you at a ten, but that's not enough. I love you at a twenty-five. I love you at a two hundred." Hot tears stream down my face. "But those numbers aren't enough. They don't quantify it correctly. They don't say it right." I hiccup a sob. "All of them. All the numbers. I love you all the numbers, Luke Granger."

He stands stock-still, only the muscles at his jaw twitching rapidly.

"I'm a mess. My life took a sharp turn. All my plans went out the window right along with my ability to execute them. I can't do the things I usually do to cope with life. To perform. To prove my worth. I just have to sit in this season of life, wondering what's going to happen next. I'm emotional." I swallow. "I have no idea what to do with these tears, or with this love for you. It's messy." I sear my gaze into his and point my finger to the floor. "But for the first time since my mother died, I'm living. Fully. Feeling. Risking. Living. And I have you to thank for that."

I calm my breathing, step toward him, and place a hand on his arm. I gentle my voice and say, "My question for you, Luke, is are you living? Fully. Feeling. Risking."

His body stays rigid, and I know I have to go.

With no response from him, I walk to the exit. I pause at the doorway, holding the frame and turning his direction. "You once said you wanted to be the safe person for me to love. You got your wish, Luke. I love you. I can't be bothered with whether you're still safe to love or not because it's already done. I love you. Wholly. Completely." I sigh. "So I'm going to return the favor to you. I'm going to be the safe person for you to blame. And I say this with full understanding that I don't know the future, and this might not ever come to fruition. But I'll also be the safe person for you to love."

All my feelings. All the numbers. I leave them scattered on the floor at Luke's feet.

But I take one thing with me.

Peace.

And maybe a significant amount of sadness.

27

I THREW AWAY my armor.

The four-inch heels. The pencil skirts. The flowing silk shirts that screamed femininity with no small amount of power.

I threw it all away.

Okay, in reality, I moved each piece to the back of my closet.

There will be a place for them again, someday. Maybe.

Today, I don upscale gray leggings with a silvery shimmer, a long, navy tunic sweater belted at the waist with a silver chain-link, and a pair of suede platform Steve Madden slip-ons. Gone is the sleek, tight power ponytail. In its place is a clip that holds my hair loosely at the neck.

It's not that I don't like my new clothes. It's that I'm uncomfortable with this new kind of exposure. But there's no place for my armor anymore, no need for it now.

A knock sounds at the back door of Twelve Bluebells, and I reach for the doorknob. Deep breath. Here goes.

When I open the door, Meredith's eyes travel down to my toes and back up to my face. We haven't seen each other since the funeral, but I texted her with the news of Luke's decision about our relationship. "You look amazing," she says, leaning in for a hug. It's a long embrace, a wordless clutch full of the things girls say to each other when they experience a breakup.

I grab a bottle of water for myself and offer Meredith the cup of noncaffeinated hot tea I prepared before her arrival. "Do you want anything to eat?"

"I want everything to eat," she says, patting her stomach. "But I already had breakfast. Thanks, though."

On the way out the door, I pick two folders up from the kitchen counter. Meredith grabs the blankets I set out, and we make our way to the chairs. The heavy metal scrapes against the concrete as we situate them. The second-floor balcony provides ample shade for those who want to lounge on the porch, but this morning, the sun naps behind billowy gray clouds.

Meredith flips the space heater on and drapes her blanket over her legs with one hand, careful not to spill her tea. "Honestly, it's kind of annoying how great you look. When Harlan and I broke up, I didn't shower for days."

"I'm a doer. I went shopping."

"I can see that. And thank you for not asking me to go with you."

I try to hold back a smile.

"I would have gone with you if you had asked, you know. That's how you know I love you."

I tuck my blanket tightly around the edges of my legs, leaning forward to cover the draft between my leggings and my shoes.

Once settled, we both stare across to the vast boardinghouse that sits behind the main house on the ranch. The construction crews blew out a wall and poured concrete. A buzz saw grinds on the other side of the house, prepping two-by-fours for the wooden skeleton of additional square footage Meredith is adding to the existing structure. The smell of fresh sawdust mixed with a hint of the neighboring cow pasture floats across the porch on a chilly winter breeze.

She draws her cup up to her mouth, the steam swirling off the top of the tea. "Do you want to talk about it?"

"Not particularly."

"I figured as much." She takes a sip and swallows. "May I ask you just one question?"

"Yes."

"Did you lean in?"

"With everything I had."

She nods once. "Then maybe there's nothing to talk about."

Nothing except the twisting pain in my stomach that reminds me of the gaping hole that no amount of tasks could fill in the last two days.

I think there's always going to be a twelve-year-old girl in me who aches to be chosen. And I think there's always going to be a trailer-park boy in Luke who doesn't know where he belongs. The triggers will dissipate, but those wounds will always whisper to us.

Both Luke and I have tried for years to prove our worth. But somewhere along the way, we got lost.

The truth is, we're enough.

I'm enough.

Which is why, heading into this meeting with Meredith, I have peace. If this doesn't go the way I want it to, I'll be okay. I will find something different. I'll take a risk for something different. Whatever the case, the urgency I felt for proving myself is no more. I am Penelope. I have strengths. I have limits. No matter where I land, I am enough.

But that doesn't mean that the stakes for the conversation I'm about to initiate aren't high.

"There is something I wanted to discuss with you." I angle my chair so I can face her.

She nods, moves her chair to mirror mine, and resettles the blanket over her body. "What's on your mind?"

I inhale, gathering my courage. Exhale, releasing the outcome of the conversation. "I want to work at Twelve Bluebells."

Her brow furrows. "But you're already involved with the ranch. What do you mean?"

"I want to resign my position with Harlan's company and officially be your program director."

She mouths, *Oh.*

I scoot to the end of my chair, hands folded tightly in my lap. Darn it. I want my pencil skirt. There's too much at risk here for me to be wearing a cousin to yoga pants. "I know I messed up and probably shouldn't be considered for the job. But will you please hear me out?"

"What are you talking about?"

"I was going to ask you to consider me for the position awhile ago. You and Harlan went on your honeymoon and entrusted me with the care of the girls. It was the perfect opportunity for me to show you how I could excel at the job." I sigh, looking over her shoulder. "I knew I didn't have the qualifications, but I thought I could show you what a good fit I was for this facility."

"Penelope—"

"Then I failed. I lost Finley. I failed at my job and I tried to fix it. Made it worse, became injured, and then I wasn't able to work." I shrug. "Not the most ideal candidate for the position."

She opens her mouth, but I hold up my hand and continue. "I brought you two options." I run my hands over the red and blue plastic folders with my possible futures tucked inside its pockets. "The red folder has my proposal for the program director. I know my education isn't an exact match for this job, but I found several graduate programs that would ramp up my qualifications. I've started the application process."

She nods.

"Esther Haverty operates Safe Cove right outside of Dodge City, Kansas. She runs a similar facility and spent several hours helping me map out what I'm about to show you."

"And what's that?"

"I know that in considering me as a candidate, my health might be a concern. The folder contains a contingency plan."

"What does that mean?"

"My headache treatments have gone well, but I'm still managing more migraines than I was before the accident. Dr. Ridding says it's just going to take time." Pictures of the recent brain maps pop into my head. Angry red and orange patterns dissipating, giving way to the more gentle greens and blues. The burning sun finally resting behind the calm of the ocean countryside.

I rub the spine of the red folder. "Knowing I have physical limits was a catalyst for me to brainstorm. I was forced to look at the job differently, and I'm really pleased with the outcome. I created a program I think might be valuable to the girls' leadership development."

A sparkle hits Meredith's eyes, and a surge of confidence runs through me. "Go on," she says.

As we sit, I walk her through the pages in my folder. The overall concept is to give the girls ownership of parts of the functioning halfway house. I would essentially delegate pieces of my job to them. They would act as my assistants. This would serve as a leadership development program while doubling as a backup plan for days when I can't perform all my job duties.

Meredith lifts each page as I talk, stopping a few times to focus on one detail or another. She holds up a piece of paper with a map of South America. "What's this?"

"That's for a more advanced stage in the program." I bite the edge of my lip. "Something to think about in the future."

"Yes?" The question lingers in her eyes.

"Overseas service work would expose the residents to other cultures, develop other-mindedness, and instill compassion. I don't have all the details fleshed out, but I was looking at different partnerships for this kind of thing. It would involve support raising and cultural training. A kind of graduate-level work, if you will. Something to cap off the leadership program as a whole."

"And does the partner you have in mind come in the form of a man in well-fitting cargo pants?"

Heat hits my face, and I feel sadness. "It did at one point. But there are alternate options out there."

She leans back, places the papers in her lap, and folds her hands. Using a tone that's half business, half plotting, she says, "I would think you'd need extra travel days in your schedule for you and your partner to scope the locations beforehand, get the lay of the land."

Meredith is such a romantic, I know she's talking about partnering with Luke. But my broken heart keeps me grounded. "Meredith, as much as I want Luke to show me the world, I can't depend on him to come around and be on board."

"Maybe not." She taps on the folder. "But this is a good idea. It has potential."

Yes. It has potential.

"Anything else you want me to know? Since, in spite of me wearing sweatpants, this is apparently a job interview?"

I stare her square in the eyes. "Meredith. I belong here," I whisper.

Leaning forward, she grabs my hands and whispers back with a watery smile, "I know." She nods to the blue folder in my lap. "What's in that folder?"

This moment is like the Choose Your Own Adventure books my mother bought me from the used bookstore around the corner from our apartment. Choose the red folder and Penelope stays in Colorado Springs. Choose the blue folder and Penelope moves away.

I hated those books. Why did a story have to change? "Predictability is a luxury you don't want to afford," my mother would say. Maybe she was right.

The beauty's in the wild. Lean in.

"In the event that you deem it necessary to hire someone else as program director," I say, "the work files are organized in such a way that the transition will be seamless."

Meredith crosses her arms over her chest. "Let me guess. You have recommendations for your replacement?"

"Yes."

"That sounds about right." She taps her finger on her lips. "Three candidates?"

"Five."

"Of course."

"Four of them are local, including Daphne Fielding, even though—full disclosure—I think she would rather focus on developing the art program at the ranch instead of running it. You should hear her talk about a project she wants to do with the girls that ties into her graduate studies." A project she's almost heartbreakingly passionate about, and the longer I watch her at work, the more I want to know. "But I really like the candidate from Virginia. She's willing to move, and I wondered if it would seal the deal if we paid her moving costs."

"Your five candidates, even Miss Virginia, won't have what you have to offer these girls."

"You haven't seen their résumés yet."

"Penelope," Meredith almost growls. "You wanted to prove that you were capable of taking care of the girls while we were on our honeymoon? When we returned, Bianca spoke her first sentence to me that wasn't filled with a bad cliché from her past. Nothing remotely coherent for the first ten weeks of her stay, then I leave for my honeymoon, you set up drum lessons for her, and she's speaking sentences."

Luke is the one who bought her the set. I open my mouth to point that out, but she says, "And I suspect you are the reason why, for the last four days, Tanya has walked around with her head held a little higher, using advanced vocabulary correctly for the first time in months."

I look away, sigh, then focus on her again. "And what about Finley?"

"I don't blame you for Finley. You're the one who has to forgive yourself for her leaving. And, I'd like to point out, it's wasted forgiveness because it wasn't your fault she left in the first place."

I purse my lips. Maybe someday her words will sink in, but today Finley's situation still stings.

"I have news that may come as a shock to you," she says, leaning forward. "It may be very true that you love these women more fiercely than the rest of us."

Not knowing how to reply, I tuck a strand of hair behind my ear, warmth spreading through my chest.

"And you have something that only you can offer them. You and I might not talk about it a lot, but your history gives you great strength at Twelve Bluebells. You know what people need and how to get it for them before they understand what's happening. The tasks you do behind the scenes protect and love the girls in ways that they won't ever truly understand. What they do know is that instead of feeling sorry for them, you respect them. You hand them their dignity without having to say a word about it. You forge a complete and total belief in each of them that spurs them to grow as women."

I hold out my hand. "That's you, Meredith. That's not me—"

"Oh, Penelope. Twelve Bluebells may have been my creation, but you? You breathe life into it."

How can that be? I would have lived all my years working on the west side of the fence property line with Harlan. But the east side of the fence beckoned to me. Pursued me. Gave me a place to belong.

Twelve Bluebells breathed life back into *me*.

She leans back and picks up her drink. "Do you have a paper shredder?"

"Of course I have a shredder. What respectable working

woman doesn't have a shredder? That's like asking if I have a label maker. Or Post-it notes."

"Post-it notes are a modern-day miracle."

"Exactly. And paper shredders are an office supply evolutionary phenomenon. So yes, I have a shredder. Why?"

"I'm hiring you as my program director, and I need you to take whatever's in this blue folder and shred it to pieces. Then throw it in the recycling for good measure."

Several days have passed since I've felt like smiling, but as I stare at Meredith Holcombe, our future sitting in the boardinghouse in front of us, I smile so wide that my cheeks hurt.

"Consequently"—she takes a sip of her tea—"what was your backup plan? Where would you have gone if you didn't get the job here?"

"Blake Hartwright wants me to be his personal assistant."

"The head coach of the Arizona Cardinals?"

"Yeah."

"But you don't know anything about football."

"Apparently I studied enough that I aced my interview."

"Figures," she said, glancing across the field. She throws a hand over her mouth. "Oh, wow. My husband's about to have a very bad day. He lost his assistant. And he lost the opportunity to steal your free game tickets, which you invariably would not have used. Both because his wife stole you right from under his nose. He's never going to forgive me."

"You're going to have to play the baby card."

She snaps her fingers. "I'm going to have to play the baby card. Brilliant." She leans over, takes my hand in hers, and lowers her voice. "It's going to be brilliant having you on board, Penelope."

My eyes well up, and I whisper, "Thank you."

I lean back in my chair, drawing my knees to my chest. But as I pull the blanket up, something shrill whines out.

Meredith sits up straight, eyes shooting to the boardinghouse. "What was that? Was that the buzz saw?"

I shove to my feet just as a flailing girl turns the corner of the main house and comes into view.

The sound isn't the screech of the buzz saw. It's the high-pitched, scratchy yell of Finley. A struggling, bruised, bloody, and broken Finley.

28

"LG SECURITY. This is Mary. How may I help you?" the woman asks at the other end of the line.

With Finley's injured body slumped against me in the back seat of Meredith's Jeep Grand Cherokee, I hold the phone up to my ear. "Mary, my name is Penelope Reid. Our property at Twelve Bluebells Ranch is an existing client. I need to report that a threat has been made."

"Yes, ma'am." I hear clicking in the background. "Have you called the police?"

"I have. They're sending a unit over now." One to the house. One to the hospital.

"Are you on the property now?"

"No. I just wanted to call this in. Luke—" Shoot. "Mr. Granger set up extra security for us about six weeks ago. I thought he would want to know. I called him directly, but my call went to his voicemail." Twice.

"Yes, ma'am. He's unavailable. But I'll send another associate out to the property right away to see if there's been a breach with the system cameras or wires."

Unavailable. Unavailable to everyone? Or just unavailable to me?

"Ma'am, you mentioned a threat?"

I shake my head. I can't go down a rabbit hole and make assumptions. He could be out of town, for all I know. *Focus, Penelope.* "Yes. A threat. Marcus Skelly assaulted one of our residents while she was off property, then threatened to track her down and kill her if she returned to Twelve Bluebells. We're taking her to the hospital now." While I give her the location and ETA, Finley moans, her arm clutching her side.

"We're almost there, sweetheart," Meredith calls from the front seat.

In the few minutes of chaos after her arrival, Finley told us that she left Marcus's place after he passed out. With no way to know how long before he would wake up and go on the rampage again—and who knows what recreational drugs he might have consumed—Meredith and I decided everyone should leave the property. We relieved the construction crew of their duties, loaded into Meredith's car, and I started the process of texting and making calls.

Harlan's cutting a business meeting short so he can meet us at the hospital. For good measure, Harlan's mom has Alex and they are heading to the mall.

After I call the hospital to let them know of our impending arrival, I tap out a text to Bianca and Tanya.

> Girls, please do not go to the ranch after work today. Marcus is unstable and probably headed there. Meredith and I are taking Finley to the hospital. I will send updates as I receive them.

With a wheelchair and hospital attendant awaiting us, Finley receives immediate attention. I'm only able to catch a few of the words flying around the room before we're asked to leave. Possible broken ribs. Need to check for internal bleeding. Facial X-ray.

I instruct the nurse manning the ER desk of our whereabouts in case the police or anyone else arrives.

Meredith and I enter the waiting room, and I point to a light blue couch. "Sit."

She paces three steps. "Sit? How am I supposed to sit?"

I had no choice but to allow her to drive, but her high-risk pregnancy was adding weight to my shoulders the entire car ride to the hospital. I place a hand on her arm, stopping her movement, and gentle my tone. "Please, Meredith. I need you to sit and take some deep breaths. And I need you to let me handle the remaining details."

She stares at me a moment, nods, and sinks into the thick damask fabric. The pastel painting of the Rocky Mountains sits crooked above her on the beige-colored wall. It seems to be the only thing out of place in this well-kept room. Even the coffee maker offers a designer label and various pod flavors.

A sharp pang pounds in the left side of my head. I take a deep breath. That's fine. Expected, even. In light of these circumstances, a migraine is inevitable. But I'll take a headache over the kind of consequences Meredith could experience if she puts too much stress on her body.

Digging through my purse, I find the medication I'm looking for. After grabbing a free water from the mini fridge, I gulp down the pill. Out of habit, I glance around the room for Luke. No matter where I am, I've been doing this for several days, and I get the same disappointing result each time. No Luke. But this time more than the others, it feels like he should be here.

"Ms. Reid?"

I turn, and a uniformed police officer looks at me in question.

"Yes," I say.

Harlan storms into the room, a thunderous look aimed at Meredith. He takes a knee in front of her, cups her face, and kisses her gently.

I look at the officer, and he offers a kind smile through his thick gray mustache. With his robust belly, I wonder if he doubles as Santa Claus at Christmastime.

Once Harlan is convinced that Meredith is fine, she and I debrief the men.

"What are we going to do?" Meredith asks. "She needs protection."

"I don't know that I'm comfortable bringing Finley back to the ranch." Harlan runs his hands through his hair. "I want her to be safe. And I don't want to endanger anyone else."

"I think I know how to help her," I say. All heads turn toward me. "But she's going to have to want to go."

I walk to the corner of the room, sit in a chair, and start making calls, hating every piece of pain that led Finley here. But hoping it gives her the resolve she needs to leave.

Marcus's boot broke three of Finley's ribs but, thankfully, didn't hit any internal organs. Her retina is in place, but her cheek is fractured. The emergency room doctor quietly declared Finley lucky, but as the purple bruising deepens its color across her pale face, it's hard to agree.

With all of us in the room watching, Finley sits on her hospital bed and responds to the police officer's questions with short answers. She's not avoiding the questions, but her winces tell me short answers minimize the pain.

There's nothing jolly about the officer when his concerned eyes focus on Finley at the end of the interview and he says, "I'm worried about your safety."

She holds up her hand and whispers two words, her voice cracking, making them indecipherable.

"What's that, sweetie?" Meredith asks.

Finley clears her throat. "No more." Her scratchy voice projects into the room.

Meredith steps toward her. "No more what, Finley?"

"I can't do this anymore." She looks at me. "I can't be around him anymore."

"Okay," I say, touching her leg. "You don't have to be around him anymore."

A tear runs down her fractured cheek. "He's going to kill me."

"No. He's not."

"What am I going to do? I can't go back to Twelve Bluebells. He'll find me." She draws a hand up to her face and covers her eyes as the tears run more quickly. "I don't have any family. I don't have anywhere else to go."

I pull a chair up to the side of her bed and take her hand in mine. "You have family. You just don't know them yet."

By the time I finish telling Finley about Safe Cove, she's ready to get in the car and leave Colorado Springs behind. Program director Esther Haverty and I formed a tight bond while I was doing research for my job proposal. When I called earlier today, she confirmed that they have a bed for Finley, as well as a job interview upon her arrival. But there are some contingencies.

"Finley," I say, "everyone is on board with getting you to your new home, but we need to know that you aren't ever going to contact Marcus again."

She wraps an arm around her body and grazes her knuckles over her injured ribs. "I won't. I promise."

"You have to give me your cell phone. We'll buy you a cheap burner to use until you get your feet on the ground. But if he's been paying the bill on this one, he'll have access to it and track you down eventually."

Finley stares at her hands, nodding slowly.

"Harlan's going to go to Marcus's place accompanied by an officer. He'll get your things for you. Do you have any instructions you want to give him?"

"I don't want my things," she says to her lap. "It's just clothes."

"Are you sure?"

She looks up at me with fear-filled eyes and lowers her voice. "I don't want anyone to go back there."

Once we solidify the plan, everyone disperses. Meredith places a quick phone call to Tanya with instructions. Tanya and Bianca will get off work for lunch at noon, head to Walmart to stock up on clothes and toiletries for Finley, then drive to the hospital to say their goodbyes. Harlan fields calls to LG Security with updates on the ranch. He also fills Meredith's car with gas for the trip.

I'll be taking Finley to Dodge City. Meredith can't make the drive with a high-risk pregnancy. Harlan offered, but he should stay home with Meredith. Luke is—well, not here, I guess. Or maybe he is here. Whatever the case, the drive's just over five hours. Finley and I can stay at a hotel if we can't make it all the way to the facility, but if we drive straight through, Esther herself will be waiting to welcome Finley to her home.

I'm not sure what kind of threat Marcus poses. But the more we plan, the more peace we all seem to have about getting Finley to a safe place. It feels to our advantage to move quickly while Marcus sleeps off whatever substances he has most likely consumed.

Short-term safety is important, yes. But with each discussion, Finley's voice becomes a little stronger, and it seems that she knows she's making decisions for her long-term safety as well. She only asked a few questions about the facility. But that's a good sign in the midst of a terrible day.

With little traffic during a midday drive and Finley sleeping in the car most of the way, our trip to Dodge City went well. Aside from the part where I had endless time on my hands to think about Luke. Miles and miles of concrete passing under the tires. Miles and miles of second-guessing passing through my head. Thank goodness Finley didn't see the tears I wiped away while we drove down the road.

But now, standing here in front of the doorway of Finley's new home, I'm not sure I can hide these tears from her.

Finley slowly turns in a circle, looking around. "This place isn't bad."

No, the huge colonial home doesn't seem bad at all.

"I never thought not having a family would be a good thing. But it made it easier to leave Colorado Springs," she says.

Yes, I suppose not having family connections would make it easier to leave.

"Except I don't want to leave Twelve Bluebells." She takes my hand. "Or you, Penny Lady."

"You haven't lost us. The officer said the prosecutor will contact you at some point, so be on the lookout for that call. If you need anything during the court proceedings, we'll be available. But past that, Finley, I'm sorry. There's just no way you're getting rid of us."

A half smile tips her mouth. "I keep thinking that I should be stressed out because I don't know what's going to happen next. Where will I work? How will I find friends? But I'm just so relieved to be getting away that I don't care right now."

"There's freedom in not knowing, isn't there?" I cock my head, pondering my own words. "In the meantime, we have phones and FaceTime, and five hours isn't that long of a drive."

She studies me. "You're working on one of your headaches, aren't you," she says as a statement. Finley, my sweet caretaker. "You need to get some rest."

"I will."

"Marcus is the one who trashed the chapel the night before Meredith's wedding. He told me after I left the ranch. He'd been stalking me and saw the wedding preparations."

I nod. That information doesn't seem important now. Except that it led me to Luke.

Her face crumples, and she wraps her arms around me. "I'm so sorry. What he did to you. I just didn't—I thought that I could change him—" Tears engulf her apology.

"You can't control Marcus's choices. I don't blame you for what he did to me. You shouldn't either." I pull her in, trying not to squeeze too tightly around her ribs, but not wanting to let her go. "You'll get through this, Finley. You'll heal. You'll find your bouncy step again. And you will shine. You'll shine so brightly."

Dead to the world. I want to be dead to the world. After an unbelievably long day that ended with a drive-through dinner and a healthy dose of migraine medication, all I want in life is to continue this nap. But my feet are so cold that I've started to shiver. What is wrong with the heat in this hotel?

I check my phone for the time, but it's dead. Shoot. With such an intense day of phone calls, texts, maps, and web searches, it's no surprise my battery ran out of power. I fumble through my purse, find my backup charger, and get my phone set up.

The digital clock tells me it's almost ten, which means I only slept ninety minutes. With the lamp on. Such a dissatisfying nap. But the good news is, my migraine is gone. I'll probably have a few more hours of being sensitive to triggers, but I should be able to sleep off the tail end of this headache.

Scanning the walls of the room, I find the thermostat. I walk over. "Sixty-three degrees?" I say to no one. As I punch the up arrow ten notches, my phone alerts me to a new text.

I crawl back under the puffy white duvet and curl onto my side. Before I can check my messages, the phone rings and Luke's name pops onto my screen. My stomach flips, and I pause just a second before I answer.

"Hello?"

"Where are you?" he barks into my ear.

I glance at the caller ID, making sure this is his number. "Luke?"

"Where are you?"

"Is something wrong?"

"Where. Are. You?"

Something must have happened at the ranch. I sit up straight, my legs hanging off the side of the bed. "What happened?"

"Penelope, are you at your hotel in Dodge City?"

"Yes," I say, holding my arm out in exasperation. "Did something happen at the ranch?"

He sighs. "You about gave us all a heart attack."

"You're not making any sense."

"I'm not making sense?" he yells. "We've all been trying to get ahold of you for over an hour now."

"Stop yelling into the phone, Luke, or I'm going to hang up."

He gentles his voice. "You've got a headache. Of course you have a headache after the day you've had. Is it a bad one?"

"It was bad. But I took my meds and took a nap." I rub the scar at my eyebrow. "Can you please explain to me why you're so upset?"

"Yeah, actually. I'd really like to explain to you why I'm so upset." His deep voice hints that he's not just talking about this phone call.

I pull the phone down to see the screen. Nine missed calls and fourteen texts from Harlan, Meredith, and Luke.

"Penelope?" Luke calls.

"Hang on. Let me text Meredith and Harlan that I'm okay." I make quick business of sending apologies to the Holcombes while Luke remains on the line. Then I rummage through my purse, find my AirPods, place them in my ears, and settle against the faux-leather headboard that's screwed to the hotel wall. "Okay, I'm back."

"Why weren't you answering your phone?" he asks.

"It died while I was taking a nap. Again, why are you so upset?"

"How was I supposed to know Marcus didn't follow you to Dodge City—and harm you—if you weren't answering your phone and no one had heard from you?"

"Fair enough. But Meredith knew I made it to the room."

"Look at your hotel phone, Penelope."

"What?"

"The hotel phone. Probably by your bed. What is it doing?"

One glance and I know why he's so upset. "It's off the hook."

"Yeah," he growls. "It's off the hook. And your cell phone was going straight to voicemail."

"Sorry," I say sheepishly.

A text alert dings, and I smile at Meredith's message.

> Glad you're fine. I told Luke you were. Mr. Cargo Pants can get bossy.

Everything must be well at the ranch if Meredith's making jokes.

"Are you okay?" I ask.

"Am I okay?" He blows out a long breath. "I was surveying a farm in the middle of nowhere Nebraska, with no idea that I didn't have any cell reception until the owner finally tracked me down. He told me Mary called and said it was urgent. Then I spent the rest of the afternoon trying to manage the situation in Colorado Springs remotely while figuring out how to get home as quickly as possible."

Good. I'm glad he checked on the ranch. "That sounds stressful."

"That's not the worst of it."

"No?" I ask, drawing my knees up to my chest.

"Ever since Mary said Twelve Bluebells was involved, I've had trouble breathing. It's like someone's sitting on my chest." He pauses. "I was so worried about you." His voice cracks.

"Luke." I pick at a spot on the bedspread. "I'm okay."

"All I could think was that something was going to happen to you, and you'd never know."

I wrap my arms around my legs and hug them to me. "I'd never know what?"

"That I got it wrong." His deep voice sounds thick. "I didn't know it, but I got it wrong."

A cautious hope trickles down my spine. "What did you get wrong?"

"There was a woman at Robert's funeral. She came with her two daughters and some friends of theirs. Carol Reynolds."

He must be talking about the woman I noticed crying. "Carol Reynolds?"

"Robert's fiancée."

Luke's mentor had a fiancée.

The air hangs heavy between us.

"I had lunch with Carol. She laid out their entire relationship. Met him a few years ago, and he fought their connection the entire time. But she said he broke down and they got engaged. He wanted to tell me, was waiting to introduce me, but he got cancer. Then, she said, it was all about him trying to beat the cancer in time for their wedding. Didn't let anyone know, really, how bad it was." His voice clogs with emotion, and he's silent for a few beats.

I turn my head to the side and rest my cheek on my knees, trying to imagine what it would be like to learn too late that your friend had met his future wife. But more, that he was sick.

Tragic. At the very least, profoundly sad because you didn't get the chance to say goodbye to the person you revered, the only father figure in your life, the one who shaped you into the man you are today.

"I've spent the last week trying to wrap my head around something Carol said."

I clear my throat. "What's that?"

"She said Robert told her he had one regret. That he fought his feelings for her and lost time he could've been married to her and doing life with her." He pauses, and I can almost feel his pain through the phone. Then he whispers, agony in his voice, "That's what I got wrong, Penelope."

"What did you get wrong?"

"I shouldn't have wasted more time. I should have told you the truth. I should have told you what I wanted."

Lean in.

"And what do you want?" I whisper.

"I still want to do what I've been doing. I like my business. And I want to continue traveling for service work."

Tears sting my eyes, and I cover my face with my hands.

"I just want to do it all with you by my side."

A sob escapes my lips.

"Or maybe it's me by your side."

My shoulders start to shake.

"Baby?"

Baby. Tears stream down my face.

"Penelope?"

"I missed you," I whisper, and my lower lip wobbles.

"Baby." His voice rumbles through my ears, down to the very tips of my toes.

Three knocks sound at the door, and I jump, my heart pounding out of my chest. "Someone's at the door."

"Then you need to answer it."

"What if it's Marcus?" I pull the covers up to my chest. Great. Now Luke has me freaked out.

"Penelope." Luke's voice gentles, sounding closer to me than through the phone. "I think if you answer the door, you'll find that the person behind it knows how to back a trailer."

"What?" I shoot out of bed, throw my AirPods and phone on the side table, swipe away my tears, and rush to open the door.

With his hands braced on either side of the doorframe, Luke crowds my doorway. I barely get a look at his layer of stubble and bloodshot eyes. Intense eyes that burn the moment he sees me, just before he steps into my room, wraps his arms around me, and shoves his face in the crook of my neck.

I run my fingertips up and down his cropped hair. "I thought you said you were going home."

He lifts his head so his face is just a few inches from mine. "I am home," he whispers against my mouth. He presses his lips to mine with an urgency, as if he's scared that if he doesn't communicate everything he needs to in this one kiss, I'll run away. He gives me deep, wild kisses with his hands cupping my face, then moving through my hair. Then the kisses turn beautiful as he cradles my head, holding me to him, slowing us to a sweet, gentle ending.

He pulls back but keeps his forehead pressed to mine, our breaths tangling, fighting for oxygen. "I'm sorry, Penelope. I got it all wrong. And I took my grief out on you. And I'm so sorry."

"It's okay." I lift up to kiss him once.

"And that speech you gave me the other night—"

I stand on tiptoes to kiss him again.

"It was wild, out of control, and the most beautiful thing I've ever heard."

One more kiss.

"And I love you. All the numbers. I love you too."

I wrap my arms around his shoulders, pulling him down to me, and nuzzle my face into his neck.

He tightens his hold, angles his head down, and says into my ear, "There's my kitten."

My mother's words almost float through the air. "*The daughter of a lion is still a lion.*" She would have loved Luke. She would have loved Luke for me. Puzzle pieces that need each other—that fit together.

"Wait." I draw back and look around the room. "How did you get here?"

"I rented a car in Lincoln and drove almost six hours."

"I thought you went back to Colorado Springs."

"My guys have a handle on things. Plus, I didn't like the idea of you driving Finley here all by yourself."

"Does that mean you need a ride back to Colorado?"

"Am I going to have to listen to hippie music all the way home?"

"Yes. Are you going to chew on a toothpick all the way home?"

He grins, his eyes glittering. "Yes."

"Then let's get the heck out of Dodge," I say. When my words hit me, I cover my mouth and let out a combination laugh and snort. "Get it? We're in Dodge City. Get the heck out of Dodge?"

Luke pulls me in tight, his hands splayed on the small of my back. His lips twitch, but his voice takes on a serious tone when he says, "Before we go, I need to lay something out in the open. A confession of sorts. Give you the freedom to change your mind now before we take this any further."

My spine straightens, all my senses on alert. What on earth . . .

"Not too far down the road, I suspect there will come a time when I'll give you a piece of jewelry for your finger, and we'll wear specific kinds of clothes to say certain vows, and we'll figure out where we want to live. Together."

The air swooshes out of my lungs, and I sway in his arms. I swallow. "You don't waste time, do you?"

His eyes flash. "Not when I know what I want. You belong to me."

"Yes," I say, breathless.

He kisses me. "And I belong to you."

"Yes."

He kisses me again. "And I can't actually back a trailer to save my life."

My body had already decided to lean in for the next kiss, but at his confession, I freeze. "What?" I blink.

He shoots me a blinding smile. "Baby, I can't back a trailer. Never have been able to. Collectively, I think I've destroyed three pieces of property while a trailer was hitched to the back of my truck."

I giggle. "Three?"

"U-Haul won't rent them to me anymore."

"Are you serious?" I ask through my laughter.

"As serious as the stop sign I mowed over in college when I was moving into a rental house."

I shake my head. “This is amazing.”

“What I need to know is, in light of this information, will I be able to show my face at the ranch?”

Cocking my head, I tap my lips as if I have to think about this. “Well, as the official program director at Twelve Bluebells Ranch, I feel like I could pull a few strings. Give you a pass.”

His beautiful face lights with recognition, then softens with pride. “You did it.”

I beam at him. “I did it.”

He kisses me again, this time drawing out sweet affection.

When we break, I gaze up at him. “Good news for you, though, that you’d end up with me.”

“Oh yeah? How’s that?”

“I’m excellent at backing a trailer. It’s like threading a needle.”

29

"SIX?" I ASK LUKE, rinsing off a plate in the kitchen sink at the ranch. "Did you say six?"

"Yeah," he says, taking the plate from my hands and drying it. With the sleeves of his Henley rolled up to his elbows, his sinewy arms working while he helps me with the dishes, it's hard to concentrate on this morning's topic. But when he mentioned his latest idea, I became laser focused on the conversation.

I turn to him, resting my hip on the counter. "You want six kids?"

"Yeah."

"Why?"

"The roller-coaster effect," he says, as if I have any clue what that means.

I raise my eyebrows.

"You have to have your kids in even numbers so when you go to an amusement park"—he sets the plate in a cabinet—"everyone has someone to ride with."

My mouth gapes. "You're either completely lovable or totally ridiculous."

He grins. "I vote for completely lovable."

"But why six? Why can't you start off with two kids? Or even four?"

"Ah. So you'd consider four." He throws the towel on the counter, slips his arms around my waist, and pulls me to him.

I shake my head, placing my hands on his biceps. "You did that on purpose."

He moves slowly toward me, a sly look in his eyes, then he kisses me once. Quick but sweet.

"You did," I say. "You maneuvered the conversation so I'd agree to four kids."

"I've got to get my hits in while your brain is still healing. I won't have a chance in this relationship when you're running at full capacity."

"Well, I'm rethinking this entire relationship." I'm rethinking our relationship, the jeans and fitted flannel tunic I'm wearing, and my invitation for him to come to breakfast this morning.

One more kiss, this time soft and slow.

And now I'm rethinking my rethinking. Or really, not thinking at all. I'm just breathing heavy.

He smooths his hand over my back. "What do you have planned this morning?"

"Tanya mentioned she wants to get baptized, but she wants to do it in the chapel on the Holcombe property. I'm going to take measurements to see if we could use a big water trough as a baptistry. It might be a tight fit on that small stage."

"I'll walk you over there. Harlan and I are going to sight in our guns today. He's getting the target set up now."

"Sometimes I forget I'm dating an Olympian." I give him a kiss, then step out of his hold. "Are you making him do all the dirty work?"

"He's in charge of the protective eyewear and headphones. I have to give him something to do that he can feel good about. He's a terrible shot."

"Worse than his dancing?"

"It's a toss-up."

As we walk down the hallway to the front of the house, we pass by the wall of family photos.

Luke stops and points to one of my mother and me. "Hey, this one's new."

I smile. "I hung it yesterday."

Of the entire lot of ruined, double-exposure pictures from the day my mother and I shared at the beach, the best picture is a close-up of our faces. A selfie taken before selfies were all the rage. It was a spontaneous shot my mother took.

I couldn't believe she was going to use one of our precious twenty-four pictures on a shot that might or might not turn out well. But looking back, I realize it was so very much my mother. She saw a moment, drew me close, and risked taking that shot. It came out perfectly. Or almost perfectly. Our faces are at a diagonal just a touch. What is truly exquisite about this double-exposure photo is that the flower shot taken from the week before layers our faces in a delicate border, only overlapping in a few spots.

Running my finger down the edge of the black frame, I say, "It's my favorite."

"Do you want your coat?" he asks as I open the front door.

"No. I'm not going to be that long." I slip my phone into the pocket of my tunic.

"Did you hear from Jason?"

"Not yet."

"You sent him an olive branch. He'll respond at some point after he's licked his wounds a little longer."

I hadn't heard from him in so long, I wrote him a letter just telling him what he has meant to me. Not an apology for breaking his heart. But maybe some closure for both of us. And an open door to call when he's ready.

Luke and I walk hand in hand and cross west of the fence to the

Holcombe property. No wind today and the sun shines brightly, but there's still a bite in the air.

About twenty feet from the door to the chapel, I stop. "Shoot. I left the measuring tape."

"I'll go get it."

"No, no. You go on." I lift up on my toes and touch my lips to his. "It's a little chillier out here than I realized. I'll grab my coat too."

Luke splits off to meet up with Harlan, and I head back to the house. After rummaging through a kitchen drawer, I find a small measuring tape. Out of the corner of my eye, I catch my AirPods. I put them in my ears and turn on some soft piano music. Once at the door, I put on my trench coat, transfer my phone and measuring tape to one of its pockets, and head back to the chapel.

As I cross the field, my boots eat up the crunchy grass. A shot fires in the distance. I use my hand as a visor to block out the sun and squint. About half a football field away stand two men. Though I can't see their faces, one is a little more handsome than the other.

After I pull the unlocked door of the chapel open, I step inside the small room and pause, allowing my eyes time to adjust. Sunlight sifts through the windowpanes and angles toward the center aisle. Dust particles catch the light, floating to the ground on a shimmer. I walk toward the stage with delicate music in my ears and a smile on my lips and wonder if someday Luke will stand at the end of this short walk waiting for me to join him.

With the measuring tape and my phone, I make note of the square footage of the small stage. I stand on the far edge of the room, facing the eastern windows, and record my last number into the phone, the final notes of a song playing through my AirPods.

"Where is Finley?" a voice booms from behind me.

I spin around and stare at a seething Marcus. No. I stare down the barrel of a handgun about ten feet from me, attached to the jittery hands of a seething Marcus.

My heart pounds, and I gulp down a breath.

"I said, where is she?" Glassy eyes. Stringy hair. Filthy clothes. Marcus's uniform of choice. But this time a hint of eerie craze laces his expression and spikes fear through my core.

I hold out a hand. "Marcus, will you please put the gun down and we can talk about this?"

"If you don't tell me where she is, there isn't going to be anything to talk about." He points the gun to the ceiling, fires, and debris falls between us.

I jump, the loud blast from the shot reverberating through my head, rivaling any migraine I've ever experienced. Bile crawls up my throat, and I swallow it down. He didn't even hesitate to pull the trigger.

"I'm not messin' with you. Where's Finley? I've been looking for her for days. Her phone's disconnected. She stole all my money and left." Each statement he makes is filled with expletives, and his gun wobbles in my direction. Then he shoots again—this time the bullet splits the wood of a pew just two rows from me.

I jump back, my heart pounding out of my chest. He's going to kill me.

My phone rings, and I almost come out of my skin.

"Turn that thing off," he roars.

Luke's name flashes on the screen. I hold my hands out and slowly turn the screen toward him. "Marcus, it's Luke. He's not far away on the ranch. If I don't answer this, he'll come straight here."

He cocks his head, the crazed look in his eyes almost glowing. "Get rid of him. And if you say one thing wrong, I'll shoot."

I tap my AirPods to answer the call, pointing and using exaggerated movements so Marcus can see what I'm doing. "Hi, Luke."

"Hey, baby. Harlan and Meredith invited us to dinner tonight.

Before I accepted, I thought I'd do the dutiful boyfriend thing and see if we had any plans."

"No, we don't have any plans tonight." I try to keep my voice level, but even I can hear a hint of stress in the words.

"Is everything okay?" he asks.

Marcus tries to communicate something, mouthing words and pointing to his ear.

I frantically shake my head and shrug.

In a low voice he says, "Put it on speakerphone."

"Is someone there with you?" Luke asks.

My eyes widen, and I hold my finger to my mouth to shush Marcus, ignoring his demand. "Oh, it's just Jimmy. I figured out we need to bring more pews in for the baptism. But you're going to have to do it because he can't back a trailer."

A pause. "Marcus is there." Luke's voice comes through the AirPods with a deadly tone, along with some clicks in the background I can't decipher.

"Yeah," I say conversationally.

"Weapon?"

"The Nelsons are loaded, and they've already paid for two baptisms." I internally cringe. I have no idea if he'll understand what I just said.

"If he's discharged his weapon twice, he has at least four rounds left and he's not afraid to use them." Luke talks rapidly through the scenario. "I'm looking through my scope and I can see the stained glass window, but I can't see any shadows. I need you to get his center mass lined up with the center of the sun on the window, but this is important, Penelope. You need to be to one side or the other of him. When you get him lined up in front of the sun, say the word 'now' and I'll shoot. And I won't miss, baby. Promise. Do it now."

A sun sits right in the center of the stained glass window, pieces of yellow and orange glass bursting outward and breaking up the blue sky made of glass. This is all happening so fast, I don't have time to consider the implications of what Luke is telling me to do. I just know I need to do it. I need to get Marcus lined up with the sphere of the sun.

Marcus's wild eyes glare at me, the dragon on his neck breathing fire right along with them. He waves his gun and I back up, stumbling on the foot of the pew next to me.

"Talk to you later. Love you." I turn the phone to me, swiftly switching the call setting from AirPods to speakerphone. As I slip the phone in my coat pocket, I yank out the AirPods and hold them out to him. "It's over. I hung up. The call's over." I drop the earpieces on the ground, hoping he takes this as proof of my ending the call.

He holds the gun over his head and shoots a third round into the ceiling. "If that phone rings again, you're done."

I just need him to move toward my side of the chapel about two feet for his chest to line up with the center of the sun.

I hold my shaking hands out toward him, slightly bending at the knees, as if I'm coaxing a small child to come out from under the bed. "Marcus, if you'll come with me"—I throw one of my arms toward the side door next to me—"I'll take you to Finley. She's not that far from here."

"You better not be lying, or I'll kill you both," he says.

When he takes one step forward, I yell, "NOW!" at the top of my lungs.

The glass sun shatters behind him, and I dive for cover as Marcus shouts and drops to the ground.

"Happy First Partial Day Back at Work to you," Luke says with a grin, a toothpick sticking out of his mouth. It's Monday morning, a month after our trip to Dodge City. A month after Luke shattered a stained glass window. A month after Marcus lost his right arm and went to jail.

Luke stands in my kitchen dressed in black cargo pants and a black fleece bearing the LG Security logo. At least some things in life are still predictable.

He waves a rectangular package wrapped in Wonder Woman paper. Transparent tape crinkles the paper in uneven lines, resembling a child's wrap job—what I'm coming to know as Luke's endearing style.

I smile and cock my head. "Dr. Ridding only released me to try two hours, Luke. This hardly seems like a celebration." Only two hours of work, but I still did my full hair and makeup. No heels, though. I'm starting to get accustomed to my new casual wear. Though Meredith claims my heather-gray sweater dress, black leggings, and low-heel boots aren't truly casual. I told her baby steps.

"That's fine." Luke holds his gift out of my reach. "Would you rather go back to staring at the walls?"

"Never mind. Hand me the package." I stand on my tiptoes and reach for the box.

"I could also arrange for you to watch some paint dry."

I jump up, but he turns and uses his body to deflect my effort.

"I'm sure Dr. Ridding could come up with more treatment plans."

Placing a hand on his chest, I slowly lean in, yank the toothpick out of his mouth, and press my lips to his. He wraps an arm around me and returns the kiss.

I pull back. "I've been wanting to do that since that first day in the chapel."

"Which part? Yank a toothpick out of my mouth or kiss me?"

"Both. So it's a total bonus that I got to combine them for the same purpose today."

He grins. "You're such an overachiever."

"Efficiency is my—"

"Love language. And in this case, I'm very grateful it is," he says right before a short kiss.

"Does that mean I get my present now?"

He hands the gift to me, and I unwrap the box. Shining at me from a bed of tissue paper is a colorful new clipboard with three lines of engraving on the silver clip at the top.

Penelope Reid, Program Director, Twelve Bluebells Ranch

The vibrant tones of the plastic clipboard gel together in a stunning, abstract mess of vivid greens, blues, reds, and oranges, whispering reminders of the past and present and framing them in a mesh of beauty.

A shattered stained glass window.

A foster home and a trailer park.

Neurofeedback maps.

New wounds healing old wounds.

East versus west.

All the pieces.

All the numbers.

All the love.

After we fall.

I run my hand over the glossy finish. "Oh, Luke. When did you do this?"

"The day you told me you wanted the job."

"But that was—" I stop to think through the events of our relationship. "That was before . . . that was before everything happened."

That Sunday at the Christmas tree lighting. Finley had already left, but the incident with Marcus was yet to come.

Luke takes the clipboard from my hands and sets it down on the counter. He draws me into his arms and kisses me tenderly on the lips. "I think you were mine before either of us knew that you were mine."

Yeah, that sounds about right.

All the pieces. All the numbers. All the love. After we fall.

EPILOGUE

"WE'RE NOT GOING to make it," I say, staring out the giant window at Denver International Airport.

"It's going to hold off," Luke says, his duffel bag opened wide as he sifts through the contents. "I need to grab some gum at one of those shops."

Still looking out the window, I say, "Check my backpack. Front compartment, third of four sections on the second row of pockets." Sheets of rain hit the glass. "We're not going to make it out of here."

"It's going to hold off," he says again.

Lightning strikes in the background.

Luke stands behind me and works to open the backpack I'm wearing. "I wanted to get you the pink weekend travel tote."

"And I believe my exact response was, 'How can I travel the world with so few pockets?'"

"Which is why I got you both. Because I know secretly you thought that bag was beautiful even if it was impractical."

Which is why my heart swelled when he bought it for me, and said tote sits at my feet with rolled-up clothes in vacuum-compression, space-saving travel bags for efficient packing.

As opposed to Luke's clothes that get strewn all over the place when he has to get into his duffel for anything.

"I still can't believe that you pack so disorderly."

"Disorderly?" he says in a fake-offended voice. "I'm a priority packer. I have the essentials. Everything else I might need, I'll figure out along the way."

"How did gum not make it on the essential list?"

"I thought I had some from my last trip." He closes up my pack, yanking me a little to the side, but then steadies my shoulders to set me right again.

"But you made sure cargo pants were in the bag before you left because those are quintessential Luke Granger."

He kisses my cheek. "You know it."

"We're not going to make it."

"It's going to hold off." He stands next to me, both of us with our arms crossed. As we look out at the numerous planes docked at empty gates, a sheet of rain hits the windowpane so hard we both jump.

He nods to my backpack, still attached to me. "What else you got in there?"

"Maps."

He grips my backpack and shakes. "That's a lot of maps."

"Our itinerary."

"I thought we were just going for a few days. This feels like a lot of paper. Or something." He pats it down. "Seriously, what is in here?"

"We're not going to make it, so it doesn't matter."

"It's going to hold off." The lights flicker. "Why do you need printouts of maps and itineraries?"

With our travel taking us to a remote location in Costa Rica to scope out a new aid project, I did some prep work.

I sigh and turn to him. "I printed the maps, itinerary, copies of our passports, and my spreadsheet. I packed gifts for the families that are hosting us, printouts of the contents of each of our bags in case our luggage is lost, and, against my better judgment, boarding passes to the flight we aren't going to make. Do you want to know the exact contents of the small liquids I put in a quart-sized baggie?"

"Maybe." He glances outside. "It's going to hold off."

A small child runs in front of us, and we hitch back before he crashes into our legs.

A man rushes by. "Sorry! Little buddy doesn't know what to think of it being so dark in the middle of the day. This weather is throwing everything off."

Luke smiles and nods at the man, then looks back at me. "Go back. Your spreadsheets?"

I hold up a hand to count the list on my fingers. "Travel times, mealtimes, where to eat, when we're meeting with people, transportation, backup transportation, backup to the backup transportation, confirmation emails, confirmation numbers, receipts, international travel insurance, health insurance—"

Luke goes from wide eyes to chuckles.

"What's so funny?"

"Nuh-uh." He holds a hand out in a "gimme" fashion. "What else is in this backpack?"

I huff, even though my heart's not in it. "Well, if you must know, I have my migraine meds, extra malaria pills, a first-aid kit, over-the-counter anti-inflammatories, Kleenex packs, wet wipes, and extra socks."

His eyes sparkle. "And . . ."

I slide my eyes to the side and mutter, "A clipboard."

He all-out throws his head back and laughs, picks up an abandoned empty water bottle off the ground, and chucks it into a trash can a few feet away.

"I don't know what's funny."

"You should by now." He stalks toward me, a gleam in his eye. In one super-smooth move, he runs his hands over my shoulders, catching my backpack straps and gently sliding them down my arms to release the bag onto the floor. Then he wraps his arms around me and bends down to kiss me just a touch more than PDA might allow at an airport. But only for a quick few seconds. "You should know by now. You're funny—"

I open my mouth to protest, but he continues. "And brilliant and generous and kind and oh so beautiful." He kisses me quickly. "And you have done more packing and planning than I ever did for any trip that Robert and I went on."

I blanch and pull back but stay in his arms. "What? How is that possible?"

"I don't know," he says with a chuckle. "Robert would call and tell me when and where we were going. He always had contacts. I always had my passport current so I could pack a duffel and go when he called."

"That's—" I'm dumbfounded. "That's ridiculous."

"No, baby." He curls a strand of hair around my ear and looks at me with all the affection in the world. "That's why I need you."

"Oh." Tears prick my eyes. "Oh, okay."

Concern fills his face. "Penelope?"

I let my head fall on his chest and burrow into his heat. A few tears fall. After a couple of deep breaths, I look back to him, wiping at my cheeks.

"What just happened?"

"I was just trying to be a part of your life. See your world. I wanted it all to be perfect because you've spent so much time taking care of me. After the accident. After Marcus. I just wanted to be able to do something for you." I lift up on my tiptoes and kiss the underside of his jaw.

He pulls me tightly to him, and I wrap my arms around his waist and squeeze. But then something occurs to me. "Just out of curiosity"—I draw back—"what was your plan for this trip?"

He grins. "I was going to show up, find our contact, and figure it out from there."

"That's appalling."

His shoulders shake with laughter. "It would have worked out."

"How can you live like that?"

"I can't wait to show you." He leans down and kisses me.

"That's appalling," I say again, unable to find other words.

"Just out of curiosity, is this the way you're going to run our household when we get married and have six boys?"

"You're going to have to ask me to marry you to find out." I place my hands on his chest and push up to whisper in his ear, "But first we have to get out of this airport because we're not going to make it."

He rubs his cheek against mine and says, "Oh, we're going to make it."

DISCUSSION QUESTIONS

1. Gary Chapman wrote a book called *The 5 Love Languages*, where he claims each person has a preference for one of the following love languages: words of affirmation, acts of service, receiving gifts, quality time, and physical touch. As a humorous claim, Penelope's love language is efficiency. What is your love language (one of the five, or a humorous one), and why?
2. The first time Luke met Penelope, he said, "Excuse me, ma'am, I don't think you've had the pleasure of meeting me. I'm Luke." How would you have responded? Share any other cheesy pickup lines you find amusing.
3. Penelope earned a master's degree in business administration that prepared her for work with Harlan's company, and a master's degree in misery from a group home that prepared her for work with Meredith's halfway house. What fake degree have you earned in life? (For example, a master's degree in listening to your friends from the University of Compassion, or a master's degree in loading the dishwasher from Clean University.)

4. Luke claims "the beauty's in the wild." What does that phrase mean to you? Is this something you could connect with in the book? In Penelope's journey? In your own life?
5. The scene where Meredith drops a piece of chewed gum on her wedding dress came right out of Deborah Clack's life. Ten minutes before her own wedding, her father leaned over to pray for her, and his gum dropped on her pristine white dress. Nervous laughter became joyous laughter when they extracted the gum and saw that it left no mark! Did you ever have a time when you laughed off a serious moment?
6. Both Luke and Penelope grew up in homes without marriage, good relationships, or fatherhood modeled. Other people came into their lives to fill the gaps. What do you think their lives would have been like if others had not come alongside them to help? Did anyone come alongside you to mentor you or encourage you over the course of your life?
7. Penelope goes against Luke's wishes and risks talking to Finley without him. The conversation results in a life-changing injury for Penelope. Have you ever tried to take something into your own hands, only to have made the situation worse?
8. Harlan surprises Penelope with his big-brother protection and support of her when he asks Luke what his intentions are with her. Have you experienced a time when someone else's act of protection for you made you feel unexpectedly safe and cared for?
9. Migraines plague many people. This story gives an account of one person's experience with them. In her personal experience as well as in her research, the author found numerous causes of and treatments for migraines. Do you have different insight or experiences?

10. Have you ever had a dream for yourself that fell apart, but the pieces that were left came together to be something better for you in the long run? What did that look like and feel like? What do you dream of now? Is there a baby step you can take to capture a piece of that dream?

Read on for a sneak peek
of *Still Here After*, the final book in

THE
SHELTER AND SKY
SERIES

AVAILABLE APRIL 2027

1

"DO YOU THINK she shot her husband with that old rifle?" I ask Professor Evelyn Wimberley out of the corner of my mouth.

"Probably," she answers. Her posture mirrors mine, relaxed in spite of her formal attire, arms crossed. The sequins dotting her emerald jacket are flashier than the ones at the hem of my secondhand cocktail dress. "Probably dug up a grave behind that sham of a house and stashed the body, never to be found again."

I tilt my head and study the painting on the ballroom wall in Colorado Springs' prestigious Broadmoor Hotel. A weathered woman on a sagging porch white-knuckles the long barrel of an antiquated gun. Tall reeds of yellowed grass in the painted country scene coax me to believe, if I take one step closer, I can brush my fingers along their silky frayed tips and smell the backwoods breeze.

The professor clucks her tongue twice and points one authoritative, stubby finger toward the picture. "If I'd buried Howard behind my house, our loyal dog would've dug up the grave and given him mouth-to-mouth." She turns her stocky, impeccably dressed body toward me. "I'll take the painting."

I shake my head at her on-brand generosity. "Evelyn, you're here as my guest. Please don't feel obligated to purchase anything this evening."

Thirty-two pieces of donated art sprawl across the room, beckoning to generous philanthropists. All to benefit Twelve Bluebells Ranch, a halfway house for young women in the foothills of the Rocky Mountains. Patrons stride over the marble floors in their high heels and wing tips, clinking champagne glasses while they search for the perfect piece to adorn their grand fireplaces and personal libraries.

My mahogany desk chair at the hotel's Contemporary Gallery sits empty tonight while I volunteer at the late summer gala.

"I blame this spontaneously budgeted item on you, Daphne Fielding," Evelyn says.

"Know your painting. Know your buyer better." I nod to her. "*You* taught me that."

In the case of Dr. Evelyn Wimberley, I knew her well before she arrived this evening. Eighteen years ago, I ran away from home at the age of sixteen, hitchhiking myself right into the leather seats of her giant, warm Cadillac.

"I fell in love with the women at Twelve Bluebells Ranch during your presentation to the graduate committee last week." She leans in with a hint of coconspirator in her movement and tone. "I've approved the final phase of your thesis project. I'm very proud of you."

I swallow. All I've ever wanted was to repay her generosity by making her proud.

"But I'm only one vote," she says. "Dr. Sloan and Dr. Hayword will be here tonight to further evaluate this portion of your proposal."

My anxious heart ticks out the seconds. If I don't complete the project requirement for my master of art degree by the end of the school year, my ever-diminishing bank account will run dry.

She pats my arm. "I think I'm going to follow my nose and track down one of those mini crab cakes."

"Thank you, Evelyn, for your generous purchase. I'll take care of the details for you." After pointing her in the direction of the appetizers, I slide the painting information badge out of its plastic cover and turn it over.

SOLD. The bold red letters on the back of the card announce more funds raised for the residents of the nonprofit ranch.

I scan the room, and a stranger catches my eye. Tall, broad shoulders, dark brown hair clipped short. Probably a couple of years older than me. Hard lines on the planes of his face that don't age him but instead tell a story.

As I approach, I take in his well-fitting khakis and starched white button-down shirt, rolled long sleeves showing off tanned, muscular arms. Confidence. Strength. A defined jaw that might hide a dry sense of humor. But he's not to be toyed with, he's to be respected.

From years of experience selling art to personalities of all shapes and sizes, I can tell this striking man doesn't need my help to select a piece. He simply needs someone to come alongside while he ponders the world of colors in front of him.

Standing a few feet away, I clasp my hands in front of me and study the Matterson painting with him. Thin blue strokes of a waterfall plunge into the abyss of thick brown and black streaks depicting a mountainside lake. Slightly abstract but still recognizable.

He glances at me, but my stare remains fixed on the artwork, allowing him time to view the credentials hanging on my lanyard without forcing him to interact if he doesn't see fit.

But I fidget in my black dress. The embellished bead-centered flowers and flared skirt called to me in the resale shop. Now I worry the scoop neckline makes a suggestive statement about myself I swore I would never make again. I tuck a rebellious piece of my wavy brown hair under the grip of my black silk headband.

"This painting is too moody," he finally says.

Moody? Interesting. The painting matches the artist.

"I like what it tried to do." His brows draw down with his disgruntled focus on the work. "But I can't quite get behind it."

Again, interesting. His statement resembles how I feel about Pete Matterson's portfolio.

He turns his head to me. "What do you think?"

"It depends. Are you purchasing this for yourself?"

"It doesn't depend," he says, his tone flat, direct. "I want to know what you think of this piece as it hangs on the wall."

I blink. I'm supposed to do my best to sell art, but this man wants a straight answer. *Know your painting. Know your buyer better.* "My problem is that I know the artist."

He shakes his head once. "Take away what you know about the artist. What do you think of the painting itself?"

I bite my lip and release a slow breath. "The painting, while brilliant on the surface, is just that. Surface. It doesn't go deeper. Every time I study it from a different angle, I become frustrated trying to make it something that it's not."

Like the painter.

"But this one." He leads me to a perpendicular wall. "What do you think about it?"

In front of us hangs a painting created by one of the halfway house residents, Julia Keaton. All her angst, hope, and resolve wrapped up in the sweeping brushwork of her novice piece.

My throat tightens with pride. Again, I can't separate my feelings about the work from the artist.

"It's stunning," I whisper to the painting.

"This is the piece I want to buy."

I beam at Julia's creation. "The artist will be ecstatic. However, this one's not for sale. It's showcased here to explain tonight's fundraiser and the services offered at Twelve Bluebells."

He squares himself to me and crosses his arms. "I want to pay you the asking price of the other painting we looked at for this piece here."

I snap my eyes to his. "What?"

He smiles for the first time in our interaction.

I don't get the impression this assertive man offers his smile often, and wow, what a shame for the rest of the world. Lines of life experience, wisdom, and a slight hint of mischief edge a set of crystal-blue eyes that light up bright and beautiful.

So beautiful that, with just one of his smiles, I wish I was something special. Something more than my thirty-four years, shoulder-length dishwater-brown hair, and murky brown eyes. Something more than my unfinished master's degree and job that leads to nowhere. Just . . . something more.

"I have another request," he says, as if he didn't just declare he would pay four figures for an unknown nineteen-year-old artist. One who began painting a month ago in my creative arts program at the ranch. "I'll be out of town for an extended period of time. I'd like this piece to be mailed to my mother for her birthday. Could you hold the painting for me and ship it in three weeks along with a handwritten note?"

My lips part, but nothing comes out. The sweet gesture for his mother surprises me.

He stares at me and lowers his head slightly, as if prompting me to answer.

I take a breath. "I would have to ask the artist for permission to sell this piece. If she agrees, we'll count your generosity as a donation and can certainly accommodate your delivery requests, Mister . . ."

Something soft registers in his eyes. He extends his hand. "Call me Michael."

"Michael, I'm Daphne." I shake his hand, appreciating his strong grip. "On behalf of Twelve Bluebells, I cannot thank you enough."

"You can thank me when the artist agrees to let go of that

piece." With his ringless left hand, he holds up a ranch brochure. "This is an impressive organization."

"The owner wanted to create a halfway house for women who aged out of the foster care system. She reaches a population in danger of getting lost in the cracks. Gives them solid tools to live a healthy life."

"Do you work at the ranch?"

"I work at the Broadmoor Contemporary Gallery full-time and volunteer at the ranch teaching art to the residents." I cock my head. "I'm curious, what drew you to this piece?"

"I've learned in my line of work to look for the things you can't see." He turns and locks his eyes with mine. "Paintings are like people. They become more interesting when instead of focusing on what you see, you search for what isn't visible."

I tug at my dress, fighting the urge to run from this conversation and hide. He can't see my past.

He shifts his attention to the picture. "Did you teach this artist?"

"No." I clear the nervousness out of my throat. "I wouldn't call it teaching. I supplied her with a little paint and some instruction, but she doesn't need me." As I think of the magical afternoon when this piece took shape on her canvas, my voice quickens with enthusiasm and my hands become animated. "She's a force to be reckoned with, but she doesn't know it yet. What's displayed here is pure, natural talent."

On the last word, I throw my arm out to point to the magnificent painting. And knock an appetizer off a passing tray, sending it flying toward Michael.

The eggplant topped with spicy tomato sauce hits his pristine white shirt and plunges to the marble floor, leaving a red stain splattered across the left side of his chest. As if Cupid's arrow went very, very wrong.

"Oh no," I breathe.

Without hesitation, the waiter says, "I'll be right back with a towel."

"I'm sorry, Michael." Heat hits my face, bringing with it, I'm sure, a severe blush. I never could hide my feelings, something I've lamented my entire life. "I am so sorry."

Michael looks from the splat on the floor to the splotch on his shirt. He glances around the room, something working behind his eyes. He takes two steps and commandeers a stack of napkins from a nearby server. Upon his quick return, he wipes the appetizer off the ground, dragging crumbs into the napkin with efficient movements. He completes the cleanup procedure with an effective swipe over his shirt and deposits the trash into a receptacle.

The entire process takes approximately two point five seconds. Time I spend fixed in place, utterly unhelpful, with a gaping mouth.

"Are you always this good in a crisis?" I gawk at the bright red stain slashed across his heart.

He chuckles, a low rumbling from his chest. "I'm paid to be this good in a crisis."

"You must excel at your job." I realize I'm focused on his chest. His very broad chest. My face heats again, and I touch my hand to my cheek and look into his eyes. "I'm so sorry I ruined your shirt. I talk with my hands a lot. Plus, I get a little carried away when it comes to discussing the girls."

The corner of his mouth twitches. "Not at all."

"I can have a new shirt brought in from our on-site men's clothing store. What size do you wear?" My hotel employee discount will only make a small dent in the steep designer price. I'm not sure how my bank account will recover, but buying a replacement is the least I can do.

"This is not a problem, Daphne," he says with authority.

With our eyes locked, I exhale. I want to lean into his voice, absorb the steady calm. Goodness. The walls of the hotel could be caving in, but if this man told me it wasn't a problem, I'd believe him.

Patrons stroll through the ballroom. The aromas of heavily fragranced women and slices of toasted brioche float through the air. Even though I should move on to other parties for possible sales, I ask, "Do you often frequent art galleries?"

He scratches his cheek. "No. Tonight I had dinner with a colleague and his wife next door at the Golden Bee. I saw a flyer for your event."

"I love the Bee." I clap my hands once and hold them at my chest. "The old piano and ragtime sing-alongs are so much fun. I think they start at nine. You should head back to the restaurant soon."

Michael's features remain blank. "I don't sing in public."

No. No, a man like this probably doesn't sing in public. But maybe a man like this needs to take his flatlined lips and whatever weighs on those strong shoulders and let loose with a song every once in a while.

I shift forward, lowering my voice to tease, "Do you sing when you're *not* in public?"

"No." His tone is abrupt, and I'm afraid my clumsy attempt at humor offended him.

"I'm sorry." I send him a half smile I hope smooths the awkward edges of this conversation. "It seems I can't talk tonight without throwing a hand to the hors d'oeuvres or putting a foot in my mouth. I should let you enjoy your evening."

Out of the corner of my eye, I catch Dr. Sloan and Dr. Hayword approaching. The professors wear the same uniform I've come to know since I began as a grad student nine years ago. The plaid elbow patches and brass buttons don't match the high-end-dressed crowd at the Broadmoor. But with their heads in the clouds of academia, my guess is they hardly notice.

As they approach, I straighten my spine and conceal my fingers, chipping away at the drugstore nail polish on my thumb. I've won Evelyn over with the last component of my proposal, but these two gentlemen haven't offered their final approval.

Just as I free a section of the magenta polish, I catch Michael's contemplative scowl aimed at my hands. I quickly press the piece down, smoothing the wrinkled spot back onto my nail.

"Ah. I'm so glad you two found each other." Dr. Sloan dips his chin to us with a rare look of approval. "Nice to see you again, Major Knox. Good evening, Ms. Fielding." He pronounces "Ms." with a strong *z* sound.

While my name buzzes between the four of us, I desperately try to connect these men. My professor knows Michael?

Wait.

"*Major* Knox?" I ask Michael, hoping my high-pitched voice isn't as loud as it sounds in my head.

He nods, his perplexed gaze not leaving mine, as if he, too, is trying to figure out the scenario in front of us.

Embarrassment crawls over every inch of my body. I didn't just ruin the shirt of one of Twelve Bluebells' biggest donors. My actions stained a true hero.

Despite being a foot shorter and a few decades older than Michael, Dr. Sloan slaps him on the shoulder. "Major Knox, this is the graduate student we mentioned to you when we met earlier."

A flash of surprise crosses Michael's face, then it's replaced by understanding. He nods again, this time slowly.

"Instead of requiring our master's degree candidates to compose a thesis, we ask them to complete an extensive culminating project using curriculum content." Dr. Sloan rocks from the tips of his toes to the backs of his heels, looking at me over his bifocals as if I should speak.

"My project analyzes the emotional impact of art on individuals." Sweat turns my palms clammy. "I created a program teaching various forms of art to the halfway house residents at Twelve Bluebells. We'll include their creations in care packages we send to our troops."

I dart a glance at each of the three men. Realization topples into place like slow-motion dominoes falling one after another.

My professors mentioned me to Michael. Michael's in the military. I need a military contact. They want—

"Mizz Fielding brought us an impressive proposal," Dr. Sloan says to Michael, "but she needs a military contact to accomplish the application task of the assignment."

Oh no. Oh, please don't put this officer in an awkward position. I open my mouth, but Dr. Hayword beats me to the moment.

"What do you think, Major Knox? Would you be willing to assist with her project?"

My eyes widen at his audacity to ask an active serviceman for help with a mundane civilian task. Shaking my head in short, panicked movements, I say to Major Knox, "I—um, you don't—"

"Dr. Sloan. Dr. Hayword." Evelyn ambles to the group. "It's nice to see you boys amongst the art this evening." Her Southern accent seems amplified with the not-so-subtle dig.

I close my eyes and swallow down my acute discomfort.

The bizarre competitive nature between these professors is legendary in the fine arts department. Instead of acting like highbrow intellectuals, these three could break out in a barroom brawl at any moment. The only truce came after Evelyn's husband died. For a few months after the funeral, her voice softened when she spoke of her colleagues.

"Of course we get out to support the arts. Our students as well." Dr. Hayword stares down his nose at Evelyn. "I'm not sure what use you've made of yourself tonight, but we found Mizz Fielding the perfect military contact for her culminating project."

Evelyn moves her focus from me to Michael, her eyes narrowing when they land on him.

I bite my lip, worried she's going to transition from proud professor to mama bear. Her name might not be on my birth certificate, but she's played the role of mother since the day she picked me up and brought me into her home.

She shoots her hand out to him, and they make quick introductions. "Is this true? Will you be helping Daphne?"

"I don't believe I have enough information about the situation to make a decision." He looks at me. "I PCSed to Fort Carson only a few days ago. I don't know my on-post duties. I need to take the request under advisement." His words may be stiff, but his reply is gracious considering his surprising position in the spotlight.

After two months of dead ends, I can't help but hope he's the one to put my proposal into action. But I realize it's not simply the matter of my project.

This thoughtful, forthright man who exudes integrity is worth knowing.

With the attention of my professors, a steely gaze from Major Knox, and the weight of my looming deadline, I'm standing in a pressure cooker.

I sneak a glance at Evelyn.

She purses her lips and peers at me. There's that protective mama bear.

And now I'm worried she can see right through the blush I know must cover my face.

One glimpse at my watch, and I think of the only feasible excuse I can under the scrutiny of my professors. Keeping a straight face, I say, "Well, we need to let Major Knox enjoy the rest of his evening. He's got to get back to the Golden Bee at nine for the sing-along."

Major Knox clears his throat, but I don't dare look his way. After saying goodbye to Evelyn and my professors, I hold an arm toward the exit to usher him out of the conversation.

"You spell trouble," he murmurs as we approach the ballroom doors.

"No." I shake my head, biting the inside of my cheek in a failed attempt to contain a grin.

"Yes. Whether it's the Golden Bee or a spelling bee, you most definitely spell trouble."

"Okay." I giggle. "Yes. But only as far as staining your shirt and my professors putting you on the spot. If you go to the Bee for the sing-along, you'll have so much fun that I will have redeemed myself."

We step into the mezzanine, the ornate silky furniture and spectacular sparkling chandeliers reminding me I'm employed here but I don't belong here.

He turns to me. "As I said, I don't sing in public."

"Are you telling me that when you go to a birthday party, you don't even sing the happy birthday song?"

He stares blankly at me.

I hold a hand to my chest in feigned offense. "Even at a *child's* birthday party?"

"I give good gifts."

The painting he purchased for his mother flashes through my mind. Yes. He gives good gifts. Gifts that scream thoughtfulness and generosity without actually saying the words. What else is this man saying without words?

"I'm sorry my professors asked you to help. They mean well." I clasp my hands together. "You are officially released from Daphne duty."

"Daphne duty." The edge of his mouth tips up just a notch. "I don't remember being trained for that at ILE."

After almost two decades in a city filled with military personnel, I've picked up some of the lingo. I think he means intermediate-level education. He might have recently become a major.

"It's a highly specialized class," I say with a smile. "Are you deploying overseas?"

"Yes. I leave in three weeks." He widens his stance and crosses his arms over his chest. "What are the specs for your military project?"

My belly flutters at his interest, and my excitement pushes me a step closer to him. "What I want to know, what I want to test, is what happens to the human spirit not just when we *create* our art but also when we *share* our art?"

He rubs his chin. "And you want to share your art with me?"

"No," I say a little too loudly, then cover my mouth when I laugh. "Sorry. I need names and addresses of five deployed women. We're going to send care packages to soldiers full of items they need as well as one selection of art from each halfway house tenant."

He narrows his eyes, and I worry my idea sounds stupid to him. But I want him to understand. To see what I see.

"The project goes beyond the basics of art and art appreciation. It will open doors for discussions about gratefulness, encouraging others, and the impact of military service. But it's more than that. Sending a piece of something you created to a complete stranger just for the sake of sharing a part of yourself can be powerful." I smile on a wistful sigh. "I think it has the potential to be beautiful."

He shakes his head, his sharp eyes intense. "I only recently finished ILE. Then I got called up to be an XO. My PSC orders were expedited to get me to Fort Carson because the 2IBCT already deployed and have boots on the ground."

With so many acronyms, it's hard to translate exactly what he said. But the strain in his voice is enough to communicate he's under pressure with his new post and duties. "Really. I understand, Major Knox—"

"Call me Michael."

"Michael." My thumb itches to scratch at the nail polish. "I'm sorry my professors mentioned anything. When I envisioned this project coming to fruition, I pictured asking some as-yet-unnamed grandmother for help. Possibly the spouse of a retired public servant. In no scenario did I picture a . . ." I hold my palm out and gesture to him.

He tilts his head. "A what?"

A single, attractive, sightly taciturn but entirely intriguing officer.

He continues to stare at me, my face flushes with heat, and I unsuccessfully rack my brain for an explanation. "A . . . you. I didn't expect to ask someone like you."

He raises his eyebrows, the left quirking a bit higher than the right, but instead of feeling flustered, I pause to look at him. To see what he's saying without words. To take in the hard planes of his face and the way he carries his body like it's never allowed to rest.

Compassion. This warrior needs compassion.

"Michael, I didn't expect someone on active duty to help me. Please don't feel like you have to do this. I can't imagine the pressure you're under with a move, a new job, and an impending deployment."

He exhales, turns away from me, and runs a hand through his shorn hair. "I'm in over my head," he says in the faintest of voices.

His words surprise me, but not as much as the vulnerable tone. I'm tempted to offer him a light touch of support, but he whips back around, his mouth set in a grim line. "I'm sorry, Ms. Fielding. I haven't had time to orient myself to my duties or personnel. I'm afraid my focus needs to be on my new post. I can't be of service to you."

He thrusts his hand toward me, and when we shake goodbye, the heat of his palm and the disappointment of his answer hit me at the same time. With a brusque nod, he shifts and strides to the grand mahogany staircase that leads to the lobby.

No. No, a man like Major Michael Knox wouldn't commit to anything he couldn't do well. A man like that doesn't buy a painting he doesn't care for. And a man like that doesn't need anything messy in his life. Or anyone.

"It's okay," I whisper to his retreating figure. "I know what it's like to be in over your head."

DEAR READER,

It's not lost on me the millions of books we get to choose from. Also not lost on me is how little free time we each have. That you would pick up Penelope and Luke's story means so much to me. Truly. Thank you.

I fell in love with Penelope in *Even After This*, and I knew she was beautifully more complicated than her type-A personality wanted us to believe. I also knew she needed a man who would be irreverent of her clipboard. Writing began with finding much glee in borrowing the pickup line my father used on my mother. But the guts of this story came from my personal struggle with migraine headaches, the longest of which was twenty-one days and occurred while working on this story.

Penelope's story isn't mine. And hers might not be yours either. Approximately 148 million people worldwide experience migraines, all with different causes, triggers, treatments, and journeys. One intervention does not fit all. And for two percent of us, most interventions don't work. But even if you have no experience with migraines, what's universal about this story is the fall. Migraines or not, we can all fall in so many ways.

What happens when we look for our worth in what we can do or achieve but we're no longer able to do or achieve? Are we still lovable when we can't earn everyone's love? What if we have to adjust our lives or ask for help? It can be gritty. Awkward. And we can be uncomfortable in our own skin. Fortunately for

Penelope, her journey also included the gleam in Luke's eye and his mile-wide protective streak.

I'd love to stay in touch. The fabulous Team DC runs my social media, but I'm not there. Maybe someday I'll write about why. But for now, I would love to connect with you through my monthly newsletter at DeborahClack.com. When you sign up, I've got a free novella for you with an opening scene that may or may not be based on one of my most embarrassing moments.

And if you enjoyed getting a whisper of Daphne and want to read the story of the beautifully disheveled volunteer art teacher for Twelve Bluebells Ranch, check out bookstores in April 2027. Major Michael Knox looks for things that most can't see, and what he sees in Daphne is breathtaking, heartbreaking, and powerful. *Still Here After* is not the story you're expecting, but it's full of swoon and beauty all the same.

And finally, my thank-yous.

Kelsey Bowen, I still can't type words about partnering with you in the editorial process that don't make me tear up with gratefulness.

Jessica English, this manuscript and this author needed a lot of grace and elbow grease during galleys. Thank you so much for both.

To Rachael Betz and the marketing team, the title of this book fits this story on so many levels. You guys continue to be such a bright spot in everything that you do.

Laura Klynstra, you and your team create covers I want to live in. Goodness, this one is truly stunning. Thank you.

Emily Vest, you are a blessing to me, handling one of the most stressful parts of this career. Thank you. Truly.

Tamela Hancock Murray, thank you for believing in Penelope and Luke.

Thank you to Julie Marx and her fabulous crit group with Brittany Ali, Bill, Loved Carmack, Jennie Gorman, Tonya Hamilton, Jim Head, Marie Sontag, Byna Whitlock Terndrup, Alicia Van

Huizen, and Jen Weaver. I read the first chapter of Penelope to you guys, and your excitement breathed life into me to continue. Thank you.

Becky Wade, Lynne Gentry, Sherrinda Ketchersid, Kay Learned, Shelli Littleton, Kelly Scott, and Stacy Simmons, thank you for the crowns, fun paper clips, and laughter.

Bethany Kazmarek, I'm still in awe of how you show love through your edits.

Kelly Jo Fernandez, it's the fun part!

Lynn Blackburn and Debb Hackett, bring on the oversharing via texts.

Thank you to the Ride at Dawn crew. You saddled the horses and told me you were ready, and you'll never know what that meant to me.

Thank you to Dr. Pamela Bell at the Neurofeedback Center of Dallas. Thank you to Dr. Carey Penniston at Speece Family Medicine. Thank you to medical consultant Debby Clack. All mistakes are mine. Every last one of them.

Joy, your GIF game is strong. So is your friendship.

In-laws are the best. Thank you to Trevor Jordan for the trailer line and Crystal Alley for the codependency line.

Thank you, Dad, for letting me borrow the pickup line you used on Mom for this book.

T and M, there aren't enough words to tell you how deeply I love you.

Lance, I fell a little bit in love with you when you told me we were trying to have a civilization here. And for so many other reasons. Also, I'm sorry I couldn't fit the paranormal flying people scene you wanted into this story.

To the Lord. Every word is Yours. The path to here was paved in so many ways that could only be You. I pray I never forget to trust You with whatever comes next. In anything.

I love you guys,
Deborah

Deborah Clack is a *Publishers Weekly* bestselling author and native Texan who believes in the power of fiction, in the lost art of lip-synching, and that chocolate should be eaten without nuts. A high school AP history teacher for ten years, Deborah earned a master's degree in education and was awarded Teacher of the Year for arts in education. Now she creates stories of her own filled with endearing characters and a hard-fought romance. Learn more at DeborahClack.com.

Sign Up for Deborah's Newsletter

Keep up to date with Deborah's latest news on book releases and events by signing up for her email list at the website below.

DeborahClack.com